RAIN

By

Michael Irons

for Eileen
from Michael

RB
Rossendale Books

Published by Lulu Enterprises Inc.

3101 Hillsborough Street

Suite 210

Raleigh, NC 27607-5436

United States of America

Published in paperback 2014

Category: Fiction

Copyright Michael John Irons © 2014

ISBN : 978-1-291-72337-3

This is a work of fiction. Names, characters, corporations, institutions, organisations, events or locales in this novel are either the product of the author's imagination or, if real, used fictitiously. Any resemblance to actual persons (living or dead) is entirely coincidental. Any relationship to existing or former organisations and individuals is purely coincidental and such a relationship is not intended and should not be inferred.

Dedication

To all those who have helped me through life

Acknowledgement

Grateful acknowledgement is made to Peter Connolly whose 1983 school text book entitled 'Living in the time of Jesus of Nazareth' (Oxford University Press - ISBN 0 19 918142 X) provided a general template against which it has been possible to set the general background to part three of this story.

CONTENTS

IN THE BLEAK MIDWINTER

WHITE

20 October 2131

The snow had smothered the valley of the Thames. The change was as complete as if a pot of white paint had been carelessly tipped over a chart film at the offices of the Ordnance Survey. The snow had begun to fall overnight on Saturday, quietly and softly. It had been an especially cold October but few people seriously expected snow. Many had no doubt been looking for a change for the better, an Indian summer to make up for the dismal months of July and August. Weather satellite data had clearly marked up the unusual sun-spot activity. There were forecasts of colder air masses off the North Atlantic, but newscasters would only grudgingly concede the possibility of some minor sleet flurries. Home meteo-kits, popular among children some years before, had correctly warned of snow. Grown-ups had mumbled uncharitably 'you must have calibrated the thing wrong', and turned back to the home view-screens. No, it wouldn't snow because no-one expected snow – the traditions of centuries were not to be denied.

Nevertheless, as daylight expanded on the morning of Sunday 20th October 2131, the citizens of southern England woke to find thirty centimetres of white snow, a leaden sky and no sign of a halt in the steady fall of fresh crystals. The initial burst of irritable surprise was overtaken by fatalistic resignation – well after all it was an excuse not to travel. Children began to delight in the possibilities of snowmen and sledging. By noon the falls were too deep for convenient horseplay. Families were consigned to viewing the scene from behind domestic glass. Just before thirteen hours the England Weather Centre advised the cessation of private air traffic; three hours later the State Governor signed an order stopping commercial movements using airspace above one hundred metres. As darkness fell, a collective chill ran down the spine of the south. People didn't need government exhortations to caution to know that things were not good. Movement had virtually stopped. On the H14, the main arterial route out of London to the west, more than sixty cars plummeted into each other as snow clogged air intakes and hover control vents. Fire melted the snow, twisted metal squealed and molten plastic burned into flesh as eighty seven travellers perished. Black acrid smoke rose over Basingstoke marking the funeral. Night closed its door on the terrible scene as blue flashing lights of emergency services fluttered round like blinded butterflies. An unorthodox imaginative controller in Greater Reading, throwing away the rule book, had ordered in ancient mothballed helicopters in place of the modern hover ambulances. This bold decision saved eleven terrified travellers trapped on the eastern edge of the carnage, but farther west there was no help. 'South at 18' carried live pictures and many parents shielded junior eyes as view-screens showed torn bodies in the blood-spattered snow. Inter-State reports conveyed similar stories – from Nantes to Newcastle, Glasgow to Genoa, the snow had caught everyone unprepared. In only three short years, since the Atlantic conveyor had shut down during 2128 switching off the boon of Gulf Stream waters to northern Europe, the spectre of reality in living with its 55 degree north latitude was now hitting home hard across England and the northern states.

In her living unit on the northern outskirts of the ancient city of Milton Keynes, thirty-one year old Mary Trent paced slowly up and down. As her finger jabbed at the view-screen controls a stab of anxiety hit her heart; a little piece of her died as the brightly-lit screen died, leaving an almost oppressive silence. The window blinds had slid closed automatically an hour earlier but now she manually overrode the control to release them, staring out at the cotton-wool blanket falling steadily through the light cast out from her home. The shiver running through her slim body was not caused by damp or cold – the heating elements had cut in on time under computer control – she was simply afraid. Her five-year old daughter was asleep in bed but her nine year old son was late home from a friend's house.

"Oh, Matthew," she breathed almost inaudibly "where are you?"

Her stomach started to throb with worry. She shook herself awake and crossed quickly to the phone. Fingers that were beginning to tremble jabbed at the buttons. A woman's face expanded onto the screen.

"Cheryl, is Matthew still there, please?"

Cheryl Gordon noticed her friend's anxious look straight away.

"Frank left with him about fifteen minutes ago, Mary. They took one of the main air lanes. It should be passable and still patrolled. Please try not to worry."

"OK, love. Thanks. I'll call when they get here. If the snow gets worse, Frank can stay the night."

Mary pressed the off button. The stomach throb began to develop into a craving for a cigarette. She reached for a small white plastic packet. Only four left….she sucked her lower lip nervously. There was no chance to get any more now until Tuesday when her next supply would become available. She was licensed to smoke so there would be no delay in the corner kiosk accepting the validity of her tobacco card, but how on earth could she suffer on only four cigarettes not knowing if her son was safe? She pressed one to the desk hot-pad to light it, drawing deeply on the smoke. She glanced at the clock – 19:45. She inhaled again and tried to think. The Gordon's lived just over eight kilometres away among the trees. A private hover car would normally take seven or so minutes to cover the distance, so allowing so for the weather she told herself to stop worrying until 20:00 hours. Released from the strait-jacket of worry she went to look at her daughter. She squatted near Saffron's bed and gazed at her sleeping face.

'You're like your father,' she thought, 'the same naïve toughness – please don't leave me like he did.'

A soft kiss on the forehead and she was back pacing like a lioness near the still-open window blinds. As the small clock in the corner of the view-screen rolled over to 20:45 Mary decided she could wait no longer. She strode to the main wardrobe. Checking the screen inventory she chose her heavy grey cape. It took a few seconds longer to find appropriate footwear – boots and heavy duty shoes had been placed in deeper storage and would not normally have been to hand until November. Silver insulated snow boots appeared on the chute and Mary pulled them on. The decision to act brought solid relief. A gentle hiss as the door slid back was followed by a sharper one in an intake of breath as the cold air struck at her face and throat. The snow curtain fell steadily, damping out the prospect of sound. Struggling to the lane fifteen metres away left Mary with a dry sore throat and the realisation that she had forgotten gloves. With a rushing, gurgling sound giving warning of its approach a silver and black car moved by barely seven metres overhead, banking left slightly as it shot towards the city centre, sucking dizzy flurries of snow in its wake. It was gone in an instant, leaving Mary gripping the wall's stonework at the garden's edge. The sudden shock of the reckless driver's noisy passage had overbalanced her taut nerves; tears welled up melting the snowflakes on her eyelids. The rush of emotion sapped her resolute spirit. She was sobbing freely by now, raw sad emotion freezing on her soft worried cheeks. She turned and stumbled home. She sat numb by the phone, staring at the instrument as if willing it to warble and tell her Matthew was safe at a neighbour's door. A shiver pulsed through her slight frame reminding her she still wore her snow-sodden cape and boots. Mary hugged the cape tightly about her as if to insulate herself against the nasty world. The phone sang. Instinctively she pressed 'respond'.

"Mary.....Cheryl.....are they there?"

Mary swallowed, but the aching lump wouldn't leave her throat. The anxious phrases flooded out to stem the flow of tears again.

"No, Cheryl. I don't know where they are. I went to the lane to look but the weather's so awful. I don't know if they've crashed or stopped with a neighbour or anything. "

"Keep the line open, Mary. I'll call the Law and ask if any patrol cars have flown that way in the last hour. Stay with Saffron."

Cheryl had cut in with an authority in her voice that she didn't share, but Mary was on the point of hysteria. She couldn't trust herself not to follow her friend over the edge. Her face moved out of sight of the phone cam. Mary reached for another cigarette. 21:55 – Cheryl's voice returned to the phone, followed by her face.

"I've spoken to the local Law office. No sightings at the moment, but they are still out there."

"Oh." A short silence followed, heavy with nerves. Mary spoke again.

"I can't sleep."

"I know, my dear. I'll clear the line in case the Law are trying to get through. I'll check back with you soon."

Mary turned to the windows and stared dumbly at the falling snow. Sick with worry, she sat and closed her eyes........

The phone warbled, the urgent sound striking an immediate chord in her brain. She woke with a start, realising she was feeling cold. Cheryl's drawn face made her feel colder. Although the snow had stopped there was no news to warm her heart. No trace had been found of an abandoned car.

Monday 21 October

Monday morning had dawned crisp, clear and bitterly cold. The hearts of many thousands of gardeners were squeezed with unbelieving emotion. Everything smaller than the chrysanthemum displays had been smothered completely. Taller blooms had died in the frosty onslaught. The duty officer at the municipal transportation depot was not a gardener. It was just as well; there would be no time for grieving with his workload this morning. Jack Smith grumbled and swore under his breath, but he was good at his job. Jack was a short stubby man. He did not easily fit into the plough's driving seat, but he knew that in such extreme circumstances he really did have to include himself on the duty roster. The service these bright yellow monsters provided was not primarily for airborne motorists. Farmland needed clearing and walkways for pedestrians made safe. The only time that drivers felt their presence as a blessing was when lane-side refreshment centres were kept clear of snow for the cheaper vehicles, those without telescopic support stalks, to be able to flat-land and leave again. Jack knew the access route to the main Buckingham air-lane had such a centre and that he would be needed there as the morning's activity picked up. Swinging to the right with a tremendous roar of power he sent his plough up over the small hill before him. A blanket of white smothered the earth all the way to the horizon. Through the tinted windscreen he could see the sun glint brightly on the immense silver domes of the giant satellite control centre at Akeman Path far to the north. Nothing but snow lay between.

Yes, he knew he was some kilometres off the Buckingham air-lane access point but he was intently watching something black almost directly below him. He craned forward against his flight harness and peered down into the snow. A black tail-fin of a hover-car was sticking up out of a hummocky drift. Jack's stomach moved. He knew he would have to go down and do it the hard way. He chose a level area some fifty metres away, setting the plough down in a burst of flying snow. The fin wasn't visible at ground level; 'now, which way was it?' He took a few seconds to gather his thoughts. With a scratchy hydraulic hiss the roof slid back. Cold air poured in, clearing the driver's brain and pulling him alert. Jack breathed deeply and climbed out onto the side wing. He looked up as a controlled scream of engines built rapidly to the rear of the plough. Four military craft in diamond formation skimmed a bank of trees on the middle distance, roaring by barely three hundred metres overhead. Jack glimpsed the European insignia of the golden star circle on their sides and then they were gone, plunging into the morning sun. He was alone again, alone with his black fin and a job to do.

He pulled a snow shovel from its magnetic fastening and jumped down onto the ground. The snow was knee-deep, fluffy and cloggy. The hummocky drift was much more formidable than it had appeared from the air. Reaching the buried vehicle, he plunged the shovel in and began clearing snow, each spadesful more wearying than the one before. There was a dull thud as steel struck plastic deep inside the drift. The shock of contact stung Jack's wrists bringing pins and needles to his tired arms. He cleared a small patch of side-plate; tapped and waited. There was no sound. He waited a few seconds more, while his painful breathing eased. A vicious cramp bit at the back of his left thigh. Clutching and rubbing the protesting muscle he surveyed the task before him. He reached forward, scraping more snow from the hard plastic coaming. It was clear that the car had twisted sharply on impact, almost as if it had screwed itself into the snow when it crashed. So very little of the tail-fin had been visible from the air. A crash within the last few hours since the snow had stopped would have left much more of the car showing. From the extent of burying, Jack guessed that the car had gone in at some time before midnight. He took a deep breath and plunged the shovel with determination. Slowly, the snow was cleared round the top of the car. He scrabbled nervously over the bonnet, slipping on the wet surface. The blue sky spun wildly before his eyes. His head landed with a sickening thud against the windscreen. His gaze came into focus across the few centimetres of glass separating him from the crushed eggshell of a man's skull and the blank stare of a boy, with cold congealed blood plastering the sallow skin of his neck and a dead tongue frozen to the windscreen.

SILVER

Monday also dawned bright and unusually chilly in western Portugal, though there was no snow. Overnight frost had come to many areas as far south as Estoril. The southern Algarve had escaped, though holidaymakers considered they were being badly treated, it still being the English half-term holiday. The frost shimmered as it began to melt on sun-facing roofs of the State Capital and clung crisply where shadow still protected it. 08:00 local time – Lisbon was already awake, slowly shrugging off the shock of such a cold night. People were out and about. Green and black taxis, still made by the Mercedes Corporation, hovered gently at street corners or glided on their air cushions around the Praca do Comercio.

At his vantage point on the eighteenth floor of the European Union offices Hans Muller gazed thoughtfully through the triple window unit at the city below. Standing still, he cut an imposing figure, the shock of grey hair in rippling shiny waves setting him apart from his fellow delegates and enhancing his seniority. The grey moustache added ten years to his fifty five, underlining his command and charisma at the negotiating table. After nearly eighteen years in the diplomatic service his presence had become synonymous with the granitic, unyielding tradition of the European Union. Yet as his gaze followed the early morning traffic down the Avenida da Liberdade, Hans Muller was deeply worried. Wednesday this week would see the start of the final plenary session at the World States Council on the matter of World Bank distribution for the decade 2136-2145. Traditionally, this had presented no problem. After the World Bank's re-formation in 2037, European influence had been strong, only behind that of China and the United States. The imperceptible shift of world events over recent decades, however, had now led to a situation where a worrying outlook faced the Europeans. Muller turned from the windows and sniffed thoughtfully.

"We will have trouble, Manuel."

It was a firm statement, calm but with a tinge of resignation so untypical of his superior that Manuel Perez looked up from the table full of documents with some surprise registering on his round brown face. The two men were alone in the room, the briefing with other members of the delegation now over. Muller walked back to the central work surface and idly toyed with one of the white plastic sheets now scattered like old-

13

fashioned confetti over the marble top. By some eccentricity of tradition the medium of world diplomacy was still the plastic typed word and not the visi-screen. The standing joke told to all new initiates to the service being that it was the need to keep alive the phrase 'not worth the paper it's written on'. The language on these sheets was English, standard throughout the Union since the Treaty of Carlisle in 2091 cemented the present-day grouping. The European Union had grown steadily since its original inception in 1957, the Treaty of Accession having been signed by more Member States by the Single Market watershed of 1992. The new millennium saw integration and enlargement gather pace with the Treaties of Lisbon and then Madrid bringing more unity. Direct elections had eventually led to direct action. Europe's economic problems began to fall away after 2020 in the face of the concerted onslaught as common need developed a common identity, overseeing original nation states and turning them towards states of a union.

Eleven years from 2030 to 2040 presided over the most prestigious changes – the consolidation of the unit of currency, the Euro, and the accession to the Union of many former eastern and northern states. Independence from the United States of America was assured. By April 2051, on the signing of the full federal charter at Versailles, only Liechtenstein and Switzerland remained as separate nation states in much of the continent. Full status had been accorded in the previous sixty years to former satellites of the eastern Soviet bloc. The only change then was in 2088 when in January of that year England, Scotland, Cymru (formerly Wales) and Ulster chose separate statehood within the Union. Europe in its widest sense was a success story, but the heady years of the late 21st century were over.

In common with the United States of America and the Confederation of States allied with the Russian Federation, the Union had not seriously attempted to help the southern half of the planet, beset as it was with problems of horrendous magnitude. The Third World had made a valiant attempt at catching up, despite enormous handicaps; from 1950 to 2020, the Asian, African and South American states had truly deserved the name 'emerging nations'. The way became harder, however, and as surely as foothills lead to mountain crags, nation after nation fell by the wayside. The reasons were complex but the paths of history fell into two main strands. Mother Nature, of course, never gave up her grip.

Earthquake, crop failure, monsoon, disease and over-population continued to drag at the heels of the climbing fledglings. The developed northern hemisphere found it could not simultaneously give to others and

14

increase its own share of the world's resources. China bought up vast tracts of commercial and rare-earth metals. Western copyright was jealously guarded, even in areas of medical breakthrough. There was always tribal fighting, but it was with guns and bullets sold at a good profit by northern world companies. Cancellation of third-world debt was tried, though after the great recession of the early 21st century, even this began to peter out. Technical excellence brought money and money brought power. Frustration and bitter desperation grew in the southern world.

So, Muller was worried; he knew that from Chile to Cambodia the starving tiger was about to bite. In a mild gesture of resignation he let the plastic sheet fall from his fingers onto the marble table.

"Massive transfers of world money are hardly plausible, Herr Muller. The disruption to our trade....to all our trades....it would bite the hand that feeds them, surely?"

The senior diplomat shrugged his shoulders.

"That may be so, but I recall the situation in '21. Final voting was fifty eight to forty three with twelve abstentions. That was close, too close. Ten years is a long time and things are getting worse, not better. Morocco, New Zealand and Venezuela have left us since then. Rumour seems to be saying that Mexico and Israel are on the brink, close to believing a major financial shift would help them. If that is the case, how can we stem a tide on Wednesday?"

Muller stood up, the nervous tension holding him alert but uneasy.

"Are our travel arrangements ready?"

"Yes, completed. Our delegation flies from Portela airport direct to Malta. We are scheduled to leave at ten tomorrow morning."

Muller made a snap decision.

"Bring it forward. We'll leave at fifteen hours today. Our suites at the Council buildings will be reserved, anyway, and there are people I must talk to in private before any voting goes through."

"Very well, I'll see to it straight away."

The young Spaniard left the room. Muller was again gazing from the window, but his eyes were vacant, dreaming of the hours ahead.

Controlled activity fluttered round the executive VTOL airliner as it stood in the sunshine at a far corner of Lisbon's Portela international airport. Europe's delegation was loading. At the gate of the four-metre high security fence passes were being checked. Diplomats, advisers, aides and support staff intermingled on the concrete apron. Silver, magnetic-lock cases shone intermittently, reflecting shafts of sunlight as their owners turned. The mood of those assembled was mildly tense; the bringing-forward of the departure was most unlike the strict regulation metronome against whose tick much of European business was conducted. Rumours had rolled around like distant thunder - 'this will be the final meeting of the Council' and 'the black nations will boycott the Assembly', even 'disaster will stalk the northern world's corridors if certain needs are denied'.

The four members of the BBC's Diplomatic Unit loved rumour, especially heady, doom-laden rumour. It added spice to their work. Each in turn presented credentials at the security gate.

Forty five year old Craig Landon was the World Finance Editor - solid, intelligent, smartly-dressed, with the Corporation's insignia at his lapel, effortlessly endeavouring to ensure with every interview that 'nation shall speak peace unto nation, but only if there's an angle that suits us'. Landon's grey-specked eyes were not visible behind his chromatic flush lenses, but they moved endlessly, watching anybody and everybody. His artificially-dark brown hair was swept back at the sides, adding to the well-groomed impression. One metre eighty five was an impressive height. He played it to full advantage. He gave a palm scan and a well-practised smile, and he was through towards the plane.

Peter, 'Pip' Ashton, Sound Recorder, with sandy, fly-away hair, speckles and old-fashioned external spectacles balanced on his nose. This was his first major international assignment, and it showed. Flappy nerves bubbled as the twenty seven year old shuffled through his identity cards. Chubby fingers pressed to the palm scan, throwing up a small red light. The Portuguese security officer smiled.

"You have much sweat. Dry your hand."

A wipe down his sky-blue shirt and Pip pressed the screen again. The green light was accompanied by a noticeable sigh of relief. The BBC man blinked widely like an owl caught in a beam of light and walked through the gate.

Paul Devine, the Senior Holographic Officer, was ten years Ashton's senior. He was stout and florid, but a master of his equipment. The change of diplomatic plans had rushed them all to Lisbon for the flight and Devine in particular got out of breath when he was rushed.

The fourth member of the Unit stopped at the guard's side. Felixana Smith aged 31, World Correspondent, was petite. She stood at only one metre fifty two, had long dark brown hair and warm dark brown eyes. Her hair lay carelessly over her shoulders. The warmth of the eyes spread to the face as she smiled easily at the officer. Then she too joined the small queue at the steps to the plane.

"Hello, Toni. How are you?"

Landon had spotted a former colleague now working for Reuters International and he moved towards him, hand outstretched.

"Fine, thanks Craig, it's good to see you again. Still with the old firm, I see?"

A soft chuckle escaped Landon's lips.

"Yes, the Corporation has looked after me. I get around and the pay is good; well, good enough for the moment."

Felixana Smith had come alongside and Landon turned to introduce her.

"Felixana, my dear, meet Antonio Zarbelli, the finest investigative reporter this side of Washington. Toni, this is Felixana Smith, our World Correspondent on this trip. I'm sure you've seen her on many recent clips - she's on the way up."

The Italian's smile revealed perfect white teeth. The instant attraction between the two hit the warm afternoon air like an electric spark. Landon sensed it instinctively through the almost imperceptible tensing of his colleague's slight body next to his. His eyes narrowed. He diplomatically moved away to walk up the steps alone. There would be an opportunity to reminisce with Toni later.

At 15:03 hours, the jetliner lifted off Lisbon's soil. The blue and gold Air Europa livery crackled with reflected sunlight as it rose powerfully to its holding float at one hundred metres. The sky was cloudless, the city magnificently sharp in the clear autumn air. The fifty seven passengers gazed from the square panoramic windows. The small circular portholes of early air travel had disappeared more than sixty years earlier. By the early 2060s, plasti-glass technology had reached the point where it was almost possible to construct transparent aircraft. Two factors had reined in the eagerness to do this, however. Flag carriers needed opaque surfaces to carry the flag, but more importantly, the travelling public, with its innate fear of exposed heights, did not relish the thought of hurtling through the atmosphere in a goldfish bowl. Compromise was reached in large viewing windows similar to those in high speed land trains.

The airliner shifted into forward flight, banked steeply over the city outskirts and sliced through the air towards the state border with Spain, the afternoon sun at its back. Restraining seatbelts fell away and several travellers took the opportunity to stretch their legs. Chief diplomat Muller was not one of them. He sat quietly at his secluded rear seat, already at work playing the numbers game, shifting theoretical voting patterns around on a small magnetic board; blue for first world western, red for Russian Federation associates, amber for Asian, white for non-aligned and black for the third world's developing and emerging remainder. He sighed. Already it seemed to Muller's cautious mind, there were too many black pieces for European comfort. The jet sped on in the clear air. A course set direct for Malta would have involved crossing Algerian and Tunisian airspace, so the chosen route was entirely within Union air territory - Toledo, Minorca, Sardinia and then to Valletta Air Reception via Masala on Sicily. It was nineteen hundred kilometres, one hour twenty minutes flying time.

As the jet slowed and dipped over the eastern coastline of Gozo, Craig Landon saw the outlying buildings of the World States Council complex from his starboard window. The buildings were a rich, honey-sandy brown, in keeping with the Maltese backdrop. He noticed squat administration blocks, then soaring utility towers converting the Mediterranean sunshine into electricity. Closer to Sliema, the Council chambers themselves came into sharper focus. Those seated passengers who had never before been to Malta buzzed with interest, restrained as they were now by their landing belts from craning closer to the viewing glass. The heart of the complex presented an impressive sight. Barely two hundred metres from the edge of the coastal cliffs the huge central block began its rise. Thirty two floors of staggered rounded facing, like a gigantic pile of golden coins, swept up at the same gradient as the cliffs, to drop away vertically on the landward side. Landon had seen the sight before, but he still smiled at the perennial golden-coin simile. The World States Council was rich in power. Like the European Union itself, majority voting had led to actual decisions and it had the World Bank to back it up. The decisions of the Council were invariably implemented. Delicately and appropriately poised between the European and African continents, the Maltese complex represented the ultimate in world power.

The jet swung easily into Valletta Air Reception, the pilots switching over to auto-land to allow low-intensity lasers to channel the aircraft down through the final ninety metres. Even before the hum of flight died away, Landon and his team were rising from their seats to catch the opening interviews of the Council summit. Discussions with diplomats had not been permitted in flight, but now the media's own representatives moved into action, rushing to the bottom of the plane's steps and flicking on cameras and microphones. When Hans Muller and his ten fellow negotiators walked down to ground level they were greeted by a seething mass of European broadcasting personnel. Muller had not before experienced dinky little Felixana Smith at work - the modesty had fallen away as she went straight for the throat.

"Chief Diplomat Muller, is it true that the Southern Brotherhood now has the northern world in its power?"

Muller's face remained non-committal, but his stomach churned.

"I don't see how we can say that. Voting patterns are by no means clear. My understanding is that all contributors to this meeting will wish to decide what is right for the well-being of the whole world, and I believe that means putting one's trust in stability."

"Does that mean the status quo?" the man from Paris Match interposed eagerly.

"As I said, world stability is vital. I have nothing further to add at present. Excuse me."

Muller pressed on towards the waiting sleek black limousines. Their butterfly-wing hatches opened and the diplomats stepped in. The German was already regretting having been so brusque, but the young thing from the BBC had somehow got under his skin with her forthright attack. Yes, he was worried about the Southern Brotherhood; but, he told himself, it is not good to be so edgy so early in the diplomatic game. The four limousines rose on their cushions of air and rolled away with the European flags fluttering on their bonnets, towards the security of the residential suites. The representatives of the press pulled together their equipment and made their own way to the main areas of reception.

Residential units for the world's media were reserved in a separate wing of the complex from the diplomatic corps. Felixana Smith stood for a moment looking after the disappearing tail-fins of the official limousines, a soft smile ghosting from her eyes and round her face. Then she clutched her hand-grip to her side, jogging after her colleagues. Outside it was nearly dark. The little white lights of isolated shipping sparkled out at sea. There was a tangible chill in the air so uncharacteristic of Maltese evenings in October. Locals stayed indoors and so did the visitors. Inside, from the vantage point of the ninth floor of the press residential wing, guests could look out northwards over the rapidly-darkening Mediterranean Sea. It was warm here, and many were tired. Time enough tomorrow, Tuesday, to wrap up that exclusive interview, that shock disclosure. Tonight was for relaxing.

"May I sit with you, Felixana?"

Toni Zarbelli's soft Italian voice seduced its way gently into her brain, waking her from her quiet reverie in a softly-lit corner of the bar. He knew she did not permit the shortening of her name to Felix. A naturally-sweet smile gave him an answer. As he settled into a body-contoured chair next to her a squat silver drinks unit rolled towards him. It stopped, politely waiting for his voiced instructions to activate its controls. The delay served a double purpose; until the customer spoke, it would not know which language to use.

"I would like a scotch whisky, please - and you?" He looked at Felixana.

"Thank you. A dry martini with lemon and no ice".

The unit responded with a row of twinkling white lights at its midriff.

Thank you, both. Please place an identity card in my slot.' Toni leaned forward, slipping a piece of plastic into the horizontal cleft at the front of the unit's dome. Information flashed instantly on short wave to the residential reception desk: *'Zarbelli, Antonio - Reuters International - Room G71 - seventeen euros fifty'*

The unit rolled away again in search of the drinks. The Reuters man leaned back against the comforting upholstery, his eyes on the woman. He asked about the weather in the northern states.

"It's bad. We left Maplin for Lisbon at eleven this morning. Many plane schedules had been disrupted even then. There were no flights overnight, of course. The snow was a terrible shock; I'm glad to be out of it. What about you?"

"I came from Washington. The cold was unusual, but no heavy snow like in Europe."

The unit trundled back. Zarbelli took the drinks from its open front.

'Have a nice evening' chimed the servant, rotating slowly and moving away.

'Nice touch,' thought Zarbelli, 'this one's programmed for the time of day.' They touched tumblers and their eyes met briefly, flashing unspoken messages of attraction.

"How long have you been with the BBC?"

"Just over three years. I majored in global communication at Harvard Business School. My mother moved to North America from England when I was ten. I still have happy memories of the English Peak District of my childhood before my father died. Parts of the State Park are still preserved as it was centuries ago. Anyway, America was too hectic for me. My roots were in Europe, so I came back. I took a job in Birmingham with an opinion research company and the chance came up to work for the Corporation."

She chuckled softly, laughter chiming enchantingly into the Italian's ears.

"I mean, Britain as an entity hasn't existed for fifty years - some would say longer - yet the BBC serves those islands, and the world, as imperiously as it has for the past two hundred years. Such an international institution was a real attraction to me."

Her enthusiasm was flowing; he was pleased to listen.

"I joined as a junior interviewer, yes, even at my age! I was assigned to Craig nine months ago, just after the Midwinter Festival. We fitted well straight away; it felt good to be part of a good team. Together, we've travelled around, hitting stories hard wherever they appear. I'm reasonably happy."

There was a natural pause. The man sipped his whisky and glanced around the bar. He noticed three or four couples, a group of four men and two solitary drinkers - a well-behaved end to the evening. The clocks recessed into the arms of the body-contoured chairs were softly glowing 22:30. Felixana finished her drink. She smiled charmingly.

"You worked with Craig," she said. "Did you travel widely?"

"No. In any case, we never worked closely as such. We met in London on a training weekend - collaborated on an assignment to cover the Punjab food riots in May '25 - and that's about it really. Nevertheless, we became good friends. I left the BBC to join Reuters in early '26, but kept in touch with him. Apart from that one trip to the Indian sub-continent, I've never worked outside the Union, so I'll always remember his company and professionalism."

"Do you live alone?" That disconcerting bluntness again; this time Zarbelli was not thrown. He took it in his stride, smiling broadly.

"Always have! I come from a large Italian family and I'm afraid I found it claustrophobic. I enjoy the solitude of living alone." He smiled again. "Of course, that doesn't mean I'm a hermit. I do enjoy company, but not on a permanent basis."

The approach could not have been more obvious. Felixana laughed cleanly. She responded equally openly.

"I'm pleased to hear it," she replied. "The world is not a safe place to have someone, anyone, depending on one."

To Zarbelli's surprise, she rose from her seat.

"Well, it's twenty two, forty and I have to make a call. I do want to see you tomorrow, but there are several important interviews to tape first. I hope we can lunch together; say, thirteen hours at the Asian restaurant on the ground floor?"

The man was taken aback this time; he had not expected such a surgically-clean incision to end the evening.

"Well, yes, of course, fine. Thirteen hours it will be. Goodnight, Felixana."

Her dark brown eyes flashed warmly at him and then she was gone, the indefinable scent of her perfume hanging in the air. He exhaled with a resigned finality, finished his drink and stared out over the darkened Mediterranean. Her laughter echoed in his brain.

Tuesday 22 October

06:00 hours - Craig Landon rolled over in bed and woke up. He showered, shaved and dressed, pressing his BBC badge to his outer tunic at the magnetic square over his left breast. Almost instinctively, he passed his hand over the sensor control for the radio.

'There is severe weather again throughout northern states. Reports from Scotland indicate almost total disruption to transport, involving the isolation of many towns. Denmark, too, has suffered particularly badly. Thirty three people died in a crash on the Kobenhavn-Malmo Bridge in heavy snow blizzards and high waves. Our correspondents tell of minor snow flurries as far south as Perpignan and Bologna.'

Landon walked round the room, checking everything was tidy before breakfast. The radio caught his attention again.

'The World States Council meets in full session in Malta tomorrow for a two-day summit, amid increasing rumours of an impending major shift in world financial resources. There will be regular reports from our special team in Malta during the summit.'

He left his room and walked along the corridor towards the elevator section. 07:15 hours - breakfast first, then a swift visit to see Michael Ben-Tovim, leader of the Israeli delegation. Felixana and the team would cover the European press conference at 09:00; that would form the first 'regular report' to London mentioned by the BBC's World Service. Landon himself was playing a hunch. He had seen Chief Diplomat Muller's stone-faced response to Felixana's question on the Southern Brotherhood and he wanted to investigate further. He knew Ben-Tovim, had met him many years before in Tel Aviv. Warning bells of a good story were playing softly in Landon's head; he sensed that in some way Israel might hold the key. Landon presented himself at Ben-Tovim's door on the third floor of the diplomat's residential tower. The neat, dark-haired fifty five year old diplomat beamed as the door panel slid back.

"Craig Landon! Come in - come in! It's good to see you. I wondered if you would be covering the summit."

The nearby security officer, satisfied with Landon's authenticity as a friend of the senior diplomat, quietly moved away to resume his duty position at the end of the corridor. Ben-Tovim's outstretched hand drew Landon into the room. The visitor noticed it was larger than his own; no surprise, because diplomats would have better accommodation than pressmen.

"It is such a pleasure to see you again, Craig, but I can only let you stay a few minutes. I have a briefing at ten hours and such occasions are obviously not for the press!"

Landon sat at the invitation of his host.

"To renew a friendship is a good thing, Michael, but I also come to seek some advice."

"Oh, you would like some advice, eh? That's a new word for an interview!"

The mutual laughter came easily - the two men were boxing with each other, aware of hidden strengths and yet determined to maintain the niceties of unspoken confidences. After his initial tentative thrust the BBC man backed off slightly to the calmer waters of family. Ben-Tovim smiled.

"They are well, thank you. Young David is now seven, and we have a daughter, too. Rachel is four. Yes, I know I am almost too old to be a father, and I must admit I do get very tired! I am blessed that Anna looks after them well, she's a good wife. And yourself, are you still with, er…." He snapped his fingers to pull in the memory. "Jane."

Landon sighed. "Jane and I have parted."

For some strange reason, Landon felt slightly uncomfortable. He envied the Jew his solid marriage, the warmth and comfort of constancy in a shifting world. The slow death of religion as a powerful force in much of the developed world over the previous century had led to a corresponding decline in the institution of marriage. The majority had found that without spiritual strength the cement wouldn't set. Landon pulled himself onto a tougher subject.

"Michael, I won't ask about Israeli intentions, but I would appreciate an opinion on likely voting patterns seen through your eyes, on tomorrow's early financial decisions."

Ben-Tovim's face was impassive, giving nothing away. "Why is my opinion important, Craig?"

The diplomat's olive eyes gazed into Landon's. He had known the Englishman for eleven years, having been interviewed first by him in 2120 on the point of leaving the Israeli army. Landon did not know of his Mossad connections. Ben-Tovim was a devout Jew; Landon certainly knew that about him. His wife, Anna, was a liberal secular Israeli; perhaps he would have been more comfortable if he had been talking with her instead of her husband.

"I know Israel stands at a sort of bridge between two worlds. The western nations have shared much of their technology and achievements with your country, and for your part we have benefitted from the advances in artificial horticulture over the past fifty years. I sense, however, a link to the under-developed world."

Ben-Tovim did not respond other than to confirm with his eyes that he was concentrating on the Englishman's words. He knew Landon would develop his argument quietly and with penetrating logic.

"That's partly due to your history over two hundred years," the guest continued. "When the State of Palestine was created in 2046 as part of the Three States Agreement the old fears of extinction began to haunt Israel again. The strain of maintaining the world's fourth largest army has clearly continued to build up to the point where real poverty has begun to bite into parts of the nation. There is your Faith, as well. Judaism has enveloped your political consciousness completely now. There is a secular strand, but it has become smaller. Only that strand bridges your country to the west these days."

Ben-Tovim permitted himself the ghost of a smile. Landon continued.

"How much do you know about the Southern Brotherhood, Michael?"

"Probably no more than anyone else does." He stood up and paced his room slowly, giving him time to weigh his words.

"Rumour has it that certain nations are pooling their diplomatic resources." He shrugged, and continued pacing, speaking softly to his visitor.

"It's something I suppose has been growing since the last world summit in 2121. The frustration and anger were there then, but it wasn't quite organised into a coherent-enough weapon. Times haven't changed, they've only got worse. The world's developed nations have tried to hold onto their monopoly of wealth. China and some of the middle-eastern states, those known over one hundred years ago as sovereign wealth states, have joined that unholy club. Despite advances in medical science the health problems of much of Africa and South America and, indeed, even pockets of southern Asia, have been so immense as to be untouched

25

by these advances. Wherever stability has established itself and begun to trade at tough competition with the northern powers, certain interests have seen to it that any serious competition, however early its stages, has been nipped in the bud to ensure supremacy of the northern product.

This attitude over the years has set a divide, and, some would say unfortunately, the aggrieved felt they had to respond. You will have seen how, for example, medical organisation in Africa has begun to be self-contained. Any discoveries which until now had been made widely available are being jealously guarded. There is still a strong attempt to prevent the Zambian breakthrough on artificial eyes spreading to the northern powers. The Brotherhood is organising disadvantaged nations, helping them to conserve their strengths and diminish their considerable weaknesses."

The Israeli diplomat paused. Landon spoke softly. "Who does rumour say leads the Brotherhood?"

"Brazil."

"How do you think the voting will go tomorrow?"

"I think the under-privileged nations will see things turn their way. I may be wrong, but in any case the current is flowing that way."

The two men fell into silence for a few seconds. Landon then rose slowly. He sensed a new gulf between himself and his friend, but one which was tinged with sadness rather than bitterness. In order to maintain the semblance of seniority he decided to retain the initiative in the conversation.

"I wish you well, Michael. Thank you for inviting me in."

Ben-Tovim smiled; sincere kindness flashed between them. Landon felt better. A few moments later he was walking across the honey-coloured concourse between the residential towers, towards the press quarters. He gazed up at the morning sky, the rich blue of a Mediterranean autumn holding a blazing sun. There was only a slight hint in the air of the meteorological terror unfolding barely a thousand kilometres to the north.

10:05 hours - the throb of an intercontinental transport pulsed overhead, circling to the south and east, blotting the sun momentarily like a giant vulture thick with menace. Landon glanced up and noticed the Air

26

Varig symbol on the plane's tail. The arrival of the Brazilian delegation, having flown direct from the large air and earth port at Recife, was noteworthy. The northern Brazilian city boasted the world's only joint airport and earth-port, carrying travellers from around the world, the orbiting residential and scientific stations, and the Russian, Chinese, European and American bases on the moon. The transport dropped from sight, over to the east where the Valletta Air reception would deal with its cargo of people and diplomatic baggage. Landon walked faster - he had to check on the outcome of the regular report to London for the BBC's news service. He reached the rising pavement and stopped walking. The gently-moving incline would take him in through the glass frontage of the press building and lift him in a series of wide circles to the seventeenth floor if he wanted it to do so. His reporting team was waiting for him, however, on the second floor. He stepped off the walkway there and joined them near the large window overlooking the sea.

10:20 hours - Landon slid a payment card along a wall slot to collect a glass of iced orange juice from a recess. He sipped slowly, gazing out to sea as Felixana ran through the electronic sheaf of press hand-outs. He concentrated on her voice; the aura of fatefulness had clung about him from his meeting with Ben-Tovim, but the rigours of professional training prevented the mood from gripping him to the point of day-dreaming. He was watching a small boat about five hundred metres off shore when Felixana reached the schedule of lunchtime briefings.

"The three main reception interviews are with the U.S. main delegates, the Russian and Chinese deputies. Broadcasting at that time will be live."

Landon turned, his mind made up.

"No, we'll interview the Brazilian diplomats at the studios in the Mezzanine Concourse."

Devine and Ashton looked up from their equipment in surprise; Felixana merely waited for her colleague to expand on his point. He didn't.

"What time do they expect journalists?"

She checked her list again, the tiny wrist screen flashing through digital details until the Brazilian entry glowed. "Thirteen hours."

She hesitated again, willing Landon with her silence to be drawn out. This time he was.

"I think we may have some inside information. Brazil, it seems, is going to play a big part in the summit. The BBC ought to get in early with appropriate questions even if we don't get specific answers."

He finished his juice, placing the plastic container back in the wall alcove. A door closed and the plastic was vaporised to the accompaniment of a soft hum. Felixana suddenly remembered her lunch date with Zarbelli.

"Excuse me a moment. I must cancel a lunch engagement I'd made."

She walked over to the bar reception and punched a sequence of numbers on the room-pad in a spare booth against the wall. Her voice was soft and honeyed.

"Toni, I'm busy at thirteen hours; can't make it for lunch. I'm afraid. If you can, please meet me in our bar at twenty one thirty, later."

The message was stored. It would be replayed automatically by the computerised room service when Zarbelli himself returned to his room. Felixana re-joined her reporting colleagues. Landon wrapped up the session.

"We'll meet at twelve forty five on the Mezzanine Concourse. I'll report our intention to be present at the Brazilian press session. Felixana and I will piece together the questions we intend to ask in my room at twelve hours."

Nods of assent all round. Pip Ashton was pleased; he'd met a young Japanese interpreter the evening before and he could certainly use a spare hour or so to press home his advantage with her.

Romero Duarte entered the mezzanine studio at precisely thirteen hours. Accompanied by two young swarthy colleagues, their black eyes darting ceaselessly, the balding diplomat walked to the presentation dais and sat down. There were few people in the room - the BBC quartet, two reporters from South American news channels, three Council security guards and Duarte himself with his two 'supporters'. The official security guards wore stun weapons below their white tunic tops. The corners of Landon's mouth lifted in a barely-discernible smile; in any other set of circumstances it would have been Duarte's thugs who would be armed, but Council protocol made arming of diplomatic personnel strictly forbidden. Ancient Vienna Conventions had been flouted in London nearly one and a half centuries before when Libyan diplomats had resorted to gun warfare. Ever since then, an increasing number of nation states had agreed not to abuse diplomatic immunity. Libya itself was by now a solid peaceful democracy of over one hundred years' standing, well-respected in the Arab world for its stability. Like all nations, moreover, it possessed x-ray lasers, so diplomatic bags were about as secret as goldfish bowls in what they could hide.

Duarte recognised the BBC insignias straight away and his eyebrows moved. A soft patina of sweat appeared on his brow. He didn't have Muller's Teutonic drilling, just bluff, bluster, and in the right circumstances, barely-veiled threatening poses. None of these would serve him now. He hadn't expected neutral or possibly hostile coverage this early in the world summit. He waved a chubby pink palm at the man from Brasilia Tempo, wishing to warm up with a few puppy shots.

"Are Brazil's finances going to be a major bone of contention here tomorrow?"

"Sim, that is most sure."

The voice was soft and almost gruff. Not surly, but quite close to it, Landon felt. The Brazilian reporter continued.

"Do you have any intention of holding back on sharing any of Brazil's medical advances if there is no progress in financial matters?"

Duarte pursed his ample lips. "That is a possibility, certainly, but I feel the United States of America and others will see the importance of sharing their wealth for the good of the whole planet."

The Brazilian diplomat was warming to the task. He felt it would be a magnanimous gesture to introduce the global perspective, the mark of a statesman. He threw an inviting hand at Felixana Smith, dressed in mid blue tunic edged with dark blue piping, long dark hair tumbling easily over her shoulders.

"Senhor Duarte, will Brazil be working with any other nations in the discussions in the Council chamber tomorrow?"

"Brazil has friends, it is true, but Brazil's voice is to look after its own people."

Devine's holographic equipment purred softly, recording the Brazilian whose tubby colour image would be pumped into millions of European homes that evening on news broadcasts. Felixana continued.

"How many nations have joined your Southern Brotherhood now?"

The word 'your,' stung Duarte.

"It is not 'my Brotherhood'; it belongs to the poor people of the world."

"Is Brazil poor, then?" The diplomat couldn't answer such an innocently-simple question with deeply complex connotations. It was never meant to be answered, anyway, only designed to throw Duarte off-balance for a further punch.

"What do you say to the rumours that Brotherhood power over the past ten years is now changing and slipping away from its leaders?"

Duarte snapped at the bait. He glared witheringly, his Portuguese accent rushing back into his English.

"We shall continue to lead the fight for human justice!"

His hand flicked back to the man from Brasilia Tempo, choosing to spend the rest of the interview voyage in less tempestuous waters.

14:15 hours -

"You hit a nerve, Felixana." Craig Landon smiled with satisfaction.

"It gives us enough to build a report around a shift in control within the Southern Brotherhood."

The two were sitting on a rocky outcrop above the high water mark. The mid-afternoon sun at their backs was just warm enough for the shedding of an over-tunic. The climatic shift now terrorising northern Europe was noticeable even in the southern Mediterranean. Landon's gaze followed a sea-bird, dipping and whirling above the endlessly-restless sea.

"The question took me by surprise, I must say. What made you assume Brazil was losing its grip, anyway?"

"The way Duarte stated 'it's not my Brotherhood'. It smacked of petulance. If all was well within the ranks he would have been only too quick to crow about his world leadership role. As it is, I played a hunch to see if he is about to be toppled."

"We still don't know what form the changed Brotherhood will take. Something fairly substantial or Duarte would still be content. I've spoken with my friend Ben-Tovim, the Israeli diplomat. Something is building, something powerful."

Landon rose to his feet and walked along the beach, away from the World States Council complex. Felixana walked alongside. Her colleague continued with the logic of his argument.

"It was a sort of scoop to have identified a probable shift in power before tomorrow's opening session. We'll build a full report for live broadcast at the BBC News 18:30 scheduled programme."

The girl kicked idly at the sand with a soft fabric slipper. Landon watched the dry grains fly out in a perfect fan and fall back, continuing his thinking out loud.

"There's little else we can do at the moment. The pieces are all here now; we can only wait and watch."

Wednesday 23 October

Toni Zarbelli felt good. Whistling with unrestrained gusto, he combed his hair. It had been a fulfilling night. He could still sense the warm slight body of the BBC girl, pressed against him with unexpected strength. Her cool white neck and shaking thighs, the moans of her orgasm; the memory had lingered satisfyingly. Loneliness had drained from his body as he had reached his own fulfilment. The relaxing drift into sleep followed, accompanied by thoughts of a young Italian girl he still remembered from years before. Streaming sunlight had awakened him. He rolled over to find himself alone. It had not been a dream; the bed still bore her imprint. He had sighed contentedly, laying for a second, reliving the night.

The pressures of the day had slowly filtered back into his consciousness. It was Wednesday; the day of the opening session of the World States Council's ten-year Full Congress. He stood beneath the micro-shower unit, his skin being tingled clean and dried in a few short seconds. He dressed - white underpants, a cotton top in white with blue piping and silvery-blue trousers. Casual slip-ons in rich burgundy sheathed his feet. He felt on top of the world. There would be no opportunity to speak with Felixana at present; seats for the media were strictly allocated for the start of the first plenary session of the Congress. He guessed she was already planning her professional day. He rode the elevator down to the smaller of the two restaurants in his residential tower. There was seating here for two hundred, beneath a cantilevered glass dome which would open later in the day to provide a barbecue patio, like a giant flower unfurling its petals.

He sat at a vacant eating surface. A small screen glowed into life at his right hand. He placed a finger against the spot marked 'italiano'. The breakfast menu strung itself out in soft green letters for him. The choice was massive - he touched the roll-on square and page two appeared. He sat back, waiting for his orange juice, warm toast fingers, honey and black coffee to arrive. The restaurant had human waiter service. After about three minutes a young Maltese man in white uniform moved purposefully through the dining area to where Zarbelli sat. The white tray he carried bore the items ordered. The two men exchanged smiles. The good feeling continued - even the fact that he had forgotten to press the butter button for the toast did not irritate him. The orange juice chilled the back of his throat beautifully. He ate at peace with the world.

Two hours later he stood at the entrance to press gallery 41 at the main Congress chamber. The security guards watched impassively as he placed his flattened right hand, palm downwards, into the admission slot in the side wall of the doorway. The tracer analysed the whole hand in a fraction of a second - finger and palm prints, thickness of flesh, residual perspiration - this was Zarbelli. He was ushered through into the press gallery. It stretched out on either side to an overall width of about fifteen metres. In front of him, the floor sloped slightly downwards to a spot four metres away where a glass-fronted overhang enabled reporters' eyes to look down into the Congress chamber itself.

10:05 hours - the chamber was beginning to fill. The sight below was impressive. Concentric circles of silver consoles with softly-glowing blue lights were being attended by an increasing number of delegates. Wine-coloured upholstered seats were not staying empty for long as the senior representative of each of the one hundred and thirteen nations took their places and settled down. Zarbelli watched the principal Congress administrators in the centre of the chamber going through the steady routine of electronic security checking. There were no imposters here, at least not in the normally-accepted sense. Only time would tell, thought Zarbelli, if any were merely masquerading in the role of world leadership. He sat at his allotted place and pressed the roll-up button. A thin glass bubble rose up round him, cutting off the shuffling expectant sounds of the press gallery. Reporter bubbles had disconcerted him in the early stages of his career but he was now accustomed to their claustrophobic effect. That effect was easily outweighed by the remarkable advantage they held. The memory of the press gallery faded; the sounds, odours and growing tensions around him now were those of the main Congress chamber below. The blue lights on the chamber's consoles turned red simultaneously - the Congress was in session.

Congress Secretary Lee Kuan Lee rose to his feet. The desk-top cue screens cast a small image up against his head visor and he read the words appearing twenty centimetres in front of his eyes. He spoke in English. His words rang crisply and clearly around the chamber.

"Representatives - I welcome you on behalf of the peoples of the world to the Eighth Economic Congress of the World States Council. The decisions you reach here will control the course of world financial events for the decade ending in December 2145."

The main console lights stayed red to indicate that voting could not take place, but the subsidiary communication indicators twinkled on and off incessantly as messages were transmitted into and out of each representative's desk unit. Zarbelli shifted his weight in his seat, renewing his concentration. The Indonesian Secretary continued. There was no need for him to turn to the different sections of the audience in the circular chamber. As he spoke, the raised dais turned slowly, presenting the speaker to all in turn. The chamber's natural light twinkled on Lee Kuan Lee's epaulettes as his body turned.

"I now introduce Representative Pierre Faulkner of the Canadian delegation, current President of plenary Congress, to open our deliberations. Please refer to your agenda papers."

Zarbelli shifted again. No applause greeted the President from the chamber. 'World conferences these days were nothing if not business-like', reflected the reporter. That business ebbed and flowed. Then the United States representative read out the set proposal before the Congress, that the World Bank's distribution of resources for the decade starting on 1st January 2136 remain in the same pattern at that currently obtaining. The representative presented her statement in rich, ringing, authoritative tones. The chamber audience moved slightly in restive response. The proposal came to an end with the words - 'I so move', and she left the dais. Zarbelli was watching Representative Muller at the European Union console, noticing the concern still etched into his features. He saw him lean forward, speaking into the intercom unit to a colleague outside the chamber.

Eyes shifted to the display boards hanging round the upper walls. These told that Representative Doctor Austin Mbene would oppose the motion. Zarbelli checked with his personal information screen, learning that Mbene was the voting representative of the newly-independent Republic of Transkei. The African had a limp in his left leg, walking slowly to the central dais. The matt of his sand-brown tunic served to highlight the glossy black of his skin - more like a Nigerian's than that of a Transkeier. He hesitated at the rostrum, calm eyes gazing out on a sea of expectant faces. His voice was firm as it began, not loud but letting each word and phrase hang for a second in the mind.

"There is snow and bitter cold over much of the world which lies north of this place. It is surely an unforgiving October. Industrial nations are watching while a citizen dies every five minutes from the extreme temperatures. It is not that extreme I have to speak of now. It is not that bitterness. I have to speak out for the other world, the world to the south, the world where an untimely and unnecessary death occurs not every five minutes, but every five seconds. I speak out on behalf of those who taste the bitterness of hunger, of disease, and of neglect. What is the most terrifying aspect of this? It is that for these peoples, this October is not so memorable. October 2131 is no different from October 2031, or even October 1981, one hundred and fifty years ago. Countless millions of souls have passed on in that century and a half, paying silent testimony to a harsh economic creed that puts cars and technological gadgetry above bread and clean water. Famines and droughts have stalked our world for many generations.

I turn my eyes to the heavens and what do I see? There are steel islands spinning in orbit far above us which pass daily over a world which continues to cry out for life itself. Those islands spin quite oblivious to the desperation far below them."

Mbene hesitated, letting the images of Copernicus Centre and the three other orbiting stations settle into the minds of his listening audience.

"The bitterness of an early winter reflects the bitterness we feel, and have felt for an eternity. We have been made to wait for too long for

34

God's true justice, but we wait no more. I call upon all brothers and sisters to vote out this obscenity before us, by supporting the following amendment."

Mbene gazed out at the assembly before him and spoke slowly and clearly, so there could be no mistake.

"This Congress supports the present distribution of world financial resources for no longer than the end of December 2135. Thereafter, in five succeeding years on each first day of January, one tenth of international funding at the starting day, calculated as Gross Domestic Product identified by the Bank of International Settlements in its immediate preceding annual report, be transferred to nations presently in full membership of the World Faiths Congress, from nations not so in membership, in order that by 2140, one half of the North's industrial reserves be reallocated to the starving world; and may God's Will be done!"

The chamber buzzed with emotion. Congress Secretary Lee pressed the control pad to grant the right to speak to the United States' representative. The voice of Josephine J Summers dived into the diplomatic maelstrom.

"The world deserves better than this! Industrial nations do much for the whole planet. It is a partnership - to break that partnership now would serve none of us any good. The poorer nations would never cope without technological support."

A few metres to the left of Zarbelli's reporter bubble sat Craig Landon, his attention frozen on the events unfolding in the huge bowl below him. He was anchor for Felixana in the BBC bubble, feeding her with background information to flesh out her commentary. Landon's eyes lifted to the indicator lights high above the Congress Secretary's position, the white circle shifting the right to speak to Japan. One by one the representatives gave their nation's views on transferring financial resources. When contributions had nearly finished, Landon leaned forward on impulse, hairs itching on the nape of his neck. He found himself speaking to his colleague.

"Things are speeding up - slip in something about a momentous decision about to be taken."

Felixana hesitated, the thought flashing into her mind 'that can't be, they haven't put the automatic voting sequence into operation yet.' The

35

trusting working relationship with Landon took over. She spoke to her audience.

"The ordered way of the world is about to change as". She got no further, her mouth open in forgetfulness as her eyes fixed on the main voting console, blazing in a green mass, inviting representatives to start casting their votes. The assembled representatives watched as the automatic voting sequence started. Mbene was back in his seat again. He thrust out his hand theatrically onto his console to extinguish his light in issue of a vote in support of his amendment. Like a mighty tide, other hands followed. Craig Landon watched while his chest tightened with nervous tension. Pinpoints of green light winked out into eloquent darkness on the main voting console, bearing witness to the soul of the southern hemisphere. Landon's eyes desperately tried to follow the arithmetic. Were there thirty or forty already? He found his eyes drawn towards one particular light, still glowing steadily. How much time had passed since the start of the voting sequence? How many of the allotted ninety seconds remained for votes in favour?

The Israeli light winked out! Gasps rose from the chamber now as a second wave of darkness bathed the console. Pakistan, Bangladesh, Southern Iraq, Kurdistan, Morocco, Iran, then the Korean Federation, followed. Within seven more seconds the target was achieved. Enough nations had signalled affirmation of Mbene's dream. A total of sixty one 'yes' votes had been registered. The rest of the automation was hollow theatre. The palms that registered 'no' votes shook with anger, despair and fear - among them Canada, Japan, United States of America, the European Union, the Russian Federation, the Peoples' Republic of Greater China and the Australian Republic. The abstentions - Trinidad and Tobago, Turkish Cyprus and a few more - were hardly noticed in the turmoil of shock and confusion. Vivid cameos flashed into Landon's eyes, cameos that were to haunt him in the coming weeks: Hans Muller's grey face, grey as granite and just as hard; Josephine J Summers burying her head behind her hands as she slumped forward in her seat; the squeal of released elation and glowing bright eyes of the Jamaican representative as he flew across to grasp Mbene's arm in jubilant greeting.

The reporting chambers were in equal turmoil. In tens of languages the message was instantly beaming around the world. On World States Council and World Bank wavelengths the same message bore the ring of authority and the command of instruction - ring mains of computers bowed in technological obedience to the voting decision. The credit balances of the commercial and socialist power blocs were being automatically locked into a new direction to await the arrival of the year 2136. Landon rose from his seat and whirled from the reporting chamber, moving to the down walkways. The buzz of the Congress chamber was sound-proofed away behind him. Clenched fists by his side betrayed his tension. He was tempted into a restrained jog until the glowing red plastic beneath his feet warned him to slow to a walk again - he had forgotten that running was forbidden in the Congress buildings.

He wanted to get down to the main chamber level, to catch the representatives as they emerged. He reached one of the main exit doors as the Russian representative stormed out, his round glowering face almost merging in colour with the regulation brown of his clothing. He swept past Landon who was jostled aside by a bodyguard. The BBC man bounced against the wall, catching only a glimpse of the guard's face as he recovered. A mild sensation of revulsion followed the sight of the Russian's earless right profile; merely smooth skin covering his flesh from his collar to his hairline.

Thursday 24 October

"Howl!"

Pip Ashton's use of the expletive in fashion was his response to the biting cold hitting his face at the external doors of reception at London Maplin. Landon chuckled softly with a humour he didn't feel and pushed his colleague playfully in the back.

"Go on, a young fellow like you can take a bit of a chill, surely?"

Ice gripped through the banter; they both knew this was more than 'a bit of a chill'. The airport out in the Thames estuary was more exposed than its predecessors at Stansted, Luton and Heathrow. Prime land was at a premium, and the former sites had been relinquished many years before. The isolation of the maritime setting added violence into the climatic strangeness afflicting England as with all Europe's northern states. The circlet of raised helipads at the centre of the complex had taken on the appearance of a giant frozen statue. A cutting wind blew in from the North Sea, buffeting the odd gull spinning over the water. Grey puffs of cloud smudged the crystal-blue sky, swept into its clarity by the astringent wind. Landon's throat tightened. It was difficult for him to recall a winter like this, never mind an autumn.

The memory which clung with greater force, however, was of the day before in Malta. In varying storms of confusion, recrimination and elation the Eighth Economic Congress of the World States Council had dissolved away on the day it had started. The welter of emotion had proved too much of a strain for the delicate lattice of mistrust in the world's international diplomatic arena. Within fifteen minutes of the Wednesday vote having been taken, there had been insufficient numbers of representatives remaining in the Congress chamber to form a quorum. As twilight fell, many delegations were finalising hastily-arranged departures. The BBC team had bought space on a Thursday morning flight to Maplin via De Gaulle, buzzing with the dramatic turn of events. A flurry of movement behind him caused Craig Landon to break from his grim reverie and turn to his up-coming colleague. Paul Devine was out of breath, as usual, puffing away as he caught up with his two compatriots. Landon smiled.

"Fine there's no interview, Paul."

The holographic officer took the soft jibe of a rebuke in good heart.

"My equipment is the heaviest." He patted his stomach. "That means the flesh as well as the plasti-metal!"

The three laughed into the teeth of the wind and walked down the outer reception ramp to their waiting Corporation hover-car. The nearside panel slid back with no audible hiss against the background of weather. Warm air from the plush interior fanned out into the three tired faces. The senior executive ushered his juniors into places behind the driver, then slid in himself. The car slipped smoothly from its parking hover into forward drive, dipping away to the right down the exit road, curls of white snow dust rolling out in its wake as it rode a metre and a half above the plastic concrete. Young Ashton voiced the thoughts of the three.

"I wonder how Felix is getting on in Italy."

Devine's hum was heard, as he absent-mindedly watched the grim whiteness flash by outside the speeding car. Landon himself merely smiled, though it was tinged with some resigned sadness. Felixana's predilection for male companionship was well known within their small circle. The pally shortening of her full name, though, would never have been allowed in her presence. She was now in Padua, visiting Zarbelli's mother, no doubt, thought Landon.

"Felixana's a big girl, Pip, and she has rest due to her. We have to wind things up here; there's little else for us to do. Whatever stories come out of this situation now are far above our level."

Ashton shrugged his acceptance and returned to contemplation of the snow. Since the snowfall had stopped, the hover-routes into the State capital had been reopened.

'Centre traffic congestion at Chigwell; turn north at Billericay.'

The driver swung the car to the right in response to the automated call, heading north to gain entry to central London at the huge Harlow interchange. Between Chelmsford and Ongar the rural zones of Anglia finally gave way to London's urban order. Landon leaned forward.

"How long before we get to Broadcasting House now?"

The Corporation driver checked his controls. "Another hour, or just under, I suppose; say, fifteen hours thirty."

The car slotted into traffic lines at Harlow, streams of vehicles in hover lanes above and below separated by the regulation five metres in each direction. The car's computer spoke again.

'Move to radar spacing. Thirty second warning at Broadcasting House intersection.'

The driver relaxed as the automatic pilot cut in. The massive stream of cars flowed into London like water down a drain. The BBC car joined the second stack. Two-storey housing units rose on either side, the rows distanced some seventy metres apart, separated by the surge of traffic. Lights in window slots were winking on; twilight was coming. Snow clouds were rolling back in. Devine broke the silence, turning to Landon.

"How will yesterday affect ordinary mortals like us, Craig?"

Landon's lips pursed; he was unsure of how to reply.

"Half of the northern world's financial resources will be shifted by the time the next nine years are over. The effects don't really bear thinking about. Incomes and investments will be halved while prices stay nominally static. I say 'nominally' of course, but the social and emotional upheaval of the stripping away of half of a person's finances is certain to increase anxiety and even fear. Fear is the most powerful negative emotion in existence. Inflation will get out of control. It will pull along with it the second most powerful - greed. Most people will look for ways of recovering the lost ground, and only the ruthless will survive. Individually, there could be ruin for many, and even for those who manage to adjust to what it means, will suffer as a part of the culture shock. Not just our economies will suffer. The Chinese communist world will feel the shock as well. We've been linked now for over fifty years in our treatment of the African continent, and indeed parts of South America and Asia. Moscow and Beijing will be just as worried today as Washington and Brussels."

It was all too much for Devine; he fiddled absent-mindedly with his holographic camera for the remainder of the journey.

The triple pyramids of Broadcasting House at Shepherd's Bush stood solidly against the first flurries of the afternoon snowfall. London was bracing itself for another bitterly cold night. The snow over the previous two days had not achieved the comprehensive efforts of Sunday or Monday, but the relief was hardly noticeable. Unseasonably-low temperatures continued - the lying snow would not easily go away. The depression of car pad four had been kept clear electrically. As the motor died the sounds of the gusting wind swept in, easily swamping the barely-audible rustle of the BBC car's heating unit. Landon thanked the driver, commenting on the smooth ride.

"No problem - from what I hear, the bumpy times are yet to come!"

The vehicle lifted off for the car pool, leaving the three passengers to walk through opening pad doors to the Broadcasting House interior.

Wednesday 30 October

'Good morning. Here is the BBC world news.'

Craig Landon was standing at the window of his housing unit in Windsor. His gaze rested delicately on the weak morning sunshine lighting on a small group of oak trees as he listened to the radio stream online.

'Last week's decision of the World States Council's Economic Congress continues to have a catastrophic effect on financial markets throughout the world. In New York at the close of Tuesday trading the Northern Average stood at fourteen thousand seven hundred, down four hundred on the day. Markets are bracing themselves for further fall this morning when the European bourses open. The money news in the past few hours from the far- east has not been good.'

Although Windsor Great Park was only one third of the size it had been in the late twentieth century, it remained the largest open green

40

space in central London. Ten -day old crunchable snow lay centimetres deep across the normally -green expanse stretching out from the housing areas towards the castle. 'Was the Princess Regent in residence today?' he wondered. His eyes were vacant, the whitened tracery of the trees framing a tranquil backdrop to the wasp of worry buzzing and baiting his troubled mind. Something from Malta had refused to settle to his satisfaction. The radio cut into his thoughts again.

'Heavy snowfall has again disrupted air traffic and commercial life generally in northern States. Seventeen people died in Bremerhaven last night when a cargo airship carrying materials for the new Friesian hydro project was blown into a harbour-side hotel. Senior engineers from the French Mystere Corporation will begin the final demolition of the Eiffel Tower early in the New Year. The two hundred and forty two year old tower has been closed to the public for over thirty years and the dismantling will leave the site clear for redevelopment. Sources close to the Union government have indicated that the Trocadero site was still being considered for Europe's third earth-port.'

"Craig, sorry to break into your news broadcast this early, but I need you. Please switch to visual."

The mild urgency in the voice of Outside Broadcast Controller Stevens brought a shutter of concentration down over the autumnal scene. Landon turned on his heels and swept his left hand over the screen console. The Controller was clearly excited. His sandy-red hair tousled about his head, betraying his early rising despite his clothed appearance. He grinned spontaneously on seeing Landon's bedroom-clothed figure expand onto his screen.

"Good morning, Craig. You'd better dress quickly and get over to Kingsclere. At the private airfield there the American Secretary of State is scheduled to arrive at ten hours this morning. We don't know why he's coming and we haven't even been told officially that it's happening. A leak in Washington to our private sources is all we've got. Security's bound to be tight. I don't expect an interview, obviously, but I do want some pictures. Anything to give the BBC a scoop would be great."

Landon was not on screen as his Controller jabbered on. Tunic, slip-ons and outer weather-jack were thrown on feverishly as he listened to the voice.

It beats me why England was chosen for a secret visit. If we get enough that's substantive they won't even be able to deny that it's happening. I'm assuming it's the Union government that's flicking the

41

switches on this one; a top-notch Yank is hardly likely to come over to see the State Governor."

Stevens heard the apartment door snap shut off screen.

"Craig, are you still there?" He squinted at the furniture in the empty room.

"Craig? Craig?"

Bitterly-cold air followed Landon into his hover car. A succinct stab at a heater control brought warmer air whistling into the unmarked car with the early morning sun on its tail fins. At nine hours the flood of traffic was eastwards; comparatively little moved west out of London. The BBC man spoke softly to the car's guidance system, his voice taut with the nervous tension bubbling inside him.

"I need ETA Kingsclere, given present conditions."

'Twenty five minutes.'

A thought struck Landon. "Give me a less conspicuous approach, please." Only a moment's hesitation followed.

'Head via Fleet and Basingstoke. ETA would be forty minutes.'

Landon touched the automatic pilot. "Execute."

The one word of command was sufficient. The BBC car banked south at Bracknell's hover interchange and accelerated. A short sequence of buttons put the driver back in touch with his O.B. Controller.

"Approaching Fleet and on time. I have a few tricks to evade the outer security rings, but we'll likely have nothing spectacular at this short notice."

"Understood, Craig; just do what you can. Close down transmissions now. There'll be automatic monitoring of all frequencies once you get within eight kilometres of Kingsclere."

"Fine, John. I'll be in touch." Another sequence and the contact went dead.

Beyond Basingstoke in the final approaches Landon began his descent following the Hover-way Code. A ghost of a smile played across his lips.

As expected, his instrumentation was alerting him to security surveillance at eight kilometres from the airfield perimeter. He reached for a small box on his car's panel. He synchronised a green blip with a hairline cross and set a ten-second manual timer. The car sped on as the timer reached contact and activated. The green blip peeled away sharply to the left at a hover-way interchange, just as its twin was doing on a security screen somewhere ahead. Landon's eyes flicked onto the surveillance light. The glow disappeared - security had lost its interest in him, for the moment.

An earth bank appeared ahead and to the left, three metres high and stretching away for a kilometre or so, running parallel with the car's flight. The airfield boundary would be topped by a lattice of electrically-charged particles. Their controlling mechanism would inspect every transgressor, ignoring the birds and stunning the humans. Landon switched his tachograph off, dropping to two metres, well below the minimum legal flow height. His jaw set firmly. A stationary hover was all that was permitted at two metres; certainly not twenty five kilometres per hour. The immediate danger would be running into stray pedestrians, but he had to stay out of view below the boundary earthworks. The concrete hover-way swung in a wide arc to the left, following the raised earthwork. Landon risked lifting to three and a half metres to survey the field. On the far side, over six hundred metres away, the low white administration block stood like a squashed mushroom. There appeared to be no sign of activity. He dropped the car again to avoid detection, checking the dashboard clock - 09:50. He let the car gently slow to a stationary hover behind a small copse of trees, his fingers drumming absent-mindedly on the dashboard as he considered how to proceed. He was surprised that the trees were even there. A military base with a higher security rating would have circumvented the European Woodlands Acts and cut them down. Either the Secretary of State was in a hurry or there was something special about the location of Kingsclere.

Steering further behind the copse to hide him from the airfield he lifted the vehicle to leave the roof just level with the top branches. Sliding the roof-light back he took a deep breath and heaved himself upwards. The cold reality of open air stung his head; a momentary feeling of vertigo passed and concentration returned. Lying on the gently-throbbing roof he looked beyond the frozen leaves towards the airfield. A bright yellow windsock rose and fell fitfully at the left edge of vision. He checked the time - 09:57. He became conscious of the thick condensation of his breath and resolved to exhale into the car. He slid back down onto the soft seats to gather the black delta-shape of his radio binoculars. Back up on the roof, his fingers found the dorsal spine, activating their screen.

Black cross-hairs against white snow leapt into view. There was no sign of life below the mushroom. To the building's left, three airport luggage carriers hung in parking hover like three black slugs. Landon glanced again at his wristband - 10:00 hours.

Forsaking the binoculars, he looked up at the blue sky, westward, searching for an incoming dot. Beyond the airfield, perhaps still five or so kilometres away, he saw it. The redirected optics trapped the sight. They panned down, following the craft until the powerful moan of the nuclear engines died and it was down. The black slugs were no longer rider less. Landon watched one sweep across the icy concrete towards the taxiing plane, followed closely by the other two. They took up position on either side of the nose assembly, escorting the large jet towards the administration building. Landon checked the calibration of his binoculars - one point five - just above minimum power and not enough to alert the transmission sniffer mounted atop the mushroom. The plane's door slid back and out, leaving a black hole in the shining surface. A man came into view; short, stocky in a light grey tunic. Low intensity on the binoculars wouldn't reveal his face at this distance. Despite the warning of danger, Landon eased the power of the glasses up a notch, causing them to purr softly in his hands.

The image which rushed into focus was that of the Vice-President of the United States of America, Harold P Lutz. The BBC man drew a breath sharply and lowered the glasses power again. Excitement and emotion burned in his cheeks. It was not the Secretary of State, but a bigger prize. Laying his head on the cold shell of the car roof he struggled with the implications thrown up by the appearance of the Vice-President. Steven's source had said the Secretary of State. A reliable source, high up no doubt, but not high enough, Landon concluded. Whatever had brought Lutz over the Atlantic was probably known only to himself and President Korda. Lutz walked briskly down the concertina walkway to the ground. The young man with flowing blond hair at the base of the steps was obviously Michael Thorson, the England State Governor. No surprise anymore; indeed, Landon expected such a high-powered reception after the shock of seeing Lutz.

The two men shook hands and forearms vigorously in friendly greeting, climbed aboard one of the slugs, and disappeared towards the buildings. The plane's power flowed back momentarily, it lifted on its cushion of air, and it peeled away to the enclosed hangars on the far side of the field. Landon swept his glasses the full cover of the field one last time to wrap up the final scene - there was nothing else worth seeing. He had already slung his cold legs back into the car when a sharp flash winked in the blueness of the sky, pulling his attention up again. At first he thought he was mistaken, but then he heard and saw it; a silver fuselage, a nuclear whine, another incoming aircraft. Binoculars swung to the base of the mushroom as he hastily resumed a prone position on the car roof. Sure enough, the slug carrying Thorson was returning to the centre of the field. The plane swept in like an eagle. It was smaller than its predecessor. Once it had landed, a tall slim man in black descended the steps.

Mild irritation at the absence of clues continued needling Landon to the point where he lifted his binocular power again. His eyes followed the stranger across the short span of open ground to the waiting escort vehicle. Two bodyguards nudged up alongside. One turned to look back at the plane. Shock hit Landon's stomach, bringing again the tightening sickness of excitement. There were surely not two security aides in world diplomacy with no left ear. "Russians!" gasped the BBC man aloud.

His attention was held by the disappearing slug, so he didn't see the security vehicle speeding across the snow to his point on the perimeter. He did notice it at five hundred metres and tumbled back into the car. His desperately-moving fingers jerked the car out of stationary hover into manual control. A lurching dip to the left was quickly corrected. The airfield Law vehicle slid through the temporarily-neutralised security field atop the earth bank, coming in low. Landon threw the BBC car forward and down in a tight circle to the left, banking round the trees to quickly come atop the metallic-blue military Law vehicle.

Full downward thrust at barely one metre had a devastating effect. The two security officers in their vehicle were pumped the short distance to the ground as firmly as a stopper bursting from a carbonated drinks flask. The shell of their car cracked on the frozen grass, splitting apart with a scream of tearing metal and plastic. Landon glanced down briefly over his shoulder as his own car recoiled into the sky. One of the men was visible near the wreck, having been thrown clear. The other must have still been inside the torn shell of their vehicle. Plates of earth-clogged ice and grass had scudded out from the point of impact. Landon steadied his vehicle at twenty five metres and hit forward drive. Three more security cars fanned out from the far side of the airfield buildings, but the BBC car was already slicing south through the brittle sunshine beyond their reach.

Saturday 9 November

"I don't know where Craig is, no-one does. Nobody's seen him for ten days."

Moon glow shimmered on the ice of the Thames, the same ethereal ghostly white of the Tower of London's ramparts nearby. Tower Hill Trattoria was full this Saturday evening; humanity huddling together for warmth and comfort against the bitter weather. But then the Trattoria was always popular. Like a huge flat wheel, tilted upwards towards the river, the structure was reminiscent in some ways of the former Atomium in Brussels, and the London Eye which had once existed a little further up the Thames. The five steel balls each housed a restaurant. The hub was built on the river bank, the restaurants arcing out over the river as the building rotated slowly, giving diners a complete panoramic circuit once every forty minutes. Toni Zarbelli's face turned from the spectacularly-lit Tower Bridge to look at his dining companion. He saw the concern flickering in Felixana's dark brown eyes.

"Who saw him last?" he asked.

"John Stevens, his O.B. Controller. Paul Devine told me that Craig missed a scheduled press conference a week last Thursday. I contacted John who said Craig had been sent on a rushed assignment the day before; that would be the 30th."

"Did he say what it covered?"

Felixana leaned forward slowly and lowered her voice.

"There was a secret visit to England due by the American Secretary of State. It was presumably to see the Governor, although John had no further information from his Washington source. There's been no news coverage of a visit, but that's to be expected. Whatever Craig found out has either forced him into hiding, or....."

She hesitated, catching a lump in her throat. Zarbelli acknowledged her fondness for her boss, reaching across and touching her hands.

"I'm sure he's alive somewhere. He's clever and tough, very tough. Remember I've seen him in action in India. He's well able to protect himself."

Felixana relaxed, the confidence flowing back into her fingers. Zarbelli eased back slightly, opening the way for her to regain composure fully by taking the initiative himself on the conversation.

"Look, I'm here as you asked me to be. You return to London on Tuesday and yesterday I get your message to come. Will the Law take any action to find Craig, or is there any reason to suspect their involvement?"

"No particular suspicion there, it's simply that State law in England requires four weeks' absence before they'll treat it as a possible crime."

"If Craig is hiding, or actively following up this American connection, there'll be no trace, anyway. He should be able to evade detection by the Law; if that's the way he's playing it."

"How long can you stay, Toni?"

He made a small gesture with a strong, tanned hand. "Three or four days won't go amiss. I have to report in for duty every Wednesday, wherever in the world I happen to be, but I have no Reuter's assignment at present."

The dinner passed, the open discussion of options and plans of campaign taking away the anxiety of the unknown; the gnawing feeling in Felixana of something being terribly wrong, but not knowing how to grasp it or bring it into focus. Around midnight, automatic units brought their outer jackets and they left in Felixana's vehicle, cruising silently through the deep canyons of the City's financial sector to her housing unit in Shoreditch. Zarbelli stretched his body in the warm cocoon of the car as tiredness began to creep into his limbs. An outstretched finger towards the radio activated the 'on' function. Music flooded the car and washed over him; soft, vibrant night music with wide shells of violin sounds eddying into his mind and splashing over his brain. She turned her head to him, smiling in the soft green glow from the instrument panel.

"Where do we start?"

The Italian smiled back. "We start by getting a good night's sleep, and I do mean a good night's sleep!"

They laughed together. The car became a nugget of warmth shooting through the vast frozen city.

Sunday 10 November

The sandy-haired man in a green tunic lay back in a conscious effort to release the tension in his body. He shifted his weight from one side to another, snuggling back into the red and white upholstery as the United American Airlines T94 Air Bullet pierced eastwards through the sky over the north Atlantic Ocean. He lifted his right arm to his ear to learn the time from his wrist band; in one and a half hours he would be in London. Professor Jon De Haag had been blind since birth, seventy one years before. Strong, sinewy fingers rested delicately on the grey plastic file on his lap. He could guess why he was wanted in England - his theories were needed. Yet they were only theories to him, born of the darkness in his eyes. It had taken someone else, another Dutchman, to bring them into the light of reality. The seductive drone of the Air Bullet's nuclear-powered flight brought sudden memories of the noisy bees around the hives of his childhood near Den Helder. Tension flowed out like a haemorrhage. Behind the closed eyelids, he dozed. A businessman with a pencil moustache seated at the opposite window turned his head away to gaze at the bottomless indigo of the threshold of space. He even closed his eyes for a few seconds, trying to imagine the kind of black universe in which his fellow traveller lived.

As the Sunday noon Air Bullet landed at London Maplin, Toni and Felixana were some kilometres away to the west, checking information records on her domestic screen in Shoreditch. A combination of BBC and Reuter's passwords was bringing rich pickings from the world's computer banks via the new organic web. Hospital and hospice entries, reported accidents, air and sea passenger manifests, earth port departures and arrivals, appointments in the business world and in politics; they were all trawled through until digits swum before the eyes. There was no trace of Craig Landon. The Italian downed his third coffee and let his fingers punch on, deeper into security. Felixana began to worry about her BBC clearance. The spoils that were being turned over were becoming more and more secretive. She was uncertain at what point Toni's higher clearance would leave a trail for the authorities to use to invalidate her own investigative licence. The lists became more sensitive; missing persons, inter-State law information, persons wanted for contravention of dangerous drugs regulations, unlicensed dealers in cigarettes, persons sought for extradition, lists of............Zarbelli stopped short, retraced the screen's last few steps and looked at the woman with a wide grin on his face. On 'information hold' the screen glowed brightly.

48

'LANDON, Craig, aged 45, World Finance Editor, British Broadcasting Corporation, is required for questioning in London for alleged serious fraud. Statement listed at Oxwich Bay Law Unit - 22 hours, 9 November'

"Alleged serious fraud?" Emotion trembled slightly in Felixana's voice. The relief at finally finding a clue had lifted her spirits, bubbling into her tone in wobbly excitement. "There's nothing fraudulent about Craig! It's obviously a trick."

He sensed again the fondness she held for Landon. "Where is Oxwich Bay?"

The girl shrugged. "I don't know; never heard of it. Let's look it up."

The gazetteer responded. Her confident movements were beginning to return. Her fingers flowed over the instruction pad, switching the screen to a graphics mode. The Gower peninsula throbbed in outline. Two brains buzzed aimlessly, like gears not engaging. Their eyes met, quizzical concern bouncing back and forth.

"Is that Greater Swansea?" The Italian had a rough idea of the local geography.

"Felixana nodded. "Luxury housing, I think. It extends out to sea as well, but, why Cymru? Why a welsh connection? I suppose he's followed a lead there, or something."

"We ought to go."

She knew he was right. She simply nodded again.

Red Dragon House, Gorseinon, was unassuming, the small red plasma-filled heraldic beast set on its frontage barely succeeding in qualifying as an attractive feature in the quiet residential backwater of a Swansea suburb. The two figures stepping from the roof lift were tired. A black hover case hung at the side of each, moving like obedient puppy-dogs as magnetic belt fields tugged them out of the lift with their carriers. The small reception area was hardly four metres across. Pastel shades, subdued lighting and a human reception clerk greeted them. They had sought anonymity, but hardly expected such frugal facilities. All hotel chains and many smaller hostelries now had purely electronic registration; employment in the leisure industries was almost at its nadir. A welcoming smile greeted them.

"Good evening. Are you Mr Todd from London?"

Noticing the fingerprint identifier on the reception desk caused the Italian to hesitate, smiling broadly as he swiftly improvised.

"No, my name is Zarbelli. Mr Todd is our Corporation Director. I assume the booking may have been made in his name."

So saying, he slipped his right hand, palm downwards, confidently into the machine. The receptionist looked at the girl. Tossing back her hair and smiling sweetly, she said

"I'm Felixana Smith. One room will be fine." They were shown to a ground floor room, cosy but gloomy.

"It would have been foolish to try to avoid a fingerprint check. We'll have to drop back on an official presence here." Felixana shifted on the bed when he had finished speaking. She flopped back from a sitting position, slender fingers massaging her delicate forehead, still aching slightly from the long journey. The room was warm. She turned her head to the wall screen, looking at the soft green numerals - 21:33 hours.

"Let's run the news."

Shots of ice in the Camargue dissolved into a young newscaster's face as the flat screen glowed into life.

'Although there remains the possibility of an end to the most extreme features of the current cold snap by early December, forecasters are expecting that regular autumn weather will not return...

'Following the completion of his visit to Pretoria, American President Korda has today arrived in Juba on the fourth leg of what has become a pan-African tour. This is widely seen as an attempt to raise support for the reversal of the World States Council's decision to move half of the developed nations' financial reserves to the southern world by 2140. The President's discussions in Dar es Salaam and Kinshasa do not appear to have met with much success.

'Meanwhile, at home in Washington, the mysterious reported illness of Vice-President Lutz is keeping him out of the public eye. A White House press statement confirms that the Vice-President, now aged forty seven, is again cancelling all planned engagements. He has no history of bad health. His private residence remains closely guarded.'

Zarbelli peeled off his upper tunic in the warm room, the soft voice of the newscaster serving only to lull him into relaxation.

'Turning to local news, tomorrow's NVL march to the State capital is now expected to attract over five thousand demonstrators, despite the bitter weather. Law units have indicated that feeder routes to the starting point in Quadrant Park will be patrolled from first light. State Governor Wilkinson said in Cardiff this morning that any violence manifesting itself would receive severe responses from riot control officers.'

A jostling mass of people gelled onto the screen, interspersed with the bright flashes of laser posters. The newscaster's voice continued.

'Non Voluntary Leisure demonstrations in recent months have caused considerable damage, as these scenes in Greater Oxford show. This event was in July this year. The fear for the authorities must now be that the threatened reversal of the world's financial systems to the detriment of the older nations will stir great passions and lead to even more damaging violence.'

Zarbelli pointed to the phone. "I should call London; that's our reason for being here; to tell them we can cover the start of the march. It's an ideal opportunity - they have no-one else of your standing." He sensed he had almost pulled a blush out of her, but perhaps it was only the weak glow of the table light as she reached for the phone buttons.

Monday 11 November

The sun rose, an insipid orb out of which the brittle morning air had sucked the warmth. Four Law riot vehicles hung at ten metres at the eastern rise of Quadrant Park. They throbbed in the crystal air like huge mosquitos. 8:15 hours - several hundred people had already gathered on the hoary grass slopes, wrapped warm against the weather, smoky breath writhing up in a wall of distrustful fog. Toni Zarbelli cut the drive of his horse, letting the tripod of stubby legs settle on the frozen ground.

"Look for the leaders while I prepare the recording equipment."

Felixana had stopped alongside, slender and business-like in a warm, metallic-silver overall with the BBC insignia at the slight swell of her left breast. She nodded, pulsed her steed back to life and rose, banking to the right up the rise towards the front of the gathering crowd. Her eyes behind the visor swept across twenty or so nearby faces. Some were young, out for the excitement; many were older with worry and uncertainty etched in deep lines, on men and women who exuded a strange mixture of resignation and determination.

"Stay calm and they won't have any excuses."

The thin, reedy squeak jerked her attention left, onto a surprisingly-bulky man for such a transparent voice. Felixana stopped in a puff of frost crystals as her colleague slid alongside. Practised, professional habits took over - the smooth familiarity of a microphone in her fingers and the friendly yet authoritative way her words could open the floodgates of speech in those she interviewed. Torrents of fact, interest, opinion or just plain prejudice; it made no difference. Others would edit, delete, warp or concoct; not Felixana.

"We must have work," the reedy voice was saying. "State gifts of food are being reduced. The bad weather will be simply another excuse to forget us, to push us into nothing. We won't be ignored. We won't be brushed aside."

An intensity of feeling bored its way into Zarbelli's portable lens, aching through the glass onto screens in cosy homes across three States.

"We want money," stated the bulky demonstrator in finality. The group huddling nearby, trying to squeeze into the fame of a BBC shot, took up the chant. "We want money! We want money!!"

Felixana remembered they had to advertise their presence to Craig. She switched off sound and spoke to Zarbelli. Her gaze into the camera was clear and sharp.

"The people are gathering; the mood is rock-hard. We must expect a rough day, many messages will be sent out before the settlement later in the State Capital. We hope we will not see violence, but I'll be here following the head of the march as it unfolds. This is Felixana Smith, for the BBC, in Quadrant Park, Swansea."

Zarbelli's right hand lifted from the camera in a gesture of approval. The fact of her being in Cymru was announced; now it fell to Landon to make a move, if he would.

The screen darkened as Michael Thorson swept a hand peremptorily past the control. The England State Governor turned to the five other people in the burgundy room.

"You see what trouble we will have if we don't succeed. Those live scenes in Swansea this morning will be nothing compared to what would happen if we were to be bled of our commercial power."

Harold P Lutz looked up momentarily from his breakfast kippers. He grimaced slightly as if he preferred not to think about what would happen, which was true. He returned to his warm plate. At his left, the slim fifty five year old figure of Mikhail Vorshin of the Russian Central Praesidium sat in a well-concealed state of unease. The impending financial disaster was casting its shadow over his Federation as well as those of the rest of the northern world, so he was here to play a full part in trying to avert it. In his opinion, what had happened in Malta was tantamount to terrorism, and Vorshin knew all about that. It was no reason, however, why he had to like the American Vice-President; besides, he didn't like the smell of kippers.

The third person present, the Chinese Premier Lu Wan Tao, sat back, quietly and inscrutable. Further round the kidney-shaped table sat the fourth, younger man, dressed in white and drinking coffee. He spoke softly.

"The President is due at ten. Your English security units are covering the arrival?"

"Yes, that is so." Thorson felt slightly irritated that his arrangements were being questioned, but he let it pass. He considered it important to rise above such things, and learn to be a world statesman himself. He even permitted himself a diplomatic smile. He reminded his ego that he was the host to this auspicious gathering.

"Regular security cover will stay operative until our task formally begins. At that point, when the European President indicates, your role would commence. It is expected, Mr Atkins, that you would recruit and deploy entirely to your own discretion. Our operation is to remain a closed affair."

Simon Atkins nodded, a slow methodical nod, his eyes fixed on Thorson; for a second the Governor's unsettled state returned. He felt uncomfortably like a mouse being fixed by the hypnotic gaze of a snake. Then the feeling was gone. The young white South African put down his napkin, pushed away his coffee container, rose and strolled slowly to the huge, magnifying, laser-proof windows overlooking the front lawns of Chequers, the country home of the State Governor. 09:25 hours- a sudden shaft of sunlight pierced a snow cloud, striking a sundial pedestal some twenty metres away across the whitened grass. He automatically estimated the pedestal's worth as a hiding place, accurately measuring in his mind's eye the angles in which a sniper would have a view of the house. 'The Secret Man who Never Relaxes'. He smiled inwardly to himself, recalling a news headline from a few years before. Well, he could soon afford to relax now - only just thirty years of age and he could actually retire if he wished to do so.

His mother, Sheila, would have been proud of his achievements. She had been born in 2076, the daughter of a white farmer in Cape Province, her family forced off their ancestral land by black employees in 2086, when she had been only ten years of age. Simon's grandparents had been killed, his mother taken to live in safety in a white enclave in Port Elizabeth. She had married Daniel Atkins, a white English-heritage bio-engineer, in 2096, and given birth to Simon in September 2101 while living in Rietbron, Cape Province. Simon remembered tales of great wealth told to him by his mother of times when, as a small child, she had lived in a farm homestead of huge proportions. Tales of carpeted halls, high ceilings and even some servants still remained in his memory. The landed inheritance had been snatched from the young girl when she had seen her parents murdered, staring out the back of a hover-truck as family friends had driven away at speed from the burning house. Her parents' financial assets had been safeguarded overseas, and Sheila had been reunited with them just before her death in 2120 when Simon was only nineteen. While his father had been kind, and had worked hard, the stories of grandparents' farming opulence in the early 2080s had struck deeply into him. He learned lessons at his mother's knee of how to build security by attention to detail. Simon's inheritance came early, a burning determination to remember that trust would be betrayed like a vulture if not watched like a hawk.

He had used his new wealth to buy out a string of security firms. These he had forged through hard work, expansion and takeovers to become Africa's most successful private security organisation. 'Atkins Alert' companies guarded diamonds in South Africa, uranium in the Greater Congo Republic, timber operations in Ivory Coast, and sporting events, embassies and individuals everywhere. Especially individuals - rich, famous or frightened, they all craved protection. The pulsed message to Windhoek from the European President had been personal and enigmatic.

'I require your services on a matter of severe importance. Your personal fee will be three hundred million euro, payable in negotiable minerals in the country of your choice. Military authorities at Salisbury

Plain, England will be told to expect an unmarked aircraft in the forenoon of Sunday 10 November. State Governor Thorson will welcome you.' Three hundred million! Sixty times the aggregate of project income he presently took annually from his businesses. If he chose the spread of minerals wisely he need never work again. His eyes glittered as he watched from the window. The drive for personal security was strong; it gave the cutting edge to his technique, the raw reality to his success.

The glittering eyes and the hypnotic nod which had so disturbed Governor Thorson meant nothing to his fifth guest. He smelled the breakfast coffee, lay back in a luxury side couch and sensed the polite nervousness buzzing gently in the room. The unease of the Russian exposed by the slight irregularity of his breathing caused the man some gentle amusement. Jon De Haag could follow the ebb and flow of tension better than many sighted an individual - an inflexion in the voice, a hesitation, a lie, were all so much more obvious despite the absence of an opportunity to gaze eye to eye. He stretched his long legs.

"I hope your sleep was pleasant, Professor De Haag?"

Thorson returned to the more familiar ground of political politeness. The reply was equally courteous.

"Yes, indeed, thank you. It is some years since I have been in England. 'Pleasant' is a good word to describe it." He ran his hand through his sandy hair. Flow of conversation might lessen the tension. Someone might even let slip the reason for them being here - if anyone knew it. His arrival the afternoon before had been remarkable for its achieved level of isolation. He had travelled from Maplin to Chequers in an anonymous black car and there had been no indication until this morning of the remarkably-high political atmosphere he was now breathing. The Dutchman lifted his right arm to bring his wrist band to his ear. '*Nine hours, thirty one*', intoned a gentle synthesis pitched like a female voice. Vice-President Lutz put down his cutlery on his empty plate.

"What branch of science do you work in, Professor?"

The voice was positively friendly; he seemed to be warming up his companions at last. Perhaps he had started with the Professor because he couldn't see his eyes.

"I'm a theoretical physicist, Mr Vice-President."

He gave the information freely. Lutz's people would know of his reputation and his discovery, especially as much of his recent professional work had been in the United States. It was clear to the Professor that the four power blocs were willing to co-operate on something, something of which they really had no detailed knowledge, no prior briefing. De Haag decided he would have to wait for the European President, just like the others. A glass plate on Thorson's wall console began to glow green.

"Gentlemen, the President's aircraft is arriving. Please, I must ask you to remain here. You would all present recognisable figures to anyone watching, and the Professor is, I regret, not sufficiently mobile to assist our security people. I shall return shortly."

He gave a smile as he walked to the door, pleased with the diplomatic way he had lumped them all together, especially that young South African Atkins, whom he liked less and less each moment. He left the room by the grey circular door which gaped like a camera shutter to let him out, closing after him. Atkins watched from the window as the black Presidential helicraft dropped in front of the row of trees at the right of the estate. The others sat silently, nursing private thoughts.

Atkins thought the craft was impressive. The glossy black convex saucer, fifteen metres in diameter and six metres high, shone in the weak sunshine, its European Presidential insignia of golden stars against blue appearing almost regal on the side as it descended. The five telescopic legs extended and on contact the stabilising rotor blades retracted. Atkins had never seen the Presidential vehicle with his own eyes before. It was unique, patented, deliberately designed to evoke the folklore imagery of flying saucers embedded for over two hundred years in human consciousness as a part of scientific mythology. No life beyond earth had been found, yet mankind still clung to the concept of flying saucers. No sound came to the ears through the thickened glass windows of the house. Jon De Haag sat quietly, sensing the shuffling of the others.

Outside in the cold air, openly-armed security guards converged to a matrix of protection around the settled aircraft. An enclosed walkway concertinaed out and down, the whirring of its mechanism dying as Thorson's strides brought him to the base of its steps. The cabin door was already open as he looked up. Antos Papandreou, Fifteenth President of the European Union, began to descend. Thorson's hand extended. The two men shook warmly and walked together back across the lawn.

"I've collected Atkins, the security man. He did arrive, as we stated."

"Good, - and the Professor?"

"Professor De Haag came yesterday also, on a transatlantic service. Quiet units brought him from Maplin." A silence followed. Thorson listened to richly-leathered feet sliding over frozen snow.

"Who is he?" The junior politician was intrigued by the continuing secrecy. President Papandreou kept walking, not a break in his stride. His olive face turned to the State Governor.

"You'll know in time, my friend."

The innocent choice of words shook him. His laughter pealed out. It bounced and shattered in brittle waves on the ancient house's stonework. The short plump President chortled openly. The doors opened and they went inside.

***

The pedestrian over-ways to the east of Swansea were clogging up with people. Noonday sunlight lanced in at an angle, but with blunted effect. The cold had sapped any last shreds of autumn's warmth and left a weakened skeleton of a season. Three elevated pedestrian-ways of light steel arched gracefully to city-ring woodland; dining fork tines etched in silver against the blue and icy green. Eight thousand had gathered to demand usefulness of life and gainful employment.

Felixana and Toni were becoming anxious. Press corps members were being kept at a distance from the main march by Law units determined to keep the flow going and to prevent violence getting a toe-hold. There was no sign of Craig, though in this crush it would have been difficult to pick out his face in the crowd. Felixana noticed a gap in the ring of officialdom off to the left. She dropped a few metres, swinging away to pass into the shadow of the over-way. Emerging into sunlight again, she rose towards the far side of the path. A figure blotted the sun momentarily, leaning over the railing to drop a yellow plastic disc into the cage at the rear of the hovering horse. She ascended with a surge of power, but the figure had disappeared into the jostling stream of demonstrators, now five or six abreast on the elevated path. She dipped below the marchers again, speeding forward to join her colleague. They moved down the parkland slope, where the hub-hub of the marchers and the suspicious eyes of the Law had faded to the far background. Toni squeezed the rim of the yellow disc to reveal the silver contents.

"My play-back unit's not working. It's your message, anyway."

The girl nodded. She attached the silver disc to her wrist-band. The screen activated. Emotion sparked in the face appearing before them.

"Felixana, I saw your first broadcast this morning! I need to see you. I've dug too much and know too much. Law units have been alerted to take me and I haven't much time."

Craig's face filled the screen, leaving no background clues. The two were held by the intensity of the man.

"Please, be at the Loughor desalination plant, twenty two hours, Monday, Tuesday and Wednesday. I daren't wait longer than that. I'll watch and if it's not you, I'll not show."

The screen went blank, with no further explanation and no goodbye. Felixana disconnected the recording. The time indicator returned - 12:23 hours. She looked back through the trees where a few hundred metres away the crowds continued to course along the over-ways.

"Loughor's back on the other side of the city. If we stay here until fourteen hours we should allay suspicion."

Zarbelli turned to his horse, a white smile flashing in a stray shaft of sunlight.

"Fine, we shall do that." He fought back an impulse to kiss her. Instead, he said,

"Then we shall go to meet Craig - tonight."

***

The spectral throb of machinery pulsed out over a dark estuary, but it was more of an impression than a sound. Low tidal converters on the site of the ancient deserted village of Penclawdd offered little scope for moon shadows.

"I don't really know whether we're supposed to be open or hiding."

The whispered statement summed up her dilemma. The desalination plant was by no means a restricted area. It was unmanned - one of four centres producing fresh water for the Greater Swansea conurbation. A sudden twinge of cramp clawed at her left shin. Felixana stood, alternately stamping her foot and rubbing her leg through the black fabric.

"No!" Toni pulled her down again to a squat.

"Please, Toni, we have to take a chance. We have to be in the open."

The response was urgent, intense.

"Listen, listen to me. Just assume that tape was dropped in your pannier by the Law after taking it from Craig. The message was meant for you, it would be easy for them to plant it. We've been conspicuous most of the day."

Her tense body betrayed that she was not entirely convinced. She stared north over the estuary. Brittle pins of light pierced the night, and a green starboard channel beacon blinked sadly in the lost darkness. The message got through; the BBC woman relaxed.

"All right, we'll wait a while longer, but he did say three nights and the plant covers a wide area. Perhaps he's counting on us waiting in the same place while he clears a section a night for us."

Her colleague checked his wrist band. "Twenty two hours, twenty one. It's best we wait to the half hour."

Silence descended again over the gently-shelving beach. Then there was a faint rustle in the trees behind them and the dark silhouette of Landon broke cover.

"Felixana!" His voice stabbed in painful relief at her emotions, and then he was beside his friends, squatting on the rocky ground.

"It's good to see you; you too Toni. I'm glad you're here. I don't know how long it will be before I'm finally pinned down. I think the Law traced me here a few days ago. I must share my information quickly. Were you followed?"

"No, I don't think so."

Landon stared at his fingers as if the secret lay there and all he had to do was look deeply enough.

"Something big is happening - very big. It's so big it frightens me. American Vice-President Lutz arrived at a restricted airfield in the south

English midlands twelve days ago. A Russian plane landed a few minutes later. The Union seemed to be hosting something spreading across the whole of the developed world, and obviously in secret. I was nearly caught at that point, but I reached London and started digging. For a few days, there was nothing. Then last Monday, I tracked down some financial detail that seemed harmless enough until I put the pieces together. Large sums were moving from San Francisco to London, then from Moscow to London, and finally from Beijing to London as the Chinese came on board."

The two listeners remained silent, fearful of losing any precious nugget of information.

"I then tried to find out what their target might be. The leading forces behind the WSC decision, obviously, but who were they? I kept thinking back to the events in Malta."

He looked at Felixana, her face ethereal in the moonlight, her own thoughts switching instinctively to Toni's warm Mediterranean bed.

"Points came together in my mind. The Brazilian, Duarte, expressed anger at the suggestion the Southern Brotherhood might be changing its leadership; then there was a hesitation before Israel voted for the Transkeian motion. That was followed by a flood of Moslem and Buddhist support. It *wasn't* a sequence of political voting; the Southern Brotherhood was displaying the work of religious power blocs! Christian, Jewish, Sikh, Moslem, Buddhist, Hindu - that's a smooth display of solidarity, unique in history. The world's faith organisations acting on premeditated lines. *That's* what's unnerved the northern world. I believe we've discovered the target."

"What next?" Felixana asked.

Landon passed his left hand over his face, massaging the skin briefly. Tiredness and tension were clearly taking their toll.

"I have no idea what's being planned; perhaps an attack of some sort. I think the best move might be to concentrate on the financial angle again. If this is as widespread as it appears to be, the government agencies would need to combine. We know from experience they're not likely to share espionage systems, so a private security arrangement seems to be worth considering. Outside services will probably need to be purchased. An assassination attempt or something similar on Transkeian government figures might indicate the advantages of choosing an African company, one with local knowledge. We ought to check the continent's top three or four private security firms for any unpremeditated movements of their senior personnel."

Impressed by his colleague's logic and wanting to ride along, Zarbelli added to the mix.

"They would need a base of operations. There would be a training camp somewhere. It would have to be somewhere neutral, probably, to throw off suspicion of a direct major-power involvement."

He shivered. "It's getting very cold. We ought to plan this somewhere safer and warmer."

Felixana nodded. Plans would be wasted if arrest snipped away their new-found excitement of purpose. "Where are you sleeping?" she asked of Landon.

"I'm based on the other side of the Gower. I have a friend in the luxury sea-apartments off Caswell Bay. It's been a safe place to avoid the Law."

A friend, sex not indicated. She hid behind a statement of her own current relationship.

"We're at the Red Dragon House in Gorseinon. Wouldn't you be safer to move across? How close is the Law to you?"

Landon shook his head. "I don't know. I have perhaps two or three days, but we ought to return to London tomorrow. We can do deeper research there. Your place will be watched now, Felixana. Your appearance on News in Swansea while Law officers search for me here is too much of a co-incidence."

"I don't have your connections, Craig. There must be somewhere safe we can use as a base."

Landon's smile was warming in the cold darkness.

"I think I can find somewhere safe for you both. Do you have long in England, Toni? What of your Reuter's work?"

The Italian explained his situation.

"Fine, I suggest we meet tomorrow in the afternoon. There's a small bar, Gorgon's, three levels above the Eros Concourse at Piccadilly. I'll be there at fourteen hours. It should still be busy enough not to attract too much attention. I must go now, or I won't get back into the apartment, there's a time lock on it. Good luck and take care."

He hugged Felixana, clasped Toni's forearms vigorously, and then melted into the emptiness of the hillside.

***

Craig Landon rose on a pneumatic platform to the fourth level of the Caswell Bay apartment honeycomb. He looked down through the glass walls, fascinated by the geometric simplicity of the giant bay-wide structure. The construction was huge - its rounded top at one hundred and fifty metres could shed only rainwater or snow- it was way above the Atlantic rollers. Landon's platform stopped with a soft hiss at apartment 412. Ghost images of fluorescence lit up the edges of the entry frame. The time lock lamp was not lit. He keyed the voice-com.

"Pet?"

No answer. She should be in. There was no reason for her to go out. Concern for her safety swept over him. Perhaps it had been selfish of him to involve her. He keyed the entry sequence with his right hand, pressing his left palm urgently against the cold identity plate on the door. The panel slid away. Sensing a human presence the apartment lights came on. He stepped forward, eyes searching for the woman among the deep soft furnishings.

He caught sight of the black, melon-sized, sphere on the dining surface to his right and tensed to dive, but it was already too late. The object jerked and spun as it registered its target. A stream of steel needles spewed across the room in a clean arc. The top of the stream pierced the walls and the final missiles ripped the floor covering, but the central element of the burst had traced a perforating diagonal line from Landon's right shoulder to his left hip. Several of the ten-millimetre long shafts passed straight through and out of his back, but many lodged on bone. Their accumulated force threw him back, his left shoulder smashing on the apartment wall near the entrance door as his body landed. The pain terrified him. Although his lungs had only partially collapsed, the effect of trauma meant he could not draw breath. Shards of intense light zigzagged across his eyes. His gaze went in and out of focus. Which was which? Why were the apartment lights going out?

62

Tuesday 12 November

The bitterly cold morning numbed the senses. The sunshine of the previous week had gone. Scattered patches of frozen snow looked no longer forlorn; within hours fresh supplies would arrive, carried by the darkening blanket of cloud which now covered southern England. Despite the weather Jon De Haag sat outside. Although, perhaps it was because of the weather - the biting temperature might sluice his mind of the tumult through which he was passing. In the darkness behind his eyes he relived the previous afternoon. The President had met him alone, before the others. Evidently, his support would be crucial, seen to be so, even at such an early stage. Papandreou had prepared his ground. He must have known of the work being done on the lunar base outside New Paris, of Pieter North's success in progressing early tentative experiments. Some of Pieter's discoveries went beyond De Haag himself - the teacher outstripped by the student, two Dutch minds thinking as one, the younger drawing strength from the elder.

The gravel crunched behind him. De Haag cocked his ears, turning his head to the right.

"Come and join me. The plastic is warming."

Simon Atkins moved alongside. "Thank you, Professor, no. This weather is not for me. I prefer warmer climes. I came to advise you to return indoors. You don't want to catch a chill, do you?"

De Haag could only imagine the South African's smile, but his stomach twitched, nonetheless.

"I am warm enough, young man. You should appreciate the elements more. Sun and frost have remained unchanged for centuries. They can be a rock of comfort in a shifting world."

"Perhaps that is so, Professor, but you should still come inside."

Atkins was standing behind the Dutchman and near his right shoulder. The severe beauty of the landscaped gardens caught him for an instant on the other's softly-spoken words. The manicured yew hedges displayed a sheen even in the gloom of the day, and the thick sturdy stems of the dogwoods were beginning to turn to their seasonal red and yellow with the sudden onset of the early winter. Then he realised that he could see and De Haag could not. He returned to the security of his comfort zone.

"Don't stay out here too long. You are a valuable person, Professor." He turned with a grinding of stones at his heels to stride back to the house. A ghost of a smile caressed De Haag's face. He found it easy enough to put Atkins from his mind. The proposition that the European President had put to him, however, gripped and played with his attention much more tenaciously. It was theoretically possible that it would work, at least in its early stages. Only Pieter could now say if it was practicable, but yes, it was possible in theory. He tugged his red padded tunic tighter against the cold. Was it morally right? What if someone died? The thought left a strange taste in his mind. Yet he was a scientist. He knew that all research, all progress in scientific knowledge, would stutter and fail if present balances did not continue. There would be no long-term benefit for mankind without western-driven science, he was certain of that.

He made up his mind - it would be OK, he would place a call to his ex-student now on the lunar surface. He pulled himself to his feet, frozen air filling his lungs as he turned from the garden, a brittle wind now blowing the first hint of snow against his face. From out of nowhere a security officer was at his side, guiding him gently back to the waiting world leaders.

***

The mid-morning gusts of light snow at Chequers had descended on the State capital several hours earlier. By 13:30 hours, several centimetres lay across the open expanse of Hyde Park. Red electric citipods were strung out along the Marble Arch interchange like holly berries against the snow, carrying Londoners about their business, a child's bead necklace moving with determination through the wintry day. To the east, in an area once known as Tottenham Court Road, the brown domes of the State Law headquarters at Europa Point were taking on the appearance of huge festive puddings. Moving walkways at a myriad of levels fanned out from the commercial blocks stepping up between the river and Trafalgar Square, dustings of snow outlining their shapes. Beyond, in seven trading floors, the huge Piccadilly Arena stood solidly against the elements. Shoppers milled along the Haymarket Concourse. Five-metre high prints studded the wall and ceiling spaces between the level two retail units. Each displayed in graphic detail a scene of ancient London, of a time when there really was a market for hay below these walkways. Pictures of flower-sellers and chimney-sweeps gazed silently at personal automated units and a scientist's teenage son phoning his father on the moon.

Felixana had chosen a grey-coloured tunic to wear. It didn't blend well with the rainbow display of winter-wear colours sported by other passers-by, but she wasn't in the fashion stakes today. She felt as if a thousand unseen eyes were watching, anyway. Toni's eyes were on the laser news displays unfolding on the level three screens as he rode with her up the moving stair.

'Brazilian floods kill two thousand......US Civil Aviation Authority investigates fraud allegations on lunar port entry taxes.....'

For a moment he fantasised *'Reuter's man uncovers attempt to foil world finance movements'.*

But the imaginary letters dissolved before his eyes. Whose attempt? How and when? He didn't know yet. As he reached the top of the moving stair he was left looking at a legend which merely read *'snow returns to northern States'.* Felixana looked up at him.

"I've been to Gorgon's before. It's a bit pricey." She smiled weakly, glancing at her wrist-band - 13:50 hours. They were early. Zarbelli sank into a padded seat, the tiredness of the day creasing his brown face. An early departure from Cymru to avoid a check by the Law at the hotel, and a breathless flight across southern England in a public airbus, were stressful enough. He also felt the reporter's instinct for the watchful eyes of authority, the queasiness in the stomach which told the hunted of the hunter. Activated by their presence around the dining surface a holographic image of a waitress formed in the centre of the table.

"Welcome to Gorgon's. May I have your order?"

The woman was closer to concentration than was her companion. "I'll have an apple clane, please."

Toni looked quizzically at her more-relaxed face. In return there came a soft burst of delight, her slender fingers stretching on the glass table top.

"It's a speciality here, a hot drink with crushed apples, spices and amphetamines." A hint of reckless mischief countered the nervousness of the occasion. "A hundred years ago some of the ingredients were illegal."

The Italian turned to the hologram. "I'll have a clane, too." The image dissolved, leaving Zarbelli to glance around at the other customers.

"It's fourteen hours, Toni. He should be here."

He nodded, his eye following a slender woman of about fifty in a silvery grey tunic leaving the bistro. It occurred to him that this was the second time in just over twelve hours that he had waited as Landon held the initiative. A worldwide conspiracy should be exposed by Reuter's, not by the BBC. He should make sure he followed up enough clues himself this time, even without the woman. Their eyes met, but he smiled confidently.

"He'll be here, love, any moment."

They lapsed into silence; each watching the crowds flow by, little eddies of humanity with secret stories to tell. Felixana thanked the young man dressed in red and green who brought their steaming glass mugs of crushed apple. Visions of Law officers ascending the walkways haunted her mind. After drinking the strange but tasty cocktail, Toni decided they could wait no longer.

"We ought to move. Something's gone wrong. We should keep moving." He wanted to add 'perhaps even separate', but realised that was premature. Neither of them knew where to go for safety. Air and seaports would be on the lookout, the two channel tunnels likewise. Outside, through the vast panoramic glass windows, snow was falling heavily now on Regent Street.

"Even the weather's against us now. How can we travel far in this?" She tugged her tunic tighter and stood up.

"We'll take a citipod, anywhere. It'll give us time to think. If anyone is following us, they should be easier to notice."

Zarbelli's tension was positive again, working for him and not against him. The downward flow of humanity flattened out onto the Oxford Circulus citipod pads, a semi-circle of four rubberised platforms, each five metres in width, open to the air at their forward edge but protected from the elements by glass roofs. Silver bollards provided guidance on pods to strange city destinations of which Zarbelli had no knowledge - Pinner Towers, Putney Hi-Park, Seven Sisters and Woppin. The pad heading south was closest. A light flashed over the door - Great Wimbledon - and then they were inside. The pod shot westwards above Oxford Street, before turning south. Movement wove its hypnotic effect. Felixana contemplated the hummocky skyline. Architecture was changing fast - the angularity and individualism of the twenty first century having given way to the graceful strength of curvature. New building materials and live-energy construction were blending in an expressive exultation of spheres, circles, domes and arches from Charing Cross to Whitechapel.

Her companion caught the relaxation. He felt her slight feminine body against his side, desire jostling with a reporter's nose for a story. The nose won. "We must find a base, at least for the night."

She turned from the window, and in a sudden clearing of thought said

"Paul Devine, my holographic engineer in Malta. He lives in Kew."

"Is that far?"

A shake of long dark brown hair was accompanied by her wafting perfume.

"No, a few pod changes, that's all. He may not be there yet, but it's all we can try."

The Italian nodded - good, it would do. By fifteen thirty, a citipod halted at Kew Gardens, sighing down on its runner in fast-fading light. This stop was quieter than Oxford Circulus; plenty of time for the silver bollard to tell visitors of the other kind of pods - seeds, tubers and plants guarded from the past. The BBC woman was a disappointment; she merely asked the way to the Crown Hill apartments. A taxi whooshed by in the gathering gloom, sucking along gouts of fluffy snow.

"We can walk. It's only three hundred metres." Silence, heavy silence, was a muffler on the world. It was easy not to talk in such circumstances. Rubberised, non-slip steps invited them up to a dark metal door at the apartments. Concierge lights twinkled brightly.

"Paul Devine, please." Hidden circuits riffled through the records of a hundred and fifty apartment residents. A warm voice spoke.

'Out, due seventeen hours. Waiting area permitted.' The door slid aside. They went in together, to a warm entrance area that matched the voice.

'Apartment number restricted. Programme will advise on arrival. Residents use separate entry doors.'

They sat, watched a view screen, and drank courtesy coffee, safe from the snow. Time passed. Devine's arrival was marked by an increase in lighting and the return of the warm voice.

'Paul Devine will see you. Move to the inner door, please.'

A partition slid away noisily, the sound pulling Felixana nervously to her feet. Her BBC colleague came through to meet them, his plump face registering a veritable mine of emotions. She discarded most but was left with a disconcerting mixture of fear and affection, tinged with confusion. Why the fear? Had BBC staff been warned about her for some reason?

"Felixana, I saw you on the news in Swansea yesterday morning! The march turned nasty."

She bit her lip. Zarbelli's lips pursed. Devine gave a smile to set them at their ease. "Please come in". They rode up together to the small apartment.

"We need one night's rest, Paul. Craig is missing, but we do know he started to reveal a conspiracy against the nations responsible for the WSC finance decision. We may be on the run - but please, one night."

Devine started to nod thoughtfully. He was still nodding absent-mindedly when the lift stopped ten seconds later. The apartment was strewn with pieces of machinery. Cameras, holography lenses and curls of leads lay in profusion around the furniture.

"Come in. Come in. Excuse the mess. I'm always cannibalising things for experiments. I never find the time to tidy." He bustled about, finding space for his guests to sit. Felixana sank into a chair, the homely attitude of the host breaking the dam of anxiety to let tiredness rush in. Three hours, a meal and much conversation later the tiredness lay heavily on their shoulders.

"I must sleep now, Paul. I'm sorry."

"The spare bunk is available. No night clothes, I'm afraid." He looked at Toni. "It's only a small bunk" he said with meaning.

The other man shook his head. "I'm tired too. I'll sleep here if that's alright."

The girl kissed both men gently on the cheek, and held Devine's hands together in her own. "Thank you for helping us, Paul. We'll feel better tomorrow." The partition closed behind her.

***

The dark concrete tunnels echoed as Felixana ran from her pursuers. Corridors spun in mocking confusion. She ran on, but they were coming closer, hurling glasses of hot steaming apple drink at her shaking body. She knew she had to reach the door, the way out. Where was it? The darkness was clearing. The voice calling her name would help. Paul Devine was shaking her into Wednesday, his eyes urgent, the fear returned.

"Toni's gone, Felixana! I've been to the living area, and he's gone!"

Thursday 14 November

Minus Celsius temperatures still held their grip in the pre-dawn. Meagre shrubs on rocky slopes were hard with frost. An owl stared with huge, philosophical eyes at the eastern horizon where a softening of night's blanket was beginning. The rumble far to the north bordered on imagination. The owl fluffed its feathers against the cold and rocked from side to side in uneasy movements. The rumble grew; the bird could stay no longer. Launching itself skywards, it silhouetted for an instant against a gibbous, blood-red desert moon and spun back to the south. The delta of seven black industrial hover-dozers screamed low across the border, a vampire cloak of red and silver stars heading south through the hills. Their speed slackened, nuclear engines throttled back in anticipation of the first evidence of population ahead. Among the hills several kilometres north of the small settlement lay a natural bowl in the land, a circular depression still steeped in darkness. The dozers sank to surveying height and spread into a ring round the slopes, facing inwards towards each other. The first pulses of excavating lasers cut in unison into the frosty ground just as daylight tinged the east-facing scrub. The new day had begun.

Fire flashes dissolved rock in four concentric circles within the basin. Pulses of light momentarily lit the hill slopes, sending grotesque shadows of a giant's gnarled hands leaping in response over bush and sand. A shepherd ten kilometres to the east leapt to his feet in fear and irritation as his flock broke nervously apart. A lost lamb now, when the light was not yet good enough for retrieval could break a leg and be easy prey for the eagles and foxes. But the noise had died away, the earth no longer shook. Foundations were flowing into the basin. Plasti-concrete in a sand-brown colour levelled out, congealing and forming as live-energy electric rods lowered beneath the dozers sparked out the setting current. Within ninety minutes the work was done. A circular arena was laid waiting for construction teams that were only an hour away to the north, teams which would airlift buildings, equipment and personnel. The dozers left. The owl and the shepherd were sole inheritors of the sun-touched slopes.

Far above, an insignificant Australasian mining satellite, no longer listed as working, logged the activity as man-made and went on its way. Its polar orbit should have decayed years before; but then, Perth Tracking had rarely received a transmission over the years, anyway.

Saturday 16 November

Pieter North sat at the viewing window and let his mind follow his eyes downwards. At five thousand kilometres the earth does seem at a distance, nestling snugly like a brightly-lit jewel on a pitch-black cushion of eternity. Distant enough to encourage harmless day-dreams, yet tantalisingly close enough to reach out and touch, to turn in the hand, to day-dream further, and place back gently on its starry mount. Copernicus Centre was not in synchronous orbit, so the earth turned clockwise below. The European Union's orbiting station was showing its age now, being the first of the four in existence to have been built. It was sometimes known affectionately as 'copper knickers' by staff and visitors alike.

The doctor's gaze watched the eastern seaboard of the North Americas cross the terminator into brilliant morning sun, the intensity prodding him into turning again to the blue plastic folder on his lap. It was no good, he couldn't concentrate, and his mind was too full of speculation. His eyes returned to the glorious view beyond the glass. A soft, wry smile creased his face, squeezing up his grey eyes and flattening his receding hairline. He knew his inner turmoil and surface calm were reflected below. The planet was a beautiful cosmetic advertisement for unsuspecting visitors yet shielded great tensions and powerful forces in the endless chess game of history. Dr. North let his bubbling thoughts bounce off the earth below.

Returning earth-side was always a time to take stock, of oneself, one's friends, career and nation. Here he was going down for the second time in four months. Jackson Matthews had said fifty years before that space travel turned people into philosophers; deep, taciturn serious thinkers abounded. The matter-of-fact, objective professionals of the twentieth and twenty-first centuries had been excited by the technological miracles before them. Here in the year 2131 ordinary people had experienced space

70

travel and it had touched some deeply. 'But not me', reflected Pieter North. 'It's just what it looks like - empty space'.

He was pulled out of his thoughts by a soft electrical spasm which pulsed against his left wrist. His touch band was reminding him that boarding of the earth shuttle would begin in fifteen minutes. He gazed around inside the waiting area at his fellow travellers, a comforting wall of reality against the heave of his thoughts. Ordinary people, but a few stood out from the twenty or so who were waiting. A middle-aged couple who were obviously finishing a retirement cruise, a few exhausted scientists, two men who looked like civil servants of some sort, and a young lady with auburn hair wearing the Air Europa stewardess's uniform. North smiled briefly as their eyes met, hoping that his smile didn't betray his lust too much. 'She really is gorgeous', he thought, admiring the swell of her breasts against her steel-blue tunic top. Sadness welled inside him again. He hadn't known a woman sexually since his personal assistant had died over a year before. There were so few people in his branch of science that it seemed to him that he spent much of his time alone. Now at the age of fifty he felt that such life, or at least romantic life, was about to leave him behind.

He had been born in April 2081 in Harlingen on the Waddenzee, where the grey skies meet the grey North Sea. Not that he had any recollection of the area - the North family had been forced out in 2085 by the Great Flood when he was barely four years old, going to live in Enschede on the State border with Germany. He often wondered in later years, if science had been developed further and faster, whether knowledge and technology could have saved his birthplace from premature inundation. Pieter's aptitude for science had blossomed early into an obsession. After obtaining his first degree in Rotterdam, he undertook important post-graduate studies, first at Trinity College, Cambridge in 2103 and then John Hopkins University in Maryland in 2105. His work in theoretical and applied electrical physics had carried him through a succession of private corporations between 2106 and 2121. It was in March of that year, just a month before his fortieth birthday, when the European Union had appointed him as Head of Lunar Research. Over the period of ten years since then he had taken Jon De Haag's theories and brought them to the brink of reality.

He shook himself visibly and turned back to the splendid panorama of the earth below. Fifteen minutes would soon pass, he told himself. Two hundred years whirled and pirouetted in his mind's eye as the earth turned before his waking eye. The slaughter of two world wars had been

71

followed by around fifteen smaller ones in the name of parochial nationalism amid a surge of materialistic peace. Corporate and individual uncertainty accompanied the over-riding obsession of the 1970s and 1980s of a nuclear war that never came. The closest event to a major atomic disaster was the destruction of Caracas by an accident in a nuclear power station in 2039. Through the early years of the new millennium mistrust turned slowly to a mutually-beneficial game; the protection of northern cultures at the joint expense of the southern half of the globe. Military spending had sucked deeply at both capitalist and communist economies. On both sides of what once had been bamboo and iron curtains, ordinary people had come to seek greater commercial expression in the things that technology could offer.

Militarism ran out of steam on grounds of cost and through the tense decades after the year two thousand, northern eyes turned with irritation on the way the third world was attempting to catch up, soaking up as it did the planet's dwindling natural resources. By the year 2100, considerable north-south tensions were building up as the fully-developed world struggled to keep its materialistic economies intact and growing. The World States Council decision in October was shocking, but hardly surprising. Northern cultures had lived on borrowed time for too long.

A soft tone and a second pulse from his touch band told North that boarding of the shuttle was requested. Already the lights were dimming to prepare his eyes for the much lower transit luminescence, chosen so passengers could better appreciate the visual luxury of a descent to an earth-port. He moved quickly in the hope of getting near lovely Miss Breasty Auburn, but it was not to be. He saw her disappearing on a gravi-lift. Instead he was compelled to follow the softly-glowing arrows on the floor through the shuttle-way. Strapping-in wasn't necessary; each seat sensed the natural earth weight of its occupant to automatically exert a sucking force on the body. North settled in and closed his eyes, shutting out the rich burgundy and silver of the shuttle's interior décor. The background buzz of conversation died as the shuttle broke free of Copernicus Centre. The gravity induced in the seats gave a minimum impression of 'up' and 'down', but this only served experienced travellers. Floating out of a shuttle bay was always the worst part of any trip; worse, in fact, than the traditional experiences of coming in to land on the earlier models. He was tired. Reaching out a finger to a button on the right arm-rest, he caused the ear lines to swing in to his head. Music gushed soothingly into his brain, easing the turmoil of speculation.

The message he had received had simply read -

'Pieter, northern alliances are prepared to offer unlimited funds for your services. The project is interesting. Please meet me Saturday at Humber Earth Port, England. Jon.'

He noted the strange juxtaposition of the superlative 'unlimited funds' and the modest 'interesting'. It was a clash of approaches guaranteed to tantalise him. Questions rose and burst and rose again in his mind like bubbles in hot custard. The blind Professor came into his thoughts. Though Pieter was twenty one years the junior, they had been friends since University in England twenty eight years before. They were soul-mates in high energy physics, tutor and student, from the fens of Holland to the fens of Cambridge. North suddenly shivered. In under an hour, he would walk out of the Humber earth port into the worst freeze in recorded history, according to some news reports. Minus temperatures in controlled scientific situations on the lunar surface were acceptable, but numbers of Europeans dying each day while going about their ordinary business was not good. It was still only mid-November.

A more tangible phrase from the message stuck in his mind - 'for your services'. That could only mean one thing following his visit to earth in July. He searched his memory for clues to his forthcoming meeting. He had submitted brief details of his work to the Forum of World Science in response to their advertisement for research projects to be discussed at the Faraday Conclave in California between 5th and 27th July 2131. The scientific gathering was set to mark the 300th anniversary of Michael Faraday's discovery of electro-magnetism in 1831. Pieter's project had been chosen to form the final element of the Conclave. Packing had been difficult; the sudden death of his assistant Diane in May 2130 had left him bereft of domestic continuity. The final approach to Los Angeles had given a good opportunity to see the urban network spread out below. The city of the angels was not what it had been in the late twentieth century. The terrible earthquake of 17th November 2039 had destroyed a fifth of the city and killed over seventy five thousand people, many because the worst shocks had occurred in the early evening. That was ninety two years before. He had made a mental note to visit the 2039 Museum if the chance arose during his stay.

The Conclave had been a dizzying experience. Rounds of speeches, dinners, seminars, dinners, presentations and dinners had been almost too much for his digestion. On the early afternoon of Thursday 25th July he had stood before nearly three hundred of his fellow scientists. The first part of his presentation would be predictable - talk of the latest work being done with quarks and leptons and the still-unresolved problem of

73

discovering super-partners of known particles when super-symmetry is broken. The final theoretical bosons had remained elusive. North heard himself speaking the next few sentences.

"Colleagues will recall our predecessors tried without success to establish by experimentation if a maximally-extended super-gravity has a completely sensible quantum version. We now know this was because the earth's gravitational field was swamping attempts to isolate the necessary super-partners. Our chance came only three and a half years ago when we opened new testing stations on the lunar surface where the gravitational effect is smaller. It was to prove crucial to our success. Within two years, we were on the point of identifying the first super-partner - in this case, that of Hadron 315. Our initial research led us to predict that the super-partner would appear at a given strength in the special power surge built to produce it. We named the super-partner the dantino, after Edward Dante, the Scottish physicist, who died in 2063."

A pause followed, and a gulp of water.

"A year ago, the dantino appeared. It was a major breakthrough in our search to finalise and apply certain new theories in quantum physics." There was a courteous ripple of applause. The Dutchman had smiled inwardly to himself. *Just wait until you hear the next bit'*, he remembered thinking to himself.

"However, there was a disconcerting irregularity. The dantino had not appeared in the instant we had predicted, but nearly three seconds prior to that point. Obviously, we assumed an error in calculation and tried again. Once more, streaks of two dantinos showed two point eight seconds before the time our computations had indicated they would appear. There were only two possibilities; either the basic hadron equation was wrong, and we've been using that for over fifty years, or our particular power lattice was causing something else to happen with sub-nuclear particles. We tried again. Three days later, on precisely the same power lattice, but with increased magnitude, the dantinos appeared eleven point five seconds prior to predicted origin, with their effect lost at that point of origin. There could no longer be any doubt over what had happened."

The shuttle skidded on a cold air layer, banking as it neared the troposphere. Bumped from his reverie, North opened one eye. The curve of the Atlantic horizon arched away into the forward distance, planet and not space now filling the view. The scientist and his fellow passengers were plunging closer to the discontent of England's early winter. A stewardess paused on her way aft to prepare for landing, now no more than twenty minutes away.

"Have a pleasant stay, Dr. North."

"Thank you. I shall try." His voice came out perfectly normally, somewhat to his surprise. He even managed a smile. The captain's voice caught the attention of the passengers with the now-standard phrase of interplanetary flight.

"My fellow travellers, we approach the Good Earth."

A pause was followed by two musical tones, then more information. "The temperature outside the earth-port is minus nine degrees; air clear, no wind, no precipitation. Please do not attempt to leave your seats until the red light at the front of the cabin goes out. We shall land shortly. Have a good time earth-side and take care. We trust you will travel again with Air Europa soon."

Through the port window near his seat North could see the English countryside bathed in brittle sunlight. The land was covered in a stifling white shroud. Then there was no more time - the shuttle was down. He stretched his legs. The attempt at relaxation was only partially successful. The leaden lump of nervous anticipation remained in his gut. The shuttle power died as the reception bay umbilical latched on to the forward exit-way. Quarantine and customs formalities would be at a minimum; Copernicus Centre was part of the European Union so shuttle AE301 was purely an internal flight. Personal magnet-bags clutched tightly, the passengers disembarked. The earth-port was well-insulated, but even so the new arrivals heard the subdued roar of a shuttle leaving the port on its journey up-side.

The passengers collected their luggage and went their separate ways. Silver information bollards in the arrivals lounge attracted considerable numbers. Pieter North had no opportunity to walk to one. At the foot of the gentle down-slope of dark-green floor fabric in the exit zone, two young men moved in protectively. The one to North's left spoke softly.

"Doctor North, you are most welcome. Professor De Haag is waiting for us outside. Please accompany us to the reserved exit."

A plastic-textured hand of perfect manicure panned right, drawing the Dutchman's eyes to the far wall panelling. He followed his welcoming committee as it flowed with professional inconspicuousness through the crowded lounge. The area beyond the panelling was unheated. In an echoing space stood a vertical take-off jet of the Union government, at its steps his old friend Jon De Haag. The Professor's ears separated three sets of footsteps and he smiled. "Pieter, is that you?"

"Jon." The words and the handshake were outward signs, sufficient to calm North's fluttering caution. He told himself he should do well to follow his tutor's restraint in calling the affair 'interesting'; he had no idea at all why he had been called to earth. Aboard the vehicle they sat quietly. De Haag sensed the patience in his pupil and smiled to himself. It was good - although he had convinced himself the project outlined to him by the European President was worthwhile, there was no point in opening his private thoughts here and now. North himself seemed to be prepared to keep his mouth shut. The older man also realised he now had a pair of eyes on his side. The hangar doors parted. Beyond in brilliant sunshine the English countryside was in deep freeze. The pilot opened her door momentarily to give final instructions. Her smile was real enough - the younger Dutchman had a vision again of Miss Breasty Auburn on the Copernicus shuttle. He smiled back. Light-sensitive windows darkened against the snow's glare as the craft rose steadily into the sky.

"Have you taken breakfast, Doctor North?" asked one of the chaperones. The two of them seemed quite content to allow the scientists to sit unobserved to their rear.

"I had a coffee and some sandwiches in Copernicus, thank you. I would like something when we arrive." The invitation to prompt a response as to the destination was not taken up by either minder. North turned his attention instead to the countryside below. Obscured at dotted random by smudges of ice-cloud, the landscape offered a vista of unremitting white. Even the straight line of hover traffic on the H15 route south to Lincoln appeared as puffs of white smoky traces.

"What is the moon like, Doctor North?" asked the other official.

A faint lift of eyebrows was the response, unwatched by the men who had not turned around.

"You only have to look below. It's not the temperatures that bring the cold; it's the absence of trees, grass, birds. There's just the cold hand of man on the moon. It's quite boring, really."

Was it a put-down or a philosophical truth? How could life on the moon be boring? The agent grappled silently with the balance of options. The grappling consumed the remaining time in flight to Chequers.

***

"This is very much a personal invitation, Jon. What would happen to both of us if I were to say 'no' to whatever it is they have in mind?" The lilt of the ancient Dutch language bestowed an additional intimacy to the surroundings.

The blind man's face registered a soft smile. His answer came in a voice that was perhaps unnecessarily low. An instinct that was just as ancient as the language meant that the echoing space in which they sat urged speech to be soft and intimate.

"I expect we'd both be allowed about our business. Funds for research would perhaps start to disappear. Don't forget the World States Council took some momentous decisions last month. You are also on the payroll of the Government in any case. A Head of Lunar Research must have some wings clipped, I suppose, though you could seek a post back in the private sector."

"I don't mind so much about the funds disappearing. Could we disappear ourselves? I mean, the stakes are very high in this game, if all northern alliances are determined to co-operate on something."

"We are precious commodities at present, Pieter. I think we are relatively safe."

The younger man thought of the money and raised the possibility that without this opportunity they might never be in a position at all to proceed further. He added, "The experiments we have completed so far have been very expensive. We keep bidding for the next year's funds with no guarantees. On top of that, the lunar leasing and oxygen fees just keep going up."

Jon De Haag responded with a positive nod of the head. "Science must progress, Pieter. I know you agree with me on that. The thinly-spread wealth that the southern world wants may indeed bring temporary comfort, but mankind has moved on too far with science and technology to let things go now. The northern nations are the ones grappling with intensive food production, medical security and land reclamation; indeed, a whole host of initiatives on which we all depend. Only scientific endeavour can prepare us for the future, sometimes many decades ahead." He paused, and then added, "How far has your team progressed?"

Pieter North looked around him, a luxury denied his companion. It was a quiet, dark place, with subdued lighting, old pictures and old fittings. "Are we safe here to talk?"

Caution, ever caution.........he had tutored his student well.

"Oh, yes. The chapel at Chequers hasn't been used in over fifty years. There are no listening devices here. I explained to the President I would have to speak with you alone. Now, what can you tell me about the research? How are things coming?"

Pieter looked up at a stone figure of an angel, gazing into the dusty eyes as if seeking an answer. He could hear the blood gently throbbing in his ears.

"Our early work has been completed. We have shifted inanimate material through a gel of ninety three years and returned it intact. Rats were initially retrieved dead from a distance of thirty years, but over the past few months we've achieved successful live return from twenty years, after ensuring a safe oxygen supply could be carried with them. They were physically perfect, but we're not certain how to test their mental condition. Bureaucracy has intervened as well; we can't get import permission to test with rabbits. It's all in lunar gravity, of course."

"When would you be ready for primates?"

"We could try lower species in about ten weeks. It would be a bit reckless, though."

"Have you had any thoughts about man?"

The sense of unreality already engendered by the unfamiliar surroundings edged up a notch. For a few surreal seconds Pieter North thought he was going to laugh. Instead, a gentle snort of exhaled air echoed in the quiet chapel. He found he was tracing with his fingers the ornate curled wooden end of a pew. Such exquisite artistry performed by a long-dead skill in the human hand. He looked up again. The stone angel returned his stare, unable or perhaps even unwilling to offer him guidance in his reply.

"It'll be years before we get round to that! I'm not at all sure we'd even get a volunteer." He sensed it was not the reply his mentor wanted, so added "They don't want me to move a man, do they?"

He received a slow, somnolent nod. He looked around, grasping for order in the chaos. The timeless aura of the small chapel faced backed at him, unblinkingly. He heard again the rhythmic flow of blood in his ears.

"It's not a game we're playing, Jon. It's very dangerous. Do they know that?"

"Believe me Pieter; their earnestness is just as deadly." The Professor's hands swept up in an expressive arc. "The things that could go wrong are known to me. The logic of the theory has been in my head for so long that we are old friends."

"What do they want us to do?" He hoped the Professor had not noticed the use of the word 'us'.

"I'm told they want us to place someone back four weeks or so, to prevent Austin Mbene from addressing the World States Council and stop the proposal to move finance to the southern world."

"Will that work? I mean, assuming we can get someone there, can we really change history? It's happened, hasn't it?"

"Yes, but it can change. As long as no-one dies as part of the process, I believe it will work."

The younger man could not really believe he was holding this conversation as a sane person. His head was becoming dizzy.

"I don't understand, Jon. We're sitting here talking about an historical fact, something real. Does it mean we would no longer be here, would never have been here? It's terrifying. Where would I be, for example?"

De Haag chuckled. "On the moon, I would think; carrying on with your experiments. Besides, over the past two hundred years or so, spin, opinion and prejudice have produced many versions of historical fact. Just look in any history database or old-fashioned history book. Which one is right?"

Pieter North shuddered. "I can't handle the theory, Jon. The physical problems are nightmarish enough on their own. I've already mentioned the matter of mental well-being. If we push development too fast people

79

will die anyway, regardless of theories about....about..." a hand waved unheeded in the air, searching for words, "temporary history!"

There was another pause, during which De Haag remained silent. Two cycles of soft breathing circled in the peaceful air of eternity; then the cadence of one eased down a notch.

"We would obviously need facilities for accelerated development. My senior colleagues from the moon are essential. As you know, interdependence across several disciplines is the only way we can make progress at the limits of knowledge we're working at."

'This is just mock now', thought De Haag. 'He's decided to do it'. North continued talking, perhaps to convince himself it would be all right.

"Does the President know we can't make spatial and temporal shifts simultaneously? We're hardly likely to be granted permission to build a generator in southern Africa and anywhere else our agent will have to travel to find Mbene. These journeys would be fraught with possible dangers, deviations from plan.....anything to disrupt a smooth change of history."

"I have explained to him some of the difficulties, as well as I know them myself. Clearly, a secret generator somewhere near southern Africa will be needed. Some sort of infrastructure in support taken back too, to facilitate a safe return?" The upward inflection lobbed the conversation back to North.

"That would seem desirable, yes." He hoped he didn't sound too sarcastic; he didn't mean it to be. "Howl! We don't even know precisely what happens at the far end of a connection. No-one's been there to carry out tests!"

Something akin to recklessness touched North. Perhaps it was a mild hysteria, born of the unreality of the conversation and the quiet, timeless chapel. It all sounded so implausibly grotesque he may as well take the research money and let nature run its course.

"How long do we have to perfect this process?" He nearly expected De Haag to give him 'two and a half weeks' in reply.

"Next summer some time, I think. If we ever get summer again, that is. You're a good scientist, Pieter. You must have known your research was leading somewhere like this, being taken over for military or political

80

purposes. It's forever been this way. You've always believed in the supremacy of science to solve any problem, and this is just the other side of the coin."

A cramp in his arm forced North to his feet. The other's head rose as if he were looking at his colleague. The younger man spoke in response.

"I should have expected it, it's true. I miss the earth, Jon. Since my assistant's death the moon's been crowding in on me. It's too isolating, it forces one to brood too much. Perhaps this is what I need for a fresh start."

The chapel suddenly looked more welcoming. "Anyway, my personal reasons sound a lot more convincing to me than any professional ones. The technical problems of the task are terrifying."

De Haag deemed the conversation at an end and his undertaking to the President to speak with his student successfully completed. He rose to his feet, a knee-joint sending an echoing crack round the quiet chapel.

"We must report, Pieter, and begin work. I would certainly hope to stay closely involved, even if my blindness is seen in some quarters to be an irritating intrusion into the scheme of things. I ought to give a gentle word of warning to you, however. Do not become too enmeshed with the security man, Atkins. I fear there will be tumult."

Sunday 17 November

'Lucky' Len Horton screwed up brown eyes in a weather-beaten face and tried to concentrate again on the laser matrix. The argument with his woman had left a bad taste in his mind. She went to her mother's every Sunday, despite his clearly-expressed irritation. 'It's deliberate' he thought chauvinistically. 'She knows I want a meal after finishing this urgent work, and she still goes.'

He yanked the magnetic couplers too hard, the digital readout spinning crazily as the security beam slipped off-centre. "Damn!"

Another figure in blue overalls several hundred metres away among the rocks stood up angrily.

"What the hell, Lucky! Are you trying to kill us? These beams are still lethal!"

81

The shout carried easily through the crystal air. "We don't have time to power down. The base must be ready today. Now, take it easy!"

A heavily-gloved hand waved back in guilty acknowledgement, its owner returning to his task. A recalibrated beam struck its triangle post on the far side of the valley. 'Lucky' straightened up as the indicators purred a perfect line of zeros. A bird caught his eye, a bobwhite quail, stark against the sky. It circled overhead to disappear behind the watcher, down the far flank of the hill. 'Lucky' was a country man, at home in these hills. It was a real pleasure to work here, on the only military base permitted in the Wichita Mountains. There were no roads; everything had to be airlifted in. He listened to the wistful sigh of the ceaseless wind and let his domestic troubles blow from his mind.

Way off to the north-east, in the direction of Oklahoma City, he saw the glint of an aircraft as it caught the noon sunshine. He finished packing his instruments and began the descent to the compound, picking his way round the rugged, ancient boulders that littered the hillside. A glance to the sky confirmed the aircraft was coming closer, the whine coming to his ears across the silence of the desolate landscape. Fifty metres below and over half a kilometre out across the valley he noticed the landing-pad at Pichot Base attract a small knot of military personnel. A smartness and an urgency of movement signalled to Horton that this craft was different from the transports of the past two weeks. He pressed on more quickly, sending small waterfalls of stones bouncing to the outer perimeter fence below. The silver jet swung on up the valley for several kilometres. When it returned to hover expectantly over the landing pad, 'Lucky' had reached the level valley bottom. He was sweating freely under his thermal mountain-wear. He had reached the technicians' perimeter gate as the craft's power noise died. The aircraft door panel swung out.

Horton, like other personnel in the vicinity, stood witness to the arrivals. He recognised the base commander, now walking forward to the concertina steps. A young head with a shock of blond hair emerged from the opening at the top of the steps, ignored the smiling commander and quickly surveyed the scene for possible danger. Then it disappeared. Horton saw a middle-aged balding man step onto the concertina and start to descend. Behind him came someone older, with sandy hair, holding the rail and carefully walking down. The commander was warmly shaking the hand of the first man when the blond head reappeared at the top of the steps. He reached the ground as the commander was being introduced to the older man. All four moved away to the guardroom across the frost-hard compound, their breaths bursting on the cold air. 'Lucky' turned and headed for the technicians' workshops. Excitement was over for the day. He still wouldn't get a hot meal because the normal transport back to Cache would leave in barely twenty minutes. He spat at the ground in frustration.

Monday 18 November

Major Frank Edison rocked gently in his chair, fingers tapping together on his chest in prayer-like supplication as he faced the three men before him. He spoke in a matter-of-fact way, as if stating that these three wouldn't throw him, whoever they were. He faced the balding man seated near his desk.

"I understand, Doctor North, you only arrived from the moon two days ago. It has not been an easy journey to stomach on top of that. Please feel free to rest all today and overnight. You need to know now though that I have been instructed to make certain arrangements and to receive certain equipment. I was to await the arrival of a person or persons who would know what the equipment was, and would inspect it for use. Yesterday morning, I received orders to welcome a party arriving at noon. Obviously, we may still have some preparations to complete to make you fully comfortable."

He turned his eyes to the others, Jon De Haag in a brown armchair near the room's main communications screen and Simon Atkins standing with arms folded near the doorway.

"Now, I don't know what your reason is for being here, and I don't want to know. Pichot is the most isolated base in the central States, so whatever your task is, it will remain secret. Our security is excellent."

"I am sure it is, Major, but you need to know I am taking over that security with immediate effect."

The South African approached Edison's desk, the movement emphasising his ascendancy. He handed a sheet of paper across the desk. The seated commander noticed the Seal of the President of the United States at the top of the sheet. His face remained impassive, which must have been quite an achievement, thought Pieter North. A hand swept over the communications sensor to bring the hum of a live line into the quiet room. North noticed De Haag sitting with an enigmatic look of peace on his face - what was going through his mind at that moment?

Edison lowered his eyes to the view-screen where a menu sequence of channels offered itself.

"Give me three, Internal Security. Staff Officer Josina Boon is to come to the Base Commander's suite, immediately."

Atkins returned to his place by the door, as if distancing himself from the Major to lessen the appearance of threat before newcomers entered into their presence. North kept his eyes on the door. He preferred not to look at the pulsating pink bulge of embarrassment on Edison's neck. When the door panel hissed open, there was enough to see, anyway.

Josina Boon carried her weight well. The tan U.S. Army suiting with the red and yellow lightning flashes of the security forces clothed a woman of ample proportions. Dark, close-cropped hair accentuated a plump face. Vicious-looking army boots peeped out from beneath voluminous overall bottoms. There was no ugliness; she had probably been pretty attractive in her youth, yet her size now detracted from her appearance. It seemed not to concern her. Her eyes stayed on her superior officer. He spoke in formal, clipped sentences.

"You are to accompany Mr Atkins on a security tour of the base. Put yourself and your officers at his disposal. You are to follow his orders."

"Yes sir". A Texan drawl of acknowledgement emerged from the huge woman. She turned from the room, followed without a further word by Simon Atkins. Looking down into his lap Pieter North didn't attempt to stop a smile bathing his face. Stuck with her for the duration, there was no way the South African would feel willing to try messing around with that big a problem.

Tuesday 19 November

"Josina Boon is as big as the moon!"

The rhyming cadence tickled De Haag, his face beaming in the half-light. The two continued walking.

"It will cool him, won't it? Was Atkins' room close to yours? It was not possible for me to tell."

Weak sunlight bathed through an open hangar door; although he couldn't see it he felt its gentle caress on his right cheek. Pieter North responded.

"I haven't seen him, Jon. He'll be prowling around somewhere, no doubt. He could be wasting his time. It's quite possible our power lattice won't even work in earth gravity."

The lensed aperture at the end of the hangar spun open behind a solitary guard. A sloping vista enclosed within a high white dome displayed itself beyond. Even at the entrance an uncontrolled tension gripped North. Suddenly, his nonchalant statement echoed feebly in his mind, contrasting in hollow uncertainty with the sight before him. A fear of governments' power mixed with the thrill of the scientific possibilities. He may have had doubts - might still have - but it was evident the northern powers had none. De Haag absorbed his friend's tension, catching clearly the involuntary intake of breath next to him.

"What is it, Pieter?"

"It's the equipment, Jon." The shock completed the dryness in his throat begun by the raw mountain air.

"How long has it been since the World States Council decision? Four weeks?"

"It's something like that."

"They anticipated our co-operation. They must have been moving units here for all of that time. How would they know what to bring?"

His first tentative steps into the white amphitheatre revealed more of its contents. Some were open on the floor; others were still in their toughened cocoons, transparent coats of plastic sprayed round the equipment before transit. His eyes roamed over the pieces before him. There they were, without any doubt. He could identify plasma converters, particle accelerators, charge stabilisers, and a rack of perhaps fifty or sixty silver balls the size of a man's fist containing organic liquid plastic for use as an industrial sealant. Other units contained unseen items - all were stacked in profusion, bearing silent witness to the wonders mankind could now perform. He translated the scene as best he could for his sightless colleague.

85

"This is probably going to be our main testing area. It's a prefabricated amphitheatre; a dome in semi-opaque plasti-crete, probably not charged, or it would interfere with our power pulses. Height is about twenty five metres. The diameter of the amphitheatre is massive, about a hundred metres. A three-metre wide companionway runs the full circle. There's a restraining rail overlooking a three metre drop into the working area. Walls are bare and white. Goodness, Jon, there's masses of equipment here, and it looks to be what I need, there's little doubt of that. There's no-one in the building except us."

The two began walking round the companionway to their right.

"I can check most of the pieces here, Jon, but installation and calibration are not in my expertise. I would need probably five of my team from the moon." His eyes continued to survey the equipment.

"I would need a power engineer. I'm very concerned about earth gravity and we'll need to overcome it. Then there's a plasmologist, two physicists and a science security officer. I intend to fight fire with fire, Jon. Atkins will worm his way everywhere. We must have total control of the scientific side of this. We may be able to keep him at arm's length by feeding him our version of our progress - or lack of it."

"Will he take that?"

"I don't know if we can maintain manipulation on the scientific side. He seems to be a powerful man, always interposing his will."

The two men reached a stairway on the left, leading down into the test area. De Haag's hand continued to rest lightly on the arm-rail as they descended.

"I want to study the transit wrappers, Jon, to see where some of the units come from. It all looks American, but I know some of our pressure regulators are only made in Europe. What concerns me is that someone close to our lunar staff may have fed equipment details on the restricted sophistications we should still have only on our moon-base."

North nudged his left arm against his colleague as a prompt for continuing support. De Haag took it.

Wednesday 20 November

The day dawned to a cutting north-westerly wind. Pieter North stretched his limbs languorously, returning to wakefulness under his quilt. The previous day had been tiring - lists to be checked, equipment to be examined for transit damage, storage and movement of ancillary items to be supervised. Atkins had not made another appearance. It had left North free to work with a clear mind. De Haag had needed rest around noon and had then spent several hours closeted in the communications centre making and receiving calls. North rose, a little stiffly, and walked to the oval window in his quarters to greet the cold Wichita Hills. The isolation throbbed in through the glass.

'We could be lost here forever', he thought, 'and no-one would know'. A niggling ache in his back from Tuesday's exertions had been burnt out by the heat of the shower; he faced the day refreshed and devoid of tension. The isolation seemed like a clean sheet stretched before him. He strode to breakfast with new purpose.

Black and silver furniture fittings at evening meal had been replaced by the brown and lemon hues of a new day. Chameleon furniture pleased him. There was much on moon bases where the plasma energy necessary for tubular colouring was freely available, but he was surprised that military bases stooped to such fashion. His eyes swept round the curved tiers. There was no De Haag yet, and no Atkins either. He chose a place in the top tier, from where he could best enjoy the wide panorama offered by the windows. The menu plate glowed on the dining surface before him. He touched the image of orange juice and then pressed sausages - twice. Why not? It was free. A government prepared to pay the earth for him to throw a man back in time would not worry if he wanted an extra sausage. He sat back and stretched. Military personnel moved in and out of the dining area. The pace was purposeful but not rushed.

The smell of the sausages preceded their arrival, carried on a concave serving tray by a junior ranker.

"Good morning, Doctor North." Most of the personnel probably didn't know him and he was surprised by this greeting. The dark-haired young man had a dry, crumbly complexion, his eyes intense yet friendly behind the tinted flare-protection strip mask he wore.

"Good morning." North was relaxed, quite content to share company over a meal. "Thank you for bringing this. I see you have your own meal too. Please join me."

"Thanks. I'm Robert Task, known to everyone as Robbo."

North noticed the red and yellow lightning flashes on his shoulder insignia and understood how he had come to be recognised. "You serve with Staff Officer Boon, do you?"

"That's right. If there's anything you particularly need during your stay, I'll be pleased to help. I schooled in Amsterdam for several years while my guardian worked in the European Union."

The Dutch relevance was obviously his opening gambit. North speared a slice of sausage which he carried lovingly to his mouth. They talked for a few moments of canals and architecture. The lad seemed harmless enough.

"Opportunities to speak to anyone out here must be quiet rare. Where do people go off-duty?"

Task burst a pepper capsule over his pancake. "There's only Cache. That's south, it's virtually an army town. There's nothing else in any direction. Most of us go to Cache. It can be good in the summer; the nearest Wichita peaks are open for trekking. Winter is coming, though. Do you know how long you'll be here?"

The Dutchman hesitated, just why he didn't know. He took a long drink to play for time.

"There's no way of knowing. I have my work to do, just as you have yours." He was spared further embarrassment by the arrival of De Haag, tapping his way into the closest seating area. Task quickly helped him in at the table and introduced himself. The Professor asked how Staff Officer Boon was getting along with the security man, Atkins. An easy laugh came in reply.

"I don't think she likes him, Sir. We're spared him today, though. He left for Africa early yesterday."

The fork barely paused on its way to North's mouth. He was to recall later the incongruity of a security man being open about his destination. The three talked for a while of the weather in the north of Europe; then Pieter looked at his friend.

"Can you join me in about an hour, Jon? There are some figures I need to go through with you."

The professor nodded. "That's fine, Pieter. I'm sure Robbo here will guide me to the library terminal."

"OK, I'll find you there." North moved away. The taste of sausages lifted his step.

***

Sheets of snow cut through the frozen gully, enveloping tree stumps momentarily then flying on in the leaden half-light to shroud other objects. The wooded glades slicing down to the English Channel were cutting through cliffs known locally as the Firehills but there was no fire here on this bitter Wednesday morning. Toni Zarbelli watched the sea heaving, hesitant now over what he proposed to do. Spume fanned away from each wave crest. The Italian shivered. How far was it to France, anyway? The horse would make it if he wasn't blown off into the sea. He revved the steed, sitting across the hovering vehicle. It was a smooth enough flight down the last few metres to the shore, but the cutting side-wind beyond the shelter of the cliff slewed him to the right, ploughing him heavily into the cold beach. The horse righted automatically, bobbing patiently while its rider sucked frozen air back into his shaken body and brushed away the clinging wet sand. An icy wave gushed into the stones at his feet.

He hesitated again. A whistling to the west reached his ears as a Law jet swooped low over the sea on its way inland at Hastings. If he were to be caught............... He feared that a week spent on a patchwork of enquiry woven from restricted terminal checks and his Reuter's contacts had stirred some unwelcome interest from officialdom. Leads newly-opened might give him an edge; if only he could leave England. He remounted the horse, his reporter's urge kicking down the fear. Barely three metres below him heaving restless water melted the falling snowflakes. He set full circle sweep on his radar. The cliffs showed to stern; the fuzz from snowflakes ahead. The enormity of the journey struck home quickly as he became aware of his cold isolation. He hadn't been able to get his hands on a larger vehicle. The Channel tunnels would be watched and Law sweeps searched constantly for unauthorised private fliers.

The interception occurred when he was barely five kilometres from the coast. A giant shadow, visible in the snowfall as a darkening of the sky, swept in from the starboard west, stream-hovering just higher on a parallel track, a wing of doom across the churning sea. Zarbelli recklessly

89

punched extreme power. The horse screamed in protest at being instructed to combine maximum speed with its already-difficult altitude control. Caught by the suddenness of the action the patrol vehicle appeared to fall astern and disappear in the swirling snow. Grey banks of water rushed up at the fragile hover-bike, juddering now with the stress of conflicting forces. Zarbelli's eyes flickered down momentarily to the radar screen. The patrol craft appeared to be catching again, but his eyes were forced back ahead before he could be sure.

'Stop, before we force you down!'

External speakers boomed the message out across the water. Foolishly, he turned his head, trying to look up and back to the pursuing vehicle. The shift in body-weight was enough to set the horse into a deep downward curve. There was no time to correct. He rolled clear just before impact, a wave separating rider from steed. His helmet prevented concussion, but the bitterly-cold water numbed his brain just as effectively. He came to the surface and was swept by the barrage of the high swell. The tripod sensors of the auto-grab latched one by one onto his bobbing torso, then plucked him from the sea as the Law vehicle pulled back higher. The human pendulum swung dizzily. Continued retraction of the three cables took their drenched cargo up below the side-fin grilles where restraining bands locked into place. Bundled unceremoniously, Zarbelli closed his eyes in resignation as the powerful craft turned to speed away to the Law unit at Hastings. Snow, shock and slipstream combined - he began to shiver.

***

"Is he working for anyone, or simply freelance on the scent of a story?"

The seated medical supervisor followed the weaving brain patterns on the console before him. A taller man in the blue overalls of the Law standing behind had asked the question, his face giving nothing away. The supervisor turned his head.

"It's hard to say. There's a definite trace of excitement as if he knows, or suspects, something important, something big. There's a hint of fear, too, of the something being too big, or too nebulous. I can't probe deeper on standard chemicals. His Latin characteristics overwhelm any softer subtleties. Who wanted him?"

The Law shrugged. "The Union, I understand. Though quite why, we are never told, are we?"

"Well, by fifteen hours, they'll have him. There are not many more tests I can run on his brain." His left hand moved in tired finality over the sensors. The light on the far side of the viewing window faded. The Law officer stepped back a pace as the supervisor's chair swung away from the brain-pattern controls.

"I'll tell Reading they can pick him up then." The Law officer's smile was one of satisfaction, of a task well completed. Unauthorised joy-riders in the Channel were mostly reckless youngsters; finding a federal fugitive was an unexpected bonus. He was still smiling four hours later when the woman from the Federal Detention Agency thanked him for his work. They met on the steps of the Hastings Law base, a wide white arc before an open square, where once long ago there had been a pleasure pier. The snow had stopped. A wan shaft of sunlight lit the steps, a weak beam from an ancient theatre's tired spotlight. Zarbelli was led down to the waiting vehicle.

Several pedestrians glanced briefly, but the weather was too cold to generate much interest. A rear door panel slid back and the Italian was guided inside. He looked back at the Hastings officer fleetingly, once, just before the door closed.

'*A hint of fear, too, of the something being too big*'. The words wormed back into the officer's memory, but now the prisoner's eyes were blank, merely unfocussed pools carrying the ripples of the brain scan. The vehicle lifted easily on its bubble of air, swinging without effort beyond the landing guidance pylons. The Law officer watched its departure as it became an indistinct smudge in an unhealthy sky, then wink away from sight. The young boy in a bulky black woollen coat watched it too, from several steps away. Prisoners were exciting; his face beamed. He couldn't understand why the man walking slowly up the steps back into the building wasn't smiling at all.

Thursday 21 November

"You know my authority in this matter. I did not authorise a deletion, so how did it happen?"

Simon Atkins was furious, the darkening rose of his face-tint easily visible in the holographic image appearing at the Federal building in Reading. The Controller of Federal Security Services in the main English networking base squirmed uncomfortably.

"The work was contracted out to the local Law in Cymru. Our agents picked up Landon's trail on the same day, but over-zealous officers had deleted him by the time we had fully caught up. It is very much regretted."

"Regrets are rubbish! Landon was BBC. Cut anyone like that down in a messy fashion and two take their place. It accelerates their suspicion."

The Controller was draining of courage by the second. Atkins turned his head to watch the sun dawning in a cold red nudity beyond Istanbul's eastern limits. He had urgent business in Turkey. A few days away from Pichot Base would keep him from that fat security woman, Boon, and he had cleverly sown seeds of deception as to his true destination. He let his anger drain away, returning to a dependable, thinking logic. A flash of sunlight reflected from an early morning shuttle on the zenith of the bridge arching over to Scutari; a solitaire diamond on a graceful tiara spanning the water. The klaxon of the ferry coming in at Karakoy reached his ears. It was just that the President's scheme was terrifying and if he lost his grip on security at this early stage, there was no knowing what would happen as the complexities interlaced. No-one could be trusted!

He turned back to the image before him. "This Italian you have now.............is there a clear link to Landon?"

"Yes, they had worked together before, in the Punjab. Both covered the WSC meeting in Malta last month. Records show the Reuter's man and Landon's BBC associate, the woman Smith, had stayed in Swansea on the night of the deletion. Clearly, they had time to exchange knowledge. We may need further guidance on steering them away."

The Controller was still not certain of the South African's softer tone. He had decided the humble seeking of advice was a good move to make. Atkins was too wrapped up in the permutations of espionage to notice. "What did the Italian's scans reveal?"

"He's hot about something." He added hopefully, "We may be able to stretch it further."

"Do it. Bleed him dry if you have to - and find the woman Smith!"

The image of the blond man flicked out in Reading. The Controller was uncertain whether he had survived or not. The difficulty of his task persuaded him his career was still in the balance. He terminated his end of the holographic connection. *"It would help if I knew what we were looking for,"* he mumbled to himself. *"It's always the same in our business - the blind leading the blind."*

Atkins returned to the scene outside his window. The sun, now higher, was picking out the grime of Istanbul. The Asian city beyond the water could only manage a tired golden patina where a century before there had been burnished brilliance. The day would be long in the brittle sun. Body would cram on body, Asian and European, as the urban giant struggled with another day-lit burst of dying opportunity. The twenty-year old laws on compulsory birth control would not yet be showing a significant effect on slowing the growth in population. Istanbul just contained too many people. Atkins rose from his seat and left the room.

***

The sun which earlier had lit the minarets of Istanbul was providing weak afternoon warmth to the wide valley of the Mississippi river as the pure white Amtrak Bullet sped westwards. Coil-rail expresses linked Birmingham with Little Rock four times a day in either direction. They were usually non-stop, although they invariably slowed near the major intersections south of Tupelo. The Thursday noon train westward was no exception. It accelerated powerfully to regain its cruising speed of five hundred and fifty kilometres an hour long before the mighty river passed below.

The two occupants of the third carriage's observation bubble showed no interest in the expanses of the southern States. They focussed intently on the chess pieces set out before them.

"You have a thing about bishops, Miguel." A soft Canadian drawl was accompanied by a chuckle.

The young Mexican physicist smiled in reply. "I hold a certain fondness for them; destined never to tread the regular ups and downs of their fellows. But........a diagonal path does give the advantage of always being able to look over one's shoulder. A science security officer should appreciate that, John."

Burly John McWilliam chuckled again. The passion of the two men for the ancient game had been well known among their colleagues at work.

The elder of the two by six years, the security officer from Calgary had been lunar champion three times since 2128, but had lost his title to twenty four year old Santos just three months after the young man had joined Pieter North's team. The change of title-holder had not been accompanied by rancour - eighty five entrants from seventeen bases had contested the 2131 championship; McWilliam was simply pleased to keep the honour of the top two positions in the 'family'. A substantial right hand moved forward and a holographic black knight flickered off to reappear in its commanded position.

"Check............and mate in three! That's especially pleasing, our first game on earth."

Miguel Santos' laughter in response was genuine and bubbly.

"I shall come back from defeat, John; probably tonight, when we've settled in. Where are we going, anyway?"

"I don't know. Pieter's arranged an airlift for us at Little Rock. We must simply see what happens." The Canadian rose, towering over the slight figure before him. "We ought to re-join the others. There's not much time left before Little Rock."

They moved down the stairs to the carriage's main seating area. A black woman looked up as the men approached.

"Well?"

Santos' beam was wide and good-natured. "The old master took me!"

"Two titles I have yet to achieve, old and master!" she retorted. The three laughed.

"Have you ever played chess, Caramel?" John McWilliam swung into the seat next to the Mexican. The twenty nine year old plasmologist from Baton Rouge shook her head.

"It's never appealed to me. It's too much of the indoors. I prefer all this." Her delicate hand swept across the wide Mississippi plain. "It's so warm and alive after the sterility of the moon. I think I differ from you there, John. 'Security' is a singularly human concept. The world of nature takes life as it comes - no security, but no artificial tension, either."

A new voice from behind drew their attention. "We are particularly philosophical today, Caramel."

The hairless man approaching from the rear of the carriage exuded relaxation. Paul Forbes carried himself well, despite the limp of his left leg. There was a mal-alignment of the stainless steel struts that had replaced the bones. The events of June 2127 on a new lunar building site had effectively timed his remaining life. A power surge had built too quickly for adequate compensation; only his power engineer's instinct saving himself and two assistants from death when the computer's safety programs had proved woefully inadequate. The radiation that was eating through the bone structure had already timetabled the removal of much of his peripheral skeleton. Fibula, tibia, patella and femur from the left leg and tibia and patella from the right, had all gone. Operations on his left radius and ulna had been scheduled for late-February 2132. Forbes' acceptance of the horror had stunned his associates almost more than the accident and the disease themselves. "It is the Lord's will," he had said simply. "You will realise one day it had to be." He had always carried his religion openly; he was an anachronism among many lunar scientists but quite unrepentant.

Santos looked round the train carriage. "Has anyone seen where Lita went?"

Caramel stopped sipping at her drink to reply, her eyes sharp with feminine reflection.

"You'll find her in Communications. She went to speak with her bank manager in New York. Transferring funds for more outfits, I suppose! Why she'll need high fashion if we're still pounding away at laboratory work, I don't know."

"We have no idea what it is, or even where." John McWilliam was skilfully adept at scotching rumours. He had little time, either, for feminine rivalry between the two women. "We have an airlift waiting at Little Rock. As for wearing fashionable clothes, it is certainly unlikely we are bound for New York or Chicago from the middle of Arkansas."

A soft tone rang through the train carriage. *'Fifteen minutes to Little Rock. Prepare for deceleration'.*

The compartment's rear door slid aside. Only Santos looked up, smiling with satisfaction as Lita Scarrow lurched in. "Just in time!" It was spoken to no-one in particular. The slender American physicist fell into a vacant seat behind the Englishman Forbes, her amber hair unusually tousled, a flush of breathlessness on her cheeks. She had barely completed locking her harness into place when orange strip lights on the floor turned

95

to red for the final fifteen seconds to deceleration. She knew that increased body-weight from speed reduction would affect more noticeably those with longer lunar conditioning than herself. She considered telling the others, but decided against it. She expected her advice would not be accepted; certainly not by the plasmologist, Bondi. She contented herself with making a show of closing her eyes. The train's brakes cut in.

**

Pieter North stood alone in the darkness and watched the civilian aircraft taxi to a halt. Navigation lights winked against gathering snow flurries. The Dutchman thrust his chilled hands into the deep thermal pockets of his overcoat. He walked forward onto the exposed apron. A plate of cold air whipped his face, sharpening his concentration. The soft light from the aircraft's opening hatchway was almost immediately blocked out by the bulky figure of John McWilliam moving into view. North reached the foot of the steps and smiled up warmly. A means of facing down Atkins had arrived. Santos sneezed. North smiled. "I'm glad you're all here safely. Please come into the warm."

A trolley moved alongside to collect their luggage. The security officer moved up alongside North.

"It's a military base, Pieter." McWilliam's toneless comment was spoken softly, without expectation of contradiction. There was none. North simply nodded in response. The six went inside. Snowflakes whirled across the closing door.

GREY

Friday 22 November

"How much should they be told?"

McWilliam's shrug preceded his reply. The two men walked alone across the exposed airfield apron.

"It's difficult to say. On balance, they should be told everything. They're intelligent scientists; they'll know the eventual target is to shift a human. Honesty with these key personnel, sworn to secrecy, seems to me the clearest and safest way forward. There's not just the immediate political aspect to it all, Pieter. If technical leaks raise the possibility of the Southern Brotherhood attempting sabotage, the scientific consequences could be horrifying."

Pieter North ran his tongue slowly round his teeth in concentrated reflection. Despite the after-breakfast mouth-flush the memory of hot raisin cake remained. His eyes followed a hawk across the col between nearby peaks. Overnight snow had left a cold dusting of white on the hard ground. A bitter wind in the gloomy leaden sky, scouring the Oklahoma skyline, cut into the two men with the sharpness of antiseptic on an open wound.

"Yes, that makes sense, John. The team will be working beyond normal scientific limits. Virtually everything we've achieved in the past nine months is so experimental it wouldn't surprise me if it were just a freak accident which we could never repeat. I've called an introductory briefing for eleven hours today. If we press ahead with the first stages we can probably expect four or five months of intensive work - at least. It means we'll have to shut down the moon unit. Can you arrange a closure that won't attract attention? Something that appears innocent, unobtrusive?"

The security officer stopped at the chain-link fencing. A rueful look flitted across his face. "That would have been quite difficult a few weeks ago. As it is, research projects all over earth and moon bases are closing down. Funds are beginning to dry up with the new levels of uncertainty. Our lunar operation could be shut down as part of the general malaise."

The men turned, walking back slowly across the frost-hardened compound towards the shelter and warmth of the base buildings.

"Tell me more about this South African - Atkins."

North shrugged. "There's little else to tell. I've run the available bio-graphs, which of course have been heavily edited. He was born into money and made even more, apparently. He runs the biggest security firm in Africa, lives alone, and that's about it."

The Dutchman was surprised to feel relief as he confessed his unease about Atkins. Waves of cold loneliness he thought he'd left behind on the moon had been returning with a disquieting frequency. The Canadian was a familiar rock in what was proving to be a strange and chilling ocean, with far too many fog banks.

"Be careful of him, John. There is a cold distance there. He trusts no-one. When we start experimenting he may want to force the pace, faster than safety should dictate. What concerns me most is what he might do if we're unable to deliver."

McWilliam's jaw set as hard as the ground. "From what you've told me already, non-delivery is not on the politicians' check-list!"

A tickle caught in North's throat. He coughed, once. Unreality was returning to swamp him, a sweeping wave as deceptively innocent as the cloak it had thrown over him in the strange silence of the chapel at Chequers. How long ago was that? They moved out of the wind into the lee of the buildings and the feeling passed, as strangely as it had appeared. Sensing their approach the door opened, sending a wave of warmth gushing towards them. McWilliam stepped back slightly to let the other man enter first. The door closed to shut out the raw mountain day. North saw Caramel Bondi moving through the wide corridor towards them, her deep violet overall offering little contrast with her dark skin.

"Say nothing at the moment, Pieter." The whispered warning came before she was within earshot. North smiled. "Good morning, Caramel." His eyes passed over her body, taking particular care not to dwell too long on her thighs.

"I shouldn't go outside without putting a cloak on. It's very cold."

"I wouldn't dream of it."

Military figures moved through the corridor with hardly a glance at the three civilians. With a touch of his fingers at the neck, McWilliam demagnetised the fastening on his overcoat, the heavy sides falling open.

"Has everyone had breakfast?"

The plasmologist nodded. "Yes, I think so." She moved away, adding

"I'll see you later. There's no zero-grav sports arena here, so I'll cruise around the indoor running track." A smile and she was gone, leaving the men looking at the graceful flow of muscle and flesh in a clinging violet-coloured case.

"I'm pleased she's such a good scientist," murmured North.

The Canadian nodded thoughtfully, humour touching his lips. He simply nodded assent.

***

Paul Forbes was lost. He moved along the corridor more quickly, his limp becoming pronounced. He clicked his tongue in mild exasperation; these military bases had no guiding signs at corridor intersections. Civilian lunar bases swamped visitors with too much information. A uniformed figure approached from a turning ahead.

"Would you tell me where rotunda four is? I have a meeting there."

No smile, but a courteous and efficient wave of the hand, back from where the soldier had come.

"Keep going. R-four is down an incline to the left."

The Englishman nodded an acknowledgement and pressed on. His wrist-band showed eleven hours, six. It drew another tongue-click. If the start of the meeting was on an automatic sequence of background briefing, how much vital stuff had he missed? A sharp spasm of pain coursed up his leg, causing an off-balancing judder before he resumed his passage. He knew it was earth gravity straining the strut alignment. He ran a shaky hand over his baldness, convinced he had broken out in a sweat, but the skin was dry. The incline appeared and a softly-luminescent figure four in twenty-centimetre high grey embossed relief on the door panel appeared just above eye level. A guard stepped forward. "Mister Forbes?"

He was greeted with a nod, and a smile weakened slightly by the remnant of pain.

"Go in, please. They're waiting for you."

Through the sliding panel Forbes could see the cool airiness of the interior. Greys gave way to translucent whites, the dome of the rotunda matched by a circular concave table. The latecomer's colleagues looked up in welcome. Pieter North rose smiling and turned to the entrance.

"Paul, come in. We've not yet started."

He indicated a vacant place around the far side of the table. The power engineer moved round to sit between Lita Scarrow and a sandy-haired older man whom he did not know, but whose face seemed somehow familiar to him. Mildly-tinted spectacles turned towards him.

"I believe you must be Paul Forbes. I'm very pleased to meet you. My name is Jon De Haag."

The Dutchman, De Haag! The magnificent theoretician! The man himself in real life! Forbes' stomach fluttered. He had breathed De Haag's work throughout his studies and actually to meet the man caused a frisson of excitement. The importance of the summons to Earth moved up in his estimation. He forgot about the throbbing in his left leg. North rose to speak.

"I asked you all to come Earth-side because our initial steps in temporal transference have been given an opportunity to become larger steps. I've been asked - *we've* been asked - to press ahead with expanded funding to achieve a human transference, if possible within nine months."

The room stiffened. Paul Forbes' hairless eyebrows rose; Caramel Bondi inspected her fingernails with overly-studied nonchalance; Miguel Santos exhaled audibly. North registered a slight nod from the big Canadian and continued. Why did he have the feeling of falling again?

"You will all no doubt realise it is not purely for scientific knowledge." This time, a few mild snorts puffed up from around the table. North pressed on.

"The financial changes coming from the World States Council decision in Malta last month are starting to have effect. We've all seen the news. The northern developed world needs to care for an ever-increasing population world-wide. This would be a particularly bad time for economic resources to be spread too thinly."

He blinked twice.' 'Don't keep saying it,' he thought. 'You'll start to doubt it all over again.' He swallowed.

"A person sent back to a point before the Maltese decision could prevent that decision ever having been taken."

Any expected scientific scepticism didn't materialise; the groundwork on temporal shifts over past months had been successful to the point where individual thought processes had already made allowance for several such adjustments in approach. The opening question came instead from an unexpected quarter.

"Is there any definition of 'prevent'?" Paul Forbes was first to break into the presentation.

"No, Paul, but Professor De Haag has made it clear there is an expectation of non-violence. Indeed, the theory probably requires it, anyway. We have made it abundantly obvious to the politicians that a variety of non-violent options can and should be available, such as simply ensuring that someone other than Mbene makes the crucial speech. They have taken these considerations on board."

Paul Forbes merely nodded. The presentation was resumed.

"I am anxious to emphasise that we will all have a personal choice in this matter. The team will not be forced to act on a majority vote. The technical and other difficulties to be faced can only be tackled on a volunteer basis. However, at the limits of scientific endeavour the absence of any specialist could put others in danger. It's only fair to remind ourselves of that."

The scientist from Baton Rouge cut in, her eyes flashing in the sombre light of the room.

"I have brothers and sisters in the Third World. The spread of financial well-being is long-overdue, in my view. The decision in Malta should have been taken fifty years ago."

Lita Scarrow responded sharply. "We're not here to discuss politics; we're here because we're scientists!"

101

The plasmologist's eyes widened again, pools of white exasperation on a darkening base. "That's exactly the head-in-the-sand attitude which led to the warped development of atomic power two hundred years ago and the elitist bribery of Martian colonisation flights in the last twenty years when we cleared the way for the older traveller. Every time there's a break-through in science, the scientists themselves fail to shout the warnings loudly enough!"

"Stop, will you!"

Her volume had risen during the final few seconds of her attack. Paul Forbes' second interjection had to be untypically-sharp to slice an end to its flow.

"There's one reason why we must all stand together and see this through, now the box has been opened."

The desperate fervour in his voice held the room silent. Miguel Santos' slight frame shuddered. It was a quite involuntary nerve-twinge but it had the heightening effect of making the room feel colder. Forbes continued in the new silence.

"Caramel, you've taken us through two hundred years in a few seconds. That could now really happen. Ever since time began, the human race has been fearful of the future. It's all changed. For the first time, we must learn to be fearful of the past."

Nobody had a precise idea of what he was talking about, probably least of all Forbes himself, but the statement was sufficiently nebulous with apocalyptic overtones for everyone to draw their own private conclusions. Professor Jon De Haag nodded slightly. "A timely reminder; I apologise for the pun."

The slight touch of humour barely restored normality. Lita Scarrow's weak laugh was strangled at birth as she realised it was unintentional humour. Pieter North glanced around the table at those assembled. De Haag, McWilliam, Forbes, Scarrow; these were willing or amenable. Perhaps this would be easier than he had feared. Would the young Mexican latch on to Bondi's hostility, removing her isolation and emboldening her resistance, and that of others?

"Miguel?"

Santos' gaze held each one of his colleagues firmly before he spoke.

102

"My country has lived in the shadow of a giant for many centuries. There have been bad times, some very bad times, but I have never known the United States of America to be malevolent. I do not doubt that the African heart is in the right place, but the world is now too inter-dependent to go killing golden geese. I support the project."

The phrasing was off-beam but the sentiment was clear enough. The black girl glared at him. It was to no avail, as his eyes were on the blind professor. He continued.

"I would like to ask Professor De Haag about the practical issue of a change in history. Would our conversation here today ever have taken place under the changed circumstances? Could we be participating in an illusion?"

De Haag hesitated before answering. His face remained pointing forward, facing no-one in particular. "Yes, the words I speak might just be a temporary feature, being picked up by others merely sharing a space with the same temporary characteristics."

The timbre of his voice conveyed an easy nonchalance, as if he didn't mind one way or the other. Pieter North knew this was just his relaxed character; his seriousness was certainly not in doubt as he continued with his explanation.

"I ought to explain further, and I can a little, but the logic becomes part of a matrix that interlaces very quickly. You are best advised to trust to what I say rather than try to understand it fully. I know unquestioning trust is alien to us scientists, but please bear with me."

North could still sense Caramel Bondi's stiffness, but like everyone round the table, she was hanging on De Haag's words.

"We give the label 'history' to the record of the past passage of what we also label 'time', but here in November 2131 we are not at the front end of a vehicle forging on into the unknown. Past, present and future history is an unfolding of a tapestry, or an unfurling of a flag. What we have come to think of erroneously as an indelible mark is merely a wrinkle, a crease, on this tapestry. We shake the flag and a new set of wrinkles appears. The project we have been asked to embark on is a shaking of the flag to produce a more beneficial set of creases. Do you wish me to go deeper?"

The question was open to all and Lita Scarrow accepted the invitation. "It sounds harmless enough. I vote we go ahead."

North jumped in, not wanting to let De Haag get round to the bit about preventing the wrinkles being so severe as to kill someone.

"Well, Caramel? We shall need good plasmological control for the instant of ejection."

The girl's gaze moved off De Haag to the other Dutchman. Some resistance could still be detected in her attitude.

"There will be equality for poorer nations one day. I believe that is in the flag and not in the wrinkles, so we can shake all we like and it will do no good in the long run. As for my involvement and my co-operation, with that belief safeguarding me, yes, you can have it."

North's nod was slight and formal, but his inner relief was immense. "Thank you. We shall move to first equipment checking sequences this afternoon."

Thursday 12 December

The English city of Norwich lay frozen in the pre-holiday snow. The first ten days of December had brought several blizzards, white bursts of Arctic origin. Familiar buildings had taken on new character. The seventy-storey needle that was the Aviva headquarters rose like a giant, upside-down icicle into the winter sky. Further to the west, at Exchange Street and reaching almost towards Pottergate, the hummocky outlines of the main city mosque could manage no Arabian fire to warm the northern heart. Like the two cathedrals and a smattering of churches, it would not do much business this holiday. The day had been busy in the shops. Less than two weeks to the midwinter Bank Holiday meant that purchasing time was running out fast for the city's three hundred thousand inhabitants. This year, the festival itself would be on Monday the twenty-third; always on the closest Monday to what had once been a fixed holiday on the twenty-fifth of the month. Christmas had been the last traditional feast to move to a set government-decreed break. The re-titled Midwinter Festival of Light had moved to a fixed Monday in the year 2080.

A small flock of scruffy starlings, desperate with the weather, buzzed the grey pyramid of the Law's main buildings. Three of them flew too close to the intruder screen and were burned to death; a millisecond of welcome warmth before extinction. The sun set; ice sparkled as the frost bit more deeply, providing malevolent fairy-dust for the regional capital. Vehicles on the H47 glided slowly in a numbed response to the cold. The woman moved nervously among the homeward-bound mill of people in the city centre, all muffled against the coming night. She moved towards a grey suburban vehicle bound for Hethersett, the rectangular information patch on its nose running through the five intermediate stops chosen for the journey. She sat near the entrance, not wanting to commit herself to a hemmed-in position further into the pod. The windows turned opaque, shutting out the city lights. Warm air from the floor slots filled the vehicle, cocooning the travellers and nudging tiredness deeper; in some, over the brink into doziness.

Fighting the extreme cold was proving too much for many, especially the elderly and the very young. Strain had cut deeply into the faces on the shuttle. An old woman in a rear seat closed her eyes gratefully at being spared a wait for a later pod. Two toddlers cuddled into their mother; one with eyes in half-sleep, one with the wide glazed look of stunned exhaustion. The woman at the front tugged her brown cap more tightly over her ears, her long hair providing welcome extra warmth to the nape of her neck. She, too, was tired; a tiredness part-born of the cold and part-born of anxiety. Her eyes had swept over her fellow travellers as they had boarded. One by one, she had searched out the glance that would give away more than a disinterested spark of courtesy. There was no clue. If contact of any kind was made on the shuttle now, it would come as a surprise. Felixana Smith yawned and snuggled deeper into herself for the remainder of the journey to Hethersett.

The Blakeney Apartments were banked up the artificial hillside, black square chunks set solidly against the snow. This was not a desirable residential area, but that was perhaps all to the good. How long had she been here? Was it four weeks? It seemed like four months, with the change in scenery, the low-key investigations and life's now furtive rhythm. The cutting away from the BBC hurt almost as badly as the fear of criminal proceedings. There would be action of some sort against her, she felt sure. She trudged through deep snow to the heated stairway, set in a straight line up between groups of apartments. She shivered. The cold was encroaching again after the warmth of the shuttle moments earlier, gnawing its way back into her tired bones. Felixana sighed. She thought of Craig Landon, wondering where he was. Her exhalation of breath at the top step was part exertion, and part involuntary whimper. She turned to her left, and following the softly-luminous guard rail, walked the twenty or so paces to apartment G7. The outside frame of the entrance glowed in response to her approach. She removed a bulky mitten and pressed her palm to the key-pad. A pea-sized green indicator lit up.

"Yes, Felixana; come in."

The male voice coincided with the opening of the door. The softly-lit interior did little to alter the girl's pupil dilation after the subdued external lighting. The door closed behind her. The room smelt of plastic - the aroma neutraliser had broken down - a warm, comforting, olde-world charm pervaded the furniture. It brought afresh her memories of childhood in the Peak District. Her anxiety subsided. The room's occupant turned his head, leaning back in the contour chair in the corner. He smiled in the semi-darkness.

"How was the day? Did you learn anything new?"

She unwound a scarf, removed the brown cap and shook her hair.

"No. There may be very few chances left now. I've tried all the tricks I can on public library terminals without giving away where I am. I may have gone too far already, given new tracking techniques." She dropped her tired body into a wrap-around cushion.

"It's not fair that I should attract attention to Norwich, John. You were kind enough to shelter me when Toni disappeared from your brother's apartment. If Toni is taken at any time and talks of our night in Kew, there's a thread which could be followed here. Even without that, BBC colleagues could be having their families checked. It depends on how determined the Law is to find me."

John Devine lifted a hand in gentle dismissal of the act of shelter.

"If there is little to tell, there will be little to reveal. No-one's arrested you in the last four weeks, so the trail may have gone cold. It's clear from what you've picked up already that northern nations are ranged against the southern hemisphere. What they have in mind can only be a guess; a scientific embargo, or an economic one, perhaps? More likely is an operation to secure a military advantage or to bend international financial protocols their way without being found out. If they can break open southern solidarity a new WSC summit might be convened."

The freelance cartographer looked at the girl.

"I wonder if I can help in some way," he said. "I could try a few unconnected enquiries myself."

Felixana stirred against the yielding cushion. "You've done enough as it is. It's too risky for you."

Devine inclined his head as if to deflect and defuse the attempted rejection. "I don't know. You staying here will implicate me already. Besides, I have world-wide friends in the mapping business. We can check all sort of things innocently - geological surveys, wildlife patterns, urban sprawl, pollution densities; it would be no trouble at all to run theoretical models on where the Southern Brotherhood's weaknesses are. We may need to look at this potential story from a different angle."

He lifted his long thin body from the chair. *'So unlike his brother'*, Felixana thought.

"Have you eaten in town? Would you like a drink?" He moved to a nearby drinks cabinet.

"Yes, I have, but I'd appreciate an orange juice. What did you mean by a different angle?"

"Let's assume some physical move against the southern nations is being planned. We should be able to detect some heightened or unusual activity at military and other bases. It doesn't matter what sort of activity. Anything out of the ordinary or anything starting or intensifying in the past few weeks would qualify to be looked at. A wide range of innocuous factors is possible - co-ordinated catering developments, increases in inter-bloc electricity flows, who knows? The northern powers can hardly put a joint effort together without something being revealed. Cartographers have password access to a world of their own as well as media people, you know!" He smiled warmly.

The effect of his words on the BBC woman was positive. A way out of the downward spiral of negative results seemed on offer; at least it was worth a try. She smiled back, raised her tumbler in a grateful toast at being given new heart, and downed the juice. It was a short-lived burst of energy. She yawned. "Can we start tomorrow? I'm tired."

Devine chuckled. "I'm not surprised. The shuttle service from Norwich is enough to tire anyone out. Let's check on the world news, shall we?" He activated the wall-length view-screen.

'They were cutting through in order to reach the survivors. City, Law and Rescue officers at the scene described this as London's worst civilian tragedy for over thirty years.'

Scenes of bodies draped over department store escalators melted away as newscasters' faces returned. The two friends watched spellbound.

'Although the authorities are refusing to speculate at this early stage on the cause of the incident, witnesses are revealing the probable reason was the announcement over the store's public address system that limited stocks of fresh fruit were available in the Food Hall. Shoppers scrambling up from the floor below had jostled in the Hall and reports indicate that widespread fighting broke out. Many people fell through transparent screens onto the moving escalators, which then jammed, throwing others to the floor below.'

Pictures appeared again. Paramedic lasers lanced grotesquely past smartly-tailored mannequins. Plastic faces dripped apart in shifting beams as real flesh and blood bodies below were cut from tangled metal floor supports. John Devine turned to his companion.

"The world is getting jittery. If the Union and its partners speed up their move against the Southern Brotherhood, there may be little time for us to find out."

Wednesday 25 December

The Brazilian sun shone strongly enough over the sprawling vastness of Recife to give a special warmth. Christmas Day in this equatorial workhouse would be celebrated with vigour. Pleasure boats scythed sparkling patterns across the Capibaribe, as Romero Duarte sat pensively in the garden at the government's private dock to the west of the city's commercial centre, listening in thoughtful silence to the Christmas morning bells ringing out from the churches. A soft patina of sweat silkily wrapped his chubby features. His fall from favour had been swift. Less than three months before, the façade of success had still been in place. Duarte had felt bitterly that his final chance had not shaken out fairly. He had attended the right functions at the right time in Malta, and said the right things, but nobody seemed to be listening any more. The house of cards was falling, and though not a picture card himself, he still tasted the bitter herbs of guilt. He recalled further snatches from the pre-Malta briefing, his senior Minister's jaw set firm with fore-boding.

"Our skimming of Third World aid would be stopped if this damned God movement takes over, Romero. You for one would not only be poor, but probably in prison, too!"

The fat Brazilian began to shiver slightly, despite the mildness of the day. Prison in Latin America meant the chemical stripping of the brain. He blinked to clear a pearl of sweat from his right eye. Why were the Christian bells mocking him? He hadn't diverted that much money; just a little in the great scheme of things. The river waters looked cool and inviting. They were dirty and grey, but that was all to the good - their darkness would hide him. Duarte threw himself to his feet, stumbled across the few bare metres to the edge of the dock, and plunged into the water. His head cracked on an outcropping mooring beam, causing his obese carcase to somersault away from the shore. A circle of blood was added momentarily to the grey waters; then the slate was wiped clean. The bells continued to peal out.

Saturday 4 January 2132

A cold, north-easterly wind blew over Oklahoma. It scrubbed the sky until it was a pure blue, with the sun shining fully. Spears of icy rain had struck the frozen earth the day before, leaving a firm glaze across the ochre ground. Moaning and sighing through desolate scrub, the wind delivered its astringent message to the hills and valleys surrounding Pichot army base. The wild turkey, sheltering high on the south-facing slopes in the lee of a buffeted, stunted sugar maple, could see no changes in the base below. There was only changeless man in a changeless wilderness. Yet wild turkeys were not party to the awesome powers being tested below, so would remain unaware that Pichot had changed much over the previous ten weeks.

The air in the ground-level testing amphitheatre buzzed and throbbed gently with the nearness of electrical charges. Men and women in light blue overall suits moved slowly among the machinery. Thigh-high support trolleys rolled silently in obedient patience alongside the senior technicians, and were kept in tow by radio pulse units at their masters' waists. Gradually, since well before the midwinter holiday, the base had shed much of its military personnel as groups of scientists and security officers flew in to take their place. Now it was more than ever cut off from the world as it proceeded with its task. A soft wailing sound permeated the amphitheatre, accompanied by a pastel pink glow from low-charge plasma warning strips around the walls, ceiling and floor. A human voice broke in, carrying sharper authority than the more familiar synthetic tones.

"Attention in main test area. The primary transfer charge is building. Move from the focus area."

Figures responded to the words, leaving the circular core unit of the central focus area isolated within the amphitheatre. The black cabin stood four metres in height with a diameter of three metres. Its domed top was sealed; an elongated half-egg with a smooth matt exterior. Two half-metre diameter tunnels set forty-five degrees apart fed into the egg's base across the test-bed floor. One was a conduit for the power cables, the other the entry to the transfer chamber itself. A young technician, new to the project, moved to a wall-chart to watch the different energy pulses that would form the lattice as they grew in intensity and purpose. Coloured lights graphically charted the inexorable growth. He turned to his female co-ordinator with a sense of awe.

"They're drawing strength from each other, aren't they?"

She nodded. "We don't know quite why and how the pattern feeds on itself in this way. It's very disconcerting; of all the scientific processes developed over the past three hundred years, this is the first time we've been unable to build a simulation or a control in advance. It either happens, or it doesn't. There's no preparation and no second chances. It's a characteristic of the plasma in the lattice. If it fails, we must start all over again with a new power-build."

She pointed with a gloved hand to the steady red pulse on the left side of the chart.

"The dominant characteristic pounds like a heart-beat, orchestrating the others. Once the lattice reaches a certain point, it's like a cork being blown from a bottle. Anything in the transfer chamber winks out, catapulted backwards in time. We don't even know why it's always backwards - but that's enough to be going on with."

A beam of humour lit their faces. The lad responded.

"I should think so, too! It's an important day, isn't it? We're sending the first primate."

The woman turned to look at one of the chamber screens. The chimpanzee covered his ears as lattice sound built again; nothing painful, but noticeable enough to a trained animal.

"Yes. Stay here and watch. It should wink out in about ninety seconds."

"How far will it go?"

"It'll go about twenty years, as close as we can tell. We need that far for the chimp to retrieve an article for carbon-dating. A piece of natural wood will do. We should then be able to compare the carbon-14 result with a piece of current wood. We also need to pre-date this base so a wooded valley would be virgin ground."

"What if the return journey simply accelerates the decay process; or the chimp walks outside our tractor beam?"

His colleague winced visibly. "Don't ask me questions like that! I don't understand temporal logic. Ask Professor De Haag later."

The two watched in silence as the power lattice resonances built to their climax. There was no warning. In one instant the chimpanzee was visible; in the next it wasn't. Audible gasps and intakes of breath echoed in the amphitheatre. One operator gave a low, involuntary whimper as his entire console zeroed its indicators at registering no life within the transfer chamber. Pieter North's responses were not so obvious. There was a slight tightening of the knuckles on the perimeter hand-rail; a glance at the post-transfer pattern thrown up by the power lattice - nothing else. His brain worked furiously. Why couldn't they calculate more accurately the destination time, the time at the other end of the transfer? There was some connection between the continuance of power in the post-transfer phase and the 'distance' travelled in time, but it appeared not to be consistent in all instances. Were they wise to try a primate after only ten weeks? Early experiments with lower creatures had been remarkably successful; there was no logical reason for him to be concerned, but a primate was uncomfortably like a human being.

The blind De Haag stood at North's side, his other senses alive to the unscientific hub-hub within the amphitheatre.

"Well, Pieter. Are we standing on the shoulders of giants?"

His compatriot laughed confidently to fight off his clinging uncertainty. "No, we're standing on the shoulders of gods! The chimp has gone. It was a smooth transfer. The programs will cut power in another eleven seconds. Then we wait. It's looking good."

The power-cut came on time, with a tangible lessening of the background shimmering atmosphere in the charged room. A few checks on the control indicators, and thirty seconds later Paul Forbes limped back to where De Haag and North were standing.

"It certainly looked like a good transfer, Pieter. We'll pull the chimp back whenever you're ready."

"Just hold and monitor. Thirty minutes for the animal is thirty minutes for us. It's trained to put sticks in its basket, so we must give it what opportunities we can."

Forbes indicated agreement with his head and limped off. North turned again to De Haag.

"It would be an awful horror if we were to bring back a dead chimpanzee."

The older man smiled and nodded. "What about a live one. Wouldn't that be like opening Pandora's Box?"

"We must hope your time-stream theory continues to hold, Jon. If the animal was moved instantaneously to a point about twenty years back, it should spend thirty minutes there as we go through our next half hour, making the power parameters for its return identical to those on the outward journey."

"That's right. Two leaves in a stream, separated by distance but maintaining that distance as they float down the same stream at the same speed."

De Haag's ears picked up the soft tread of approaching feet. The arrival from behind them of John McWilliam made North jump. The Canadian security officer caught his arm, a finger to his own lips just preventing the Dutchman from speaking his name. He indicated with his face that he needed to speak privately with the Project Director. North excused himself from De Haag's presence with an explanation that there were 'figures to check', and moved away with McWilliam. Only when they were outside the main amphitheatre did the security man feel able to speak. His eyes instinctively scanned the outer concourse and corridor endings, but his face held the professional relaxation of someone enquiring about the weather or the price of lunar mineral shares. He whispered to North.

"How many plasma spasm units do we use?"

North's mind was still tuned to the morning's transfer experiments; he answered readily, copying the whisper. "Two. One in constant use and one kept as redundancy."

"Four have been ordered and delivered."

North snorted firmly. "That's impossible! Glass domes that size just can't lie around without being seen! Besides, the ones we need are very expensive units of European manufacture; they were designed especially for our use. No-one else would need them."

Speaking the thoughts and looking beyond McWilliam's nonchalance into his worried eyes, prompted the Dutchman into serious hesitancy.

"We have thirty minutes before transfer reversal. We obviously need to talk. Where won't we be overheard?"

McWilliam shrugged. "There're only two options, really. We could go outside, but it's too cold. So I think we ought to try anti-rad clothing and set the suits' communication channel to a scrambler line. Even then, we'd have to wipe the master copy when we're finished, but we have authority for that."

"OK. Let's get on with it." The two moved away quickly down an empty corridor.

***

"I thought we shipped our larger items of equipment by the military wing at L.A. for extra security."

North felt slightly foolish holding a conversation on a bench in a bulky anti-rad suit, but the seriousness of the subject kept the foolishness to a minimum. McWilliam's voice crackled intimately in his ear.

"We do, but something is still going wrong. I made a cursory check of inventory a week ago, just nosing around. I noticed the spasm unit totals and decided to run checks on all the key equipment tallies. There's no doubt of it, Pieter; from a range of suppliers and on the express orders of one, or more than one, of the senior test team, double the number of pieces of equipment actually needed are being delivered to final delivery address. I can't find out the name on the order or the delivery destination. We're not getting the duplicates here though, that's for sure."

North turned to his colleague. The eyes through the visor still held their seriousness. "Have you no idea at all who's doing it? The ordering, I mean."

"No. There are seven of us with access to the order codes. Double validation is not needed. Everyone needs to be able to order independently because of the specialisms we all hold and the speed of our experimentation program."

North stared down at his white gloves as if he could find the culprit hiding there among the folds. Thoughts ran through his mind. It could be industrial espionage. There were plenty of opportunities in successful time-travel, but who would risk a highly-dangerous theft from a cartel of powerful governments? He shared his thoughts. McWilliam nodded and replied.

"Whoever they are, they must be monitoring our progress step by step. It presents an awful set of imponderables. Either they don't know who's paying for this research, or they know and don't care. The level of funding needed must point to a similar group of governments."

"The Southern Brotherhood," cut in North firmly. "But to what purpose? To intercept the agent we send back and prevent the re-routing of history? It terrifies me, John. Why duplicate the project, why not just sabotage it? If it is the Brotherhood and they perfect this process before we do, they could wreak havoc far beyond the financial power moving their way now. We must stop it going any further."

"I suggest I ought to continue to try to find out where the equipment is ending up. That may mean a trip to Los Angeles at some point. I also need to find out who the leak is on the senior team. If it is the Southern Brotherhood behind all this, it does point to Caramel."

North nodded sadly, though the suit's helmet hardly moved with his head. They were both staring into the grey fog of uncertainty.

"I agree. She must be first choice. Her talk about brothers and sisters in the Third World was quite an outburst." He sat quietly for a few seconds; then added "Why hasn't Atkins seen it?"

"It's highly technical, so it's possible we're the first to catch it."

"If there's a way of saving Caramel from herself I'd like to try it. She's a first-class plasmologist. There's also the fear that Atkins and the Union would replace the whole of our team to make absolutely sure, and I'd be left with no influence at all on replacements."

"We'll have to hurry, Pieter. Government auditors come in at the end of February, and twice the expected expenditure is going to stand out like the Eiffel satellite."

The thermostat cut in on North's suit, its soft whirr nudging his thoughts to more immediate issues. He noticed the head-up time display on his visor.

"It's time to get back to see if we still have a monkey, John." Then he added ruefully "I hope no-one's making a monkey out of us."

TANGERINE

Sunday 5 January

John Devine was as good as his word. Throughout the darkest days of the season, when lights had twinkled bravely against the cold and the citizens of Norwich had scoured the retail outlets that tempted them through their home screens, Felixana had watched as the advantages of world cartography had revealed themselves before her eyes. The two had collected as much information as they had dared on all kinds of activity. It had been stored away into a separate file library, with so many security passwords they sometimes forgot in which order to use them. Individually, each item appeared innocuous; the hope was that search co-ordinates carefully and imaginatively chosen would spring open a lock to reveal a nugget of truth. Links and threads would probably be easy, she felt. Much more difficult would be the jumping to conclusions that would be worth following, worth risking one's life for. Their joint efforts were rewarded in the late afternoon of the first Sunday of the New Year.

The bouncing of ideas off each other had often seemed like a parlour game, a pastime quite in keeping with the mood of the season. Riddles and guesses were shared among friends, yet with the dangerous and murky edge that collecting a new piece of the jigsaw might lead to a knock at the door in the middle of the night. They looked with pensive but excited satisfaction at the plastic sheets scattered on the coffee table before them. These contained three valuable pieces of knowledge, distilled down from perhaps forty or fifty recent events. All except one had been garnered legally. The exception had only become available when they had hacked into flight plan data registered at Tangier's Ibn Battouta Airport.

The encroaching night outside had brought on tiredness. They finished their celebratory glasses of brandy and slumped back into welcoming armchairs. Felixana felt drained. Her companion watched her as she fell asleep. His own nervousness was returning. Their investigations would now have certainly invoked interest from the Law. It was perhaps time for them to move out of Norwich for safety. Their cartography research over past days had given him an idea. He crept by the sleeping form across from him. He dared not phone from his apartment, it was too risky. He slipped outside to a communal console in an adjoining

116

block. An hour later he was back searching for two overnight bags. He decided it would be best if they both left the city early the next morning.

Wednesday 15 January

The final passing of the holiday season had forced workers back to work. Despite the continuing bad weather, many fortunate enough still to be in employment had taken a deep breath and struggled back into harness. Although most would have merely remained at their domestic terminals, a fair proportion of Norwich's men and women still serviced the transport and commercial infrastructure of the regional capital.

The young man climbing down from the Blakeney Apartments in the late morning was not one of them. His employers were far away. They would receive a mixed bag from him today - some good news and some bad news. There had been no sign any more of the occupants at apartment G7. He had watched and waited for other residents along this section of the block. All was quiet. The apartment door would give no resistance to someone with his skills; he knew there would be no signs of forced entry after his silent departure. Once inside, he had searched thoroughly. Yes, there were some clues here; experienced eyes gathered that the resident had taken a female visitor for a period of perhaps some weeks. He would have to report back and move on elsewhere. He remembered to clip a bug among the furniture to watch for the future, noting with satisfaction that its small orange monitor light was winking softly. He slipped away unnoticed, only swearing softly at the base of the steps on the way out as his foot bathed in an icy puddle.

Sunday 2 March

Felixana Smith slithered on the woodland track but recovered her balance and kept running. Bursts of condensation from her mouth fell into a rhythm with the pounding in her ears. Raw dampness tickled her throat. She coughed, twice, watching her feet flash over the ground. The track widened before her; an avenue of trees and she was in the open, stumbling and running along the edge of a dark brown field. The sun had risen to her left, lighting the clumps of mist hanging in the still morning air. A few more metres and she regained the farm road, the concrete adding welcome traction to her mud-caked shoes. It was easier now. She redoubled her efforts for a final surge. The cottage door rushed at her and she leant against it, a gripping ache holding her rib-cage in its embrace. Standing alone, she watched the quiet country scene as her heart-rate slowed. She stooped, took off her running shoes, and pushed the door towards a shower and breakfast.

John Devine and Pedro Valdez were already eating as she staggered in. The Englishman looked up, a warm smile gently playing on his freckled face.

"You look better today, Felixana. At least, you will when you recover!"

Not having anything to throw in mock exasperation, she tossed her perspiration-soaked hair in a light-hearted defiance. The friendships she had been shown over the previous four months had been good for her, and she was still keeping ahead of the Law. The welcoming, enticing smell of country muffins, marmalade and coffee wrapped its fatherly arms round her and carried her lovingly through her shower. The two men had finished their breakfast by the time she returned to the low-ceilinged, sunlit dining area. The tall, wizened Colombian ex-patriot was bending at a side table, poring over computer-enhanced satellite pictures. They could have been of anywhere in the world, as far as she could tell; only the dark-brown muffins with their tangy Seville-flavoured topping on the main table held her attention.

"Help yourself to coffee." He had hardly looked up, anxious to finish checking the focus quality before parcelling the sheets for Norwich and onward transmission to the International Cartography Association in Marrakech.

His professional colleague was not interested. John Devine stood at the natural glass window, looking eastward across the sloping ploughed field to the small coppice of wood at the far side in the valley's hollow. Beyond, the mist had evaporated, leaving a view clear across half a kilometre of shabby, winter-worn grassland meadow to a larger stand of trees on the horizon, their naked arms raised in open surrender to the strengthening sun. The English countryside pleased him. Much of it was now criss-crossed with route-ways of one kind or another, as the obsession to be constantly on the move continued to grip this island people. Yet there were still large areas that lay as green and silent as they had two hundred years before when motorised transport had first become freely available to the bulk of the population. This northern lump of Anglia wasn't on anyone's route to anywhere; the sun rose to shine over Walsingham on a landscape which had frozen long before the unexpected snowfalls of the previous October.

Devine lifted a second cup of coffee to his lips as he reflected on recent events. What would his brother think of him now? Painstaking investigation was part of his nature, part of his own professional calling, indeed, but the heady scent of danger in this episode with Felixana was not at all pleasant. Map-makers rarely diced with espionage; at least, not in recent times. He might have thought with humour of tales of Portuguese explorers in centuries past, of intrigue in Spanish and English courts. Yet in his own time he found it did not grow on him, that on the contrary it was sapping his strength. The girl had swept him along in an exciting world of secrets and he hadn't even slept with her. Gradually exposing the plans of the European Union to attack the Southern Brotherhood in some way would get him, what? He cupped both hands round the hot coffee to burn reality back into his thoughts. He had a nebulous feeling that all he would get would be a laser beam in the back of the neck, dissolving his brain-stem like asparagus in acid. Would it be worth it, to die in the cross-fire between a greedy north and an embittered south? Felixana wanted a story and had been - was still - in danger because of it. Protective, yes, that was it; he felt the need to be protective towards her. He had even embroiled his fellow cartographer in their dangerous game. The wealthy Colombian had persuaded them both that a rented cottage near the coast would prove easier as a hiding place than a small apartment in Norwich. His eye caught the blink of sunlight on a vehicle hovering lazily across the far meadow. Perhaps it was sex after all, then, but would the laser beam present itself first? He took another sip of the coffee as the black hover-car lifted from the meadow and sped across the ploughed field towards the cottage. Devine banged the cup down noisily.

"There's a vehicle coming!"

The words burned into his companions and all moved instinctively towards the door, as if three human bodies would be enough to stop whoever sought entrance. Valdez's quick glance through the window caught the low matt lines of the car. It slid smoothly round to the concrete farm road, its approach completely silent. The cottage tenant indicated the rooms to the rear.

"Hide through there. It's covering the front and I can always say I'm alone."

The woman and the man scuttled from sight. Devine thought uncomfortably of asparagus. Valdez chose to walk outside. If he could keep casual callers on the farm track, it would be better than them standing on the threshold, peering in, pressing for entrance. He closed the door, preparing his mind to confront the visitors and send them packing, diplomatically but firmly. A twinge of nerves pricked at his resolve. The car hung bonnet-on towards the cottage, mirroring and reflecting back the Colombian's directness. It seemed to Valdez it would have been much more natural for it to have glided to a halt with its side in more profile. It sank onto thin, thirty-centimetre legs. Valdez stood at his door, uncertain now. He watched the car's right wing hinge up like a crow in distress. A tiny, dark-haired man rose to climb out of the wounded black crow. Across less than ten metres his smile seemed sincere enough. Valdez's legs found the strength to move. His eyes flicked from the stranger to the vehicle. He couldn't be sure if there were any passengers. He smiled.

"Good morning. May I help you?"

A nod and a smile and the stranger walked over.

"I believe you can, yes. Please don't worry. I am alone."

Again, there was a certainty, a directness of purpose, and a nerve in Valdez's neck began to twitch. Despite his greater height he felt the little man wrapped in fur against the raw morning was going to overwhelm him. The voice was extremely-well cultured, its Mediterranean lilt contrasting strongly with the wan English surroundings. The visitor continued, his next words flooding over Valdez to complete his sense of unreality.

"My name is Michael Ben-Tovim. I understand you have Felixana Smith here. She is in much danger."

The Colombian rode the emotional blow to his stomach quite well. He hesitated only for a second. Long talks with his hiding friends had told him much about the world forces being ranged against each other. There seemed little point in shadow-boxing.

"Come inside, please." He gestured towards the cottage door, standing aside to walk in with his Jewish visitor.

***

Breakfast dishes stood unwashed on the dining surfaces, streaks of food slowly congealing. Across the cottage at a lower level fresh coffee bubbled and hissed. Four figures sat in intense awareness of each other, the coffee to hand. John Devine was impressed by the small, well-poised diplomat who sat opposite him at the working table.

120

"You have taken just as much a risk to be here as we have, Mr Ben-Tovim, travelling alone like that. We could just as easily have shot first, and checked your identity on screen afterwards, as the other way round."

Michael Ben-Tovim nodded, his voice soft and melodic.

"Yes, it is a high risk, but we are in a high-risk situation. It's not getting any better. I can offer Israeli safety to all of you, but time may be running out."

His face turned to the girl, olive eyes open with sincerity and sadness. Felixana felt uncomfortable. "It is possible you met with Craig Landon in Swansea last November, and he could have told you something of importance which would help us. He wouldn't have told me direct; chasing a story on one's own is second nature to a reporter. He was a good investigator."

"Was?" Felixana's world started to fall apart. She didn't want to hear any more, but the words kept coming.

"I'm so sorry, Miss Smith, but Craig is dead. He was killed before he had chance to leave the city. We suspect it was the Swansea Law that caught up with him." Ben-Tovim was genuinely sad to bear the news.

The months of uncertainty, of longing, of anxious emotion, burst like a weakened dam. Felixana felt her face flushing up; she was already halfway across the lounge level towards the sanctuary of her sleeping room when the tears flooded into her clutching fingers. The door closed with a pneumatic sigh of tenderness as her body heaved on the bed, spurting the sobs into her eyes and beginning the painful draining of her emotion. The three men remained in their seats; all knew this was her private journey, at least for the next hour. Then she would need support and companionship.

John Devine's pensive self-examination, broken by the diplomat's arrival, was evaporating quickly. There seemed a weapon here with which to fight back at the vague and formless uncertainties. It would perhaps be a way of justifying to himself his aid for the woman. A way which, although full of danger and threat, was no longer beyond his perception of his own courage. He nodded at Valdez. The tall Colombian spoke as he spun in his seat.

"We may certainly be in a position to help, Mr Ben-Tovim. It may be that our joint knowledge will give us a better picture of what the northern world is planning. Permit me to call a world map to the view-screen."

The three swivelled their chairs to face the curved executive screen which Valdez activated by voice-print. A series of indicators riffled and spun down the left edge to provide legend colours and symbols. The main map was accompanied by two smaller ones inset into the lower right corner. *'An expensive screen,'* thought the Jewish diplomat. *'This man has money'.*

At a few instructions from Valdez, a Star of David appeared over the largest British island.

"May as well mark where we are already." The three smiled with some good humour, though dented through concern for the girl. They settled back in their chairs. Devine summarised the previous four months, explaining what he knew of Swansea, of his brother Paul in Kew, and of Toni Zarbelli's disappearance. Ben-Tovim frowned at the mention of the Italian.

"If the Union have him, he would have been questioned vigorously. He may even be dead. He may have confessed to sleeping in London, but that is unlikely, because the Law have not tracked you here yet. His brain would have fused under interrogation if they pushed him too far. We only traced Miss Smith to Norfolk quite recently and any earlier clues to your whereabouts extracted by the Union could have had you all dead by now."

Valdez noticed that Ben-Tovim hadn't clarified who the 'we' was in his explanation. He said nothing. Devine felt his nervousness returning; the Israeli was so matter-of-fact about it all. The diplomat kept talking about Zarbelli.

"Alternatively, he is still loose, following his own investigations. I don't know if Brotherhood agents have come across him. In any case, perhaps it's best not to mention it to Miss Smith. She has suffered enough today already."

The mention of the Brotherhood in the third person answered the Colombian's unspoken question. Israel, for some reason, appeared to be ploughing a lonely furrow. The other two nodded in agreement with Ben-Tovim's protective statement about the woman. Valdez spoke.

"It seems to me the trail of blood is already too red for us all. Let me show you on screen what we have. There has been enough dying."

He quoted a short string of figures at the screen. The Mercator projection glowed in response. He looked at John Devine for the go-ahead to summarise on their behalf. The Englishman nodded.

"Felixana and Toni had learned from Craig Landon that the European Union and the United States had liaised fairly quickly after the WSC meeting. The involvement of the Russians and then the Chinese was, I suppose, a surprise, in terms of the global reach that was now possible. Large sums of money began to flow across the world from east to west. Japan became implicated, too. It was perhaps payment for services rendered, or to be rendered. But what services? Something massive was being planned. We feel it likely that it would need a dependable security operation to run it."

Valdez smiled as he continued. "Cartographers have many contacts world-wide; perhaps as many as do diplomats, though I don't doubt the Mossad do much better."

The mention of the Israeli secret service caused Ben-Tovim to smile as well. His host wasn't yet telling him anything he didn't know, but he was a patient man. The Colombian continued.

"Landon had suggested that a private security company was probably going to be involved, one that could understand how the Southern Brotherhood might react to threats against it. An African connection therefore seemed the best place to begin looking. We started at the top - Atkins Alert is the biggest around, headquartered in Namibia. Their boss makes a big point of the personal touch. He's famous for a hands-on approach; always handles things personally, despite the secrecy of the business he's in. We looked at the timings involved and the likely journeys that would have to be made. One seemed particularly to fit. A small unmarked airliner had stopped in Tangier for refuelling last November, in the early hours of Sunday the tenth. We took a risk in breaking into flight data at Tangier airport, but it was worth it. It was on a stop-over from Windhoek to an undisclosed destination in England."

John Devine picked up the presentation.

"The timing is too good to be co-incidental. The boss, Simon Atkins, hardly ever leaves southern Africa, apparently, so it's likely he was on the plane. It was timing that led Felixana and me to our second of three discoveries."

He spoke to Valdez. "Can you show us the string of locations, Pedro?"

"B seven, C nine, H five, necklace sequence, tangerine nineteen."

The letter 'S', the nineteenth in the alphabet, glowed orange across the global map at six locations; San Francisco, Mexico City, Dublin, Paris, Stockholm and Jerusalem. Ben-Tovim was impressed, and this time not only by the screen's sophistication. If these people had strung that sequence together and drawn some reasonable conclusions, there was indeed a chance to perceive a fresh factor, a small key that might unlock the dark mind of the northern powers. He sidestepped the implication and merely asked, "Why pick the letter 'S'?"

Valdez laughed. "It's because they're suspects, my dear man!" They all smiled. The Englishman returned to the serious business, warming to his achievements.

"They all represent people who disappeared in mysterious circumstances in the few weeks before the midwinter holiday. Dr Paul Carter, nutritionist, failed to arrive for work one morning at Cross Food Laboratories in Dublin. A Professor Lundquist took a short skiing break from Stockholm University in early December and never went back for an important conference. Apparently, he's an acknowledged expert in civilisation sociology. Pierre Lucas resigned from the International School of Oriental and Tropical Medicine in Paris the same week. The media said it was professional pride after an internal argument, but rumour has it that no such argument ever took place with anyone there. Ten days or so later, a nature conservancy expert on wildlife went missing from Mexico City zoo; same as Carter, just didn't turn up for work."

Devine turned his head from the screen and looked at the Israeli.

"No surprise, I'm sure, about the event closer to your home. Professor Samuel Meir, in central Jerusalem, jumped into a jet car which sped away, leaving his woman partner on the shopping trip with no explanation for his sudden departure. There's been no sign of him since. He's Principal Professor at the University School of Languages. Finally, on the twenty first of the month, there was a break in the pattern, and perhaps the most ominous of all. Philip Allen, former hand-weapons adviser to the U.S. State Department, was actually abducted in daylight along the

Embarcadero on San Francisco's waterfront. A nuclear helicopter whisked him straight out to sea. We've monitored events ever since - not one of the six has been seen in 2132."

Valdez picked up the story as Ben-Tovim nodded gently, almost imperceptibly.

"The pattern is clear. They're world authorities on nutrition, medicine, wildlife, language, civilisation and weaponry. Their specialisms also tend to knowledge of the middle-east. It seems to us that a secret military strike is being planned against the ruling powers in, perhaps, Jordan or Egypt, to break them apart from the Southern Brotherhood. These experts would be needed for training purposes."

Valdez paused at that point, his eyes back to the visitor. "How are we doing so far?"

"That's very good. Our own professionals could not have done it better. We, too, suspect a military strike. The point is, just where and when? You mentioned it as the second of three discoveries. Do you have more?"

John Devine spoke again, his nervousness returning.

"I'm sorry, but I think we would prefer you to help us for a change. Our lives are in danger, by your own admission. Simply to suck us dry of information with nothing in return, does not seem right."

The Colombian nodded in support. Ben-Tovim sat silently for four or five seconds. His voice came softly.

"You're right. There is little point in not sharing with you. Friends and allies are hard to come by. We do not know what the Union is planning or how quickly it may become too late to stop it. Would you put a question mark on your map, please, on the American State of Oklahoma?"

Valdez responded. Ben-Tovim pointed to the glowing enigma. "Israeli and Mexican operatives have traced Atkins' activities to a military base in the Wichita Mountains. Our agents in Washington D.C. intercepted a high-level message destined for the base on the twenty third of November. It simply read 'Methuselah approved.' There was nothing else. We don't know what it means. Considerable amounts of scientific equipment are being delivered to Oklahoma. A strike against any nation in today's world would only carry high chances of success if some terrifying new weapon were to be used. It seems likely that something is under development at the Pichot Base. We have no agents inside and cannot tell."

A thought struck Valdez, who sat up with interest. "Are satellites registering power emanations from this, what is it, Pichot Base?"

"Yes, quite powerful, and in irregular bursts over periods of time, as if trial and error testing is going on. The registration is increasing."

"Can you call the picture graphs to the screen? Believe me, it may be important."

"I don't know, but I can try. The use of my call-sign to Walsingham may make your life here untenable if the Union is monitoring screen-frequencies, but we may be past the point of safety, anyway."

Ninety seconds later, considerable in screen response time, a series of peak-and-trough patterns sprang into one of the rectangles in the lower right corner of the main screen. The legend read temperature, radiation, gravity oscillation; even a plasma-bolt reading. Valdez's lips tightened and he responded with commands of his own. He finished with one word. "Superimpose".

The peak-and-trough patterns marched across the screen in near unison. Valdez nodded with satisfaction. "They're almost identical, wouldn't you say? The differences can be explained by latitude, although strangely enough, the latitudes are not all that different. We could compensate for that, but it's hardly necessary, I think. Case proved!"

"Where is that?" Ben-Tovim's voice was showing real excitement.

"It's our third discovery. Colleagues in Australasia dragged up a report at Perth Tracking from a defunct mining satellite that by rights should have burned up years ago. The radiations are coming from a deserted mountain region in Turkey, south of the Georgian border. That's much better for a middle-eastern strike than launching an attack from Oklahoma, wouldn't you think?"

Valdez and Devine glowed with satisfaction. Ben-Tovim nodded, clearly impressed.

"We must get someone into Pichot Base to find out what's being built there. That we can do; much easier than Turkey at this stage."

None of the men had heard the woman return to the room. She spoke with quiet determination, her red-rimmed eyes still hard with pain.

"I want to go in."

Saturday 8 March

Mary Trent bubbled with anticipation and barely-suppressed excitement. David was coming to pick her up for an evening out. She lit a cigarette quickly, and just as promptly stubbed it out. *'No, that wouldn't be a good idea,'* she told herself. David didn't smoke and perhaps it was time to turn over a new leaf. Saffron was with a neighbour. She hoped it was safe to leave her overnight away from home; Mary had kept her close all winter, during the six terrible months when they had struggled to come to terms with Matthew's death. She shivered again with anticipation, checking her short dark hair for stray strands that would detract from her appearance. She wanted to look at her best. David Thorpe was her age; at least, she thought so. A neighbour and a friend for several years, he had been a great support in the weeks following the crash of the Gordons' car. His current woman was away in Scotland for the weekend to visit an elderly parent. Mary still couldn't believe that she had agreed to a clandestine dinner-date. The secrecy made her throat dry but she couldn't snap out of the feeling that this was what she wanted. The doorbell rang, her heart jumped, and she was with him. Nothing else mattered.

The meal was good and the occasion satisfying and natural. The weather of the winter had given way to a damp spring, the melting snows being joined by persistent rainfall to give flooding over lower-lying land. The overcast skies had carried out their threat of heavy rain by late evening; both she and David had become drenched in making the rushed journey from their homeward taxi to the door. Stripping off wet clothes had seemed sensible; his eyes on her lacy, orange bra cups had seemed equally natural. The night melted into glorious fulfilment for her.

Sunday 18 May

Paul Forbes stood at prayer. The stainless steel skeleton in his legs would not accommodate kneeling, so he had forsaken the western supplication for the upright Christian Orthodox stance. In the silence of his room his closed eyes shut out the world. It had been hard to maintain a weekly rhythm when Sundays were timetabled into work schedules so completely; but then, Sundays were only special to a handful like himself. Certainly, no-one else in the senior team professed a Faith. This particular Sunday was needful of prayer - the first attempted transfer of a human was only hours away. His lips audibly carried the Lord's Prayer in its traditional 2050 version: *'please pardon our wrongs when we pardon wrongs against us'*.

He felt a twinge of emotional feeling. After six months of intensive experimentation, he prayed for the safety of all involved. He was conscious of his own contribution to the project. A few more moments of silence and all tension drained away. He pressed his tunic edges together, setting out for the main amphitheatre with a calm acceptance of what might come. He didn't have long to wait for his first shock. At a junction along the corridor a smooth voice reached him.

"Permit me to join you, Doctor Forbes. I understand we have a big day today."

The Englishman winced inwardly. Atkins! What was he doing here? He had only seen the chief security officer three or four times in the previous six months, yet here he was turning up at such a crucial time. His use of the word 'we' grated particularly on the power engineer, who shifted deliberately to the personal pronoun.

"Well, Mr Atkins. I shall have to see. Nothing is guaranteed, not in this particular business."

The soft laugh and the dead eyes showed that the South African was not convinced. He merely commented "Indeed, indeed", and fell alongside Forbes in silence on the way to the amphitheatre. The bland façade came naturally to the security man, but behind it Atkins was expectantly nervous. Six months had passed since he had taken the European contract and it had seemed like an eternity. It wasn't just the horrendous magnitude of what he was guarding, it was the way it had sucked him into setting aside the usual habits of his profession. It demanded his personal attention to so many aspects of the assignment. He had dared not relinquish the ultimate project to others. Somehow he knew if he once let it go, it would unravel. He couldn't trust anyone. It was beginning to be an obsession. His thoughts threw up pictures of the past months. His first visit to Istanbul had been followed by two more. When he had found that the Federal Detention Agency in Reading had raised the possibility of a brain-sear result on the fugitive reporter Zarbelli, he had himself gone to England to question the man. It had been too late. The fools had overdone it and killed the Italian.

So, here he was back in Oklahoma. The senior scientists here would remember him from his few visits. He braced inwardly. It was the blind Dutchman, De Haag, who made him wary. He could see more than the sighted ones! Yet Atkins' confidence was flowing back. Equipment and data were reaching Turkey in a steady stream and the base there would soon be ready for the senior scientists. The equipment had been tested on the new site, power had been gradually increasing, and the laboratories were working. Information from every success in America was being conveyed secretly across the Atlantic. His informant on the senior team was doing an excellent job. He would have to remember not to throw any knowing glances in that direction today. If the test went well with a human it would certainly be a great step forward.

He left Forbes at the door of the amphitheatre, striding away towards one of the back viewing galleries. He turned momentarily to watch the Englishman as the various pre-test checks were run. A pathetic sight, he thought, content to follow orders until his crumbling skeleton collapsed within him. Nothing anyone could do for him now, that was for sure, yet he seemed untouched by it all.

A wall door slid open on the far side of the amphitheatre, causing Atkins' attention to abandon Forbes. The man in shining white who entered seemed to be in his mid-twenties, slim and fit with short dark hair. Doctor North appeared from behind a wide bank of instruments, strode to the newcomer and started speaking. Two technicians holding low-power monitors proceeded to check the transmissions from under-skin sensors implanted in the younger man. North nodded vigorously. He glanced at his wrist unit and pointed to the entry tunnel for the black central cabin.

Atkins' eyes swung with experienced perception around the amphitheatre. There were ten, perhaps twelve, people only, none of them displaying any particular excitement. He felt like an outsider. He took a deep breath and tried to look nonchalant himself. He almost succeeded, yet there remained an indefinable anxiety. These people around him were displaying so little emotion. They were scientists, and it was a world of which the South African had no knowledge. Without knowledge, he felt he could not be in control. A row of screen monitors to the right picked up the man in the enclosed chamber. Who was he? There was some anxiety there too, surely? Perhaps he could see a slight tightening of the skin around the eyes? It was hardly surprising, of course. There was history in the making and perhaps much more to come. The man would be highly trained, thought Atkins, and keeping himself under control, but no-one could tell the South African anything about detecting symptoms of an underlying fear. His whole life was tuned to exploiting such emotions. Yet he couldn't escape from the feeling that he was an outsider.

The power in the amphitheatre built. Atkins' eyes narrowed, willing the man into the past. Was he strapped down? The monitors didn't show it either way. Atkins blinked at the instant of transfer, unnerved by the emptiness in the blank cabin. His eyes flew round the room, seeking to recover his alertness by seeing shock in others' demeanour. There was none. He could only detect the control of the scientists professionally and calmly handling their latest experimental cargo. It unnerved the layman.

Monday 19 May

The President of the European Union materialised into the reception area; or rather, his holographic image did. There was almost enough presence about Antos Papandreou, Atkins thought, to will himself there in person. Black, curly hair in a tight mop topped an impassive, tanned face. The electric blue uniform with its circular insignia of golden stars clung immaculately to his solid frame. Atkins sat two metres from the incoming projection, noticing the shimmering and flashing halo round the President that signified this was a high-security transmission into the Pichot Base.

Atkins smiled. He was tempted to feel impressed that the President had chosen personally to speak with him; but perhaps it was only evidence of the intense secrecy involved. "Good morning, Mr President, or is it afternoon with you?"

"It's afternoon here." The hologram didn't elaborate on where 'here' was, but came straight to the point. "Was yesterday's experiment successful?"

"Indeed it was, Mr President. North and his people put a man back in time three years. He brought back photographs of the base as it looked at the time; astounding really. It hardly seems possible. Apparently, the transfer is instantaneous, although it must be a jolt to the system. The Air Force Sergeant who went reported terrible stomach cramps. The scientists are talking now of fasting before a transfer."

It was not a detail to impress a President. Papandreou dismissed it with a twitch of his jaw, focussing on the main point. "I am pleased with your security control. The Southern Brotherhood is fixing its hopes on

130

the Israelis, but it seems they are not getting anywhere. You are to be congratulated."

Atkins glowed visibly at the compliment. It was a pity he didn't feel so pleased himself. Through the confusion of feelings he became aware that the President was still speaking.

"We can now press ahead with Project Methuselah. I require your continuing work on that, too; especially as teams are moved across to Turkey."

Atkins dared to voice his concern. "Their security officer, North's I mean, name of McWilliam; he's been making enquiries of some equipment suppliers in California. There is suspicion on the diversion of key pieces of equipment. They probably think it's the Brotherhood, but if the disclosure of the new base's purpose is not managed to the Union's advantage, it is possible that key members of North's team would not co-operate further. The deception will need to be handled sensitively; many of the other disciplines are in plentiful supply, but the time travel people are pushing back scientific boundaries through hunches. We could never replace their unique abilities."

Atkins was unsettled by his admissions on ownership of the project and recognition of the scientists' worth. This was certainly not in his nature. He explained to the President that he did not trust the balding Dutchman. The politician for his part was feeling expansive. He responded well to the sensitive perceptions put to him.

"They will respond to the challenge, the ultimate test. They will have to be told soon, anyway. Once the technique is mastered, De Haag's scientists will be expecting to move the operation to Africa. If you are concerned about secrecy, you must inform only the Professor of the true state of affairs for the present. Do so as soon as you can."

The President smiled and the line went dead. Atkins felt numb. He sat in silence; unease and irritation growing at being sucked in and used for so much more than a security control.

Friday 23 May

The girl shook her head, golden locks tossing prettily. "No, sir, I'm sorry. Professor De Haag left yesterday with Mr McWilliam."

131

Exasperation welled up in Simon Atkins and he exhaled sharply.

"Why?"

"'Library and Research Work' it says on the chart. He often goes to California with one of his personal assistants, but this time he travelled with Mr McWilliam."

The base's External Reservations Officer seemed not at all unnerved by the South African, who now raised his voice.

"I was not made aware of his departure. I did not give clearance." His tone was acidic.

The Officer's fingers keyed the board for clarification. The screen glowed, confirming the security codes for De Haag. "That was not necessary, Mr Atkins. The Professor has senior team classification. He's exempt from your transit codes."

Atkins fumed with irritation that the codes had not been more assiduously assigned in the first place. It showed him that even the senior theoretician was not to be trusted. Why was this young officer so frank and outspoken, anyway? He thumped the desk top, causing its contents to jump wildly.

"I'm going to have a change round here! I'm not having this happening again!"

The echo of the roar followed him as he stormed from the room. A pen rolled off the edge of the desk to the floor. It laid in silence as the girl bit her lip and shook. Had she said something wrong?

Tuesday 27 May

The light golden dome of Los Angeles' 2039 Museum glowed in the midday sunshine like a huge upturned grapefruit. The matt-black lines that zigzagged artistically across it in representation of earthquake chasms were clearly visible at a height of a thousand metres from the twin-seat craft closing on one of the city's northern airports. The passenger looked through the windows as the jet banked and then levelled. Greater Los Angeles was massive. Streams of cars at different heights were criss-crossing the conurbation. The city now stretched south along the coast for over eighty kilometres. The aircraft centred itself on the landing strip and lost altitude. Piece by piece, the city panorama narrowed, until with a dying of power, the pilot and passenger could only look out on a bland and anonymous three-storey airport building, sand-brown and shimmering in the heat. More than fifty years of development to the south had left this northern spot relatively quiet.

The quietness suited Simon Atkins. He wasn't yet sure how to proceed and needed time to think. The journey to the rented apartment was uneventful; by 14:30 hours he was seated at the accommodation's view-board. He drank coffee as he keyed instructions; a black and astringent drink that matched his mood. A flurry of passwords and the screen brought him the security world's messages from around the globe. He noted with satisfaction a political assassination prevented in France and a political assassination achieved in Senegal. The deck of cards he played had no saints or devils, no good or bad. The high-security business was nothing if not amoral. It accurately and soullessly reflected the societies it served. The money kept rolling in and the blind Dutchman kept appearing in his mind.

What was he to do? He would tell De Haag about 'Methuselah', yes; but where and when? McWilliam would be chasing the equipment duplication and it would only be a matter of time before he realised the Union was playing a double game. It might blow up in his face if he didn't steal the thunder by bringing De Haag into the picture very soon. He might even be able to leave his contact in North's team in place. Yes, he would have to get to De Haag fast. He would be on one of the UCLA campuses, probably. His Faculty would be listed. The University registers confessed to three De Haag's, but only one was Jon, working as predicted in the realms of theoretical physics. Atkins keyed the journey tag to the route-planner frequency of his hire car for the data to flow across; no point in wandering across this vast city, he felt. The feedback information told him how many other vehicles had logged the same route for the same time co-ordinates, and suggested a fifteen minute delay on his start time. He sat back and picked up his coffee, feeling slightly more relaxed. The view-screen sensor picked up his next command. "Roam, fast."

The screen responded, running in increasing wavelength sequence through the forty two local information and entertainment channels available in this sector of town. The screen lingered for five seconds on each, providing a pot-pourri of images and sounds to tickle his brain.

'The weather in the mountains will be changeable.'

'He stands accused of murdering his neighbour.'

'Welcome to the third day of the North American Gliding Championships.'

'Only the right answer will get you the prizes, Clementine.'

'We are seeing the biggest movement of people in Africa for more than fifty years.'

"Stay!" Atkins' word stopped the sequence just in time. The word 'Africa' had triggered his instincts. A reporter was visible, behind him an African plain partly hidden in the pall of dust thrown up by a vast army of feet.

'Estimates are putting the total travelling from the south at between a quarter and a third of a million people, with other large movements from the north and east. Their destination is clearly the area around Kolwezi, in Zaire, from where rumours of magical and unsubstantiated appearances continue to emanate. Some governments in this part of Africa are maintaining this is a destabilising attack on the labour force of fragile local economies by the United States. Any such counter to the financial changes being forced on world governments must be regarded as possible, though Washington and other key capitals in the north deny any involvement.'

The reporter turned and gazed out over the teeming masses, then faced the camera again.

'Your correspondent here has seen these migrants at first hand, however. They appear genuinely entranced and are moving in on Kolwezi clearly determined to gain what they keep referring to as 'salvation'. If we obtain any further news on the appearances we shall obviously bring it to you. Remember, you heard it first on this channel. This is Jermaine Soto for Worldstat Fifteen, in the plains of southern Africa.'

Atkins cut the link with a dismissive gesture. He remembered being told how hordes like this had swarmed all over his grandparents' happiness. He gulped the last of his coffee. Contemptuous of the ant-like images half a world away he swept out to the hire car. It lifted off into the hot blue sky over Los Angeles. He considered his options as the vehicle sped across town. Certainly, he did not relish his task. There had been no love lost between the Professor and himself. The few occasions they had met had been marked by a distinct wariness. His natural expectation of total obedience had been countered by a quiet, almost submissive, enigma - a sightless old man who saw through him. What did he see? Why was he so confoundedly gentle all the time? Whenever the cold professional approach had undercut sensibilities before, the response had been sharp. He could handle that, citric sharpness, but who could fence with a bank of sea-mist? He would be business-like and brisk, he decided. He would simply tell the Professor about the true purpose of the experiment, with the clear implication that North and the other scientists would be expected to co-operate. After the excitements of success so far, they would surely be hooked on the potential for further, greater, things. But, was that the way? He thought of the sea-mist again.

The decisive descent of the hire car to a parking hover at Compton Campus jerked the South African from his cotton-wool of indecision. A green sward stretched away from the vehicle areas out towards the jagged outline of the university buildings, stepped up in rectangular blocks to reflect western afternoon sunshine. Balmy air spilled into the driving seat as the vehicle cover opened. A reception unit rolled over. Atkins placed his request; an interview with Professor Jon De Haag, if possible, this afternoon. The processing took place silently within the enigmatic, orange-coloured unit.

'One moment please. A re-route is requested.'

The metallic, artificial voice fell silent. Atkins glanced at the hire car's time display; 15:30 hours. The loudspeaker spoke again, this time carrying a human voice.

"Mr Atkins, my name is Carrera. I am the Campus Security Controller. Would you come over to the main entrance, please? Follow the unit."

The visitor grounded the hire car and complied. He found Carrera coming halfway down the steps to greet him. The man was as young as himself, a fit man with dark Mexican bone structure and friendly eyes. His hand-grip was firm.

"Your reputation precedes you, Mr Atkins. I am honoured to meet you."

"Thank you. I rarely travel, but recently I seem to get everywhere."

The blond visitor was genuinely courteous to a fellow security officer. This was the central campus, and the largest. Carrera would have held not inconsiderable power and responsibilities. The host smiled, indicating the doorway. "Please come in."

Atkins was shown to a first-floor office via a wide marble staircase. The imposing surroundings, with sculptured busts of classical, medieval and lunar scientists, were not surprising to him. Universities were among the oldest institutions in the developed world; for many hundreds of years now scientific knowledge had meant power. Command of the physical world had kept ordinary citizens in respectful thrall of the seats of learning. *'Yes'*, thought Atkins, *'puny scrawny Africans shuffling across a dusty plain deserve to be swept aside by the natural superiority of the northern scientific world.'*

He sat down in a comfortable leather cup at two metres' distance from Carrera's desk. The Mexican leaned forward on the concave side of his kidney-shaped console. The scene was set. Atkins waited. Sunlight shafted in through slatted windows, throwing golden bars onto a honey-coloured plasti-wood floor. Carrera's voice was as rich and mellow as the atmosphere in the room. Somnolence tiptoed up on the visitor; recognising it, he shook himself alert.

"It is not for me to ask after your reasons for being here, Mr Atkins. They must indeed be compelling to bring you here in person. There is nothing I can do for you, however. You see, Professor De Haag died of a heart attack less than two hours ago."

The South African's world was beginning to tilt. "That's impossible! Surely you have compatible units here, to cope with regular staff if not for every visitor?" The irrational feeling presented itself that security officers should not allow important people to die. "Where was he?"

"In his office, Mr Atkins; believe me, there was nothing anyone could do. It seems his will had left him; as if his work was over. I always attend incidents of this kind in case campus security is compromised. The medical people were surprised that they could do nothing, despite having spare heart units to hand."

Atkins stood, fighting off the dizzying frustration. It would do no good to vent anger here. His hand reached out for Carrera's, himself just rising from his desk.

"It was good of you to see me, anyhow. I shall just have to pursue my enquiries elsewhere."

Atkins was shown from the room, but walked back down the marble staircase alone, cocooned in a sense of unreality. His mind was in a turmoil that contrasted with the confident timelessness of his surroundings. Perhaps, as he had been tempted to think only three days before, the whole thing was beginning to unravel in his hands. The more he pushed for control, it seemed the less he had. He regained his car, upping the air-conditioning to force an end to the sleepy warmth of the day which had been sapping his determination to the point of fatalism.

'No, this would not do,' he told himself. He would find McWilliam and tell him of the project instead. Why should he shoulder this secret alone any longer as a puppet of the world's politicians? There would be no sea-mist with McWilliam, no enigmatic cotton-wool of an answer to confound his wishes for progress. The project would proceed on time.

The Canadian was a no-nonsense security man; North's own security man, it was true, but that wouldn't matter. The lunar people were in too deep to back out now, their scientific curiosity captured by the two guaranteed temptations of unlimited funding and surprisingly-quick initial success. They would embrace the real task with enthusiasm and he, Simon Atkins, would keep a strong grip all the way back. Besides, the blind Dutchman was dead and out of his way. Perhaps that was all to the good. Supremely confident again, he punched the hire car skyward. He re-joined the northbound rush hour traffic, not noticing the small vehicle that had also lifted from the university campus and had slotted itself a few cars to his rear.

Wednesday 28 May

The high, feathery cirrus cloud was tinged with orange as the day came to its close. The sun had dipped below the Wichita hill-line only a moment before, but already the valley in which Pichot Base lay was gathering its evening cloak around itself. Lumps with no outline were visible beyond the perimeter fencing. Were they boulders or clumps of brush? Felixana Smith couldn't tell. She sat tensely silent as the small shuttle-bus flowed in towards the buildings from the air-strip. She was not alone in avoiding conversation. Most of the ten-strong calibration team members were tired and simply gazed from the windows. The only sound came from two middle-aged males sitting at the back, chuckling in soft ragged tones as they shared a lewd joke. The English woman had hoped that the speed of developments would have outstripped the growth of her nervous anticipation, keeping her feelings well under control, but she was uncomfortably aware of a fluttering inside. She looked through the windows on the other side of the bus, letting her eyes drift over others' profiles. She relaxed slightly; no-one was remotely interested in her.

It was as she had been told. Calibration teams rarely contained elements of fellowship as their members often didn't know each other. The anonymity was in their nature, swooping in a non-predictable time-table on secure bases to change access frequencies on locks, safes, fencing, stores, meeting rooms, data repositories; everywhere to foul up any chance of a concerted attempt at gaining unauthorised entry. She had been told this was her best way in, perhaps her only way in. Her Mossad guides had decided to act quickly once it was known Atkins was in Los Angeles. His personal presence always increased security alertness. It would be marginally lower in his absence, perhaps just enough to make the difference between access and detection. Would that be sufficient? She had no way of knowing. She wasn't even sure that she was ready, that she looked and felt the part.

The butterflies continued when the shuttle-bus stopped. A hiss of air and an opening door preceded the appearance of a Base duty warden, climbing the two steps inside to smile at the arrivals. Felixana's fluttering quietened. The demeanour of the warden showed clearly that calibration visitors were treated with the nervous reverence accorded to auditors the world over. The imposter would have little difficulty here. The team leader rose, momentarily blocking the warden from view of Felixana's column of seats. The English woman squeezed her eyes shut to clear her mind, opening them with renewed confidence in her frightening yet necessary mission. The team leader turned. "Please follow me, everybody."

The last hint of daylight had gone as the calibration workers filed silently into the Base. The English imposter was thankful for the anonymity of the night, but for how long would the darkness hide her?

Thursday 29 May

The first hours in Pichot Base passed uneventfully enough. Security changes proceeded in an orderly fashion, the work of the calibration team achieving remarkable heights in repetitive boredom. Much of Thursday morning's work involved perimeter checking. Felixana was appreciative of the outdoor nature of the duties, the fresh air countering the deadening and unexpected claustrophobia of being a spy. She worked enthusiastically enough, making acquaintances among the team members, her eyes and ears constantly alert for clues to the purpose of the Base. None came, except for awareness that whatever it was, it was intensely scientific in nature.

Around noon, she was crossing the edge of the airfield apron as the jet came in high over the hills to the west. She had reached the shadow of a hangar when the fierce reverse roar slowed the craft's final momentum. It taxied to a stop less than a hundred metres from where she stood. Two figures came down the steps. She recognised Simon Atkins easily from sight of his shock of blond hair, but the burly figure behind him she did not know. Atkins! Her mouth dried; for an absurd moment she even imagine he would stride across the apron to clasp an arresting hand on her shoulder, to grip her as a bird of prey would a mouse. Yet he didn't. The two men moved briskly to the administration entrance and disappeared inside. The girl continued round the hangar, rubbing palms sticky with nervousness against the side of her overalls. She felt as if a bridge had been burned behind her, that there would now be no going back. The sense of her vulnerability was almost overwhelming. Atkins' arrival from Los Angeles struck her as proof of her mission's reality. It was perhaps to be expected that the closer she came to uncovering her story, the more the symbols of opposition would press in on her. She had put herself in a position where conjecture and theory were no longer the main tools of her trade. Now there would be merely the sharp stab of success or failure, striking into her like a sword.

Even the cloak of her deception bore threads of fatalism. This morning's calibration work had completed much of the exterior activity. Every session would now take her nearer to the most secure parts of the Base. She gazed up at the slopes of the Wichita hills, drowsy in the May heat. They beckoned to her, safe and uncomplicated, changeless and open. She thought of the gentler hills of the Derbyshire of her long-past childhood. The inner depths of Pichot would hold the secret she sought, but they would also carry the greatest risks of detection. Which would come first - knowledge of the flame or death from burning? How fortunate were the simple moths and butterflies up in the hills around her. There was a natural order, a balance, to their activity, yet for her, there was no such balance.

"Hey!"

The sudden jolt of the shout almost brought stomach bile to the back of her throat. She was conscious of a deep flush rushing to her cheeks. She turned.

"Outside calibration's finished. It's time to start inside."

The team leader was smiling, beckoning her over. Felixana could read sexual desire in his eyes. That was useful; he would misinterpret the nervous blush and the downturned face. She walked with him to the nearby entrance door.

Friday 30 May

It was as she had thought. Friday's work drew her closer to whatever secret the Base held. The number of restricted rooms and corridors increased. Complexity mushroomed visibly in the calibration charts which pointed the way to the successful completion of each new task. She was no scientist, but she was well aware that the Mossad had trained her well. She silently thanked them. Throughout the course of the day a picture took shape. She already knew that the secret was held multi-nationally; nonetheless, seeing a few Chinese technicians and project officers in a restricted American military establishment jangled on her perceptions. There was also the gnawing fear that Atkins himself would walk around the next corner, read the deception in her eyes, and it would all be over.

It occurred to her that clues could well be laying all around and she would be unable to interpret them. She took every fleeting opportunity to scan any screen that came within reach, being careful not to appear too obvious. Row upon row of data soldiers marched tantalisingly before her in their unfamiliar uniforms; half-life quotients, surge-delay factors, tunnel activity identifiers, they all intrigued, but did little else. Mid-afternoon duties brought her to the central experimental chamber, empty and silent as it awaited access re-calibration. She spoke to the woman with her, older than herself, someone with relative kindness in her eyes.

"We've completed nearly three days' work now. Do we get time off?"

The woman chuckled, a deep soft gentle sound. She didn't turn to look at her younger companion, but continued checking a string of figures on a wall display.

"Yes, four days on and one off. Two shifts should complete the work this time. You'll have Sunday evening and all day Monday to yourself."

"Do we have to stay on base? The social arrangements here seem designed round service personnel."

"Clearly, they are. Calibration people can go off-base, but there's only Cache. It's virtually a base town, but the bars are less stiff and formal there. As for daytime activities, you could hire a jeep and fly up to the hills to film wildlife."

The checking continued. She was courteous enough but was obviously content to take the conversation or leave it. Felixana scratched the side of her nose. Steering the talk nonchalantly to the base's experiments was not going to work, so she stayed with the off-duty theme.

"Are there available men in Cache?"

The checking stopped. The woman's head turned.

"I hear tell there are, but it's not something I pursue myself."

The English woman felt she may have touched a chord, but the gentleness was still clear as the response continued, a crystal sincerity edging into the voice.

"You should save yourself for someone who loves you."

Felixana's cheeks flushed into exposed colour, born partly of the woman's candour and partly of her message. She was to recall the words, and the particular way they were phrased, at another, more terrifying, time. Now they caused a mild twinge of indefinable longing, sufficient to send her diving for escape into the colder waters of her main purpose.

"I've seen people from many different countries here. Is it a big international project?"

There was no sense of tensing, of cautious parrying, as the other replied.

"I think it is. We shouldn't talk of such things, though, and certainly not off-base." She looked about quickly to check that no-one else was around. The chamber was silent. She lowered her voice, a mischievous smile ghosting across her mouth.

"Do you believe in teleportation?"

Felixana's stomach fluttered. "Oh, that's all theory, surely?" The stomach muscles were bringing on a hint of change to her respiration. She sensed her fingers tingling. A part of her brain suggested that the breathless, wide-eyed kid approach was perhaps not inappropriate, after all, though it was best not to overplay it. She glanced round the chamber herself.

"Is that what's really happening here?"

The woman shrugged. "I hear rumours. This is my second calibration visit to the base. I came last March, and I get to read between the lines. I

141

suppose it's something to do with Africa getting their hands on our money in a few years' time. That would explain why there are no third-world scientists here, anyway."

"Where would they teleport to?"

"That's where I get a zero-row. Even at a high level, no-one appears to have any idea. I have found out one thing for sure, though. A duplicate base is being kitted out elsewhere. I can only assume it's in Africa, as that's clearly the target. Billions of dollars are going in; they appear to be in a hurry. But….enough is enough." She smiled. "We didn't speak and I've heard no rumours, OK?"

Felixana smiled back. "OK." She said nothing about Turkey.

Saturday 31 May

As Friday wore on and gave way to Saturday there was plenty of time for conjecture, but little tangible to build on the misty mountain of rumour. Felixana saw nothing of the other woman as she herself carried out new tasks around the base's living quarters. She dared not speak with anyone else about what she had heard; indeed, she was not yet settled in her own mind on how to think it through further. A military operation and teleportation could make sense, but who would they attack? The nasty feeling grew that the Southern Brotherhood's leadership could be wiped out by a teleported assassin, just as one wipes clean a computer disk. A black sense of unreality wrapped her in its cold embrace as she checked and rechecked access codes with almost robotic repetition. The unnerving part was that no-one else would notice her inner turmoil. The world within the base went about its business with a self-assured certainty that all was well.

Sunday 1 June

Saturday turned to Sunday. Perhaps the Mossad could spring the lock, could apply this key usefully to the other pieces of the riddle. Her mind moved forward. The evening would bring an opportunity to leave the base. Perhaps in the town of Cache there would be a chance to send a message back. A row of three green lights on the wall-pad lit, breaking into her thoughts to remind her that another calibration re-alignment was complete. Only three more along this corridor and she could rest for several hours until a short evening shift was due.

She moved to the next wall-pad, an orange- coloured rectangle where inlaid sensors could carry fingerprints presented in a specific pattern to open or close recreation bays. There was one bay for each resident - except that calibration personnel were not classed as residents, so there would be no point in getting excited about the brain-calmers that these bays contained. Felixana knew of their existence. They were machines whose energy grew alongside brain patterns until they were duplicated, in order to steer thoughts and mental images into pre-set scenarios for relaxation. Tropical beaches, classical music concerts, sexual orgies, whatever pleased the user. Elsewhere, only the finest hotels boasted such attractions. She had longed to experience one, but they did serve to stress for her the lengths to which the governments were prepared to go to keep a precious workforce contented and innovative.

She keyed the reminder list of new codes up onto the screen of her portable calibration unit out of its memory. There were seven codes for the seven inhabitants of this corridor. She paused, noticing that the seven held the highest civilian security clearances registered on the base's official lists. She gave a quick scan of the names - Bondi, De Haag, Forbes, McWilliam, North, Santos, and Scarrow. They meant nothing to her. She had run the first test on the wall-pad a few moments later when the sound of raised voices came to her.

SCARLET

Miguel Santos gazed into his drink. The music this evening had been too loud for his liking, but now they were giving softer sounds. Bodies moved on a darkened dance floor to laser flashes that were more diffuse and seductive. If he turned his glass slightly he could catch a fantail reflection of aquamarine shot through with bright red from a nearby light source, ghosting delicately across the surface of the liquid, cold liquid, but burning warmly inside him. He took another long sip. He closed his eyes, running his memory across two dizzy days.

Early on Friday afternoon, Pieter North had called an unscheduled team meeting of those from the lunar base and several other scientists. It had caught the Mexican unawares. A few days before had been his twenty fifth birthday and Thursday evening had witnessed some serious Latin American drinking in the base's social areas. It was quite frowned on, of course, but how was he to know that big chief Atkins had arrived back earlier that day? Not that it would have made much difference. Tequila can be smuggled anywhere, anytime if the desire is strong enough. There was still a gentle but insistent throbbing in his head as he had taken his place at North's table for the afternoon meeting.

A frisson of expectation not present before had rippled through the gathering. He had noticed that Jon De Haag and Lita Scarrow were not there and had thought it most unusual. He could easily remember North's opening words, 'I am sorry to have to tell you that Jon De Haag is dead'. The matter-of-fact finality of the tone had stunned his audience. Even the enormity of what followed had not fully shaken the listeners from their sad and reflective resignation. Santos had looked around the table, his eyes passing from one stone face to the next, scientists whose efforts over the previous six months were now etched in their faces with deeper pain. The odd word had trickled here and there through the unblinking, unbelieving walls of each personal thought sitting around the table - 'sudden', 'heart', strength', 'continue'. North's round face was also drawn; the two Dutchmen had been very close. Someone had mentioned Lita Scarrow's absence and North had glanced at his security officer, before volunteering the explanation that she had left the base. No further detail was forthcoming. The Dutchman's discomfort at concealing his irritation had been evident. No-one had felt inclined to press the matter.

Santos raised his drink to his lips again, but he couldn't bring back the numbness. The recalling of the remainder of the afternoon's meeting was

144

acting on him like a cold shower. He winced wryly when he recalled the words, 'Project Methuselah'. He felt it was hardly an appropriate name, but he supposed the world leaders found it gave them an adequate enough link. Perhaps they couldn't be expected to know any better. Excited nervousness had permeated the meeting as details became clearer. Santos had watched Forbes closely. The Englishman's face had turned white and then ashen, but he said nothing. It was only when North had finished speaking and had asked for questions that he had stood up shakily. His voice, however, had been firm as his eyes held North's.

"I'm sorry, Pieter. I will have nothing to do with it."

He had then hobbled from the room, leaving the others with an even greater sense of stunned unreality. A few seconds' silence was broken when the black girl, Bondi, spoke.

"*That* was to be expected! It should not stop us going ahead. The world depends on it. I'll support the venture."

Noises of consent had risen elsewhere. Santos recalled he had nodded, so North had got the near-unanimity he wanted. Even so, he had assured the gathering he would speak with Paul Forbes. The Mexican had made a similar mental note; if terror was ahead the more solid they were, the better.

He noticed his glass was empty. The unit that glided up to refill it did not bring the companionship he sought. The bar-room was so dark and the music had begun to be loud again.

The new drink burned fiercely. Its cutting edge recalled for him a more recent memory. He remembered the ferocity of this very afternoon's exchange when the security man, Atkins, coming to Forbes' room while he himself was there, had also failed to turn the Englishman's mind. Atkins had seemed to be obsessed by Methuselah, although the stiff formality of the rejection clearly irritated him as well.

"I'm sorry, Mr Atkins, but it is so important to me that I cannot be involved, not at all. If it means I must be shut out of developments, then I must accept that."

Atkins had unwisely stood close enough to the room's entrance door for it not to have sensed the need to close. Anyone in the corridor could have heard what followed.

145

"Look, I understand you don't have long to live, anyway. Why not make your mark on this big chance and go out in a burst of glory?"

"You have no idea how long I may live! It is not up to you!"

The voices were getting higher and Santos had turned to the blank view-screen, unwilling to attempt a separation. The Mexican wasn't feeling physical.

"Oh, come on, Doctor Forbes! At least the girl Scarrow had the sense to gain financially by helping us prepare for it. We have the other base set up now. There's nothing you can gain by this approach. We shall go ahead anyway."

Santos had turned at that point. Something about the look on his face had sucked the sting from Atkins' rage. It shrunk and warped into the formality that Forbes had employed.

"Very well, Doctor Forbes, leave the project if you must. I am sure your scientific talents will be missed by your colleagues, but I'm equally certain we shall replace you. Why make a pointless gesture?" There was not a glance at the third man in the room as Atkins had turned and strode away with an air of dismissive disdain.

Santos finger moved delicately round the top of his glass as it sat on the table in front of him. He grimaced silently and his stomach tightened as he recalled what had happened next. It had been foolish and inexplicable and so out of character. Atkins had disappeared into the corridor when Forbes called after him, "Who knows who I might tell about it!"

His friend had reached across and touched his arm, but the damage had been done. Atkins had not come back, had not replied, and had simply continued along the corridor. The eye-contact had been sufficient to give Forbes a pained reproach and receive from him a patina of hastened regret.

The eyes still haunted Santos as he continued to drink. He had failed to turn Forbes' mind and presumably North had tried and failed also. Atkins had displayed little finesse in his attempt, a thin veil of diplomacy over an obsessional pre-occupation with forcing through the project. There was little doubt that he had the upper hand; half a year of Forbes' engineering talents and experimental efforts had probably been logged, copied and practised now by several senior power engineers on more faithful service to government. He took another gulp of tequila. His friend's refusal to budge was understandable, and his genius unquestionable, but the gesture would surely be side-stepped and his non-cooperation as useless as his crumbling skeleton.

Santos' nostrils caught the seductive wave of perfume before his eyes noticed the girl's nearby body. She seemed friendly, a companion at last. He smiled, though whether she saw it in the near-darkness was not known. Perhaps there was just a flash from his white teeth. She sat without invitation, but his body language told her he wouldn't refuse. He was about to offer her a drink when he noticed she already carried one; a long cool ice in long cool fingers. The perfume hit him again.

"Hi." Her voice was soft, the sound clear and pure.

He heard something that sounded like his own voice, disembodied as if from across the table. "Hello, I'm pleased to see you."

She was unknown to him, although the pleasure he felt was real. If only it wasn't so dark. He couldn't see her face clearly in the semi-darkness of the bar, but was sure it was beautiful. The music was soft again now, lulling him gently. She seemed too smooth and polished to be a call-girl; no, she couldn't be one, surely? He smiled again.

"My name is Miguel Santos. I work up at the Base."

"I'm Belle Porter. I work there too." She didn't reach across to shake hands. Santos was glad. He visualised an opening for something far more intimate. A stray shaft of light from the ceiling display spun across her body. It caught the red and yellow lightning flashes on her shoulder insignia. He nodded in their direction.

"Security; that means you're on Josina Boon's staff." There was humour in his voice, which she didn't understand.

"Yes, I am." Felixana was pleased that she had found the courage to steal some spare insignia and fix them to her partly-unzipped overalls. No-one in Cache would question a security officer, though she knew she would be skating on thin ice if she had tried it on the Base itself. The Mexican was clearly struggling under alcohol and Felixana decided that attack was the best option available. She leaned gently across the table, making sure the rounded outline of her small breasts came into the light. She spoke in a confidential tone, taking a chance on the rumours she had picked up.

147

"I must confess I do know you, Senor Santos. I'm one of the two Directors with Base security. Josina assigned me to Mr Atkins to control the movement away from the Base."

"Atkins? Poor you; is all I can say to that!"

It worked. She could scarcely believe it. The door she had pushed at almost fearfully was falling open in front of her. The man nodded, hypnotically, sadly.

"Well, we'll be on our way soon, and that's a fact." Was he talking to her or to his drink? There was no surprise in his voice, anyway. Perhaps he had already been thinking on the lines of this matter. She pushed the door further.

"There is evidence of some dissent, Senor Santos. It is not at all clear that we shall hold full security. Josina Boon has asked me to check with all senior scientists on their reliability."

Santos sighed. So, this was business, and he had thought she had been interested in his body, or at least in his money.

"What can I say, Belle? I'm fully committed to the project. You'll have no trouble with me." He wished he could add some stronger innuendo to let her know he was still keen. Nothing came to mind; the alcohol wouldn't let his brain function. Felixana reached over and placed her warm hand over his.

"I'm very pleased to hear it, Miguel. I wish everyone was so honest. I've spoken with Paul Forbes, but he won't tell me why he's upset. Surely there is nothing in this to upset him?"

"Paul is a good man, Belle." The intimacy of first names was adding to the intoxication. "I honestly don't think he would tell anyone about the project. He is so loyal to his friends. But what can he do?"

He opened his hands as if to indicate the dilemma facing his colleague. Then in a moment of candour, he summarised the project.

Felixana felt so sick with excitement in her stomach she thought she must pass out. How long was it before she dared trust herself to speak? The Mexican seemed unaware of the passage of time. He was swallowing again from his glass. A flash of light from a ceiling spot caught her eyes, its after-effect leaving greenish fudge on her retina. She was conscious of shaking knees and a drying throat despite her drink. The pieces were coming together, the picture becoming clearer. She could understand Turkey instead of Africa, but surely not what she had just heard? She grabbed desperately at the pieces in her mind, anxious to press home the advantage. He was falling, and she had to keep him off-balance; talking and giving more to her picture.

"Equipment in Turkey has been duplicated wherever possible, I suppose, but there must be some items that are only available here. How much do we have to transport out of Oklahoma?"

Santos had been resting his head in his hands. Now he lifted it and turned his palms upwards again in a gesture of invitation for guesses. He was co-operating beautifully, she thought.

"Not much. Depends on how quickly we have to achieve the transfer. Not been told yet." He still couldn't see her face clearly, but it didn't matter. He could smell her perfume and sense her body. Her voice was soft and faintly foreign - English perhaps, or Australasian?

Felixana pressed on with another thrust. "It all seems so unnecessary to me. It increases the risks of broken security to build two bases and transfer people and materials across the ocean. Why not just move from here?"

Santos waggled a shaky finger like a schoolteacher pointing out something clever. His coherence was beginning to break up. "We can't move in time and space sillil......simultaneously. If we went back in Oklahoma............no way we could get to Turkey. But a base there; and we can use donkeys or camels, or whatever they used then." He finished his drink, setting down the glass with an air of finality.

"Do you still have any work to do here?" she asked again.

His head slumped forward, his hands cradling it on the table. "No, all finished." The words slurred out thickly, bubbling through the treacle of his hazy awareness. Felixana looked around. No-one was taking an interest in them, there was just sound and shadows and flashes of coloured light.

"Miguel, what's going to happen in Turkey?"

The figure opposite her began to snore. She spoke his name again, more urgently.

149

It was no use. She stood up and slipped away into the semi-darkness of the room, barely conscious of her legs' ability to keep on walking.

Monday 2 June

The snake stopped, its tongue tasting the air in short thrusts. It had picked up the presence of a human and was instantly wary. Sunlight and heat baked down comfortingly onto its scaly back, motionless against the scrub and rock. The figure upwind hadn't seen it, but the kestrel far above was much more vigilant. The blink of a shadow against the sun sent the reptile scurrying away in a spasm of muscle into a rock crevice, where it coiled in safety. The man's eye had caught the final flashes of action over to his left. Was it a cottontail rabbit? Probably, he thought. He was beginning to get used to them now after six months in the Wichita Hills. Pieter North shaded his eyes from the sun and watched his stocky security officer clamber over the last few boulders to join him. The Canadian was breathless; North felt a mild twinge of self-satisfaction in having shed five kilos of excess weight himself in the time spent at Pichot. The initial greeting from the climbing man was pained.

"This is very high, Pieter! You've never climbed up here before!"

The Dutchman felt magnanimous. The splendour of nature was comforting him. "I'm sorry, John. I needed the silence."

The security officer arrived, settling heavily on an adjacent rock. The two exchanged a smile. Perspiration glistened across McWilliam's face and dripped into an eye. He wiped it clear. "I understand you wanted to see me."

North nodded. "Yes, I wanted you to see this message. It came in this morning, coded onto my wrist-band alone." North pulled his band from his left wrist and held it for both to see, shading the sun from its screen with his hand. He set it running. The figure of Papandreou, the European President, appeared against a background of bright red curtains in an indoor setting somewhere. The two men watched in silence. Professional and confident charm flowed out of the picture. Another tear of sweat dripped into McWilliam's eye.

"I would like to congratulate both you and your team of scientists on such a momentous achievement. Your place in history is assured, Doctor

North, although I suppose you would now tell me we are all in a position to re-write history!"

Avuncular humour flitted across his face. North sat as motionless as the stones about him.

"I have heard of Professor De Haag's death and it saddens me. I am sure he would want the work to go on, to see us achieve the result we want and to protect the stability of the world. You will know by now that a base is being established in Turkey for you. Much equipment is there already, although doubtless there are some pieces which you will all need to transfer over when you move. We shall need another team of experts for our purpose; perhaps more than one team. They are being gathered together now. Your own flights out of Oklahoma are being organised within the next three weeks.

"Mr Atkins has been successful in retaining our security levels and he will now control security on Project Methuselah. I send my thanks and those of the whole world for your remarkable achievements." The recording ended with a smile. There was real pain in North's face as he turned to his companion.

"Despite the vast amount of money and resources being poured in here, I really do feel it's being invented as we go along. The President mentions 'experts for our purpose', but we don't know precisely how that purpose is to be achieved. Who's going to maintain overall security from now on - Atkins himself?"

"He's just a security officer doing his job, Pieter."

"I still don't like him, John. Lita Scarrow's double life was almost like treachery and the work she did in giving the Union a base in Turkey still upsets me. We're being used more than I ever wanted to be. Jon De Haag warned of tumult. That's what he said. 'I fear there will be tumult'; his exact words. As for me, I fear the unknown now more than ever before. We're being told very little, except that the solidarity of the southern nations will be destroyed by the proof we are going to get. How is that going to happen? Is there to be a kidnapping, or an assassination?"

"Honestly, Pieter, does it matter? Our chances of success must be very high indeed. The blind faith of these nations against northern scientific achievement is surely the weakest link in their chain."

North waved his hands agitatedly. "I know all that! I have no doubts we'll achieve some proof. That's pretty obvious. It's not that which makes it so dangerous. A temporal shift of nine months to tamper with a Congress decision is delicate enough, but a confident expectation of harmless interference with history over a longer period would be humorous if it wasn't so terrifying."

McWilliam looked carefully at his friend, sensing the beginning of an obsession. "Are you upset about the project or Atkins?"

North sighed deeply. He watched the heat haze shimmer on a nearby rock.

"Atkins, I suppose. We all knew that time-travel itself would be laid open to use by bravado more than by a surgical incision. It always had that potential for the grand gesture. Using Atkins, though, would be folly. The whole point of the project is to give proof of a falsehood to people who would otherwise stay solid in their allegiance to each other. There seems little value in bringing such evidence to the attention of people in the European Union and the industrialised northern nations alone. Atkins' whole nature is about hiding things, keeping them secret. He wouldn't know where to start in the matter of revealing things. In fact, if it were not revealed to maximum effect the whole affair may rebound and the Southern Brotherhood would be the stronger for it.

"Yet I must stay with it and follow it through, John. Science will triumph in the end, just like it did with Galileo. I don't mind the Southern Brotherhood having their silly principles as long as they don't get in the way of science. The President is right about Jon De Haag's legacy. I opened the lid to his box and others will not let me shut it. I owe it to science to try to avoid a disaster in the use of this new toy."

McWilliam watched the dust from a hover transit vehicle on the valley floor rise and disperse in the warm clear air. He felt his friend was beginning to wash his hands of this discovery, despite his confident declaration of staying to hold responsibility for what might befall. A description as dismissive as 'this new toy' would never have left his lips a few weeks ago. Obviously, De Haag's death had saddened him deeply, and there was this obsession with Atkins as well. The Canadian mopped his brow again in the silence, his thoughts continuing to unravel. The scientific assessment appeared correct in a layman's eyes, but the technical complexities could certainly mount up more rapidly now. There was work for a security officer there, for certain. He must keep a good grip, keep the lid on, and maintain discipline within the senior scientific teams. He could give security a human face and perhaps write a page of history himself.

"We'll be ready in a few days, Pieter. Have you had any success with Paul?"

"No. I've spoken with him and so has Miguel. This feeling he has cannot be shaken. I can hardly blame Atkins for that, though by all accounts he made it worse by a clumsy attempt at persuasion. Paul's a good engineer, but the problems of power have been solved now, so others could just as well take up his role. It's just that we're falling apart, John. Jon is dead, Lita has sold us out and deceived us, and now they give us a project that Paul can't swallow. It's always been the same throughout history. Science has been opening doors constantly, and then it sees politicians ruin it all. I hope when we beat the Southern Brotherhood that it's all been worth it."

McWilliam nodded and smiled. Perhaps his friend would see things straight after all. He picked up a stone, tossing it in a high arc down the slope before them.

The natural break in both men's thought patterns was accompanied by a bleeping of North's wrist band. The face of Josina Boon appeared; its features tight and worried.

"Doctor North, could I ask you to come to my office right away? I do need to see you very urgently."

He acknowledged and gave his location, furrows appearing on his exposed brow. The two men descended the hillside together.

Monday 9 June

The Kenyan fishing boats bobbed in the early morning swell coming up out of the vast Indian Ocean. The night's catch had been good; stomachs and pockets would be filled. Tired and happy faces were startled when the first of the aircraft swept in from the east. The fishermen stood up in their boats and watched as five manta-winged jets screamed by in a succession of black shapes, heading for the coast and Mombasa. The fishermen smiled and chattered excitedly. The craft were friendly; although they saw no insignia, they knew that African air forces had all adopted the brooding shadow of the giant manta-ray for their airframes. Pointing fingers followed them out of sight; confident, proud, pointing

153

fingers. Africa was getting richer now. The Brotherhood would lead its peoples to great peace and freedom. The boats sailed happily for harbour.

Scented air-conditioning ruffled the smooth garments of the Foreign Ministers as they rode the roof elevator. Security was low-key; the occasion important but totally unannounced outside its immediate circle. Some of those who congregated in the spacious roof-garden had not met before and introductions flowed. Within ten minutes of the first arrivals the Ministers were seated and ready. Four from south-east Asia and the Indian sub-continent, two African representatives, three from the central and southern Americas and three from the Middle East. The arrival of the Israeli Foreign Minister, carrying documents from his country's Defence Minister, completed the gathering. Representatives from the Southern Brotherhood's Diplomatic Under-Council were finally in session.

The Israeli Minister looked round the table and spoke without rising.

"My colleagues, just a few days' notice of a meeting is not usual, but there are urgent and serious matters to discuss. My Government thought it appropriate also that we do not use holographic conferencing as we cannot guarantee its security." A few nods bobbed around the black ebony table.

"I bring the possibility that we may be subject to a military strike of some kind from the northern powers."

Mumblings and facial expressions of concern rippled through the gathering. The Minister continued. "I do refer initially to Israel, but if my Government falls, the right-wing alternative will stop co-operation with other Faith Nations. The Brotherhood may then not be able to force economic changes in the world." He tapped the sheaf of papers lying in front of him.

"There have been disappearances of scientific, military and other senior figures during the past six months. At first, suspicion was not aroused; they could have been harmless, coincidental occurrences. Then a pattern of expertise became clearer, though the voluntary nature of the disappearances was still apparent. We have certain pieces of information and some surmises built on those. An attack may take the form of an assassination or a series of assassinations, because no large-scale build-up of a military presence is being detected. Perhaps they are intending to use a new weapons system, but we just don't know. The centre of development and training is an American forces' base in Oklahoma."

"Oklahoma is a long way away. Are Brotherhood scientists disappearing?"

The Nigerian who spoke sat opposite the Israeli Minister, the blackness of his face shining against the resplendent yellow and scarlet bursts of colour in his dark gown.

"They are not all northern people, it is true, but the clear impression is that wherever world scientific leaders are involved from backgrounds that are reasonably sympathetic to our cause, the disappearances are taking place under duress."

One of the Islamic Under-Ministers spoke out. "You may need our military and diplomatic help in stopping their plans."

"Not at present, I think. However, the additional information we have obtained may make your active participation more likely and appropriate in the future. We learn of a subsidiary base sited at Siverek in eastern Turkey. The World States Council has this registered as a monitoring plant for the ozone-replenishment program, though no inspection of the base has yet been possible. We believe this to be a cover program. What the true intent might be, however, we are no closer to knowing."

The men and women round the table sat silently. There was no need for screens or coloured graphs in this gathering - each held an adequate mental picture of the geography of the Middle East and vague sinister images of a high-technology murder plot being assembled in the mountainous Turkish wastelands. The particular help the Israelis might have in mind could be revealed soon enough. The gradual revelation continued as the Israeli Minister spoke.

"We should all keep a close watch now on the base at Siverek. There may be environmental equipment going in, but we should be alert to whatever comes out, of any description. Our options for intervention at this stage are limited, unless any of your governments have sophisticated ozone programs?"

The question hung half-expectantly, half-forlornly. Shakes of heads confirmed the worst.

"In that case, we have no direct reason to seek entry to the base. We could ask for access on grounds of atomic energy safety, but the World States Council would need to give approval for that. It could take several months to set up. Northern powers have chosen their cover well."

155

The Trinidadian Foreign Minister, a plump woman in her late forties, indicated her wish to speak. "How do you know of the American and Turkish bases?"

The Israeli's face was impassive. "Our clandestine staff world-wide can only work effectively if they remain anonymous. You will understand that. I have a briefing document for each of your governments. We have some of the pieces of the plan against us in place. We know 'who' and we know 'where'. We shall all soon know 'what', and that will just leave the 'when' to be revealed. I suggest it might be useful if we go through the monitoring and logging options open to us in order to reduce still further the possible danger of being taken by surprise."

'What a long way to give no reply', thought the Trinidadian. She remained silent. Nods and murmurs of assent were followed by a dealing of red plastic data sheets around the table.

Wednesday 11 June

Felixana Smith sealed her shoulder bag. Lifting it from the floor, she walked towards the open exit-way. Her shuttle would soon be leaving. She joined several other calibration team members near the external door where they exchanged tired smiles. The past two weeks had been long and hard, but for the English woman it had held greater significance. The days had been harrowing, her mind not letting her drop nervous questions. Had Santos become suspicious? Would he check with base security? Yet above all, the enormity of the quest loomed over her like a prehistoric winged reptile - grotesque, gnarled, threatening, mysterious. The proof they sought would shatter the Southern Brotherhood. Even over the past six months the base of their threat to northern commercial strength had been evident. Further developments now would place the northern world in an unassailable position for the future. Their scientific consumerism, rampant over the past one and a half centuries, would be vindicated as the human way forward. Any differences under the skin of the southern world's solidarity would be exposed, and many nations would rush to explain that they still stood on firm foundations. She felt she needed to grapple with the implications on a personal level, too, but such luxury would need to await her safe escape from this isolated American base.

A warm evening breeze spilled down from the Oklahoma hills, teasing its fingers through her long hair. She thought of her new paymasters - telling them of the threat against the Southern Brotherhood would not in itself be an answer. African and South American nations were not ideally placed to counter these developments militarily; perhaps the best defences would be in harnessing and steering public and world opinion. The thought intrigued her. Organs like the BBC could decide who would win in such a war for hearts and minds. Steering public opinion had been their stock in trade for two hundred years. There might even be a financial gain for her in what could emerge.

The departing members of the calibration team converged on the evening shuttle. General tiredness was evidently affecting the base security personnel as well. The man at the steps of the aircraft was waving people past without even looking at lapel identicards. Felixana Smith was excited and nervous, but not fearful. The weeks on the base had begun with her feeling very conscious of the danger she was courting, but its closeness had acted almost as a drug. The awesome secret she now carried had been well worth the exposure. Yes, Craig Landon would have been proud of her independent courage.

She was at the shuttle steps, reaching for the handrail. The base security man was now behind her. The balding man on the top step inside the aircraft gazed down at her in an almost fatherly way. Their eyes met momentarily and with a sinking stomach she knew that he knew. She hardly noticed the lapel button displaying 'Dr Pieter North'. He reached down and guided her back down the steps and onto the airstrip apron. It was so natural and quiet that she was not even sure if anyone else knew what was happening. His voice was as soft as his eyes.

"Ms Smith. This is no place for a BBC person, you know. I really can't let you go."

Were they out of earshot of others when he next spoke? She couldn't be sure. She was aware of his soft voice, conversationally asking if she had been in contact with anyone off-base since her arrival. It all seemed so unbelievable, but she found herself hardening up fast. There was no need to tell him anything. She looked again at his lapel button. She knew he was the senior scientist; if he knew, or suspected, then others did, too. Yet, why the personal approach? Why not arrange her arrest by security guards? She looked back at the shuttle, to where passengers were climbing unconcernedly on board. There was no point in running, there was nowhere to run. The door ahead slid open and he ushered her politely inside. If she could be sure her voice wouldn't waver it would be worth an opening shot. Further silence might weaken any opportunities still open to her, so she spoke out.

"There must surely be some mistake. I've been calibrating your systems, not interfering with them."

The door slid shut behind them. They were alone. He guided her into a side office, its lights coming on automatically as the system sensed their presence.

"Please sit down, Ms Smith."

There was only one chair in the room. She chose to do as he indicated, but kept her hand on her bag as it rested on the floor. He paced slowly, his awkwardness apparent; grilling obviously didn't come easily to him.

"There really isn't much point in you protesting your innocence. I know who you are, who you work for, and what you're doing here. Certainly, you're not going to be allowed to leave the base, I'm afraid."

She thought how best to negotiate into a better position, considering he would want to be satisfied on how much she knew. She needed to give an impression of uncertainty on that matter for as long as possible. If it became so clear that she hadn't got anything out, her safest course might be to appear as ignorant as possible. She felt suddenly trapped. There were no windows in the room and the sense of claustrophobia this gave imposed itself on her by adding to the content of their supposed dialogue. What would happen to her? Would she be locked away until it was all over? Would she just disappear? How long would it take, anyway? How 'long' is 'long' in a frightening world where time itself could be squeezed or stretched by devious and determined scientists?

The skin on her arms began to creep with anxiety and the coolness of the room. She smiled at North as sweetly as she could. "You must expect an investigating journalist at least to investigate."

His awkwardness seemed to ease a little; her admission had given him a peg on which to hang a dialogue. He stopped pacing and faced her.

"We are far away from world events here, Ms Smith". He kept using her name to press home his advantage, fully aware it was not the name displayed on the gentle, beautiful swell of her tunic. "It is possible, however, that in two weeks you have found out the purposes behind this base, and we shall need you to tell us that as painlessly as possible."

She found his presence increasingly disconcerting. She also didn't like the word 'painlessly'. He was standing over her now, waiting for her to respond. She found her nervousness compounded by uncertainty on his intentions. He was pressing her with his words, but somehow in an indefinable way, not so strongly with his demeanour and bearing. She hoped her voice remained soft and neutral as she said "I honestly have nothing to say."

He turned to the door. "Well, I'll give you some time to think about it."

The word 'time' almost caused her to smile in a spasm of response, but her muscles didn't move.

"The air shuttle is departing without you. When you do not report back, your employers will know something has gone wrong. They can then either throw more people after an enterprise which has already failed - because we are forewarned - or they can merely forget about you. I'll leave it with you to consider if there is any other alternative for you."

His eyebrows rose pointedly at the last remark, and then he was gone, the door closing with a sigh of resignation as if passing a sad comment on her plight.

Friday 13 June

Simon Atkins woke in a cold sweat. It was two in the morning, still dark in the dead hours of Friday the thirteenth day of June. Twelve days of obsession had eaten into him, twelve days of projected imaginings built round the premise that the crippled Englishman Forbes would betray the project to the Southern Brotherhood. He had said as much to Santos' face, hadn't he? Perhaps he had done the deed already. Any senior member of North's team could come and go as they pleased, and although he knew Forbes had not actually left the base, there was no knowing what messages he had contrived to deliver. The project was now unstoppable, he kept telling himself, but the propaganda wouldn't sink in. Somehow he knew that the European President was holding him personally responsible for keeping that grip on things for which he had become well-known in world security circles. There was little time remaining before they left Pichot. Forbes would not go to Turkey. He would pack his bags and disappear, and there would be no control over him after that. As for trust......well.

When the coming weekend was over there would be essential work of a security nature to be handled on the other side of the Atlantic Ocean. The South African knew he could just not afford to leave such a sensitive thread hanging - it could easily become a noose to throttle him. Unpalatable as it was, he would have to confront Forbes again before it became too late. The decision made, his body relaxed; but only slightly, and there was still that insistent sound of the blood in his head. He called to the screen of his wrist-band a pattern of colours and whorls designed to reduce tension and induce sleep. The creations swelled and retreated before him in the darkness. Although he kept imagining that cursed Englishman's limp, the abstract pictures fulfilled their purpose and tugged down his eyelids. Sensing the rhythms of sleep, the wrist-band switched off the display. The steady tread of the dread hours of Friday advanced alone through the darkness.

***

He awoke early. The wrist-band showed 5:15 hours. The certainty of action lay on his stomach with a lead weight. Somehow he would stop Forbes, neutralise him; wipe out the possibility of betrayal with the completeness which marked his profession. Atkins massaged his eyes, rubbing his forehead to try to clear the vestiges of the night-time headache. A stinging shower and he would be ready for the day. The seventh hour changeover of security personnel would bring a heightening of activity to the Base. A visit to Forbes at six, when the man would be sleepy and receptive, could well pay dividends.

All the residential units were sited together, so a quiet passage through a few empty corridors proved very easy. If anyone who didn't recognise him did happen along, a veritable battery of identicards and skeleton keys would move him quickly on - but there was only silence in the Base that Friday morning. A ripple of simple electronic security couplings along the final corridor tickled softly into his trained ear as the sixth-hour automatic changeover of frequencies occurred at ceiling height. They would not be a problem - his lapel badge being set at the highest security level would instantaneously deflect the new frequencies and the couplings would let him pass without an alarm sounding. He reached Forbes' door with still no sign of movement along the corridor. His right palm pressed against the entrance pad, eliciting a red light. He wiped his perspiring hand on his white tunic front and tried again; a green light now showing his name would accompany a soft calling tone on the bedside console of the room's occupant. There was no reply. His drier hand tried once more, but there was still no response.

160

He entertained for a fleeting moment the possibility that he should break in and confront the Englishman. He could certainly over-ride this door lock on his security clearance. He rejected the idea; persuasion or threat had to be more subtle than that, had to bear the mark of innocuous action or even seduction. He started to nose around, the frustration at missing Forbes urging him to flex his security role and check out the area in an impromptu, unscheduled audit. He had rarely before used the code sequence he held as overall Chief of Security. Its use now brought him an increasing sense of power as he opened door after door in the vicinity. He felt like a magician with a magic wand, lock after lock bowing before him in total obedience at his commanding presence. No-one was around. Why couldn't he catch a sleeping junior unawares and exercise his authority with an icy reprimand? The jewels that revealed themselves to Aladdin were proving to be merely paste. Operating gowns, oxygen cylinders, five or six surgical units standing silently in a line and still on their overnight re-charging program. He heard a rhythmic pumping sound coming from the next cubicle. He moved on to investigate, the frosted partition standing aside with due deference.

The South African burned with pleasure - lying on an automated exercise bench and supported by gleaming rods and pistons was Paul Forbes undergoing a skeletal workout. Did fear flicker in the prone man's eyes? Atkins couldn't be sure. It was gone in an instant, but he hoped it had been there. What a marvellous position in which to be overawed in an argument! The security man resisted the itching that called for an overbearing approach. He began pleasantly enough.

"Good morning. This is a surprise."

Forbes looked up into a smiling, tanned face set with blank snake's eyes. He stopped exercising and sighed deeply.

"Good morning."

He reached forward and cleared the magnetic couplings holding his ankles, swinging himself remarkably easily to a sitting position. A patina of perspiration on his brow shone in the surgery lights. Atkins had to hurry; the man was moving to a position of equality for the conversation.

"I wanted you to know how much we shall need you and your skills in Turkey. There would be no need to be involved in the project itself; you could certainly keep your conscience, but the team needs you."

Atkins' throat tightened on the words. He could hardly imagine himself saying them. They almost made him gag, but he was accustomed to being cold and incisive. When that required smooth honey he prided himself he could deliver as effectively as anyone else. The approach seemed to work. Forbes sighed again, this time with noticeable sadness. He kept his eyes on the floor.

"I know the team needs me, and that makes it unfortunate, but I cannot take part. Any further work I do in the knowledge of what you're planning would be wrong."

He looked up at Atkins, emboldened now by his stand. "You may press on with your project, Mr Atkins, but you will do so without me."

Blood had rushed to his neck as he fought the man with his words. Atkins' smile froze. Increasingly, he wanted to own this project and he readily interpreted this response as a personal attack on himself. The rejection of his kindness was insulting. This obsessive fool was dangerous and should be silenced. He turned from the sitting man and strode away. He had since turned over in his mind countless times the events which followed, but they didn't seem to flow with any logic, in any natural ordered sequence. Justification may have later lain tantalisingly out of reach, but at the time it seemed clinically necessary and fulfilling. Forbes just couldn't be trusted.

The tray of scalpels lay on a bench just beyond the partition. He never questioned their existence, why they should be lying in unsterilized abandon, or indeed why the more recent laser scalpels hadn't replaced such ancient instruments in the minor surgery areas. He scooped up the one which had glinted most wickedly in the light and turned back to the physiotherapy area. Forbes saw him, saw the firm set of his jaw and the knife in his hand. He started to lift himself from the bench, but it was too late. Atkins thrust the scalpel up under Forbes' rib-cage, piercing his heart and killing him instantly. The body slumped forward. Atkins was surprised at the dead weight. He took a faltering step backwards. He pulled out the scalpel and let it clatter to the floor, catching the body under the arms and pulling it upright. He looked around and listened, but was only conscious of his own exhalations puffing with the shock of the action. He would have to do something with the body, but he was not sure what that ought to be. Hide it, yes, hide it! If he could drag it to his own apartment he would have time to think. What was the time? He couldn't move his arm to check his wrist-band so looked around for a wall-timer. There wasn't one. Medical personnel would soon start arriving for the day's work. He pulled the body towards the door, its head on his shoulder. The first door was passed easily but he had to readjust his cargo at the corridor entrance to give him a free hand to tap out an access code on his belt.

It was then he became aware of the blood. He smelt it first, then saw and felt it simultaneously as it spread in a scarlet tide across and through his pure-white tunic. The smell was worst of all. He looked to the floor in panic expecting a pool of incrimination, but there was not a drop there. It continued to flow into his clothing as he humped the body round the room, desperate as he now looked for a way of staunching this final accusation. A cloth, a towel, a piece of clothing, or even a sponge would do - why did the damn thing have to bleed so much? He managed to drag his load to the side wall where a row of cabinets contained equipment and medicines. Trembling fingers growing weaker jabbed out a code to spring the door as he sensed the sticky liquid trickle into his navel. He felt sick. Eyes which shifted in and out of focus scanned the shelves; wadding, cotton wool, bandages, absorbent pads - none! Then he saw a can of plastic fibrinat. He grabbed at it, sending a couple of small tubs skidding to the back of the shelf. He propped the body against the cabinet and began to spray the wound vigorously. He continued long after the flow stopped, a sticky red plastic mound building up on the fabric covering the body. He had sprayed so much that the air filtration system, sensing the use of the medication, had cut in automatically. The noise operated as a background to his fevered actions, yet he wasn't aware of it.

He let the load fall onto his shoulder again, pulling himself upright and moving with an effort to the door. The blood had congealed through his tunic and onto his body. It tugged at the hairs on his stomach as he moved almost painfully along the corridor. His vision blurred over again, this time from exertion more than panic. He found it necessary to stop every few metres to wipe his eyes with blood-stained hands and shift his weight to the other shoulder. That he reached his apartment at all seemed a blessing to him; that he reached it without being seen by a soul he considered little short of a miracle.

The load fell in a crumpled mess to the floor. With the door locked behind him his first priority was to strip the horrible blood-soaked vestment from his aching chest and hips. He consigned it to the incineration chute. The sight of his stomach disgusted him; the matted skein of fair hairs polluted by dark, damning liquid that he thought would never come off. Released from the fear of immediate discovery he felt his

163

legs begin to tremble. He tried to control his muscles but found he couldn't do so.

Despite his ruthless history in a cut-throat occupation, he had neither had occasion nor severe enough motivation in the past to kill anyone. Yes, he had fantasised often enough; it was necessary to target mentally those whom he had to beat down and destroy. Yet those targets had not been personified. He had not eaten breakfast. No matter, he still collapsed to the floor of the shower unit and retched bile in uncontrollable spasms from his empty distraught depths.

***

How long he lay on the cold tiles he couldn't say, but he became aware of the wet coldness in the air-conditioned room despite the growing warmth of the morning outside. He began to shiver. Sense and determination were beginning to return. He wrapped a towel tightly round himself, almost not daring to look at the crumpled corpse on his apartment floor. The problem of disposal remained. The incineration chute would have coped, but only with small chunks. His stomach gave a heave at the thought - no, he would have to be tougher than that to get the job done.

Thirty minutes later he had dressed. The corpse lay in a bed sheet in the corner. He sat with white rum in his hand, feeling it burning his stomach with warmth. He was alone; there was no-one he could trust to help him. Still, it had to be done. He felt better now. Oh! The scalpel! He suddenly realised it lay in stark incrimination on the physiotherapy floor! Weak with fear he retraced his steps. There it was! He scooped it up with clear relief, checking there was no blood on the floor tiles.

Returning to his rooms he made his mind up. One of the external sounds had triggered the thought of his opportunity. The squeak of an overloaded auto-trolley passed down the corridor. It reminded him that today some equipment would be in transit out of the base. The scientific elements would be going to Turkey and unnecessary junior personnel would transfer to other secure Army research sites. He emptied one of his personal clothes trunks, the possessions scattering on the floor behind him. The sheet-wrapped bundle, bent at a sickening angle, just permitted the closing of the lid. His access codes brought a trolley trundling to the door. He rolled the trunk to where the steel lifting prongs carried it to the platform behind the drive unit. He keyed in a tracker instruction to the trolley's memory and moved off ahead of his cargo down the corridor.

The first part of the journey was easy. Residential area corridors, storage hangars, loading bays, and on out through the huge roll-up steel external doors into a brilliant mid-June morning. The tyres of the trolley stirred up puffs of dust as it moved off the prepared areas onto uneven soil. The perimeter fence was now only thirty metres away. He felt for the first time that morning the beginning pangs of hunger. Still, there was work to be done and a guard to be passed. The man at the gate noticed his approach and moved to meet him. He seemed to Atkins to be of his own age, yet darker in appearance. The Head of Security handed over an identicard.

"Good morning, Mr Atkins. Can I help you?"

"I'm meeting a helicopter off-base. There's some classified material I can't trust to in-base handlers." The smile and tone were immaculate. The guard was content to leave well alone.

"I'll have to log you out, I'm afraid. Any idea when you'll be back?"

"It'll be an hour, perhaps. It's going from the next valley."

The man saluted out of habit. Atkins passed through, the trolley following obediently. A switch to forward steering and the South African hoisted himself up to sit on the lid of the trunk. The trolley moved away up the rocky slope. Atkins wished he had brought eye-shades; the mid-morning sun was striking viciously off the surface rocks, its light accompanied by a growing heat. He wiped his eyes, blinked, and clung to the jolting cart. He cursed under his breath, having forgotten to check the workload specification of the vehicle. After eight hundred or so metres, the incline steepened. The whine of the machinery began to labour noticeably. He looked back down the hill to where the guard at the gate was showing no interest in the slowly-climbing trolley.

The vehicle and its cargo dipped out of sight into a shallow plateau and for fifty metres even picked up speed. Then the incline resumed, the machinery stuttered and died, and the front ploughed into a grassy mound. Atkins tensed his muscles to cling on just a fraction too late. The sudden stopping of the vehicle slewed his body round, peeling his grip from the trunk. The world seemed to cartwheel and he landed heavily on his side. The ferocity of the fall shook his body, the rocky outcrop under him bruising his ribs through thin overalls. He moaned involuntarily and tested inhalation with pained anguish as he felt his side, his eyes tightly closed. He heard a bird's cry from somewhere in the air. Blades of grass, stones and soil came slowly into focus. He lifted a shaking hand to his ear, from where warm, sticky blood oozed softly onto his fingers. He saw his trunk nearby, one end on the ground, the other still on the trolley. He tried to pull himself to a sitting position, but fell back, blue heat from above pounding down onto a sweating face as he struggled for breath. He had to get up. He saw a vision in his mind of people from the Base, moving over the rocks and finding him, opening the trunk, recognising the body..........his stomach churched. Again he struggled up, this time holding a sitting balance long enough to gauge his predicament more sensibly.

His side ached terribly, the bruising sensitive to the slightest stretching of skin by a breath in or out. The cut on his ear was superficial. One hand was grazed sorely. The black trunk lay drunken and doleful in the blazing heat, looking like the dreadful coffin, which indeed it was. Atkins pulled himself to his shaking feet from the rock that was supporting him and lurched over to the trolley. Five minutes of painful effort put the trunk back on the vehicle, but once done he felt it was not at all a wise move. The trolley wouldn't start; several bursts at the starter, even manually delivered, failed to bring it to life. He looked around at the shimmering hills, shading his eyes against the unremitting glare, the odours of dust and sweat pulsing from his hands to his nostrils. No sound came to his ears, save the throbbing of the blood in his head. He had intended burying the body, although ideally much farther from the military base than here.

A cold panic gripped him as he realised that he had no shovel. There was no way of digging out a hole for the body. The pain in his side stabbed at him, bringing out a clammy circlet of sweat on his forehead and weakening his emotional resolve. He slumped forward on the trunk, clutching his face in his hands. Somehow he would have to get rid of the body. Despite the distaste it gave him, he knew he had to take it out of the trunk. Whether the disgusting odour was real or imaginary he couldn't tell, but it rose like a damning mist at his face when he lifted the lid. He heaved it out and it fell to the ground, the sheet becoming covered in dust as it rolled on a short incline between the rocks.

Atkins looked up the hillside to where, fifty metres away, a cluster of stunted bushes marked the top of the rise. Perhaps there was a crevice or a hole on the other side, away from the Base behind him. He knelt as if in supplication before the wrapped-up corpse, lifting it clumsily to his back. He fell three times on his journey up the hill; ripping his palms on a thorn bush the third time he fell as the weight on his shoulders pulled him off-balance. Blood mixed with the dirt and dust already staining the sheet.

At the top of the rise he sank to the ground, panting heavily. Lines of hills marched away to the north-western horizon in the oppressive heat. His hands stung and his side ached. He peered down the hillside through eyes misty with sweat and pain. Stands of trees here and there swam before him in the hot sun. Where to go? There would be no river down there, no deep wet place for his parcel. Perhaps farther away there might be somewhere? No, he just wouldn't have the energy to look. He would have to find a place nearby and leave the body until he could return. Halfway down the scree-covered slope he nearly fell down the cleft in the rocks himself. He grabbed at an exposed tree-root. The space between the rocks was tight; had he fallen further there would have been no way out. Legs scrabbled against hot smooth stone as he dragged himself away, his muscles cracking with the strain. The effort to return to the body at the top of the slope dislodged a cascade of small pebbles, their dust rising into the hot air. Grit burned in his eyes, but the way of disposal was at hand and he worked with a determined desperation.

Twenty minutes later, the shrouded body was jammed several metres down between the rocks. Stones and soil, gouged by hand, followed it down. The journey back to the trolley was easier; in more ways than one he felt he had left a burden behind. The heat was almost unbearable, affecting his breathing. He was accustomed to higher temperatures in southern Africa, but there was always someone around to fetch and carry for him. He was alone on this hillside, alone and getting seriously tired. Dusty rivulets smeared his face, dripped into his eyes and teased his mouth with strange flavours. The trolley lay silent in the sun. The trunk lay with its lid open, yawning at the sky. Atkins shuddered with a spasm of anger. Why wasn't the whole thing going smoothly? Why were problems and loose ends rearing up on their hind legs and mocking, testing, playing with him? If the trolley wouldn't start with its lightened load, he would have to find somewhere to dump the blasted trunk now!

He tried the starter almost fearfully; nothing. He tried again with vicious feeling and it sprang into life. The sound reverberated off the hot landscape and echoed away into the hills. He forced it back to the crest, astounded that it now seemed quite content to climb, while with its grisly cargo it had actually been reluctant. Confidence flowed back, dented only by the sharp pain in his side whenever the trolley jolted. On the downward side, back to the Base, he steered round several huge clumps of thorny bushes and stopped. The trunk was slid with a feeling akin to relief through a gap in the bushes. Far enough in it would not be visible from the air. He barely noticed that he had scratched his wrists and arms in the effort, and had caught his forehead on a thorny branch as he straightened up. The return to the Base continued. It must have been longer than an hour since he had spoken to the guard on duty, but his wrist-band had smashed and he couldn't tell. The height of the sun would put the time at about eleven hours. It shone into his eyes as he descended to the plain. A different guard was standing at the fence. He had clearly been briefed about the journey out-Base of the Head of Security; the salute was easy and quick, although it was followed by a frown at the man's dishevelled appearance.

"I fell off the damn trolley!"

A professional projection of injured foolishness was accepted by the guard, who joined the laughter in sympathy. Unencumbered now, the trolley bounced off towards the administration block, its pre-programmed journey forgotten. It would tell no tales of what it had done.

Thursday 19 June

"I know there's probably a simple explanation, but I'd damn well like to know where he is!"

Pieter North's heartfelt statement hung in the air as he walked alongside Caramel Bondi to the main briefing room.

"Surely he wouldn't leave the Base without saying something to us. We've worked together for too long, been too close." He shook his head, with more than a hint of self-pity, as he added "obviously, not close enough."

The black girl nodded at the last remark. "Perhaps no-one really knows him, Pieter. It's just that with Jon's death and Lita's, well, disappearance, the project's original leaders are becoming fewer. What role will we have in Turkey? Do you know?"

"We'll find out more this afternoon, I suppose. The essential equipment is now almost all packed away. They've got damn-near everything duplicated at the other Base, by all accounts."

He smiled knowingly. "The South African Atkins is obviously in a hurry. He ought to be; the enemy is getting closer."

The woman didn't understand the remark, but let it pass. At the door of the briefing room the guard saluted and stood aside for them. North's eyes looked for Forbes around the table, but were disappointed. Nothing had been seen of the Englishman since the previous Thursday evening. Now here it was a week later with perhaps the final briefing at the American base before the project moved across the Atlantic.

Over a dozen people were seated here already. They were senior scientists mainly, and a sprinkling of security and administration personnel. North sat next to Josina Boon, whose face lit with a smile. He returned the greeting and nodded, still thankful that she had spoken with him and not Atkins about her discovery. The South African himself rose to his feet and walked to the viewing screen at one end of the room.

"Your work here is now done. World leaders are very grateful for all you have achieved, but there is much more to do. All civilian personnel around this table will be going to Turkey tomorrow, twentieth of June."

He paused to heighten effect, but it wasn't really necessary. Several gasps gave evidence that not everyone was expecting that. Atkins waved his arm in a gesture supposedly designed to allay anxiety. It achieved the impression of brushing away comment.

"All the close members of your families are accompanying you. They won't know of the project, of course. Just let them think of it as a holiday. Education provision will continue for those still in study."

He smiled. A few others around the table tried, but not with any real success. The huge screen lit up, snuffing out any attempts at questions that might have been rising in several throats. A mountainous terrain appeared, its predominant brown, tan and golden hues contrasting with the tired green shrubs that still dotted the area. The sun had a brittle appearance. *'Wichita without much of the greenery'* concluded Pieter North. Long, low buildings came into view as the picture moved. Several aerials and satellite dishes and then two towers appeared, that looked as though they could be holding water or fuel of some kind.

"Siverek Base. It's our destination." Atkins had been watching the screen and now turned to his audience again.

"From this base, and with the completion of your work, our teams will spread out to continue with their work. We shall finally and fatally undermine the credibility of the Southern Brotherhood. We shall then be able to regain a majority position in the World States Council and bring financial responsibility back to the world."

"How long will this take?"

A question from a young woman; North surmised that her parents would be whisked away with her to Turkey, but what about her lover, or lovers? He liked the look of her himself............

Atkins smiled. "The truthful answer is: 'as long as it takes'. We only have a few years left before Africa takes our money. The project may need many months even now, but we shall be in time."

Some forced laughter here and there bubbled up raggedly at the unintentional pun. *'Time, time, time'*, thought Pieter North, seeing in his mind's eye the face of his old friend Jon De Haag. Sadness flooded in. The questions in his own mind were those which doubtless the revered Dutchman would have held; questions about time's fabric, and whether tearing that fabric would neutralise existence at any point. The enormity of the project's goal barely troubled him; as a scientist it held no meaning for him. The wise Professor's theories had encompassed the universe, it seemed. North himself, who had turned theory into practice, had grasped only a glimpse of that vastness. He looked round the table at the people there, their faces showing a mix of anxiety and excitement. They were nearly all technicians - brilliant, gifted even, but still technicians. No-one approached the maturity of perception he had seen in his mentor. That man had often grappled with a particularly-complex mathematical theorem by spending hours out of doors, staring up at a sky of scudding clouds that he could not even see. No, these people would have no questions which would threaten or embarrass Atkins. North decided to remain silent. He held a much stronger card. Atkins was finishing an intermittent accompaniment to the continued screening of the new locations. Doubtless it was putting his audience in the mood for a change of scene.

"The key elements on the non-scientific side that we shall work on will be how and when to play our hand. We shall need to be ready for when the scientific progress reaches the necessary points. It will be crucial to catch the Brotherhood off-guard with our disclosures. We shall have experts working on that, too."

The briefing came to an end. Chairs shuffled and people coughed. North thought about Forbes. He decided on impulse to check with the Base departures schedule. He keyed his wristband. There it was - Friday 13 June, twelve hours thirty - the lunch shuttle to Oklahoma City. So, it seemed Paul Forbes had quit without even saying 'goodbye'. North rose thoughtfully from his chair and sauntered away to start packing. There was also someone he had to see. He was pleased that Josina Boon's perceptive security screening had identified the BBC woman's profile from a chance television appearance, and had begun clandestine shadowing of her movements on base. He was even more pleased that the amply-sized Chief had chosen to alert him to the situation and not Atkins.

Friday 20 June

He revealed the existence of Felixana Smith to Atkins early on Friday morning. The security man must have been shattered, he felt, but it was covered up with irritation which bordered on anger. It never spilt over; Atkins' dislike for him was apparent, but the South African had known full well the importance of not alienating the project's senior scientist, at least not for the present. It was difficult for North to guess which had proved to be the more unnerving facet for the man; the successful tracking by the Southern Brotherhood as far as Pichot Base or the hiding of the fact by Pieter North. Atkins had appeared to be on edge over something; the Dutchman had retained the initiative throughout the conversation, which had taken place in a quiet corner of the Base.

North leaned back in his seat on the shuttle, closed his eyes and smiled at the recollection. He had won a point and gained ascendancy; it felt good. The shuttle picked up speed and roared into the Oklahoma sky. It banked over the hill-line, heading east. In a cleft in the rocks below, a small pack of rats scuttled away, frightened at the aircraft's noise. They had smelt flesh and had been tugging at the white fabric which separated them from their week-old meal. The shuttle's drone died away. The rodents returned to their task.

DOWN CAME A SPIDER

BLACK

Saturday 21 June

Glinting sunlight turned the waters of the Euphrates River copper as the airliner sped across south-eastern Turkey. Far below the travellers, the ancient land was bleak, flat and unexciting, an empty wilderness of dust and scrub and goats. The military authorities had chosen their base well, halfway between the Euphrates and the Tigris, one hundred kilometres from both Diyarbakir and Viransehir, and one hundred and twenty north of the Syrian border. In this isolation, the European Union and its allies had camped within striking distance of Israel and the Brotherhood. There was nowhere for inter-continental jet-liners to land at Siverek, so the travellers would fly on to the airport at Diyarbakir.

Pieter North gazed down as the aircraft slowed and banked, giving him a clear view of the city. Agriculture smiled back with green confidence at the sky-bound travellers - for more than one hundred years the thirteen dams of the Southeast Anatolia Project had brought water to convert hundreds of thousands of hectares of waste or fallow land to irrigated fields. This far corner of the Union was now prosperous. Large hover-tankers dotted the highway leading out over the eastern horizon to the regional oil refinery at Batman. Natural supplies of oil were nearly all exhausted, but synthetic oil had now almost replaced it in quantity and quality. Solar power screens moved automatically in their tracking of the sun. The city loomed larger as the aircraft descended. The black basalt walls of the old town stood gaunt and proud in the afternoon sunlight; during the period of the Roman Empire this key city of the south east with its Arab flavours had been called 'Amida the Black' and two thousand years later it still guarded its hinterland with brooding supremacy. Even the hill-dwelling Kurds had long since ceased their guerrilla activities. The European Union stretched its tentacles way beyond the city across the southern Mesopotamian plain towards the

Republic of Southern Iraq. The airport runways rushed towards the travellers, sucking them down to earth. Pieter North just had a chance to catch a glimpse of the Ulu Cami, the Holy Place of Islam, at the centre of the city, before the walls blocked off his view. The first of the great Seljuk mosques of Anatolia made North feel a slight queasiness; squeezed between two powerful world religions on a formerly-Russian Base built on European Asia Minor soil he was expected to perform a scientific master-stroke.

He sighed audibly as the wheels bumped everyone out of private reflection. The heat flowing in through the doorway at disembarkation deepened his depression. His feeling of satisfaction at having found out before Atkins about the English woman Smith had been short-lived. Yet he knew it wasn't surprising. He could hardly have let her go; that would have been dangerous for him in any number of ways. He could have given her back to Josina Boon or over to John McWilliam of his own staff to decide what to do with her. He could have held on to her for a little longer. Yet he was a scientist with scientific work to do and he did not need such a distraction. In any event, he knew his main reason was that he had not been able to resist the pleasure of stabbing at the heart of the South African, revealing a security coup of his own to belittle the other's performance of his work. He grimaced inwardly at the recollection as he handed his shoulder-bag to airport guards for searching. He should have thought it out more carefully instead of playing an ace so recklessly. Dangers were everywhere; throwing away cards on personal spite would be no help at all. Still, it was too late now. The girl had travelled on ahead of them in Atkins' private jet. The science team would be so busy on the project that he might never see her again. Pieter realised with a jolt that such a possibility filled him with sadness. He must be getting old, he concluded ruefully, if the principal lesson he could draw from all this complex subterfuge was that he found her desirable.

Other cares, problems, priorities had been carried to earth by the same plane. John McWilliam was feeling nervous. Internal security for the project was his responsibility, yet he had failed to vet Lita Scarrow sufficiently to detect her disloyalty. It rankled with his professional pride that Atkins had been able to pull that particular puppet's strings under his nose. The English spy was not his concern; he considered Pieter had been right to hand her over because external security was under Atkins' direct control.

Caramel Bondi's thoughts moved from memories of her mother to the wider world of humanity, especially oppressed humanity. Turkey was a melting pot of races from Europe, Asia and the Middle East. A giant on the stilts of poverty and fatalism had stalked across its dry plains and rocky hills for many centuries. European technology had brought startling changes in the twenty-first and early twenty-second centuries, but the everlasting dust still bred human spirits who could gaze through machinery as if it wasn't there. The black woman thought of the technology of the project. Hers was the responsibility of controlling the temperature and electrical charge of the plasma that would surround the traveller in a latticed cocoon of isolation. The atmosphere in the capsule would transfer with the cargo, leaving a complete vacuum. The surrounding air at the destination would explode outwards with a rushing crack of pressure as the incoming air displaced it. Nose and ear plugs and eye pads would be an early precaution to protect human frailty through the instant of transfer. The plasma would perform a different purpose on a return journey. As the tentacles of the power lattice sucked material from the past the in-rushing air would need to be filtered and collected to test for ancient bacteria, and then replaced with air from the surrounding laboratory. '*Yes,*' she thought, '*good plasmology would be important, but I still don't have to like what I'm doing against the poor people of the world*'.

Miguel Santos was also thinking of Project Methuselah as he stood in the airport terminal, though technology was far from his mind. The disappearance of Lita Scarrow and Paul Forbes caused him anxiety. He hadn't yet seen much of Turkey, but already it struck him as a strange land. His Mexican home was near the sea - another culture as alien as the moon was not going to alleviate his sense of foreboding. Why did he also retain a sliver of residual guilt over having spoken out of turn to a desirable security girl in the bar in Cache? He couldn't remember what he had precisely said, but somehow it seemed he shouldn't have said it. Goodness, he couldn't even remember now what she had looked like!

***

Felixana Smith lay on her back, staring up at the ceiling of her small room. The air-conditioning held the heat of a Turkish morning at bay; she shivered involuntarily and pulled a blanket up over her slight body. Her eyes closed. Recollections of the previous day's flight across the Atlantic Ocean ran through her mind. Simon Atkins had been courteous, but with a seemingly-detached calculating manner. It was what she had expected of him and it had not taken her by surprise. She knew he was unpredictable, far more so than the Dutchman, North. His nonchalance covered a thinly-veiled concentration as he had handed her a drink. He sat down on the soft chair opposite hers in the rich comfort of the private aircraft.

Only a slight judder every now and then had told her she was hurtling through the air; the overall effect otherwise had been of a small, quiet hotel lounge.

"Well, Ms Smith, what are we going to do with you?" There was no edge to his voice. It was all very matter-of-fact, so far.

"What do you want to do with me?"

"I haven't made up my mind, but it seems pointless to just kill you."

The easy way the remark had been made was chilling, perhaps too chilling to be real. She had to break through it somehow and improve her position. A germ of an idea formed in her head.

"Your project is unworkable, you know. You might get scientific success, but without proper publicity and media release you haven't got a chance."

The thrust had worked; a shadow of indecision and reflection had passed across Atkins' face like a cloud over a summer meadow. How much did she know? Who had she told? Was it all over, after all? Better start from square one.

"You don't know what we're doing." The statement was assertive enough, but as he listened to his own words he nearly didn't believe himself.

The girl had to press her advantage now; to be coy would have thrown it away. "Of course I do! You're planning to destroy the Southern Brotherhood's religious strength by proving that their figurehead, Jesus, is a fake. You're perfecting time-travel to do it."

Her words caught him like a blow to the stomach. His drink had shivered in his hand. He felt a pulse of blood throb in his neck. "Have you told anyone?"

The balance of pressure shifted. Now it was her turn to deflect the impression of indecision. She had masked her delay by taking a sip from her glass, and yet her eyes held his steadfastly. It was a vital moment. She could read something there for a second she had never known before; then the game took over again. If she admitted she was still alone he could have her snuffed out and still maintain the project's secrecy. If she involved a chain of contacts he might still conclude that speeding up the

175

activity was the safest way forward and keeping her hanging around was too heavy a weight to carry. He could probably check her story, anyway. A picture of Craig Landon had flashed into her mind. What would he have done? She had reached much further forward in revealing the project than perhaps he could have dreamed possible, and she must not make a mistake now and let his memory down. She decided that the South African would be more predictable if she kept uncertainty levels low.

"No, I'm on my own; but, as I said, you will need to manage the world's Press to your advantage. I have many contacts, both inside and outside the BBC." She had added mischievously, feeling bolder now that she had committed herself, "You might even want to spread some misinformation." Her slight ghost of a smile held just a hint of slyness. She sensed he would appreciate that.

It was Atkins' turn to sip and think. The woman had a point. Taking on to the payroll someone with the blue-chip credentials of the BBC might impress his masters. They could never dragoon someone, and one volunteer was worth ten pressed men. The Corporation was like any other free media unit, nosing around and trying to expose things, preferably in a contentious, confrontational manner. It sold copy. Atkins knew full well that politicians of almost every hue had to hatch their plans in spite of the BBC rather than with its support. Yet if he could keep her on a short leash, here was an opportunity to see the gamekeeper turn poacher. He smiled; too devious an individual to commit himself instantly.

She had put down her glass and leaned forward. He caught a faint scent of her body perfume. "We'll see, Ms Smith; we'll see. For the time being, you will remain in close arrest." He winced inwardly as he realised the double entendre of the word 'close'.

He drew attention to the luxury of the pressurised, well-appointed cabin with a sweep of his hand. "But as you see, it won't be too much of a burden on you."

He had finished his drink and left the cabin to talk to the pilot. Felixana had remained with her thoughts.

She was still musing on that hot, quiet morning at the Siverek Base as the helicopters carrying Pieter North and his teams of scientists arrived from Diyarbakir.

Tuesday 1 July

The wave was bigger than the little girl expected. She jumped back, squealing in fear and delight. The sea burst into bubbling foam, hissing round her legs and sending her scampering away along the beach. The man and woman lying together on the warm sand beyond the reach of the tide laughed aloud. The woman's laugh was a touch lighter than the man's, but the wheeling seagulls couldn't tell that.

"Lunch is ready, Saffron!"

The little figure turned and ran back to her mother. Mary Trent pulled herself to her knees. She dusted sand from her daughter's legs as the man moved cups and plates around. He looked up. Saffron gurgled with delight when she noticed the picnic; ham, tomatoes, crisps, and her favourite - window cake. She had called 'Battenberg' window cake since she could first speak and it was easy to see why. Mary poured three plastic mugs of lemonade. Along the beach she could see couples, some with children and some without. A day at the seaside was wonderful. She knew it had always been so. She had memories of her grandmother recalling childhood visits to the sea at Wisbech. Her own younger days had been filled with the excitement and colours of the coast at Hastings, where she had watched work in progress on the second Channel Tunnel.

A bubbling thankfulness built up inside her. It was still rare, even though nine months had passed since her son's tragic death. David was with her now; she and Saffron would be safe. There seemed to be an expectation in the neighbourhood that David would dismiss his present woman and move in with Mary, but she herself had been hesitant at first. She looked at David's strong hands as they chose and wiped a rosy apple on his check shirt. She shivered with a bolt of desire as she recalled that wonderful Saturday evening in March. She took a stick of celery from the cup on the picnic dining-sheet and stroked her fingers along its length. The excitement of the memories warmed her body as much as did the sun.

"Where shall we go tonight?"

The man shook his head. "We leave tomorrow. We should pack and sleep."

"Oh, do we have to? It's been so wonderful; I don't want it to end."

"Holidays always end, my dear. Nothing lasts forever."

"More drink, Mummy?" Saffron held out her cup, her bright eyes turning to her mother. Mary smiled gently and obliged.

Wednesday 2 July

The neighbourhood shuttle slid to a halt. Three tired figures emerged from the steps, the last to leave the vehicle. It moved away into the dying suburban sunshine. The journey from Dorset had been strangely quiet; Mary knew something must be wrong. Saffron had slept but David had avoided his woman's eyes on several occasions. The pneumatic mechanism on the outer domestic door had sighed softly in sympathy as the panel shut behind them.

"What's the matter, David?"

"Nothing, Mary. Just get unpacked."

There seemed no point in staying awake that evening; the homeward journey had done little to aid recovery and refreshment. The washing unit had sorted the soiled holiday clothes automatically into separate piles for fabric temperature treatment as three pairs of lungs had expanded and contracted in rhythmic oblivion. The third cycle of drying and pressing was nearing its completion as the figure moved silently past the kitchen and utility areas. The machine took no notice. Why should it? It was built to serve, not to tell tales.

Thursday 3 July

Mary found the memo marker light near the view-screen glowing when she woke late the next morning. The digital recording was barely more than a minute in length, yet she watched it four times before the message could be accepted by her anguished emotions. She recognised bitterly that a small plastic camera lens was easier to talk to than a distraught lover. The sentences were short and to the point; one didn't have to spare the feelings of a camera with a circuitous or sideways approach. Still, some words stung more deeply than others - 'no excitement any longer', 'this new girl at the bank', 'tell Saffron I'll miss her'.

Her hands flew to cheeks already flushed up, and she screamed. Hysteria overwhelmed her in vast, unremitting waves. She was still screaming as the first drugs were injected by the paramedic who attended at the call of the distressed neighbour. The woman held Saffron close and tried to calm her as the young girl watched her mother being taken away. The incident upset some neighbours; some were angry that their morning tranquillity had been shattered by the noisy arrival of the hover-ambulance. The flight to Milton Keynes Memorial Trauma Unit took only a few moments. Mary's sedated body was wheeled to initial assessment. Vital signs, blood pressure, organs, breathing, all were stabilised. Yet it became clear in following days that it was the patient's mental rather than physical state that would give cause for concern. The will to live had fled. She did not respond to normal stimuli. Visitors could merely sit and hold her hand, their eyes often full of tears. When it became evident that her almost catatonic state was rather more than temporary, her daughter was kept away; it was causing the child too much anguish. Saffron was sent to live with her aunt in Far Cotton, Northampton. Weeks turned to months.

Thursday 17 July

'Uproar in Paris today brought an important scientific conference to an unseemly end. Delegates gathered for the 250th anniversary of the first International Polar Conference of 1882 were stunned by the unannounced withdrawal of the American and Russian delegations.'

The presenter's face on the view-screen was replaced by scenes of a jostling, angry crowd swaying and heaving on the steps of a Parisian office tower. Someone pushed the camera operator and the picture spun and nose-dived to the sidewalk. The news presenter's features, calm in the studio, returned to face the viewers.

'The Conference was expecting to hear details of the opening-up for global use of the new international scientific facility on Alexander Island. The surprise decision to restrict its use to northern nations will undoubtedly increase world tension. This has been building steadily since last year's World States Council meeting in Malta.'

The small man switched off the view-screen and climbed from his vehicle. Although he had landed his hover-car under the shade afforded by a clump of trees the mid-July heat was weighing down like a heavy blanket on the hills surrounding Yerushalayim. Rocks shimmered and swam in the haze; Michael Ben-Tovim was feeling drowsy. He wanted to sleep, to dull his anxieties, but instead he moved slowly to seat himself on a shaded outcrop of rock to gaze pensively westwards over the valleys towards the city. He was too far away to see much, but Yerushalayim's somnolent day unfolded in his mind's eye. The stone-flagged slopes and valleys were white with sunshine; in the heaviness of the dry heat he sensed the weight of centuries of service to his Faith. He closed his eyes and travelled round the perimeter of the city in his mind. High to the north, the square Knesset lay in its now-ancient wood. The hills to Samaria rolled away beyond. Mount Herzl lay to the west, and lower down was the memorial of Yad Vashem. He envisaged Hadassah Hospital at the city's farthest reach, with its twelve lattices depicting in glass the twelve tribes. His mind roamed south, to the Sion Gate and then the ever-present hills again, this time the Judean hills running down to Bet Lehem. The timeless sense of history calmed him. He began to piece his thoughts constructively.

The English woman he had turned into a spy had not returned from Pichot Base. Seven weeks had now passed; there was no doubt in his mind that she had been found and captured, perhaps even killed. Had it been a mistake to have sent her in the first place? Surely a trained agent would have been much better suited to the task? Two months of preparation had been insufficient and she was not objective, that was the worst part. Why on earth didn't he see the foolishness of sending in someone with a personal involvement, someone with a black monkey sitting on her shoulder and goading her on into perhaps unnecessary risks? But then, the Mossad had no-one else to send and the opportunity would never have occurred again. He sighed aloud, the sound dying instantly on the flat, scorching air. He thought of the man opposing him - the South African, Atkins. Where was he? What was he doing? What was in his mind? Triumph at having caught such a prize? Where would he be, Oklahoma or Turkey? Siverek would be much the closer of the two. He looked towards the north, trying to visualise what the opposing powers were planning. He failed.

Sunday 24 August

Experiments at Siverek proceeded more quickly than anyone had dared hope. All equipment had been delivered and commissioned weeks earlier and only final calibrations were necessary to reach the point where human transference would again be possible. At eleven hours in the morning, three military officers, two men and a woman, went back and came forward again on the power calculated for the target date. They reported a deserted scrub landscape, baking in summer heat. They carried rocks for

180

radio-carbon dating. The mood in the Base was one of excitement and nervous anticipation.

Pieter North knew his work was nearly done. Early briefings had taken place with the handful of specialists who would lead and control target activity. The Dutchman had taken an interest in the start of medical, linguistic and other preparations designed to ensure safety and anonymity in a strange and ancient world. Equipment and clothing imbued with mysterious unfamiliarity began to arrive in the Base. It would not be long now. Sadness began to develop in him. He had spearheaded so much, turned a theory into reality, probably earned himself lasting scientific fame; yet the personal experience of time-travel would not be coming to him. He had spoken with one of the military travellers who had 'been through'. The man had told him of a blinding, instantaneous light, even with the protective eye-pads, and a stomach-wrenching spasm that left muscles aching. The desolate scrub was simply desolate scrub. Obviously, no journey had been made to ancient towns and villages, so the destination had been an anti-climax. Nevertheless, the air had smelt differently; presumably, it was the absence of pollution.

The scientist longed for the experience. He would spend hours on the periphery of the Base, sitting on a rock in quiet solitude, trying to imagine the surrounding countryside as being that of the past. He had seen the English woman once since their arrival in Turkey, and she was now constantly on his mind. He longed for her so much, to walk with her down the long avenue of the past now opening up before them. What of the Southern Brotherhood now? He looked towards the south, trying to visualise what the opposing powers were planning. He failed.

Five days later, he received a message which was to rip away his pensive reflection.

Friday 29 August

Yerushalayim baked under the summer sun, its houses and walls shimmering in the honey-tinted light. Hover-cars lifted from their landing-pads at the World Faiths Congress buildings like bees leaving a hive. Michael Ben-Tovim watched them thoughtfully from a window high up in the Israeli wing. Power was gathering its forces. Would it soon have a purpose for which to fight? The Southern Brotherhood, now securely under the sway and influence of world Faiths, was beginning to buzz round its adversary, looking for where and when to sting. Yet time could

181

be running out as the planet was in increasing turmoil. Pictures of the morning's gloomy news telecasts flickered across the diplomat's mind.

'Yesterday's earthquake and tsunami in Southern India continue to exercise the world's nations. The World States Security Council has met in emergency session to consider a draft resolution condemning the refusal of donor nations to relieve the tragedy. Aid agencies have indicated their stocks of water, drugs and shelter are inadequate, though some reports from Europe and North America do seem to reveal unwillingness by governments to believe this. The International Red Cross and Red Crescent are trying to do what they can in the early days of a frightening disaster. Other aid organisations and NGOs are complaining of government hesitancy to provide logistical and transport support, or even to grant permission to log flight plans for mercy missions. The Indian Prime Minister continues to ask for help. Other southern nations have been less than patient, accusing the European Union particularly of standing by while India dies.'

Ben-Tovim had once visited India as a young diplomat with Anna; he could feel pain for the anguished survivors in their heat and isolation. Far more ominous was the tale from the English Channel islands. The south-western approaches to the island of Jersey had been guarded for centuries by a marine light to guide shipping. The former lighthouse at Corbiere Point had been replaced in 2089 by the present-day white tripod, twice as tall as the structure it succeeded and equipped with the new high-luminosity, low-intensity navigation lasers. A cargo vessel passing to the north-west towards Guernsey had been strafed at 0200 hours on the previous night by a laser beam from Corbiere without warning and with devastating effect. The vessel had been rocked by explosions, and had then sunk with no survivors. It had been sailing under an Egyptian flag. The newscast had reported the opening of investigations by Trinity House, the London-based controller of navigation lights, but as yet no explanation had been revealed. The lasers were supposed to operate at well below lethal level; indeed, it was a surprise to many that such destructive power could have been available, anyway. The light was built on a promontory connected to the main island at low tide, so the disappearance of any personnel would have been easy. No comment had yet been forthcoming from the Egyptian government.

Ben-Tovim turned from the window as an aide entered the room. Referring to the Security Council's emergency session over India, he asked, "Is there any news, David? Are we still dealing with diplomacy?"

"Yes, it's still diplomacy, Michael. In addition to condemning the inaction of Europe and the United States, they decided to put pressure on

182

the north by urging the full Council to allow neutral access to the Turkish Base."

***

The evening meeting at Siverek Base had been called at short notice. As the red ball of the sun said goodbye to Friday the entire senior project staff came together in the spacious boardroom. The architecture of the room was impressive. Fingers of softly-glowing plasma-crete arched overhead in a spreading fan, holding wide windows looking out onto the western horizon. The wine-coloured furnishings of thick curtains and soft armchairs, shot through with jagged splinters of black design, counter-balanced the more solid smoother lines of the huge oval walnut table in the centre of the room. Twenty moulded chairs awaited their occupants; name plates rested in front of twenty thin writing pads on their plastic agenda blocks in the ancient and traditional blotter shape. Each blotter's computer strip glowed softly as it awaited activation, its icons lying quietly in readiness for the meeting. The room was softly lit, sensors automatically adjusting the light level upwards in perfect timing with the downward dying of the western sun.

A buzz of concern hovered like a mist as the room gradually filled up. Rumours had gone round the Base that afternoon that things were not well. One particularly colourful one was that an ancient disease had been brought back with the previous Sunday's military officers, and was even now burrowing its way with invisible deadly silence into everyone on the Base. Another was that the 'organism' known as the Southern Brotherhood had wormed into operations, putting the project in danger of imminent exposure. Pieter North smiled wanly at a couple of colleagues and moved to the space reserved for him as lead scientist. He faced out across the table and through the windows. He took his seat. The sun finally set, the windows darkened, the lights raised a notch, and the meeting began.

"I am sorry to have to bring you together with such little warning like this, but we do have a major problem. I'm not sure we can get round it easily. Tests have been completed to date the samples brought back last Sunday. They were not from the first century. In fact, as far as we can tell, they are only three hundred years old."

Sighs and soft gasps of exasperation and disbelief puffed up from the table into the warm room. North continued, his face showing concern.

183

"There are a number of reasons for our being so wide of the mark on this, none of them particularly palatable. Our calculations may be wrong. We may have suffered a power famine from this part of the European grid. There may have been some kind of temporal interference altering or slowing the transfer. Various kinds of sabotage come to mind, or it may simply be that the span of time we know as three hundred years is the natural upper limit for movement. Whatever the reason, a considerable delay in reaching the target area now seems inevitable. This will affect preparations for the final contact team, and obviously for security.

"Mr Atkins will speak to us all shortly on the security implications, and Dr Aziz for the final contact team will then speak with his colleagues. This is a new and worrying situation. I propose we tackle it on several fronts. Over the next few days I shall want technical teams to study the options. All speed consistent with a thorough review is important. We should meet again a week tonight; or earlier if a significant breakthrough occurs. Now, before I open the meeting to general questions or comments, Mr Atkins will address us."

The South African sat several chairs to North's right. He, too, remained seated as he spoke, his voice as dry as the scrubland in the blackness outside the panoramic windows.

"We have all been under pressure these past weeks, but that is the particular nature of this project. Things will not get any easier now. As Dr North has said, there could be a non-scientific reason for this difficulty, a reason stemming from political interference."

Pieter North recalled the political interference of the original deception over the Turkish Base, but said nothing. The security man continued.

"If that is the case, totally-external interference is not likely. Much more likely is the possibility of one or more persons within the Base working to corrupt our plans."

A murmur of unease bubbled up, with looks of disbelief or suspicion bouncing round the table like a bagatelle ball. Atkins clarified the action he considered necessary.

"Security is already tight, but will now become tighter; with immediate effect all personal external communications will cease. Similarly, no incoming personal calls will be allowed. All leave is cancelled; everyone will remain on Base. Certain parts of the Base will be off-limits to all but essential personnel, and present access rights will be reviewed."

Atkins gave no indication that he had finished talking. The uncertainty which that generated compounded the equal uncertainty over how to respond. Shocked silence clung for a few seconds. North ended the embarrassment by picking up the initiative again.

"So, are there any general issues of concern or non-technical suggestions we can all contribute to?" The invitation prompted several concerned comments from around the table.

"Is there any truth in the rumours of disease?"

"None at all; we're all safe on that account at present, though we shall watch the situation carefully, especially when larger numbers of people have transferred."

"If we need more power to break through a three hundred year barrier, will we give our position away to the Southern Brotherhood?"

"They undoubtedly know we're here already, though we could safely assume that if they don't know of the detail of the project, a larger consumption of power won't give them any more clues than they have now."

Simon Atkins interposed.

"We ought to increase security at external grid stations just in case our enemies guess the importance of large amounts of electricity."

Pieter North made a mental note that the South African's interruption was out of character. It had been a most useful comment, freely given, showing a genuine commitment to the team. For some reason, he seemed to North to have mellowed. The Dutchman wondered why. The questions continued for a while longer and the meeting finished to exhortations of confidentiality and perseverance.

Saturday 30 August

"It is quite possible that you have lied to me, Ms Smith."

Atkins' voice sounded hard and probing; it carried easily in the quiet room of the woman's private quarters. Throughout the previous nine weeks the days of her close arrest had been gradually eased. She had been escorted closely, to be sure, but security officers could not always be spared to walk with her. She was unarmed and alone, on a Base where it seemed that even visiting the bathroom needed a plastic security card with a hidden password, yet he continued to press his point.

"You cannot really expect me to believe any longer that this is all a coincidence. Within weeks of your appearance a serious problem occurs in the project. You could have co-ordinated the disruption, or aided external interference, or even sabotaged the equipment yourself."

Felixana Smith tossed her hair in easy defiance. She was in no mood to be defensive over his implied accusations. She felt confident enough to remain seated.

"Where on earth would I get the technical knowledge for that? You know yourself even your top scientists are working in the dark, not knowing from one day to another if the next step is going to prove impossible. If I were any longer interested in sabotage I would be looking for ways to blow the place up, pure and simple!"

Her strong and natural rebuttal reinforced his own growing disbelief that here lay the simple answer to his difficult problem. He suddenly realised he wanted to smother her attractive slightness with longing licks and kisses. The feeling shot a bolt of lust through him like a shiver. It took him a couple of seconds to recover. How best to play it now? He decided to soften; her nearness was far too appealing. How long he would want her he couldn't tell, but to keep her close was intensely important to him. He smiled, warmth spreading inside his stomach as he did so. He recalled her words 'if I were any longer interested in sabotage'.

"We do need good press and public relations. If you are really prepared to work for the project, we may see what happens."

She smiled back. He seemed to be thinking it had been his idea all along. Just like a poor man! She knew the truth in his statement, the powerful fact that she had got to a point much farther than Craig Landon had ever dreamed of reaching. Wasn't it better to honour his memory by exposing the story alongside personal gain than to snipe away from the outside? After all, the story would come out one day, anyway. She was torn between wanting the project to fail and gaining from its success. What should she do? There was no right or wrong here, no black or white, north or south, holy or secular. Wars and conflicts were for other people; her priority was to reveal the truth, to tell the story, to photograph the event. She couldn't moralise one way or the other; it wasn't her issue. Being close to the action certainly was her concern.

She stood up and toyed with a glass paperweight on the table beside her. She could sense his desire for her; it tightened her buttocks and dried her mouth. Perhaps that part of the dizzy mix could be made to work for her, too. She replied to his offer.

"I don't know what rumours the world is making of the project, but one of the first priorities ought to be to put out a believable line; to confuse and delay. I would suggest something benevolent and humanitarian, to draw the sting from the southern cause, and perhaps to divide them."

She deliberately chose not to say 'yes' directly to his offer - with the mood of the moment, it could have been taken as a 'yes' to bed as well. She wanted to keep him on edge over that. The subtlety went over Atkins, who was just pleased to be moving in the right direction. He just managed to retain a sense of formality.

"That makes sense. There's no knowing who else the Brotherhood may have put on our trail, or how close they are." Again, with his use of the word 'close' he sensed the sexual overlay. He thought he had better get out fast, before he molested her. He turned to the door.

"I'll see you are called in to some of the regular briefings from now on." Then he was gone.

Felixana undressed for a shower feeling quite pleased with the way things had gone. The only residual doubt was that she was now completely alone and living on her wits. The new tight security arrangements had reached her. There was now no easy way a message could be conveyed to the Israelis. But then, what purpose would that serve in her new predicament? She could throw in her lot with the world's rich for the moment. If all went wrong she could simply invoke the reputation of the BBC and declare herself as a double agent. That was the chameleon charm of being a media practitioner, a dabbler in the black arts.

The needle-points of heat from the shower stung away the lingering remains of a headache. A new purpose had focussed her attention. She could go forward now. She smoothed shower gel up and down her thighs

187

and with a sudden jolt of surprise found herself imagining it to be Atkins' semen. She managed to convince herself she would use every weapon at her disposal to get her story. This was just business and could be separated from love. People did it all the time. The thickening steam of the shower blurred the edges of thought and gave her cotton-wool candy confidence.

PINK

Monday 1 September

The three men from the World States Atomic Energy Authority stood in stoic silence in the spacious entrance hall. The air-conditioning kept the temperature bearable; cool in comparison with the outdoors even though it was early morning. The footsteps of the aide echoed through the stillness as she returned from the depths of the house. She smiled.

"The State Governor is in the garden, feeding the koi. I'll take you to her."

Faces smiled in return and hands gripped folios, as the men braced themselves for the task ahead. The lush garden lay before them as they emerged into the heat, its luxuriance in almost ostentatious contrast to the dun and grey dullness surrounding most of Istanbul. The four figures moved down short flights of stone steps edged by balustrades onto a sloping lawn. Fig trees and palms on the periphery were interspersed with deciduous trees from more northern latitudes and the scent of roses was heavy on the air.

The tall woman in her dark pink gown kneeling on the edge of a massive pond rose to her feet. She turned as the visitors approached. There was no attempt on either side to offer handshakes, but the greetings were soft and very courteous. The Turkish State Governor smiled as she removed her gloves. Rubiya Mabud remained relaxed. She already knew who the men were and why they had come. She gestured towards a wrought iron table and six chairs over to one side of the garden. They all sat.

"I hope your journey from Malta was pleasant?" Her voice rang like a bell with its southern Asian sing-song lilts. The language was French, handled easily and naturally.

"Oui, Madame. Nous dormions sur l'avion."

The youngest of the three visitors was obviously the most senior. Considering he had never met a European State Governor before, he too was remarkably relaxed. The Governor turned to her aide.

"Some lemonade please, Sasha."

The aide returned to the house. One of the older men watched her go. Another gazed to the city skyline with its multitude of minarets. The leader of the delegation was watching the Governor, who spoke again.

"Tell me about your request."

"The World States Council has expressed its concern that activities contrary to world atomic control agreements may be taking place at the former Russian base in Siverek on Turkish territory. The Atomic Energy Authority has been mandated to investigate. We need your permission to arrange a visit - just a preliminary one in the first instance, I'm sure; a formality, even."

"Is that a formality because you don't intend to look, or because you don't intend to find?"

"Oh, we shall look. What use the Council makes of anything is up to the Council."

The State Governor's dark eyebrows lifted slightly as she said, "Turkey may want something in return."

The young man shrugged, a non-committal, disinterested shrug, out of character now with the courteous attentiveness that was there before.

"I'm not sure how the Atomic Energy Authority can help in that respect."

"We need a more powerful and extensive irrigation system in the eastern provinces. Wind power allocations to us are too weak. An atomic system has been designed but we cannot get world approval for its use."

"You know that nuclear power is highly restricted now." The visitor did not like the way the conversation was going. His instructions had not included a piece on negotiation.

The Turkish Governor gave a small wave of a well-manicured hand designed to wipe away the difficulty of seventy years of nuclear cutbacks. "Yes, yes! I know all that! That's why my offer is on the table. It would be accompanied by co-operation and inside support from Turkish and other agencies I can influence; quite a few."

The envoy watched the aide return with the iced lemonade. He asked about the koi in the pond as they sipped their cool drinks. Pleasantries flowed around the table like the growing morning breeze. The drinks were finished and the men stood up. The senior envoy smiled. "I'll see what I can do." The aide accompanied them away up the steps of the garden.

Rubiya Mabud returned to the koi, watching their writhing pink bodies twist and turn gymnastically as they grabbed the food floating down to them. The Governor felt satisfied. Under her guidance, Turkey would twist and turn too as it tried to grab all it could for itself. Being on the edge of the European Union meant being side-lined too often. Turkey was now a poor State, its poverty extending from past histories of conquest and national rape, and from the meagre soil and often hostile temperatures which could so easily ruin agriculture. The green fringes at the edge of scrub and desert were not enough to stave off State debt.

The Governor grimaced slightly as she thought of the Siverek Base. She had been told little of its intentions and nothing at all in consultation prior to its use. The Atomic Energy Authority visit had come as a welcome opportunity to redress the balance of influence in her favour, to make amends for her weak beginning to the story. The Union and its American and other partners were playing their power games again and using smaller States and nations as pawns, just as they had done over past, colonial, centuries. She thought back to her childhood. The life of a devout Moslem family had taught her respect for her relatives and courtesy to strangers. The increasing secularity of the post-commercial northern world had frightened her as she had grown into womanhood. She remembered fighting tooth and claw in her early political career; not because she was a woman - that battle had been won in her great-grandmother's day - but because she professed a religious upbringing. She wondered what the Union was planning. She feared something so horrible that it wouldn't bear thinking about. Mankind was ever inventive, and always able to counter and circumvent international control agreements by coming up with new monstrosities. Gunpowder, dynamite and TNT had been early indicators. The years of the twentieth century had seen chemical weapons arrive, then nuclear and biological armaments, and eventually GMWs, which themselves became subject to tenuous worldwide control. There were still those who feared that genetic malfunction weapons had already been implanted in selected portions of the human stock and all that had to happen now was for the passing of time to see the consigning of targeted groups into the evolutionary shredder. The Southern Brotherhood was about to gain world ascendancy, but would this bring an equilibrium or just a southern hegemony to replace the northern one? Yet it wasn't just the poorer southern states, she told herself. This time, some rich and influential countries were allying themselves with a new global justice; Brazil, Egypt, New Zealand and Israel came to her mind. This peculiar bonding of Moslem, Christian, Sikh, Buddhist and Jew in a stated cause of the World Faith Congress' aim for human equality seemed to have the northern world mesmerised.

She tossed her last piece of food to the swimming diners, watching their pink backs thrashing as they dived away into the green depths of the pond. Her long legs straightened; if she achieved clearance for her irrigation project she would provide all the assistance the Atomic Energy Authority needed.

Friday 5 September

The swimming pool at Siverek Base was rarely used at seven in the morning. The two swimmers had the water to themselves on this particular Friday morning. They swam alongside each other, alternating strokes to conserve breath for talking. The woman was easily the better of the two, but kept her movements relaxed. John McWilliam was pleased; he knew his level of athletic ability was nowhere near that of Caramel Bondi. He also knew that the swimming pool was likely to be beyond the eavesdropping rota established by Chief Atkins. He asked about the scientific conundrum the team faced.

"How many times have you tried on maximum power?"

She shook water from her face as they turned at the end of a lap. "Twice so far, with a third attempt planned for this afternoon. It doesn't look very promising, I'm afraid. The present setup won't let us go back past three hundred years. I think the only person who could possibly design something new is Paul, and since Pichot nobody's seen him or even been able to find out where he is. Do you have anything on that?"

The man looked round the empty pool hall. "There's nothing at all. The computer's departure records showed he left right enough, yet there's no forwarding address. Pieter says he never left any messages with him. No clues as to why he went or where he's gone. Some final goodbye would have seemed natural; perhaps he was concerned that Atkins would try to track him down. Senior members of the team didn't have to get clearance; not to leave Pichot, at least."

"So you think he could have gone to ground?"

"Oh, yes. It's possible. It's not something we can work on too productively at the moment, though. What happens if we can't get back past three hundred years?"

She grimaced; then opened her eyes widely, revealing their whiteness. "I have no idea at all! That's one for Pieter to handle now, I guess. So much energy and money has been poured into this scheme, I suppose aborting it now would be unthinkable. Our historians could advise the politicians to change track and go for some significant event since 1832. It wouldn't have the same impact, though. This really is the only way the U.S. and the others can finally discredit the present southern alignment. There wouldn't be time before December thirty five to manipulate enough individual governments, there are just too many.

"If they're willing to be bought off, anyway," she added as an afterthought.

"You did express some sympathy in the past, Caramel." He tried to be neutral in his tone, but it came out slightly chiding. The comment irked her, more so with the aftertaste of talk about Paul Forbes' possible flight from Union retribution. She responded firmly.

"They may have a point, but we're all individuals. My mother brought me up to look after myself, and I'm doing just that. I can't influence world events. It would be a waste to sacrifice myself for a principle when neutrality now might give me a better chance to right wrongs in the future. Each of us has only a limited amount of power. We have to use it to best effect."

She wanted to change the subject quickly, adding "I wonder how Pieter his fighting his other battle at the moment." They turned again at the deep end of the pool.

"What do you mean?"

"I mean his attraction to that English girl, the media woman. You must have seen how he looks at her."

"Quite frankly, I hadn't noticed, but it must make life extra complicated." *'Oh, no,'* he thought, *'that's something else to dilute the bonding of the team'*. This was all breaking down into struggles for personal survival.

It made him uneasy. His fellow swimmer was still speaking as he pulled his concentration back.

"Whether or not it'll divert his energies, I don't know. He's been alone for so long, but I hope he doesn't make a fool of himself. We depend on his scientific leadership. I'm not sure really who's side this spy's on."

McWilliam snorted gently. His companion wasn't certain whether this was through the exertion of swimming or a mild expression of exasperated cynicism, a female thing hidden from his perception. He responded with a blunter instrument.

"I'm not sure whose side anyone is on! But, perhaps that's my profession speaking. I think we all trust Pieter, so any change in his attitude to the project could easily affect us all. Anyway, I need breakfast and a rest."

Caramel Bondi laughed lightly and lifted her lithe body from the pool, rivulets of water streaming down her electric blue one-piece costume. The security officer puffed out after her.

The Turkish sunset that Friday was blood-red. Pieter North remembered learning somewhere it was because of a particular density of dust and angle of light. He stopped walking and gazed to the west. Dark, red-brown shadows lanced across the scrubland from every outcrop of rock. High and sparse cirrus cloud, shot through with dark pink contrails, mirrored the random speckles that the landscape offered. A heavy silence lay on the land. He could hear blood in his ears. He imagined it coursing with the same rust-red ochre he saw all around. The main Base buildings lay some five hundred metres or so behind, hidden now by the crest of the small ridge down which he had been walking. Perimeter fences were some way off yet, but he had no intention of going that far. Just as in the greener surroundings of Pichot he craved solitude and found it in the hills. He liked hills. There were never any real hills in the Holland of his childhood. Hills gave views that expanded the mind. They gave an impression of flying; of protection from enemies below. He crouched to his haunches so he could see the setting sun reflecting in the body of water in the dip ahead. The lake had shrunk in the summer heat, but it would still be about ten metres to the other side.

Visions of the English girl swam into his mind, her long dark hair swishing gently in the silence. He had spoken to her a couple of times since 'the arrest'. Once had been to give a short briefing on the project, and he had found he could barely keep his longing out of the timbre of his voice. Eye contact had twisted a knife in his stomach, so he had tried to be light and nonchalant. Whether he had succeeded, he had absolutely no idea. How long would they now be together here in the isolation of Turkey? As long as it took to succeed with the project, he supposed. Yet, what was the way forward on that; or was it backward? It was becoming confusing. He wished he could ask his friend, Jon, but now he was dead, no longer available. This was not good enough - he must focus and think like a true scientist. What if three hundred years was pointing to be a basic rule of cosmic physics? What could he do then? Yes, they could experiment with the reasons for such a rule, but scientific enquiry was not a luxury the politicians would tolerate. They had a job to do - *he* had a job to do. He would have to deliver. The promised Friday evening meeting beckoned.

He thought back over the previous few days. He had sat through interminable meetings while historians and sociologists had agonised over alternative targets within the three-century parameters. The journey had been enlightening for someone not versed in such professional callings, but highly unsatisfactory, nonetheless. World wars, financial crises, pandemics, uprisings and social upheavals had been pored over. They had each thrown up an amazing array of leading individuals; some innocent, some genuine, some misguided, some charismatic. He had come away with the unmistakeable feeling that many had merely been in the right place at the right time. No genius, no sacrifice, no undue levels of commitment or stamina could be detected. It was all very unsatisfactory. His frustration must have shown because he had left the final meeting before it had finished. His scientific upbringing had demanded more.

He began to see purity in the original project. Nothing less would destroy the Southern Brotherhood once and for all. He suddenly sensed the reason for certainty; listening to the historians had reminded him of the eternal tension between faith and science. Only a revelation of the falsehood at source would suffice, not only for the politicians but more importantly, for human scientific endeavour. If they were successful their beautiful minds would reign supreme at last. It would be a challenge, but he would somehow have to deliver on the original task. The purity and perfection of the human psyche demanded it. Nothing less would do. Yet perhaps that would be beyond him now. He sighed, torn between the positive and the negative.

Almost in despair, he scooped up a handful of pebbles, tossing one with frustration into the silent water. It plopped noisily. The reflection of the dying sun crazed into shards of pink light. He stood up and sent a second stone scudding out over the water with greater speed. It bounced twice off the lake's surface, to clatter among the rocks on the far shore. The significance of the act stunned him. He skimmed another stone; and yet another. Each rose up in triumph from the flat surface to reward him with an echo of applause among the rocks beyond. Of course! Yes! They could all travel back three hundred years, set up a new power base, and go back again - just like skimming over water! Why shouldn't it work? No scientific reason to deny it came to him. He strode away from the last weak pinks of the western sky to share his new-found purpose at the evening meeting.

Wednesday 10 September

North's quest for a scientific solution had won the support of his colleagues. Fast progress now required two things; the agreement of northern governments to greater funding with a diversion of more power supplies, and the finding of an engineer who could break through what was increasingly looking like a solid three hundred year barrier. One of these tasks was to prove impossible.

***

The unmarked Mercedes-Benz hover-car was moving slowly in the northbound traffic across Budapest's Chain Bridge. The sole passenger, seated in the rear, was separated from the driver by a transparent screen. The car interior was pleasantly cool, keeping the late summer heat at bay. The passenger gazed out at the magnificent urban scenery. Behind, in Buda, rose the huge solid mass of the castle and the National Gallery, its green dome and green roofs standing squarely and firmly on the Danube's southern bank. The light brown massif of the central blocks with their Grecian columns towered over the lighter brown ramparts of the more ancient castle walls. Ahead, and to the left of the diplomatic car, stood the ornate splendour of the Hungarian State Parliament building, its own brown dome glowing in the afternoon sun. The car reached the city of Pest, swinging upwards and to the right onto a left-turning arc. In four minutes it was gently lowering into one of the central quadrants behind the Parliament.

Taking a blue plastic folder with him, President Papandreou moved swiftly indoors out of the heat. The holographic chamber on the second floor had been pre-set to the high security standards required by world politicians. The chamber in the Hungarian State Capital was the closest available for the President once the message from Siverek had been received. The President was shown immediately into the hologram ante-room next to the Parliament chamber. The large grey machine waited for each leader to indicate agreement for activation. It was one of the new H-5 models, with characteristics beyond previous specifications. High-definition representations of participants could now be accompanied by document, facsimile and dense-matter transfer. Inanimate objects could now be 'passed round' the discussion arena via an instantaneous technique akin to cloning. In addition to the clear physical advantages, those taking part would also experience a greater sensation of being in the same room together.

The European President placed his blue folder on the surface in front of him, wiped his face with a handkerchief and pressed the start button. The American President in Washington and the Chinese Premier in Beijing appeared around the same table. Senior advisers, two for each power bloc, sat alongside. It was impossible to tell from precisely where in the world each man or woman might be transmitting their image. President Papandreou assumed his own advisers were transmitting from Brussels, but they had not indicated this. The slim, fifty-six year old figure of Mikhail Vorshin of the Russian Central Praesidium was the last to flicker into existence. The politicians looked at each other; a diplomatic modicum of welcome was exchanged. The eight advisers looked down at their own papers. The thirteenth space around the table energised into life. If anyone did notice the significance of the total number gathered in the upper room, it went unremarked.

The Base Commander at Siverek introduced himself, coming straight to the point. "Presidents and Premier, thank you for agreeing to my request to convene at such short notice."

He continued by summarising the three hundred year barrier encountered thirteen days previously, and the unsuccessful attempts to circumvent it that had taken place. The raising of the 'skimming stone' theory caused a slight tensing of body language; its financial implications caused rather more. The Base Commander paused, and with his eyes and arms invited the politicians to begin to contribute to discussion. The Chinese Premier consulted dates on a chart that he presented to general view.

"I look at the time-scales. The initial primate was transported on January four; this barrier encountered August twenty four. It is a total of

197

thirty three weeks. Will you need thirty three weeks to build a base to go back just another three hundred years?"

The Base Commander considered this was worth countering with some confidence. "That is not likely. We have gained considerable experience and have some good resources on base. There are other changes as well. The monkey was sent twenty years; the men, three hundred. Our safety record is faultless. What we really need is an assurance of support funding to enable us to press ahead with the progress we have already made. We do not have to replicate all facilities at a new base, just the essential scientific ones."

"What will it cost?"

The American President had turned his craggy face to the Base Commander. Without waiting for a reply, he threw in a supplementary question. "How soon will you be in a position to declare you have arrived at the target date?"

The man in Siverek held up his arms in honest reply. "We need an assurance of support. We cannot say what the precise costs will be. Our scientists are projecting the completion date around this time next year."

"And how long from then to the planned humiliation of the Southern Brotherhood?" added Vorshin, keen to focus on the main prize.

The Base Commander responded quickly. "A further three months."

The Chinese Premier spoke again, his face full of mischief. "Could you plan to disrupt the Brotherhood's celebrations at their Midwinter Festival in 2133? I believe they still call it 'Christmas'? There would be significant advantages in that timing."

Chill black humour bubbled round the meeting. The advantages alluded to would be powerful; it would be a poetic justice to destroy the Brotherhood at a sensitive time of year for southern nations. The to and fro of question, answer and comment continued for twenty or so minutes. Then there were smiles round the virtual gathering. It was agreed. Only the officials who had witnessed the agreement held lumps of ice in their stomachs as they mentally projected the implications of unlimited funding.

***

Simon Atkins' search for a traitor or an enemy in their midst had come up with neither. Since his open talk with Felixana Smith at the end of August, eleven days of investigation had drawn no conclusions. One of his security officers had even been persuaded to transfer with early personnel to the down-time base, still in its infancy, because no sign of insurrection or sabotage could be detected at the original centre. The scientific project otherwise seemed to be operating smoothly, though he knew it was nowhere near its destination, and he had no way of knowing when it might succeed. He found himself wanting to see the BBC woman again. Since asking her to carve out a role she had attended two of the regular senior briefings. The project scientist, Dr North, had given him disapproving glances at the first of these. Atkins had assumed it was because the prize handed over had been turned from a liability to an asset. That made him feel good; he had studiously ignored the scientist.

He tussled with the three-hundred-year conundrum, but from a different angle than that chosen by Dr North. He had been embarrassed by the eventual realisation that their captive had been in no way responsible for the supposed sabotage. It seemed her protestations of innocence had been proven correct; he needed to build bridges. He thought again of the fee in his contract. If he were to be successful in guarding the project to a fruitful conclusion in the eyes of the politicians, whatever that conclusion might be, he considered he might negotiate a bonus. The potential for time travel haunted him; yet his eyes were not fixed on the commercial prizes that might lie in wait. Whether or not the three-hundred-year barrier would eventually be overcome was of no direct concern to him, except of course for his payment. More bases meant more security officers to be placed under his responsibility.

He found himself thinking of his childhood, and indeed further back, to the childhood of his mother. If these powerful scientists, backed by thrusting, wily politicians, could pluck something as audacious as Project Methuselah from thin air, then perhaps he could wheedle his way into persuading some to use the technique to recompense the past suffered by his grandparents. He lived again in his mind the stories his mother had recounted of speeding away from a sacked farmhouse in a friend's hover-jeep. His family history might be put back on a proper keel, his ancestors vindicated for having struggled to carve life out of their native homeland, instead of being destroyed by those perceiving them to be imposters and illegal colonisers. His family and their forebears had trusted to democracy to protect minorities, but it had been shown over the decades to have been misplaced trust. The feeling ran deep in him that he should never trust again. Now, putting right that justice wouldn't need three hundred years, just a mere fifty or so. He stretched, anxious to know whether his colleague had returned from the down-time base with any clues about sabotage.

Felixana Smith approached from around a turn in the corridor ahead, her appearance providing an electric jolt to his nervous system. Acting on an impulse he took her arm, steering her back from where she had come.

"I'd appreciate your thoughts on publicity. If you can spare a little while over a drink, there's something I want to share with you." He gave a smile, though she couldn't tell if it was genuine or not. It was disconcerting to her that both types of smile looked the same when they came from this man. She was surer, however, of his intention that she should not refuse the invitation.

Over a coffee in a quiet corner he tapped into her knowledge of the BBC's editorial policies. His skill at steering conversation was consummate and subtle. Within ten minutes she was easily giving responses to questions about her background and childhood. Then learning how happy she had been in her early years, he introduced his own thoughts on South African history, and how lives might be changed or relived. An hour later, their knowledge of each other's perceptions and wishes had deepened beyond both their expectations.

Monday 15 September

Many thoughts passed through Pieter North's mind as he sat alone in the chair.

The skimming stones had released energies in several quarters, first among scientists and then with the politicians. A pragmatic approach might not be ideal but it would give the chance of continued development, of solving the problem by trial and error, of reaching the goal. The politicians had taken the chance that a way forward could be found; the end results would justify any means. It was the technicians, the accountants, and the paper-people, who had thrown up their hands in disbelief. Vast amounts had already been spent in early experiments, in developments at the Pichot Base, and now at Siverek. If all there was to show for this was three hundred years, and investment in buildings, equipment and training was to start again, it was not at all certain to the Dutchman that resources could be found. A Siverek base in 1832 could experience the same problems before a neater scientific solution could be found. Yet as was often the case across the years of human endeavour, well-founded anxieties and well-meaning reservations could be no wall of defence against a flowing tide of power. If the scientists could deliver, the politicians would let them; force them even.

Pieter North could easily visualise the early future steps. Throughout coming months, secretive recruiting and retraining would take place, and the money would begin to flow. Larger temporal transmission units were needed if building equipment and materials were to be transported. A far greater number of personnel than originally thought would need to be shifted across time. National and international capital projects across a wide range of public and private activity would be curtailed prematurely. Investments would be raided, pension funds stripped, equity reappraised and liquidated at short notice at fire-sale prices. Emergency budget statements across the northern world would carry the same interpretation; the wicked Southern Brotherhood was forcing austerity on people - people in the northern world who had never done anyone any harm and who had merely got on with their own business.

His imagination projected the reality into the future as he waited in the chair. Redundancies began to increase in large number. Budgets that were supposed to hold good for the next six months began to fall apart. The financial reserves of organisations large and small evaporated as workers were paid off quickly. The international money markets lost faith in northern governments; governments that had been their golden customers since before the First Great Recession of 2008. Keeping a nation afloat demanded money on a constant basis, so borrowing short had become a necessity. Hot money was getting wise and ditching the post-industrial nations, well in advance of the formal institutional changes foreshadowed by the World States Council. Only the trade in technological and scientific products needed in the emerging world was continuing, and that was slowing down. Supply of food from the southern hemisphere and the tropics began to falter. The Baltic Dry Index began to live up to its name. Yet still resources were diverted to the Siverek project. A crisis of confidence had come upon the north. Governments were powerless to borrow unless the yields were unbelievably high. International rating agencies cut sovereign credit ratings. This in turn fuelled inflation, sucking more paper money into the project under quantitative easing. Pieter North could see it all in his mind's eye. It would be like 2012 to 2016 all over again, but worse this time. The die was cast; nothing could stop that now.

Sweat broke out on his face. He knew he had been, would be, the cause of so much. A palpable burst of heat swept over him, the rise in body temperature distinctly noticeable. Another mild panic pricked at him - was this natural fear or an effect of the pressure changes that must surely now be taking place around him? What had the instructor said? *'Close your eyes when you see the red light come on; there's no need for eye pads now. Try to relax and take a normal breath, but hold it in when you hear the buzzer.'*

There was no red light shining on the board directly in his view. He chanced a look to left and right through the transparent side walls of the chamber. The sense of normality beyond was quite bizarre. There was no sea of faces staring in at him; no interest at all really. He could see a white-coated technician with a clipboard standing a few metres away, but the man could not have been less interested if the chamber had been empty. Was that the last person he would ever see? The parallel with an execution scene was almost too much to bear. He had read of death sentences from the distant past, even though no-one in living memory knew of such things now, even in China. An image of the English girl came into his mind and calmed him. Why did he always think of her as the English girl? He supposed it was folklore, the romantic aura of delicate English dog roses, of Greensleeves, of Maid Marian of Sherwood. There was nothing he could do now but give himself to the power of electricity in a hot barren world.

The red light glowed. He closed his eyes tightly, screwing up his face to shut out as much light as possible. What now? Ah, yes, the buzzer. He had heard it enough times in practice so would be ready for it. The sound would last for the length of an intake of breath and there would be a second or two after the buzzer stopped before the move. He began to shake and almost missed the coming of the sound. He breathed deeply, too deeply, and let out some air as the noise cut out. Then the move hit him. A terrifyingly-white light burst in his head despite his closed eyes. His body convulsed as if he had been kicked in the stomach by a massive elephant. The air was driven from his lungs; his arms and legs tingling and throbbing at the same time. Surely something had gone wrong. He thought he was still sitting down, but his extremities were so numb that he couldn't be sure. Should he open his eyes? At least he was still alive.

"You can breathe normally now, Dr North. You've arrived safely."

The woman's voice sounded remarkably reassuring. The taste in his mouth was dry and acid, as if he had been sucking on a dead battery. He opened his eyes, taking a moment or two to let a focus settle. The chamber looked the same, and yet wasn't. A woman's face appeared at the left side window. She smiled.

"Just giving you fresh air; won't be a moment," she said almost breezily.

The taste cleared; the hangover was still there. He breathed fresh, cool air into his lungs and slumped back into the chair. The door panel hissed as it moved aside. His charming hostess reached in, offering her hand. He took it, climbing shakily from the chamber.

"Welcome to 1832. It's the fifteenth of September." Her smile and her words released a dam wall inside him, removing him from the straitjacket of guilt and recrimination in which he had wallowed. He burst into laughter, his self-confidence returning as the tension left him. Through the blur of wet eyes he looked around at the room outside the chamber. Yes, it was different, sparser. They couldn't have shifted the furniture in the few brief moments he was inside the chamber. How long would it take for the sheer enormity of it all to sink in? No matter - he was feeling dizzy with self-worth at last, shaking like a schoolboy after a long exam paper.

"We should move on to the reception area, Dr North. They'll need to prepare this area to receive the next incomer. We have only had two weeks to bring materials down, so things are a bit spartan, I'm afraid."

She cupped his elbow and guided him to a room off the far end of the laboratory. His eyes darted everywhere in his heightened state. He tried to recall earlier memories of college history lessons on Turkey. Disjointed words came to him - Ottoman; Sultan; harem. What was Turkey like before Abdul Hamid became its Sultan in 1876? Goodness, he was now breathing air that existed forty four years before that date! He lay on the examination couch in reception. The physical survey was perfunctory enough, giving the interrogation unit on its trolley no cause for alarm. The mental survey also took just a few moments as a seemingly-bored psychiatric aide tried to drum up enough enthusiasm to ask three or four pointless questions about diet and belief and the meaning of different colours. He must have passed satisfactorily as he was quickly ushered away to collect files and papers that had preceded him into the past.

The constant, instinctive search for signs of an ancient world continued, though now with an edge of disappointment. Yes, it might well be true that all around him had travelled too, the need for gadgets to sustain life and sanity being as strong in temporal terms as suits and gravity boots were in space travel terms. Would they all shrivel and die if exposed to ancient buildings, customs, food and most of all, people? He decided to push it from his mind. *'I have walked on the moon and lived to tell the tale. I am surrounded by other scientific experts, and the project has spent vast sums on historians, psychiatrists, linguists, and people and professions I haven't even heard of.'* He felt good, and given a lucky break he might never have to experience another kick from an elephant.

Wednesday 22 October

Three weeks of October passed before Simon Atkins summoned enough personal courage for his own move. Several security officers had preceded him to the 1832 base. A new pattern of life established itself. One constant real-time was maintained between the two bases to stabilise working relationships. Five days spent at the down-time base by an individual was followed by a return to a date five days after the date of origin, to reinforce the feeling of 'being away'. Communication was constant, though not direct; by mid-October, a fluency was being achieved which minimised the effects of delays.

The South African had put off his own transfer as long as he could. Much as he wanted to keep a personal control on events at the new base, he remained fearful of the trip. A nightmare world was creeping up on him. The disquieting dream that had started a little time before in his sleep could not be shaken from his memory. It had begun to nag at his mind in waking hours, leaving that mental after-taste of any vivid dream, colouring his thoughts and dragging at his plans for the day ahead. Its persistence was beginning to unnerve him just as much as the content. Increasing his workload to push it away only led to greater tiredness. Tiredness brought sleep nearer and with it came the dream again.

It had begun with him running along a beach, tripping over, and stabbing his hand on a half-hidden obstruction. The sense of falling had stuck with him the most, the piece of wood or metal being just a bizarre final twist. At first he put it down to fatigue, a late evening snack, or a mix of real events from his past. Then things had begun to change, the extremes to extend into new realms. He was no longer on the beach when he fell but two metres up on the sea wall, the jagged protuberance piercing an outstretched upper arm and not his hand. The dream would come every three or four nights. He began to fear the permutations of the disaster. The injury at the end of the fall would strike his legs or his shoulder, the sharp obstruction becoming two metal bars, growing in size.

At the jolt of impact he would wake up sweating, sitting up quickly or rolling over in a spasm, trying to get away from the pain. So he submitted to the time chamber, the action seeming just as much an attempt to escape his tormenter as to take command of operations in 1832. The move seemed to work. He couldn't guess for how long he would have relief; it was just enough to be able to turn his attention to the matters of security and secrecy of the project.

He learned from his officers that Felixana Smith was already on base, building a small team around her to test out publicity strategies. The wish to sleep with her swiftly drove away any remaining thoughts of his disturbing dreams. Things would surely be much better once he had tasted her sweet firm body, suckled on her small breasts and opened her slender legs with warm kisses. He had survived the move from the twenty-second century; his confidence was returning. Now was the time to act, before she became too involved in the preparations for media management of any final denouements. There would be a cover story to prepare, but that should not take all her energy. She ought to be able to give him some attention.

23 October 1832

He saw her the next evening, in the dining areas of the base. The atmosphere could not be construed as romantic by any stretch of the imagination, but that hardly seemed an impediment to him. Felixana was already seated with a meal when he entered. She was wearing the white overall suit now standard day-wear on base. She acknowledged his entry with a smile. He collected a meal and moved across towards her.

"I see you made it through safely from the future," he said.

"So did you. How did you find the violence?"

A nervous hesitation now from him, but it was hardly perceptible. She wouldn't have known the context, the violence in the stabbing of a man. "What do you mean?"

"I mean the kick in the stomach when you came over. The technicians told me it doesn't get any easier. Some people are beginning to bruise."

He smiled ruefully. "Mine was fine, though I don't want to do it again in a hurry."

The conversation moved into other areas. He wanted to create an island of normality in a nineteenth century ocean. She was now a little more confident that her role within the project would protect her and bring personal benefits in its own time. He found that she was willing to talk again of her childhood, of the district of the peaks in England before she was ten, and then of a life in Virginia. The earlier recollections were hazier, but even so places stood out if the faces didn't. Hathersage, Baslow, Eyam, the Linacre reservoirs............the names meant nothing to him but he was pleased to listen. She remembered a suburb of Sheffield called Chesterfield, and a strange deserted building with a twisted spire. Simon enquired naturally, "Have you any experiences of religion?"

His question made her snort softly.

"I've come across quite a few people in my reporting and interviewing with plenty, but I've no experience personally, or desire to learn more, quite honestly. I think it's a weakness. We're born, we live, and we die; that's it. Often we die more quickly than we expect. Sometimes the death causes sadness to someone else, but our destiny as a species is in our hands alone. What about you?"

"My mother served in a church for some time in Cape Province, but that was when I was very young. It would have been just after the turn of the century. I remember the stale air in the building and the awful silence, but little else. She was a good woman, though. She died twelve years ago when I was nineteen."

He smiled, adding "She was the source of my wealth; well, that plus hard work and a lot of luck in the security business. As for Project Methuselah, I don't know what to expect. If we get that far, the world will be shocked. You will have to translate that shock into destroying the Southern Brotherhood."

She lifted her head and ran her hands through her hair. "Not a very difficult task, is it?"

They both chuckled, perhaps a bit too loudly. A few heads on nearby tables lifted and turned with inquisitive interest.

***

Simon passed his hand over the electric cell, extinguishing the main light. A soft glow of moon and stars bathed the room with ghostliness, barely picking out the corners of the shelving, the door, the bed. Without his clothes his movement across the warm floor tiles caused eddies of air to flow across his skin, increasing his sensitivity to further touch. He leaned over the bed to take the hand that was outstretched to welcome him. He climbed onto the bed, fixing a warm open kiss onto her mouth. Releasing the contact after a few seconds he stroked her right shoulder softly. He savoured the satin feel of the skin, surprisingly cool now as if made of marble. He leant down and cupped her small right breast in his hand, flicking the pink-brown nipple with the tip of his tongue before engulfing as much of the breast as he could in his open mouth. He moved alongside her on the bed, stretching out next to her so his achingly-stiff penis prodded insistently against the flesh of her upper thigh. His hands held her slender waist as he straddled the body beneath him.

Warm muskiness floated up into his nostrils. Her body was incredibly warm, the flesh burning, smouldering, and bubbling with heat against his arms, legs and stomach. He kissed her mouth again, excited that it felt hotter this time. He stroked her long hair as it streaked out across the bed. Her legs opened slightly, enough to let his penis lodge naturally between them, but not so wide as to permit an early penetration. He closed his eyes as his tongue danced freely within the wet cavern of her mouth, thrusting back and forth and round and round. Felixana's mouth responded willingly. He moaned in his throat and squeezed her waist more tightly; then relaxed and squeezed and relaxed and squeezed. The ache in his penis became desperate as his organ longed to go home into the warmth now calling to it as Felixana parted her legs a little more for him. His hands moved down the soft satin slide of the small of her back to grasp the firm globes of her buttocks. Simon lifted Felixana's hips to just the right angle for possession.

Sexual muskiness again billowed over him in heady waves as he lowered his head to gaze more closely at her narrow thighs and the precious prize between them. He eased open the light-pink labia, guiding himself in with the palm of his left hand. A plaintive mew of desire caught audibly in his throat, taking him by surprise with the strength of its poignancy. He thrust with renewed passion and longing through the soft gates as her legs rose and gripped around him. He climbed to a very rapid climax, sending his semen hurtling helplessly and completely into the depths beneath him, and then let his muscles relax.

Felixana grabbed his back tightly to encourage the last few drops. She rubbed her left cheek against the uncut stubble of Simon's beard and let her legs fall back onto the bed in wide submission. Yes, he had been good and she could do with this again. She lay silently under his weight. Her breasts and thighs tingled; the feelings sharpened her mind. She had still not been certain that her short-term usefulness on base, and hence possibly her safety, would continue beyond a few preparations for media presentation. She knew she was locked into a very complicated project where the stakes were so high there might be few long-term survivors. At any time she could be scrubbed out of existence. Yet she didn't push him off, but let him take the lead, enjoying the easing of her own tension. She lay with her eyes closed as the weight lifted, then listened to the sensual hiss of the water in his shower. She showered in her own time, wrapped in her own private thoughts. When she returned to her bed she found herself alone; but her world had changed.

24 October 1832

The morning sun was already high when she activated the personal console in her quarters. As the login sequences chattered and chittered away she stretched her arms languidly in her white towelling robe and took another deep draught of coffee. The sexual reverberations had quietened in her frame. She felt relaxed and ready for the day. Almost absent-mindedly she keyed to a recording of an international BBC broadcast, sent down the line with the early morning traffic from home base. Full inward access for the world's media was possible; it was in the opposite direction that total silence reigned in both centuries, waiting for this slight English magician to invent a charmed wand of deception and presentation.

***

The screen showed the London City skyline; the male voice giving the commentary was young and earnest.

This situation remains tense. The Canary Wharf Tower, now one hundred and fifty years old and showing its age as a listed building, was the scene last night of a drama as high as the buildings all around. A crowd of very angry people, estimated at between five and eight hundred, had gathered in the late hours of yesterday afternoon outside the Canary Wharf headquarters of Global Electric. They were expressing their anger after head office employees had burst out of the Extraordinary General Meeting of the world-wide electricity generating and retail giant. The corporation had taken the unprecedented and unexpected step of planning to increase world electricity prices between three and four-fold over the coming six months. Employees are not being exempted from the new charges. Private security guards were surrounding the building. Unconfirmed reports say that at least three people were killed by stray bullets when some guards opened fire. The State Law authorities have immediately referred the alleged incident to the Independent Law Complaints Authority. There is considerable uncertainty over whether or not the order to open fire was given.'

Felixana ended the recording with a sweep of her hand. She felt a twinge of envy that she wasn't personally reporting on such events herself. Yet was she close to something far more important, something that would ensure her fame as a journalist into eternity? Or was it all a wild goose chase? She honestly didn't know; she only had scientific mumbo-jumbo to tell her that the grains of sand wafting against her window were from three hundred years before she was born. She shook herself, strongly enough to awaken from her self-induced reverie. But----to business. There was a need for a cover story, something believable to keep the Southern Brotherhood at bay, or even better, running off in a completely different direction.

She toyed with the options as her fingers ghosted over the keyboard. Somehow the secrecy had to be accounted for. She considered a medical project to find a cure for a remaining world disease. No, the southern nations would convince themselves that the technological powers would keep it for themselves. Perhaps it ought to be a space travel initiative with the prospect of major colonisation. No, that would be seen either as northern rats leaving a sinking ship or deportation of unwanted southerners. She even considered publishing a concerted attempt to improve ocean quality in the context of two hundred years of pollution, then remembered that Siverek was thousands of kilometres from any major ocean. She wrinkled up her nose at the difficulties, her journalistic pride prodding her on to do the very best job she could. She decided the best thing to do was to build on the reasons given to the Turkish State Governor. What better way than irrigation development of enticing acquiescence among nations where drought or disease-laden watercourses had plagued history over countless generations? The European Union and its altruistic friends would be working hard to conquer the problem on behalf of the poor.

She smiled to herself with satisfaction, dripping honeyed words onto the screen before her. Craig Landon's memory tweaked her conscience as if to challenge her on the issue of whether or not she should be co-operating over Methuselah. She pushed the thoughts aside; this could be the biggest story ever to break on the news-waves. An appearance of co-operation now, in the early stages, would get her closer to the best coverage of the matter. That's what he would have wanted. She tried to visualise Craig's face, but instead found the blond features of the chief security officer still in her mind. She shook her hair in a toss to clear the thoughts, resolving to stick to the task in hand. She keyed requests of the Base's networks on data relating to irrigation projects worldwide in the years 2110 to 2130. The screen rolled up, project details dancing before the eyes, parading the detail in a regimented march. The snows in the northern winters had done little to redress the awful imbalance in supply and demand from which the southern hemisphere continued to suffer. The global warming of the twenty-first century had accelerated, increasing the intensity and random incidence of droughts and floods, torrents and burning sun. She noted it wasn't simply the southern world that was suffering. Persistent malaria cases in southern England were growing in number. As she finished reading the reports, Felixana experienced a dark shadow flitting over her mind like a bat's wing. Then it was gone, only slightly denting her determination to continue.

Sunday 26 October 2132

"How easily can we get an agent into the Atomic Energy Inspectorate visit to Siverek?"

The man in Israeli military uniform shrugged his shoulders, the only part of him other than his head appearing on the visi-screen in Michael Ben-Tovim's offices in Tel Aviv.

"It shouldn't be too difficult. We've got two workers on the Malta payroll. We expect there'll be five inspectors going to Turkey. We'll need to find out who they are and apply the usual pressure."

Ben-Tovim nodded with satisfaction. "Do it then. Keep me informed."

"Are we to tell the Brotherhood?"

The Chief hesitated for a second; then decided. "No. This is our operation only. I can see no harm in handling it on behalf of the Southern Brotherhood."

He was to learn only much later of the fatal consequences of his decision.

14 November 1832

"This is the central processor unit."

There was real pride in Pieter North's voice. It wasn't just that much of the project was the product of his own imagination, his own scientific drive. He had longed to be close to the English girl for several weeks, and had never found the opportunity. Then suddenly one morning in mid-November she had appeared in the main electronics research centre at the down-time base asking for a conducted tour of the whole facility. His body had begun shaking again, as if she was a recurring case of malaria from which he would never fully escape. He had managed to think straight long enough to query whether she had sufficient security clearance. The doors on base worked by hand-print and a new system called BBI - biological breath imprint. The sensor grille at each security point would detect and screen DNA double helices from an individual's breath moisture. Crude jokes about heavy breathing had permeated the base when the system was introduced. He had even blushed slightly when he mentioned BBI to his visitor. She had caught his eyes, but it caused her no frisson of excitement.

"I have a Top Grade clearance. You can show me any part of the base."

"Well, it's not really convenient at the moment." He hated putting her off, but with the high voltages on test and with no guarantees that spare equipment would be sent if failure occurred, it was far too dangerous to be distracted. She smiled, determined not to be slowed down.

"Any time will do - this afternoon at fourteen hundred, perhaps?" And so it had been arranged.

Felixana had arrived promptly at the pre-arranged time at Pieter North's suite of offices. He wore a clean white lab coat for the occasion; she was wearing an old sweater over brown trousers.

"It will take us about two hours to visit all the main areas. I'll try and put it into some logical order so you can get an idea of the enormity of what we're attempting. We'll walk past the leisure areas, which I take it you know, and then we'll take a shuttle car. What do you know about time-travel?"

She shrugged. "H G Wells, I guess. I can't think of anything more profound."

He smiled briefly. "It's a long and interesting story, but one I can keep short enough. We'll start with the theory. From about the end of the nineteenth century philosophers were putting together two distinct approaches to time as a concept. A philosopher named Whitehead, who died in 1947, held that the flow of time is a metaphysical fact, like love and fear and pride. You can't touch it, but it exists and can be measured. Whitehead and his kind were known as 'process philosophers'. There were, however, philosophers who held that time was just an illusion and that words like 'past', 'present' and 'future' simply created a false impression that something we call 'time' existed. These were known as 'philosophers of the manifold'.

"The first great scientific breakthrough came with Einstein's theories of relativity, and Minkowski's interpretation of them to give us the single concept of 'space time'. We were no longer faced with the separate phenomena of space and time but realised they ran a double act. Just as space could be measured with its finite rules, so could time which related to it. Throughout the twentieth century, particle physics continued to develop. It was found that the three reflections of nature - charge, parity and time - only gave us an impression of symmetry when they all combined. Mankind had for centuries looked at them through what we call a CPT mirror, named after the initial letters of charge, parity and time. Once we took each reflection separately, each was found to be asymmetrical. The plasma cocoon, with its ability to suspend the CPT impression inside a given space, was invented by the New Zealand physicist, Potter, in 2053. Now with a given charge of electricity I was able to develop a theory put forward by Professor Jon De Haag of the Netherlands to shear along the fault line inherent in time, and displace it in relation to charge and parity. That displacement, only a few milliseconds at first, is in effect time travel. Once the theory had been proven the rest was easy, if extremely expensive."

The walk to the shuttle was followed with a ride to the power transformer units at the far end of the base. Felixana had remained silent throughout, but on alighting before the entrances to the large electrical consoles she ventured a question.

"Does it take the same amount of power to move someone forwards as to send them back?"

He was impressed, and smiled accordingly. "Good question. Basically, the answer is 'yes'. We thought originally we would be fighting against a forward-flowing tide to send things back, and that a return to the starting point would be an easy flow, or better still, a spring back, as if we had sent them into the past on an invisible piece of elastic. We now know that movement is equally achieved in either direction. That explodes the theory that time moves naturally in one direction when cut adrift from the CPT strait-jacket, or like gravity we fight against a particular direction with extra difficulty."

He breathed into the BBI sensor and the grey door panel slid to the left. The indefinable shimmering thud of electricity filled the air; more a sense of power held in check than anything else. Felixana looked around in awe. They had entered onto a balcony about two metres wide, running the circumference of a round chamber of huge proportions. The chamber was about twenty metres across, with a dome above of similar dimension. The floor below the balcony contained five large transformer units, each twinkling with myriad dials and digital displays. She moved to the balcony rail as her guide began speaking again.

"We get our electricity from the European grid. It's increased in voltage here. We need around forty million volts for each plasma shell, rising to sixty million for the pulse of actual temporal transfer. These units begin the process of lifting the charge, others in the second chamber beyond" he pointed across to the other side, "continue with it to the required level."

Another side exit a short way round the balcony took them along a companionway overlooking an amphitheatre with capsules she did recognise. Temporal transfer units, or TTUs, were familiar to her after the past weeks, but these were larger than she had seen before, and there were two rows of them, each with about fifteen units. Pieter North spoke again.

"These are our cargo TTUs. People don't transfer in these; they're in use almost all the time bringing machinery, food, medical supplies, that sort of thing. Some waste materials are re-cycled or disposed of here, others that need more specialist treatment are sent back to 2132."

"You said 'back to 2132'. Is there a preference for using back, forward, or up and down - that sort of thing?"

He laughed. "No. We don't use fancy words like 'upwhen' or 'downwhen'. Everyone sees this journey differently. You'd be surprised how different people react, but by and large, they treat it like a foreign country and think geographically. Which of course in one sense it is. The confusion will start when we complete the base in the year 1532, or what will probably be then early 1533."

Felixana opened her mouth to speak but he had not noticed, and his exposition continued. They had reached the mid-way part of the amphitheatre along the companionway and he was pointing to the nearest TTU. "Most materials or small pieces of equipment arrive complete. The larger units have to come dismantled and are put together here. It's rather time-consuming, but we're getting better at it all the time."

"Can you transfer radioactive material?"

Again he was caught by the intelligence of her questions. The BBC obviously didn't know what quality they may have lost from under their noses.

"Yes. It makes no difference to the strength of atomic decay. There is no backward working of radioactivity, either. It doesn't gain three hundred years in strength, it just stays at 2132 decay levels. It shows there are several time currents working together in a way that we don't understand yet." A thought came to him. He smiled. "I want to show you something. Just wait here. When I get to the other side of the chamber, put your ear to the wall."

He moved off. Her brow furrowed. She did as he asked. He raised his hand when he reached the far side. She pressed her ear to the wall.

"I know you can hear me, even though I'm only whispering. It's impressive, isn't it?"

She gasped and whispered back. "That's remarkable. I once went to St Paul's Cathedral in London. The whispering gallery there works like this. How do you do that with no stonework?"

A soft laugh spun round the amphitheatre. The scientist felt excited that he could share this intimacy with the woman. "The acoustics work the same - it's just the way the chamber turned out."

She waved, impressed. He returned and they continued their journey. They walked along the companionway, waiting for the doors to open to reveal the next huge chamber. Pieter continued with his presentation while they waited.

"There is a marked improvement in outside air quality, as you would expect. Our sensors are picking up dirt and smoke from English chimneys, though. Remember that two thousand kilometres to the north-west of here the Victorian industrial revolution is working overtime."

A thought flashed through her mind - was Victoria on the throne in 1832? It didn't matter. More noticeable was the fact that the inadvertent reference to her land of birth had struck a chord. Reverie washed softly over her, strong enough to give a keen poignancy but not so strong as to cause real homesickness. She didn't know what would happen to her resolve if her natural disorientation was struck by a maudlin wave of immense proportions; for a multitude of reasons she still felt vulnerable inside.

The door slid to one side. She was surprised to see another immediately in front of them. It was a double door - double insulation - but for what? The second barrier moved away and they entered a bare chamber. The sight to the left was unnerving; stretching from floor to ceiling, ten metres and running the whole length of the chamber, was a glass wall. She looked more closely. Well, not exactly a glass wall, more a barrier of what seemed like transparent gelatine, a jelly curtain. She could see through it after a fashion. There were one or two shimmering white-coated technicians walking on the other side. Farther away beyond the wall the lights and shadows disintegrated into meaningless shapes. She could sense the wall throbbing from a distance of just over a metre. Why was there no barrier to prevent her from falling into it? Her host provided the answer, stepping forward and placing a flat palm on the jelly.

"It's well-protected, as force fields go. There's no emission and no danger of any kind. The danger would come if we didn't have it in place. On the other side of this wall we're sending personnel and materials to 1532. The instability caused by punching one hole in time is hard enough to handle. If we had two such centres of flux close to each other, without putting a seal between them, the theory says that the whole fabric of time would disintegrate. This part of the universe would unravel and disappear into a black hole."

She stared at the wall with new respect. The awe must have been apparent in her face, for he added "It's OK, come and touch it yourself. You won't break it. In fact, we've got it so tight that nothing could get through it. We can't move to the other side of this wall while transfers are taking place."

She stepped forward, gingerly fingering the wall. "How do you erect it?"

He felt a twinge of desire at the word 'erect', but it soon passed. "It's simple enough. Glass shuttering, plasma injection, input of charge and removal of shuttering. We must walk on - there is more to see yet."

Felixana was still intrigued by the power that had been let loose in this project. She widened the subject. "Are there any explorations off-base? I mean, into the surrounding countryside or further afield? I would have thought a whole range of different scientists and historians would want to research and prove all sorts of theories."

The Dutchman shrugged. "Yes, there is some other activity, but most world effort is being put into this project. The political view is that if we can destroy the coherence of the southern nations in this major way, all projects are possible once future prosperity is assured."

The word 'future' caught her attention. "Can you send people into the future beyond 2132?"

"I don't know. We've never worked on it and it's barely crossed my mind. Logic says it would be more difficult to control because our preparations would be hardly sufficient for a comfortable stay in a time when we would have no prior knowledge of lifestyles." He shrugged again, feeling that the vulnerability of confessing ignorance might make him more attractive to her.

The thought of 'tearing the fabric of time' came to him; he caught himself up with a jolt as he realised he was getting too open and sentimental with the English girl. What was her real angle? He longed to believe she just wanted to be close to him, but she had not yet given any real clues in that direction. The rest of the journey was friendly but uneventful. They ended where they had begun; she full of unanswered and unanswerable questions, and he full of an aching in his head as he longed to lie on top of her and be loved. As she walked away he forced his attention back to the comforting realities of his work. In his office a buzzer rang. The face on the screen was barely holding back its panic.

"It's the back transfer facility here, sir. There's been a fatality in the staff TTUs coming down from home centre."

YELLOW

Sunday 16 November 2132

"Who the hell authorised it?"

Atkins was shaking with rage. The international inspection team's helicopter was visible through the glass observation port of his office, its blades still moving as the first of its occupants climbed down the exit ladder. The discomfort in the face of the security aide was obvious even on the small visi-screen. His neck flushed with blood as he replied.

"The Turkish State Governor, sir. She only told us about the visit just under an hour ago. We've sealed off the time-transport areas - that's normal procedure. What else should we do?"

"Where's North?"

The aide gulped. What on earth did it matter where the points of the compass were? He hesitated, obviously for too long.

"North! Dr North! Where is he; here or at the down-time base?"

"He's down-time, sir. He went Friday. Shall we call him?"

"Don't be stupid! It's too late, they're here now. I'll meet them. Just arrange a squad of guards to be at the main entrance. We'll frighten them into conducting a perfunctory inspection."

Atkins was standing outside in the day's heat as the five Atomic Energy Authority inspectors reached the top of the rocky incline leading up from the helicopter landing pad. Three men and two women formed the delegation, the pilot remaining aboard. The rotors slowed, sending eddies of dust swirling away in delicate pirouettes. *'Damn!'* thought Atkins, *'they're planning on staying.'* One of the women reached the main entrance incline first. There was barely a smile; Atkins read it as tiredness, though, and his confidence lifted a notch. He spoke first.

"I'm Security Commander Atkins. I'm pleased to welcome you, though you'll see by the welcoming committee it has been a surprise visit." He indicated the two arcs of armed guards fanning out on either

217

side. They remained at easy slope, offering only silent interest. "We don't know who might visit us here. The Authority will, I'm certain, expect us to operate in protection against international terrorism."

He was thinking rapidly on the spot, his adrenaline giving him a buzz that was almost sensual. The woman spoke formally, covering her tiredness well.

"I'm Jancis Pedersen, AEA inspector on behalf of the World States' Council. I will introduce my colleagues later. We would all appreciate a short rest and some water after coming so far."

The tall Swede did not elaborate on how far they had come, and appeared in no particular hurry to start inspecting. Atkins almost began to think he could even enjoy their presence, a test of a cat being around to keep a mouse on its toes. "Do come inside. We always keep guest quarters available."

The five visitors in their yellow overalls with World States' Council insignias on their breast pockets were joined by the helicopter pilot. Together they moved into the first corridors of the main buildings. It was cooler here; bodies began to relax and spirits lift. Eyes, too, began to take an interest, though years of professional training kept tiredness as the façade they wanted to present. Atkins was leading the way so was not in a position to watch the faces of others. When he did turn to guide them into the guest corridors, the blank inscrutable timelessness of the sands was all he could see in their gaze. The South African smiled again.

"I'll call for you in, say, one hour; we can talk in our boardrooms. I'm sure we can make your stay useful and pleasant as well."

The doors shut with an audible sigh, like the sigh that Atkins surrendered as he walked back down the corridor. He spoke to two nearby armed security officers, his voice as cold as ice. "Stand guard at the door. No-one moves in or out for the full hour." And so it was - Atkins did not return himself but gave instructions for the five inspectors to be escorted to the main suite of boardrooms.

There were eight in the room when they began, two more officers joining the security chief. They were introduced as an atomic energy team leader and a logistics technician. Pedersen the senior inspector introduced her colleagues.

218

"You will know we have permission from the Turkish State Government to be here on behalf of the World States' Council. There is a significant energy component being consumed here. We simply have to give assurance that safety for the region is maintained, that atomic protocols are adhered to, and that Council priorities for the region are not being compromised by the power usage. The precise usage is not within our remit; in fact, we know that the European Union quite legally carries out its own private research into a range of issues."

Atkins nodded. "If I may suggest, then, that we start with the boring formalities of showing you round the logistical sections. You'll clearly want to eat and stay a little while."

Pedersen smiled again, disarmingly this time to lower tensions further. "Of course; please familiarise us with the base."

Domestic issues dominated for a time and then Pedersen raised the central issue - the inspection. At least three days would be needed - a gathering of statistical information, a detailed study with interviews, and finally, some private work and assessment. An on-site feedback would not occur. Atkins did not like the intensity planned, or the absence of a chance to place things in the best possible light, but he chose not to argue. It was more important to him to get Dr North up-time as quickly and quietly as possible. He needed his scientific assessment of what could and couldn't safely be revealed. The South African had no real idea of which rooms and pieces of scientific equipment might jar with the inspectors as being out of place in such an establishment. At least the first day, the gathering of statistics, ought not to provide too many difficulties. He intended to keep the visitors on a very tight rein; he won the point that 'chaperones' should accompany each inspector. After all, he didn't want accidents to befall one of them if straying inadvertently into danger, did he? The visiting team was content to concede the matter. Events were going well, it seemed, and as it said somewhere, but Atkins couldn't remember where, 'the morning and the evening were the first day'.

He slept fitfully that first night, waiting for the inspections to start in earnest. The nightmares were returning. The falls and sense of spinning out of control that he had dreamed of before he had travelled to the down-time base had come back to haunt his nights. He was several metres up a sea-break wall. Losing his balance, he fell over into the incoming tide. A set of rusty railings, half-buried in the wet sand, broke his fall with a spearing of his thigh. He woke in a hot sweat, his focus settling on the time displayed on the ceiling - 6:05 hours and daylight.

Monday 17 November

A shower, as cold as crystal, only served to remind him of the pain of the nightmare. The ever-encroaching heat of the day lulled him back into a semblance of habit and self-protection. Duty data coming from the central security consoles told him that Dr North had arrived overnight from the down-time base. The physicist was breakfasting in his quarters. Atkins checked with security that the AEA inspectors were still corralled in their guest suites and then set out to meet with North.

Atkins sensed the agitation when he entered the room. The 'breakfast' was merely a half-emptied glass of water - the food was untouched. North moved from the door to the window, his eyes a mixture of fear and guilt.

"There's been a death! We've lost a worker!"

It wasn't what Atkins had come for; he swatted it aside like a small English malarial mosquito and pressed on with his own demands. "That's not our problem now. Our problem right now is the Atomic Energy inspection team. They're here and they're asking questions, and I need answers, good answers that will send them away again!"

North swung. "I don't think you heard what I said! A science assistant was - disassembled, destroyed, blown apart." He waved his hands as if to attempt to describe the horror of what he had seen on the view-screen. "Blown apart and left in a bloody heap in a back-transfer TTU. We don't know what went wrong and we need to find out!"

Atkins was not to be side-tracked. He remained cold and severe, sitting uninvited on one of the room's chairs.

"The AEA is our immediate issue. If we don't send them away contented, there'll be more deaths!"

His voice carried venom and enough mystery as to what he meant by 'more deaths' to cause the Dutchman to pause. This zealot for security would throw him, anyone, to the wolves if the project appeared about to unravel. Yet it was unravelling now, wasn't it? The fabric of time was holding darker and bloodier dangers than they had imagined at the start. He was frightened. He had to get a grip. Bile from last night's worry burned his throat. He reached for his breakfast water and slugged the taste back to his stomach. "So, how do we make them contented? Where have they been? What have they seen?"

Atkins was pleased with the scientist's response, yet knew that the other's anger against him still lay beneath the surface. "Nowhere and nothing, at the moment, but we can't hold that for long. Today they'll start gathering data. You need to feed that data to them in a way that keeps them occupied, encourages a sense of co-operation and diverts them from anything remotely suspicious. Only you can do that. I don't know what material would raise their alarm."

"The short answer is 'nothing'. It's all so strange and new, even to those working with it, that unless they see time-transference actually taking place, which they won't, they wouldn't believe anything unusual. We can explain away all our technology in any way we choose."

Atkins liked what he heard. It might be simple after all to just let them look harmlessly around and go away with drivel ladled into their brains. His confident attitude suddenly changed, as if a cold wind had blown over the warmth of the sands and rocks outside. North had mentioned a death. Just keeping the inspectors away from the time machinery might not be enough. The strangeness of the machinery they did see might only serve to raise their suspicions further. He walked to the door.

"We meet them at ten in the main conference room. Come there fifteen minutes before with a harmless introduction and show me a plan of the areas they must never see."

***

The initial briefing that morning was short. Pieter North arrived as instructed, and somewhat stiltedly introduced the main purpose of the base. The northern powers were seeking to support the world community, and especially the poorer nations, by harnessing the solar wind for electricity. North's nervousness was caused in part by the fact that his audience were accomplished scientists themselves. Yet he knew full well that solar wind dynamics and its control remained one of science's unachieved holy grails. Despite decades of off-earth research the solar wind still gushed past the planets unchecked and unused to mankind's advantage. The Union and the Russian authorities were co-operating with all advanced northern powers to find a way of helping the world as a whole. North stopped at that point; to go further would have begged the question 'why not let the southern nations' own scientific community help with the research?'

He left his presentation point, handing out a sheet of data to each inspector that included a general map of the base. They scanned the detail;

221

North's spirits lifted a notch as it became clear they were not seeking direct plug-ins, at least not for the moment. He would need at least six hours to set up a false data-stream to run parallel with the real one. Until then, he needed to keep the early steps of the inspection on a simple geographical awareness basis.

The inspectors indicated their wish to set off alone - in five different directions. Pieter North accompanied Jancis Pedersen. He was determined to work methodically through the base, but the Swede was made of sterner stuff. External connectors to the European grid, power generation rooms and step-up transformer units were rewarded with visits that morning. North excused himself over lunch on a pretext of a 'pressing personnel issue' to work with colleagues on the false data-stream. It occurred to him as he spoke the words that a personnel issue really ought to have commanded his attention - the matter of the bloody heap in the back transfer TTU could most definitely be described as 'pressing'. He took advantage of the afternoon to learn a little more about each of the inspectors. In addition to Pedersen, they comprised a Nigerian, two Chinese and an Israeli. All appeared to be experts in their particular calling.

Tuesday 18 November

North was up early, his adrenaline pumping as soon as he realised on waking that the inspectors would now begin their work in earnest. Breakfasts had been taken together, but now they might split up and set off again in five directions. The physicist's nervousness returned - he could scarcely be in five places at once. He dived in courteously and diplomatically. Had they passed a peaceful night? What did they wish to see?

The Swede and one of the Chinese were females. They indicated they would work together to check on waste products emanating from the base, including taking local air samples. *No problem there* thought north. To his great relief he was told the other three would study how the project's scientists were intending to link the solar wind with a standard electricity grid. In a flash of half-inspiration, half-bravado, the Dutchman decided to escort them to the cargo TTU hangar. It was a calculated gamble. All time transference work had stopped anyway because of the fatality. The space that the amphitheatre occupied was quite a large percentage of the total base area; too large to be 'overlooked' and therefore it was better to brazen things out. The design of the TTUs would be so alien to anyone not associated with the project that he felt he could succeed with the deception.

The visit would begin at eleven hours. North had enough time to engineer a warming up of the cargo TTUs to one third operational power. That would give a background of noise and warmth against which he could play downloads from European Union sunspot satellites. He would explain that the units were experimental generators being powered by solar wind activity. The personnel TTUs would have to remain strictly off-limits, but their smaller size meant this was not likely to be a problem.

Wednesday 19 November

Wednesday's events might prove more difficult to handle. There were to be personal interviews with key base directors. No-one was to be forgotten - security, science, administration, housekeeping, electrical, finance, waste management, nuclear - the list went on. Plus there would be random interviews with a cross-section, including those at very low rank. North had done his best to brief all staff on the cover stories but he couldn't guarantee success in every corner. It was on Wednesday afternoon that one of the inspectors managed to slip away quietly to one of those corners.

Thursday 20 November

The inspectors were leaving! North felt empty inside and drained of further emotion. The tension and anxiety of the previous three days were beginning to take a toll. He managed to pull together enough strength to see them leave and he even smiled wanly at their grateful acknowledgement of his co-operation. The false data stream held particular irony for him - he had realised during his presentations on electro-magnetism that Faraday's discovery could be dated to 1831, just one year before the down-time base they had built. Dear old Michael would have been proud of him! A further complex knitting of strings of fate, no doubt, yet the complications were now so overlaid with each other that he couldn't find the energy to try to unravel them all.

Throughout the inspection, he did notice one thing particularly; in this time of crisis Simon Atkins had acted superbly. They had been united by a common enemy for three whole days. Their mutual dislike of each other

223

had been set aside in the hard light of expediency. As the AEA helicopter lifted away to the west, North felt his coldness towards the man returning, though not quite with the same blind intensity as before.

Monday 1 December

Paul Mbeki felt the perspiration suck from his skin in the cold breeze blowing from the north across Yerushalayim. His wrist band paid off the automated taxi and he looked around. Over to the east he could see the hill on which stood the King David Hotel, built in 1931, and after two hundred years, still the most prestigious in the middle-east. Mbeki's black Nigerian skin would look out of place here, but as a devout Jew he felt at home. After a moment's reflection he turned and moved on past the Ratisbonne monastery and disappeared into the maze of small streets behind Keren ha-Yesod and ha-Melekh George, heading towards the new headquarters of Mossad. The information he carried was potentially explosive; he felt certain that Michael Ben-Tovim would be delighted. The tall Nigerian was shown straight up to Ben-Tovim's private suite of offices on the fifth floor, where the views across Independence Park were even more impressive.

Ben-Tovim beckoned his guest to a waiting easy chair. Mbeki sat, gratefully drinking orange juice from the glass which rose from a hidden niche in the chair side as his weight triggered the courtesy liquid.

"I never expected a visit so quickly, Mr Mbeki; you have barely been back ten days from Turkey. You clearly have something to tell us?" An encouraging smile was enough to start the Nigerian on his story.

"As you know, my work for the cause involved my part in the AEA inspection at Siverek Base in Turkey on behalf of the World States Council. The story we were given during the inspection is that research is being carried out on the solar wind, and harnessing it for power generation on behalf of the emerging nations." Both men smiled cynically. "Hence they profess the need for extraordinary levels of electricity generation in their early stages."

The Nigerian placed his fingertips together. "But it is clear that this is just a cover story."

Ben-Tovim tensed imperceptibly. He merely nodded. "Is it as we thought? Perhaps a military strike being planned against Israel, or another middle-eastern State?"

Goodness knows, he felt, there had been plenty over the previous century and a half, most notably that from Iran. Mbeki's face registered surprise, and even some alarm.

"No, no, it's more serious than that! I've studied our initial findings. The Europeans and the northern powers seem to be researching a practical application of time travel."

The room seemed to tilt in Ben-Tovim's perception. He found it hard not to laugh, but strangely at the same time his blood chilled. It couldn't be the modest heat outside. It couldn't be alcohol, as the Israeli didn't partake. Yet nonetheless, the world shivered and reality was definitely suspended. The dizziness had still not gone away when he trusted himself to speak. Even then, he only echoed the final two words he had heard.

"Time travel?"

"Yes, yes. It's pointing that way. The energy that is being generated is disappearing somewhere and yet it is not being registered or reabsorbed locally. Neither is it being converted to anti-matter. The only remaining explanation in quantum physics terms is that displacement in time is occurring."

Ben -Tovim was thinking again, his brain re-engaged. "Have you mentioned this to anyone else?"

"No, of course I haven't! The rest of the inspection team and our official report will have no idea of my conclusions, but I am fairly certain that this is the outcome of the work there."

"Would it be forward or backward in time?" Despite his fears, Ben-Tovim was already focussing on the words 'initial' and 'seem to be'.

"I don't know. Perhaps you have a theory that would fit?"

The host chose not to speak his mind. Laughter would not be befitting of a man in his position. Ten days would surely be barely enough to piece together a definite conclusion.

"It may be too early to say, but clearly what you have uncovered is important and needs to be kept secret from others."

"Of course - I'll let you have my written report by Wednesday this week."

After the Nigerian's departure, Ben-Tovim spun in his chair and gazed from the window again. If only he was in contact with the BBC woman, Smith; the one he had sought to put into the American base in the first place. Things might be much clearer by now. But of course, she may be either dead or held prisoner in America or Turkey, or even have been turned by the European Union and working for them now. There was no way of knowing for sure. His thoughts went back to his visit to England and the cold rural isolation of Norfolk. In his heart he felt the coldness return. Before he could set aside the ludicrous thought of time travel he felt he needed to touch the bases of possibility that the concept might throw up.

There was clearly punishment in the minds of the northern powers. Had not Israel played a key role in Malta to encourage and support the humiliation of the northern world? What could possibly be an intended historical target? Could it involve a future elimination of the Jewish identity, or something from the past? It became clear in his mind. There was only one explanation. It would be a tampering with the Holocaust, perhaps even a denial. Even after two hundred years the experience from the 1930s and 1940s scarred the corporate Israeli soul. Victimisation might continue throughout eternity. There had to be a way forward, and he would act seriously with those around him. Nevertheless, he would have to be cautious. If time travel was breathed, even as a possibility, the Holocaust would surely follow in people's minds. Besides, he would not be thought of as a fool. He would not become obsessional. A military strike was much more likely and Israel would need to watch for one. He reached forward and opened a communication channel.

"Follow Mbeki; find out where he goes and who he speaks with."

The voice at the other end responded. ""Do we delete him?"

Ben-Tovim was shocked. He dared not authorise that! He was not certain he could have drummed up the courage, anyway.

"No, certainly not; I'm not like some of my predecessors in this post!"

He returned to staring out of the window, but his eyes were glazed and not really looking.

Tuesday 2 December

The internal inquest was being held into the fatality in the TTU and senior members of the scientific team were giving evidence. The science assistant had been returning to the down-time base; a sudden and unexplained dissipation of power had occurred in the lattice. No live transfer had taken place. The assistant had exploded and there was only a bloody mess inside the chamber. The inquest had been delayed on account of the AEA inspection. There was no interest on behalf of close relatives either on or off the base - there were none- yet there was a clear need to establish exactly what had happened.

Pieter North sat at the back of the inquest room feeling distinctly uneasy. The investigating officer was a senior member of the base police contingent; it occurred to the scientist that virtually all of the technical evidence that was coming out would be way beyond her comprehension. Was the inquest merely to establish if the terrible event had been an accident or an act of sabotage? He admitted to himself that they all had lessons to learn. He had agonised long and hard over the significance of the three hundred year barrier encountered in the heat of the previous August. Now he had given his technical evidence; it had also been established that he had been in a part of the 1832 base at quite a distance from the staff TTU hangar. The investigating officer had moved on in her interests, but slender tentacles of guilt slivered into the Dutchman's mind. It had been his enthusiasm for the 'skipping stone' theory that had brought them all to the point where a down-time base of considerable size and complexity had needed to take shape. Now they were embarked on a series of mini-jumps instead of one large one. Was it any wonder that things might go wrong? Seven times the number of TTU journeys, so seven times the opportunity for disaster to strike. Unless they could identify the reason for the death of the science assistant something similar might happen again.

The inquest officer was speaking again. "Caramel Bondi is called to give evidence."

A stir went through the knowledgeable audience. Caramel was the Chief Plasmologist; a dissipation of power in the lattice could perhaps be traced back directly to the consistency or temperature of the plasma in the lattice. It was the Mississippi scientist's formulae they were all following. She took the witness stand with her head held high. Her bright eyes looked at the investigating officer, waiting for her to speak. The line taken was unexpected. Caramel Bondi responded to each question without hesitation and with no sense of undue concern. It was clear she had belief in her answers.

"Have you travelled in a unit to the down-time base?"

"Yes, three or four times."

"Did you find it a pleasant experience?"

"Not at all, though I did get used to it a little. But I'm told my experience has been no different from most other people. A sense of disorientation can perhaps be countered if one focuses closely on one's work and doesn't dwell too long on the enormity of what we are doing."

"Where were you on the fourteenth of November, the day of the incident in question, the death of Assistant Johannsen?"

"Here at centre base. I was accompanying the duty staff in the main control centre for the cargo TTUs."

"Are the cargo units powered independently from the staff units?"

"Yes. They need to be. We have to synchronise the two centres because pulses of up to sixty million volts are needed for each transfer. That amount of charge needs to be accurate. After we have transferred a shipment of cargo, for example, we must wait perhaps fifteen minutes before we can inform the staff units that they may safely send people either up or down-time."

"Were the afternoon voltages on fourteenth November hitting and maintaining accurate levels?"

"Yes, they were all stable."

The investigating officer studied a screen set flat in the surface immediately in front of her position. Its flickering luminance etched the sharp outline of her pale face. She looked back up at the witness.

"Do you ever experience instability in the operation of the lattice?"

At this point, Caramel Bondi did hesitate, though it was barely noticeable. Pieter North noticed.

"Yes, occasionally. We do experience a bounce."

A hush settled on the room. Dr North's forehead furrowed, though sitting at the back no-one would have seen.

The investigating officer looked up quizzically. "Please explain; what is a bounce?"

"Our transfers hit a barrier at three hundred years. The physical mass we transfer bounces off that barrier and our power within the lattice has to compensate for that. It happens perhaps one per cent of the time. We can control many of these bounces, and for the cargo TTUs it is not a practical problem. We estimate that perhaps one human transfer in a thousand will experience a bounce, and within that figure, one in ten thousand will need an additional power compensation for safety. The frequency is unpredictable, as far as we know. We consider lattice instability itself to be a virtual impossibility."

The plasmologist left the stand. She avoided meeting Dr North's eyes. His emotions veered from guilt to anger and back to guilt again. A senior statistician gave evidence that, if the three hundred year barrier could not be overcome, the chance of further serious harm could be estimated at one in fifteen thousand. Human activity within the project itself was planned at much lower levels than that. The investigating officer thanked all staff for their evidence. The rest of the afternoon of that Tuesday in December was taken up with closing statements. Pieter North felt sick. Caramel's early hostility to the project came to mind. *'I have brothers and sisters in the third world.'* Now, in addition to all their other problems, it seemed they would have the Russian roulette of the TTU chambers.

Sunday 7 December

In the few weeks that had passed since the inspectors of the AEA had left, Pieter North's composure had been shaken badly. Several powerful conflicting forces were pulling him violently in different directions, yet all combined to insist that he realise he had to continue with the movement from theory to practice in the great project that Jon De Haag had left him. The fear of discovery down-time, the passion he felt for the BBC woman, the temptation of time-travel, the sense that he must achieve something in his life; and the unnerving knowledge that death was now stalking the time tunnels he was digging - all were pushing him on.

There was also now the real possibility that Caramel Bondi's commitment to the project was in doubt. She must have known, or at

229

least guessed, the statistical likelihood of fatal consequences of the power-bounce concept. Why otherwise had she hidden the characteristic from her colleagues? He could still hear her witness evidence from the previous Tuesday's inquest. There was the constant use of 'we' when she really meant 'I'. - *'As far as we know'* - *'We can control'* - *'The physical mass we transfer'*. He snorted silently to himself.

There was no point in holding a team meeting on the matter. He certainly wanted to avoid one. There was no way he could confidently reassure his other scientists that he had been as much in the dark as they themselves had been. He feared such an admission of his ignorance would just as likely unsettle them further. He needed to convey an aura of total confidence, especially as some were anxious about trusting themselves to the TTU process now a death had occurred. He decided it was much better on balance to carry the responsibility of his senior role and let everyone work out for themselves that a probability of one in one hundred thousand was extremely low in any case. He was also aware that many shared his scientific excitement in pushing against known boundaries; names could be written in scientific journals and fortunes made. The power-bounce facet was no different from any other danger lurking in the practical science of time-travel. They all knew that they were working beyond the limits of normal science and had implicitly accepted the risks that went with such activity. Nevertheless, he told himself that he would perhaps do well to confront Caramel at some point in private. Time passed. The project moved on, developing a life of its own.

BLUE

Thursday 15 January 2133

"What options do we have?"

Ben-Tovim's question was short and to the point. His gaze fixed the three young security advisers seated opposite him in the sumptuous Mossad briefing room in Yerushalayim. The advisers looked briefly at each other. Despite their clear order of rank it was not going to be easy to decide who would speak first. Would the other two agree with whoever broke the silence first? Michael Ben-Tovim sensed hesitancy, and chose to fix his gaze on one of the three men in front of him. In the event, hesitancy was unnecessary; they had clearly done their work. The man in the gaze coughed.

"One, we could sabotage the Siverek base to stop whatever project they have in mind. Two, we could infiltrate the base to gain a better insight into the intentions of the European Union. Three, we could expose what we know to the Southern Brotherhood and not interfere if their leaders take action. Four, we could continue to monitor developments at the base and see what happens."

"What do you recommend?"

The adviser did not seem taken aback by this forthright invitation. "On a balance of advantage, we should infiltrate the base to obtain more information." Ben-Tovim did not mention the English woman; her face appeared in his mind's eye as he envisaged throwing another "agent" away with no returns. Yet as the adviser expanded his argument, the older man knew there would be no viable alternative.

""We cannot act decisively until we know what is being planned. We do need to pick brains within the base. We agree with the view that a time-travel project is not to be taken seriously, even with the history of our nation being the probable target. We have instigated private enquiries into the matter - it remains in the realms of theory. The only reference we can trace has been to a paper presented to the Forum of World Science's Faraday Conclave in July 2131. A Dr North gave evidence of some early theoretical work being done on the moon, but the project was shut down in early December of the same year. A military strike is much more likely. We could certainly tell the Southern Brotherhood that we suspect a military strike. We suggest we tell them we have the matter in hand and will alert them if a build-up of military hardware looks like taking place. Of course, there remains the possibility that the project's intention may be to our advantage. It would be a pity to sabotage something when we don't know what it is."

Michael Ben-Tovim liked the Machiavellian touch - this was why they paid their advisers so well. He chuckled with sincere appreciation. The summaries seemed to meet his preferences and he nodded his understanding. He brought the meeting to a close, swung his chair round and gazed again onto the eternal views across his Holy City as the advisers left to carry out their work.

Monday 19 January

"Why were we not told of the Atomic Energy Authority's inspection at Siverek base?"

The Southern Brotherhood's Kenyan representative's demeanour was not hostile; he was merely irritated and slightly impatient. He was certain of his facts, confident in his location in the Kenyan Foreign Ministry in Mombasa. He stood with his back to the wide panoramic windows through which a low morning sun was shining strongly. The Israeli Deputy Ambassador's sight was hampered. He squinted uncomfortably.

"There is no Kenyan representation at high levels within the Authority - it is certainly possible that as the official written report is not available yet, widespread awareness of the findings has not reached all parties that might be interested."

The Kenyan pressed his point. "Then here is your opportunity to tell us what you know. On behalf of the Kenyan government I do need to know if dangers to safety have been detected in Turkey."

The diplomatic fudge afforded by the phrase 'dangers to safety' caused the Deputy Ambassador to hesitate. While he could equally generalise in reply, it was uncertain what precisely the other man had meant - either in dangers to Kenya, or to the Southern Brotherhood in wider context, or indeed, what 'safety' implied. He decided it was better not to fudge in return.

"The northern powers' official line is that they are working on a project concerning solar wind dynamics. This is what the official report will confirm. However, there is a minority report that indicates the solar wind approach has not been conclusively proven. It therefore follows that a front may have been established; it may be a cover for something else. My government believes that a military strike of some kind is more likely. However, we do not know the possible target, or even what timescale may be involved."

"I see. Is your government taking steps to protect your nation?"

"I did not specify Israel as the possible target. As I said, we do not know what may be the target. It is possible of course, with Turkish land being the source of this developing plot, but any nation might be the target; your own, for example."

The Deputy Ambassador realised too late the clumsiness of his remark. The Kenyan's flat-sided palm slapped his desk.

"That's exactly my point! Any nation might be the target - like us in Kenya! It is vital that Israel should share all its information with key partners in the southern alliances. We all stand to lose if the northern powers succeed in carrying out whatever it is that they are planning. We don't know how close they are to fruition on their plans and their processes for carrying them out. I suggest you report back to your government that full co-operation at this crucial time is paramount if we are to thwart the northern powers' attempts against us. We need your clear assurance that your country will keep us fully informed. If we see any build-up of military force in Turkey, and you are clearly not countering it, we reserve the right to move into the region ourselves."

The visitor blanched at such a prospect. "I'll do what I can."

The Deputy Ambassador withdrew with as much grace as he could muster after such a grilling. Authorities in Tel Aviv and Yerushalayim would certainly need to think this one through more carefully if diplomatic equilibrium was to be maintained. He scuttled adroitly down the wide marble staircase of the Kenyan state building, and out into the strengthening morning sun.

Tuesday 27 January

It was on a bitterly cold day that the team of clinicians caring for Mary Trent decided she had to be moved from Milton Keynes Memorial Trauma Unit. Birchwood Community was only a few kilometres away. Its reputation as an institution with good long-term results recommended it well. The doctor in charge of the transfer was very caring, but he didn't understand the wild look in his patient's eyes at the sense of the deep snow outside the hospital gates, or the agitation that shook her body as it was lifted into the transfer air ambulance.

Birchwood's calm rhythms wove their soft blanket of predictability round Mary Trent's existence. She was fed by the staff gently and patiently. The soft plasma colour schemes in her rooms metamorphosed on a regular basis round a theme of soft calm blues, adding to the comfort provided by the smells and sounds channelled into her immediate environment. The clinicians knew her case was rare; they spent much time discussing the possible prognoses they could divine. A group of dedicated men and women nursed and befriended their new charge. Mary's eyes never flickered, never flinched, never varied. Drops were administered regularly to maintain moistness. Whatever she was looking at, it seemed to those around her to be far away in space and time.

Monday 30 March

On a warm spring day, with the freshness of the sun shining on early green shoots outside in the gardens, a newly-qualified psychiatrist took up his first residency at Birchwood. At twenty eight, he was some five years younger than the silent woman in the rooms at the end of the corridor. In the quietness of his room his fingers keyed her case notes onto a desk screen in front of him. He began reading Mary Trent's story for the first time.

She had been born in Hunstanton on the Norfolk coast on the first of September 2100. There was a younger half-sister, Susan, now living in Northampton, their mother having died some years before. Susan's father had seemingly never taken kindly to his step-daughter, though colleagues' talks with the younger woman had never got to the bottom of the issue. Both parents were now dead, anyway. Doctors had been loathe to press too strongly for fear of losing any hope of recovering Mary's stability. Of Mary's biological father himself there was no mention on the file.

The psychiatrist sighed, stood thoughtfully, and walked to the window. A shaft of sunlight lit a clump of yellow crocuses on the far edge of the untidy lawn. He smiled, lifted by the sight. He decided to try the new approach to psychiatric discipline. The laissez-faire attitude of the previous two centuries was disappearing. Throughout the second half of the twenty first century, psychiatrists had come to realise that the best way to recover a lost human mind was to treat the person like a human being and walk alongside them. *'Get inside their mind and let it share their own. Humans would always be imperfect, and it would no longer be sufficient to provide treatment as a disinterested professional.'* He decided he would have to think like Mary if he was to help her. He would also have to dig deeper into her past. He left the room to go to sit with his new patient.

Sunday 20 December

Nature took the northern hemisphere by the hand and plunged with it into the bottom of the pit named by humanity as the Winter Solstice. There was little snow this winter on the northern European States. There was just darkness, and with it, the cold. The wide corridors of Birchwood Community lay silent in the pre-holiday changeover of staff numbers. The cold had not penetrated here. The darkness was kept at bay by lights set discreetly into ceiling crevices; lights activated by timers, movement and staffed monitors. The metronome of time in the control centre ticked towards midnight. The middle-aged woman sitting at her console yawned. She was coming to the end of her shift. It would soon be time to depart to share the midwinter festival with her family.

In the suite of rooms at the end of the corridor Mary Trent slept, a relatively-peaceful sleep. Her psychiatrist had visited her the day before, spending time alongside her bedside armchair. She knew he had been there, solid and comforting, though she could not speak or acknowledge his presence, other than by the distinct lessening of tension in her body that told him she felt safe. He had talked for both of them - of the weather, traffic, food, wildlife, colours, clouds and music. Music especially had become a treat for her. Somehow, he had divined from her body language the kinds of music she liked, and it had begun to be softly piped through the audio channels of her rooms. This night her breathing was stable and gentle, until the corridor and room lights were extinguished by the power-cut. The source of the problem would take some days to track down. The immediate effects were of more concern to the Birchwood Community staff. The back-up generator was out of action for regular maintenance, and was not scheduled to be fixed until after the holidays. Torches were not part of the provided equipment for medical staff, nor even for administrators. The extent of the power outage seemed to be limited to the Community itself, as distant street lights could be discerned through the building windows. Nevertheless, in many pockets and corners of the large complex stygian darkness reigned, black soulless blotches of plague pock-marking the site's internal world.

Whether by sound or premonition Mary's mind rose towards consciousness. Within its recesses she sensed the darkness and the stifling fear and shame of the under-stairs cupboard. She knew the door would be locked. At first her child's fingers had tried to open it, rattling the latch with a disappearing modicum of self-worth. Mary now squirmed with increasing panic within her bed, feeling the darkness behind her eyelids. A whimpered cry burst from her throat. She had to open the cupboard door! She couldn't remember having done anything wrong. Fragments of her life spun out of control across her imagination or memory; she couldn't tell which was which. Her body threw itself out of the bedclothes in a desperate attempt to reach the door. The whimpered cry had been heard at the end of the corridor by the staff nurse on duty. Knowing it had come from Mary the woman had felt her way through the faint luminescence towards its source. Mary touched the door, not understanding why she had not felt the coldness of its imprisoning latch. This time the door was not locked. She threw it open and ran with unseeing eyes into the blackness. The nurse caught her up into welcoming female arms. Mary could only call the word 'Mum'. Her body shook, permitting the arms to carry her away to a soft bed.

The word was not repeated, nor followed by any other. Yet the nurse knew that almost a year of silence had been ended. Perhaps the psychiatrist would be able to prise open this tormented mind. He would be back after the holiday. The nurse stroked Mary's wet forehead gently and stayed with her until the rhythm of sleep had re-established itself.

The Year 934 in the Common Era

By early March 2133 the scientific foundations had been laid into the burning Middle-Eastern rocks of the year 1533. The arrival of the month of August saw the project's scientists working even further back in 1233. By early January of 2134, plasma eruptions were disturbing the nomadic tribesmen living in the year 934.

Dr North in his turn arrived at the new far-point never having fully recovered in his constitution from the kicks handed out so generously on the human body at each temporal shift. The past chronological period of ten months' experience had seemed to fly by, with scientific meetings and a monitoring of the progress through the three new stages. Thankfully, no further deaths had occurred in transfer. He had taken an opportunity within a few months of the November tragedy to speak with Caramel Bondi. Some heat had been generated, but little light. Both had stood their ground. He had emphasised the need to be scrupulously detailed over the sharing of all scientific phenomena; for her part, the key element appeared to be that the statistical likelihood of disaster had been so small as to be not worth mentioning. They had ended their conversation with feelings of wariness heightened. Neither had felt inclined to push matters to the point of the plasmologist's departure. North dwelled on the outcome in his mind.

One recommendation from the earlier inquest had been particularly striking in its impact on life in the various bases. In responding to the tragedy, emergency personnel in both 2132 and 1832 had been activated. The complexity of the corridors, hangars and access routes, duplicated on both bases, had caused some confusion and delays. Though clearly these had not had a direct input to the disaster, they would be unforgiveable if an emergency were to occur again. Yet base layouts needed to be almost identical; bulk ordering of supplies and familiarity of surroundings for staff would see to that. While several suggestions were considered for a unique character to be established for each base, the solution chosen for the base administrators and managers had been novel and would not be easily overlooked. A colour scheme was put in place, a different colour for each base. The project would work through the colours of the rainbow.

Pieter North followed an emerald green corridor to his new residential quarters. Busy schedules and demanding pressures bore down on him. He saw Felixana Smith along an office corridor one day, his passion erupting again like a re-opened wound. She acknowledged him, but he sorely wanted more. Evenings were spent in mournful reflective solitude, exhausted as he was, on low hills on the outskirts of the base, wrapped against the desert chill, gazing at the sunsets until he thought he would go blind, watching the colours shift from bright orange, through blood red to deep plum as the scrubland sands and rocks reflected the dying light again and again. It was hard for him to imagine the year that this was taking place, but easier to realise and recognise the absence of pollution in the environment. It occurred to him there must be many thousands of species of plants and animals out there in the vastness of the world. Perhaps not

237

so many in the semi-arid desert lands of the Middle East - were there still lions by this time lurking in mountain caves? He recalled from his childhood stories of lions in the deserts of Syria and Jordan at the time the Christian Bible was being written. Still, thousands of kilometres away on the un-drained and wild shores of the North Sea and the Dutch coast, there would surely be many huge shoals of fish, awaiting their extinction by the fishing fleets a thousand years later.

He tossed a stone in mild exasperation and watched it bounce down the rocky slope. All that effort and pain and cost and endeavour! They were still only halfway to their final destination, wherever that might be. How on earth could they ensure that they would arrive at a crucial time to expose the key points of Christianity? Would they go back a few years more by fine-tuning the power outputs on the lattices, and then go forward again? But surely outside the complexity of a time-travel base they could only move forward at 'normal' speed, as it were? The whole project was chunky and clumsy; if only they could build a machine that was portable without the huge umbilical infrastructure that supported their present puny efforts. But that was beyond science at the moment - they were nowhere near that. He would spend many evening through January going over such meanderings in his mind, as he tramped the lonely dusty hills around the base. Once in a while his thoughts would turn with a sense of irritation and anger to Simon Atkins and his control over the project.

For his part, also within the 934 base, the South African was just as busy and pre-occupied as the Dutch scientist, perhaps more so as there seemed to be so many imponderables to juggle in keeping security tight. All new members of staff were vetted by him; he began to develop a paranoia that infiltration of spies and subversives was occurring on a regular and increasing basis. The inspection and the high global power of its authors had unnerved him. What if they would try again? Yet all was so quiet and the scientists seemed to be making progress. He had continued lovemaking with the English journalist. She seemed attached to the physical side of their relationship. Gradually, they learned more about each other's personal lives. They talked of many things, but their sharing of confidences always returned to recollections of their respective childhoods. The unravelling of a shared historical reality was somehow reinforcing their individual perceptions of their unique past experiences. Simon recalled his mother's religious grounding, unable to understand how and why she had chosen to remain a woman of faith after experiencing such a childhood where wealth and security had been ripped away by others. He spoke of 'the importance of trusting one's own instincts'. Felixana in turn recounted how her father had been ripped away by death when she was still only the tender age of ten. She spoke of how Craig Landon had become almost a father-figure to her. Was there, she wondered, a chance to relive her recent past and regain his reality?

Simon found the subject of lives being ripped away violently was somehow discomforting to him. His nightmares had returned, haunting him with their intensity. Pulling himself back to the daily security duties was becoming particularly difficult after a night of his dreaming fantasies. The sensation of falling was no longer from a sea wall onto a beach, but from a hillside into bushes - sharp, pointed, prickly bushes. He would no longer wake after the first such tumble, but instead his rag-doll body would turn and twist and roll further down the imaginary slopes, cutting him further on more bushes. In his wakened state, he could distinctly recall the deep scratches being caused to his forehead and temples, yet on touching his head in fearful recollection after awakening, there was only perspiration.

Felixana Smith had thrown herself into her presentational role. She had persuaded Atkins, and through him his political masters, that a film crew would need an anchor, a presenter, a front person. In reality, the work ahead would need publicising and revealing to maximum effect. She was gathering round herself a team of film-makers. They were already developing techniques for showing the time-travel processes themselves and the wildlife fauna and flora of the centuries through which they were passing. While security concerns in one sense were diminishing - a community twelve hundred years from home would find it impossible to leak information - travel off-base was becoming increasingly frequent. The bases were surrounded by deserted scrubland and arid hillsides. Interference with local customs and peoples was becoming less and less likely. Pieter North had told her of the cardinal rule from science fantasy that interference with a time-zone different from your own was to be frowned on, but in reality it was turning out to be quite innocuous. Treading on an ant or worm in 934 was not going to cause an earthquake or landslide in 2134, no matter what the theorists might say. As for the assertion by twentieth-century theoretical physicists that 'the absence of time tourists proves that time-travel cannot exist', it just didn't stack up with real events. One could meet tens of thousands of individuals on the streets of 1834, 1934 or 2134 and never really know from which century they came. Individualism had become increasingly bizarre and there really was no accounting for taste. There remained for Felixana one unsolved problem. Ideally, she would need to find a way of streaming transmissions directly from ancient Palestine to twenty-second century Europe. She would need her former colleague Paul Devine for that. For all their inner turmoil and uncertainty, of whatever nature, the spring months of the year 934 allowed the players in the on-going saga to proceed with their respective priorities with a general sense of calm and order - until the evening in March when a nomadic band of thugs made its presence felt.

Four scientists were set upon in a shallow valley some two kilometres from the desalination units. Three had been killed before the fourth managed to convey a signal to the base. He, too, was found dead twenty minutes later when a hover-car and four armed personnel sped over the scrub to investigate. Major recriminations and worry ensued, accompanied by a welter of questions. How many attackers had appeared? Where had they disappeared to? What protection was now needed? The four bodies had been stripped of clothing and possessions - all had been male, but what would the attackers have done had a female been with them? Turmoil in the base and across the centuries to the other bases led to an increasingly military involvement of personnel and equipment. Bases and facilities needed guarding. Staff would not be allowed out of base during hours of darkness. Travel alone, even within sight of the bases, would be discouraged.

One effect that took some time to become clearer was that the economic costs of the enterprise began to mount significantly. Military spending was added to the scientific budgets in ever-increasing amounts. The timetable for the whole project slowed down. Individual patterns of daily life around the bases were disrupted. Pieter North's reflective strolls in the hills were curtailed. Felixana Smith was compelled to build excuses for soldiers and weapons into her early drafts of press release preparations. Simon Atkins' sole control of security was being compromised by his having to justify surveillance to military officers both on and off the bases.

Throughout May and June 934 forays of armed personnel set out from the Siverek base into the surrounding hills and scrub to search out the attacking band of nomads. Hampered by summer heat and not knowing how to read the local terrain, there was little hope of success. Flocks of goats were encountered, but of their human guardians there was barely a trace. Evidence of camp fires in isolated hill caves and animal bone meal relics were all that was revealed. Townships and village settlements were many tens of kilometres away. The Siverek base was not disturbed by a larger incursion of humanity. In an age of myth and superstition, local people would not venture into the hills to interfere with the unknown devils who could conjure explosions and booming sounds from thin air.

Across the empty expanses of the dark-age middle-east, twenty second century humans and tenth century humans circled each other's existence warily without a major conflict appearing. The mood of the project had undergone a sea-change with implications for whatever was to follow. It was a darker mood that now coloured events as the tunnel plunged deeper.

Friday 9 July 2134

"How often did you feel you had done something wrong, Mary?"

The psychiatrist's voice was soft, almost melodic in its timbre. It had become a friend and confidante over past months. The warmth of the sun in the Birchwood Community's gardens matched the warmth she felt towards her constant companion's deep wisdom. She sat of her own volition on reaching a wooden bench, its curled side arms mimicking the safety she was increasingly experiencing. She gazed at the wealth of colour in the flower-beds; salmon-coloured roses in their clipped regimen jostling with the exuberance of a giant buddleia peppered with butterflies.

"Often."

The man was used to mono-syllabic responses. Mary had only really strung words together quite recently, and even single words had taken many weeks to appear. He waited patiently. Mary turned her face towards his, the sun causing her to squint. She put a hand up to shade her eyes.

"The door was locked."

The psychiatrist took her hand. Mary had grown content with that. It did not cause her to flinch. He had not yet been able to learn who had been responsible for locking her into the under-stairs cupboard as a child. Would today be the day? Mary's revelation took another direction.

"I tried to fight the darkness with a rainbow."

The man's attention focused with a jolt.

"I remembered the brightness of a rainbow", Mary continued. "It gave me comfort."

It was enough revelation for one day. He gave her encouragement by reciting a poem. Those specific colours had been placed by Nature in their

241

particular order for a special purpose. By the time the sun fell below the line of birch trees beyond the far end of the lawn, Mary Trent had learned the poem by heart.

25 December 634

Preparations for the Midwinter Festival had culminated in the arrival of the day itself. Sufficient numbers of personnel had arrived in the new base for there to be a lusty and noisy set of celebrations. Plastic, bio-degradable baubles hung in main mess halls and corridors; denizens of the far north were incongruous in the relative heat of the Turkish desert hill areas - reindeer, snowmen, coaches and horses, snowflakes; a Dickensian feast of long-lost mythology. Equally strange were the costumes that many of the revellers were sporting. White beards and voluminous red cloaks and coats, strapped with glistening black belts on the men, and feathery-white fairy dresses for the women. Alcoholic drinks had somehow found their way down-time, none the worse for their journey. The word 'Christmas' had disappeared almost completely from regular usage within the English language over the course of the second half of the twenty-first century. The progressive and widespread growth of commercial and economic secularism had finally permitted humanism to triumph over religious faith in much of the northern half of the planet. Faith, belief and morality had been purged from the lexicons of many legal systems. Midwinter festivities no longer made reference to virgin births or cattle in stables. The former pagan significance of returning sunlight after the winter solstice now held full sway - echoes of Viking Valhalla were just good boisterous fun, and an ideal opportunity to indulge in casual sex.

Pieter North had sex in his nostrils, too. His longing for Felixana Smith had not abated in the past few hectic months. In fact, it had grown again, reaching new heights of desire and confusion. He had heard a rumour that she had slept with the security chief Atkins, but he preferred to ignore it. It was surely just tittle-tattle, anyway; no-one could know for sure who slept with whom these days. The Dutchman leaned unsteadily on a corner of a long buffet table loaded with food. He had only drunk a couple of glasses of wine, but with precious little food in his stomach, and four hard days of scientific work behind him to add to his tiredness, the effects of the alcohol were beginning to take their insidious toll. The large crowded room began to turn slowly and pleasantly to his perception. He felt a pang of warm humanity towards his fellow party-goers. Then he noticed the BBC girl at the far end of the table and his mood saddened.

242

Would he really stand a chance with her? Could he succeed? He tried to calculate the difference in their ages, but in his present state he gave up without coming to a conclusion. *'It wouldn't matter'* he told himself. *'She'll fall for my maturity and deep sincerity.'* Did he mean 'deep' or 'desperate'? A wicked voice was whispering inside his head and he pushed it aside roughly. No, it was definitely 'deep'.

He glanced around the crowd of people chattering, walking and jostling merrily throughout the hangar. There was no sign of Atkins anywhere. *'Good, I can make a move'* he decided. He walked with as much steadiness and confidence as he could muster towards Felixana. As he weaved through the revellers, he didn't notice a couple of them speak his name in social chatty introduction. He remained focussed on his target, dressed provocatively in electric blue with touches of white edging on the top and bottom of her tight dress. A deep breath, a few final, remarkably steady steps, and he was standing in front of her. The aroma of the woman washed upon him.

"Hello". His voice was firm and steady, but it didn't seem as if it belonged to him at all. Perhaps he was listening to a recording as if it came from some other source. He switched on a smile, hoping to dovetail his expressions to the soundtrack of the voice he was hearing.

"Hello, Doctor North." Her response was warm; remarkably so, perhaps, he thought. She returned his smile.

Emboldened by the early progress he looked around the room at the assembled guests, seeking to develop his next moves while trying to give the impression that his approach had been purely accidental. A business angle might well do it.

"I've been meaning to have another, longer, talk with you since we looked round the cargo TTUs together. It's just that the past few months have been very busy, and then of course the inspection visit threw everyone. Many of us have been recovering ever since."

"I understand, of course." She wished he would get to the point, but perhaps all along she really knew. A bout of raucous laughter nearby caused them both to jump. North moved his right hand to cup the girl's left elbow and steer her away to a quieter corner.

"Could we speak somewhere much quieter, please? I'm finding the noise a bit disconcerting."

The BBC woman felt confirmed in her view of his intentions, but decided to go along with the conversation anyway, at least for a little while. She allowed him to move them both to the end of the hangar and through an outside door into the relative quietness of a connecting corridor. A few members of the on-duty personnel were disappearing round a far corner - then the two of them were alone.

Pieter North cupped both of the woman's elbows and turned her to face him. His voice came with clear intensity. "Felixana, I do want to get to know you better, and not be just a distant scientist! I've wanted to know you for so long; to have you fond of me too!"

She squirmed inside. His desperate sincerity was only too obvious, but she was aghast at the situation. Surely she wasn't in a position to return the affection, yet brusquely to push him away might make things even more complicated for her. Blushing wildly, she could only stutter a response.

"Doctor North....Pieter....I don't know what to say. Surely we shouldn't behave like this in public."

Perhaps the use of his first name would soften the blow, the reminder of the public location stopping him in his tracks, while her use of the word 'we' might tie him in to her embarrassment sufficiently strongly to make him think he was not being rejected. She certainly had to play for time. His hesitation made her believe she had succeeded and she almost tugged him back to the main hangar's entrance door. Breathlessly, she spoke out.

"Please, Pieter; let it rest! I like you but I cannot do more!" Then she was gone back into the milling crowd, leaving only her perfume in his memory as he stood alone in the corridor. He walked like a zombie back to his personal quarters. Perhaps there was, after all, a comforting feeling that he was destined never to know true intimate love like other people. He had his science, his chance to be recognised into immortality by the enormity of the project, and it would keep things simple to be a rejected loner. He wouldn't have to make the continuous effort to woo her, or be faithful to her, or to get so involved that his own personality might be submerged into her own. *'Well,'* he thought, *'if that is how it must be for the rest of my life, so be it. No-one has ever really loved me, I know that. I can never know the gold of success, merely the silver of always coming second.'*

The level of personal bitterness welled up gently but firmly into his consciousness. *If she doesn't want me, then she may not prosper. I must see to it*

that I am the one who comes out of this affair well on top of the situation. This BBC woman must come to recognise that she should have loved me, and only me, all along.'
He fell onto his bed with an audible sigh, and then quite inexplicably, tears came pouring from his eyes. Equally as inexplicably, within twenty minutes he was asleep.

27 December 634

The main conference room was completely empty as Simon Atkins entered. His footsteps on the wooden floor tiles echoed into the vaulted ceiling. He made his way to the podium, laying the small sheaf of papers in his hands onto the presentational dais. The security briefing would still be over an hour away yet, but he was a great believer in preparedness. *The stone you leave unturned will be the one that trips you'*, he had learned from a former colleague. The project was moving rapidly towards its later stages; new personnel would be arriving soon in readiness for fanning out south across Palestine. The security aspects of their work would need to be properly addressed. A twinge of irritation reminded him that they still needed that damn Dutchman and his senior team members in order to keep the temporal lattices stable with so many three-hundred-year stages built into the time-tunnel system.

Atkins studied the papers before him in order, seeking to marshal thoughts and priorities that might best focus the attention of his upcoming audience. He barely noticed the door at the far end of the auditorium open and the figure enter. As Pieter North came into sharper focus the South African was instantly alert. His face barely registered an emotion of any kind, but what there was stemmed from suspicion. A veneer of efficient calm and civility smoothed his response to the scientist's appearance.

"Ah, Doctor North, what can I do for you?"

The Dutchman continued walking until he stopped at the base of the podium. He regretted that the security chief's position above him accentuated the indefinable sense of inferiority and weakness he felt. Nevertheless, he plunged in.

"Don't you think the work that English girl has to do should be left undisturbed by your attentions?"

Strangely to Atkins' perceptions, it was the derogatory and dismissive description of Felixana as 'that English girl' that irritated him the most. He told himself later that perhaps he was letting alien emotions under his skin. At the time, he was stung into a sharp reply.

"What business is that of yours?"

North stuck to his scientific role, emphasising his major credentials and stressing what advantages he could over the other man. Neither was prepared to admit that it seemed to them to be a stand-off between males, a throw-back at a more basic level to a primitive fight over mating rights, something that had been coursing through human DNA for countless thousands of years. The Dutchman bristled. His voice became brittle and the intonation of his words clipped and precise.

"It becomes my business when the success of the whole scientific enterprise is thrown into question because the publicity and media presentation is clumsily handled. The work done with BBC skills will not be completed on time if you take her attention off her duties."

"What duties? What the hell are you talking about? Felixana has no duties other than to her own destiny. The work she does, the work any of us do, is always secondary to finding her own way on her own terms and to her own desires. She does what she wants to do and that is all there is to it." Atkins felt himself flushing. Why did it matter to him that he should defend her? And to even use her name! Perhaps it was just the natural defence-mechanism of a security officer to go on the offensive once the first thrust had been parried, but he found himself adding

"You should concentrate on making the step-back process stable and not subject to fluctuation. You know the fatality that occurred was due directly to unstable influences in the main power lattice. I read the weekly reports on the temporal steps. I know that after this number of jumps, some of your own colleagues are questioning the safety levels. Stick to your own area of work, Doctor, and leave your pathetic sex-urge out of it!"

It was the Dutchman's turn to be stung, having his motives questioned in this seemingly-sordid way. "It's not a question of sex! Someone has to treat the girl as a person. We are not all like you, Mr Atkins, thinking that you are extra-important if you can spend your time scrabbling around in a woman's sewers!"

The insult burnt deeply into the man on the podium. He pushed roughly at the unfixed pedestal. It spun down onto North below, who was unable to avoid the heavy plastic and metal structure entirely. It caught him a glancing blow to his left shoulder as it crashed past, spinning his body off-balance and to the floor. The noise was probably more unnerving than the physical assault. The South African walked angrily from the auditorium, leaving his 'opponent' dazed and extremely shaken. It took North a full two minutes to come around sufficiently to stagger to his feet and leave himself. The next encounter between the two men, while being coloured by these events, would take place under entirely different circumstances.

4 January 335

The rainbow sequence had reached indigo. The colour could have created a gloomy atmosphere, but with several different perceptions around over precisely what shade of dark purple-plum the colour indigo really constituted, the overall effect was strangely chaotic. Yet that merely replaced gloomy with unnerving, as if sharp pointed shadows of a slightly darker or lighter shade of the primary one chosen stabbed at random through the corridors of the newly-built base.

Progress towards the final time-zone was reaching the point where palpable changes were occurring. New scientific disciplines were appearing on base - languages not heard before were overheard in social and eating areas, as new arrivals and old-hands alike tried out the Western Aramaic, Greek and Latin dialects they were learning. Men and women conversed nervously, earnestly and excitedly over topics unknown to base regulars. The pace of movement seemed to quicken as if unseen deadlines were conducting a new, larger orchestral work. North and his immediate group of temporal physicists began to sense that their control over the project was somehow slipping from their grasp. The concept of three-hundred-year jumps was clearly now firmly established, though stability levels were not fully stable on every occasion. Pieter North's memory was haunted by the accusations from Atkins over safety concerns; he kept an ear out for troubles in the ranks, though none came. The three-century limit was no nearer being understood. Continual testing of radioactive decay levels was being maintained, with the same results.

In the six weeks since his encounter with the South African in the auditorium he had thankfully been afforded few, if any, real opportunities to interface with him. He felt strangely embarrassed, as if he had known he had overstepped an invisible mark. All the same, just dwelling on his adoration of Felixana Smith made him burn with longing. His latent envy of the security man's sexual knowledge of her wonderful body would well up inside his being and make him bitter again. He continued to swing between two extremes of bitterness and sad resignation. It plagued his waking and sleeping hours.

12 January 335

For his part, Simon Atkins found that his demons continued to work on him, relentlessly by night and now increasingly so by day. The nightmares that had shared his darkness hours were becoming more realistic and painful, giving him uncomfortable twinges during the hours of wakefulness. The falling from walls or trees, the skewering of his palms or wrists, the slicing of fence poles or flag poles into his side, the pricking of bristly plants across his scalp - all these were tangible memories while he went about his day-time duties of security and personnel clearance. As to their origin or purpose, he knew not, but he felt the death of the Englishman, Forbes, preying on his mind, on the part of him that other, less worldly-wise people to his way of thinking might once have called a conscience. He would never have considered he possessed anything like a conscience. He had always conducted his professional and personal lives according to a simple, three-part dictum. He called it, mockingly perhaps, his holy trinity - *'I want it all, I want it now, and I don't care who I hurt to get it.'* It was a brutal world - his mother's experience had proved it.

Despite the murky, violent world in which security officers worked, up until that day on Pichot Base in America, Atkins had never even come close to murdering anyone. Yes, he had destroyed lives and careers, self-esteem and sense of worth, dreams and ambitions. He had even resorted to blackmail, while plain theft had been a thread through his life for years, but he had never snuffed out a living presence, at least not to his knowledge. Now he was a murderer, though the trail of evidence had been well covered. It was unlikely that he would ever be found out. No other person had access to the clues against him. He had control of the bases and could erase clues at will. Yet somehow he didn't feel safe, as if by some means or other he would be brought to a type of justice. No, it seemed more than that; as if he wanted to be brought to face his actions. The lessening of focus was beginning to affect his concentration and he knew that mistakes and omissions were slipping into his work. The face of the English woman would swim before his mind's eye. What would she think of him if she knew? He continued to swing between two extremes of safety and guilt. It plagued his waking and sleeping hours.

22 January 335

Felixana Smith, in contrast to the two men who fixated on her and whose thoughts revolved round her, was concentrating well on the tasks she knew she had to carry through. How and when might she find the opportunity to let Michael Ben-Tovim know of the project that now seemed to reach out towards a conclusion? She could scarcely believe the enormity of it herself. Unlike the technicians and other scientists for whom it was a challenge to be faced and achieved, her own lay status meant that her reflections on what was happening were surrounded by doubts and questions, uncertainties and fears. She told herself she had to set such conundrums aside and press ahead with seeking out an opportunity to get a coherent message to the Israelis.

The sudden thought occurred to her that, even if successful, they might not believe her. That was a chance she had to take, and its implications would be beyond her in any case. It was likely, surely, that they would take seriously any word that she might manage to pass on in such a dangerous and complicated set of circumstances. She also knew she needed to contact her former BBC colleague, Paul Devine. His stout and florid appearance came into her mind, and it buoyed her spirits. He was a master holographic professional, much more accomplished than anyone the Union had provided for her. Paul's skills would be essential in devising a technique for transmitting an unbroken stream from Palestine to the twenty-second century. A live feed would be impossible, but with a twenty- four hour delay, things could be different. Paul could surely find a way to ensure that holographic disks could retain their scientific integrity on transference through more than one TTU system without breaking up.

Paul's brother, John, would believe her story and she had to contact him in Norwich. She knew her task would be useless unless she returned to the main base in 2135. Israel had not existed in its modern form before the late 1940s in any case. The thought of agents scouring through Victorian-age newspapers for cryptic enigmas was ludicrous. Why should they, anyway? The existence of the concept of a time-travel project was not known to Ben-Tovim or his associates.

She would need to log an acceptable reason for moving between time-zones. That should be relatively straightforward; she could piece together a case for ensuring that personnel at all stages in the tunnel were properly briefed on the cover story that was still in the process of development. *'Goodness knows, it's complicated and overlapping enough in its layers to demand some pre-digestion.'* She would also have to take a decision on whether or not to try to move off-base once 'home'. Now, that would be extremely chancy. Off-base visits were approved and monitored by Atkins himself. Off-base communications might be easier. Despite the number and frequency of such high-level security traffic, it seemed the man always took a personal role in their clearance. Such an obsession with control! Yet she knew the pressures he was working under; despite trying in a sincere way to get under his guard, something darker and tormenting seemed to be working on him. No matter, that was perhaps the weakest link in the chain, she felt - his tiredness. With a forced error on his part, she might be able to manipulate more junior staff. She was more confident about her chances with other disciplines such as communications. Her senior clearance itself should ensure that she could get herself where and when she needed to be. It just required the right stratagem and sufficient self-confidence. Yet she struggled with an indefinable tug on her resolve that she must do it without endangering the man's safety. She couldn't understand the tussle within her on the matter.

26 January 335

Simon Atkins slept peacefully. The nightmares of the past nights had thankfully left him alone for once. The last few had indeed been awful - as much blood as he could stomach, blood he could almost smell as well as see, body organs spilling out of torn cavities to cascade in rippling horror to the dusty ground, a pulsing heart that died with each burst of convulsion. Why was it that he dreamed in colour with a vividness that stayed with him as a strong lingering memory for some time after he had awakened? The memory of the murder he had committed was weighing more heavily on his mind. It fed the night-time experiences and they in turn fed the guilt. The tiredness had indeed infected the efficiency level of his checking procedures, but he was sure what few mistakes and omissions there had been had not, and would not, affect the overall effectiveness of the project's march towards completion.

Yet the tiredness that had touched his mind and concentration did not for another satisfying hour affect his body. Drained of tension by lovemaking, his breathing had settled into a deep rhythm. He did not stir when the woman beside him on the bed rose quietly, pulled on her blue underwear and slipped soundlessly towards his computer console. A handful of such intimate occasions had been all that was necessary for Felixana to learn the South African's passwords and entry protocols. In the semi-darkness, fingers that had expertly coaxed the man only an hour before, now just as expertly ghosted over the thin dark keyboard to coax a personal transfer permit back to 2135, with off-base communication clearance. Then with a final deft touch she erased the source of the data request. Satisfied with her work, she left the sleeper's quarters and returned to her own. The early morning shift patterns were not yet beginning as the first fingers of dawn brushed the palette of the eastern Turkish sky.

SUFFER, LITTLE CHILDREN

INDIGO

Saturday 29 January 2135

Michael Ben-Tovim paced his office with his habitual rhythm, but his thoughts were far from the calm ordered structure that his paces might have indicated to an onlooker. He stopped abruptly and gazed through the panoramic picture windows onto the scene below. Tel-Aviv sparkled in the late winter sunshine. From his rooms atop the seventeenth floor of the Mossad building masquerading as an ordinary office block he could see the white horses on the waves of the blue Mediterranean Sea, the wake of a luxury private motor yacht and the ordered flow of hover-vehicles along the waterfront.

Yet his consciousness registered nothing of the beauty laid out there. He needed to grip the information passed to him. It had been received late the previous evening on his private wavelength from nearby in the Middle East, and rapidly confirmed as coming from the Base at Siverek. Three years of wondering what was going on in the Turkish base controlled by the northern powers had now come to a new moment. The message had given the call sign agreed with the BBC woman, long since given up as lost by the Israeli. The message had been clear and unambiguous. Yet the adherent to Judaism was in turmoil. His immediate team of advisers had shared his scepticism about time-travel. Yes, there was a line around that it had been possible across nanoseconds. His scientific advisers had found references to an obscure conference in July 2131 in Los Angeles given by a Dutchman named North. No references thereafter could be found. He had also been told stories going back over a hundred years to the first days of the hadron collider in Switzerland, when silly reports had emerged that time-travel had itself thwarted those early attempts to isolate the uncharted boson.

Now matters had taken on a new urgency. Passing on the detail about the Turkish centre of operations was not the problem; Israeli intelligence, and indeed the Southern Brotherhood itself now, knew full well about a Middle Eastern connection. A military strike somewhere would have been easily countered. Indeed, a great part of the delay and uncertainty engendered over the past three years stemmed from the simple fact that no discernible armed force was being built up across Turkey. Ben-Tovim felt sick. If only he had taken the clandestine report from the Nigerian agent more seriously that December. If only he had not focussed entirely on the implications for the Holocaust. The new information from Ms Smith was astounding, totally unexpected and seemingly impossible to counter in any meaningful way. Yet if it were true, and if it were to succeed in some measure, that would indeed be a destroyer of nations and alliances. The intention as transmitted was clear; the northern powers would take unspecified steps towards giving the world proof that the basic tenets of Christianity were a fictitious concoction of ancient imperial powers and gullible simpletons stemming from a period more than two thousand years before the present day.

Michael Ben-Tovim reflected on the world's recent past. The industrialised nations, and their far-eastern successors, had long since either given up, or never adopted, religious observance as a foundation of society. In contrast, since the end of the twentieth century, African, South American, Caribbean and unaligned countries had witnessed a growth in evangelical, Pentecostal and new age Christianity. It had been a growth over which the Orthodox and Catholic Church authorities had very little influence and absolutely no control. Organised religion had been watered down in terms of faith and doctrine. Ben-Tovim reflected that it hadn't just been happening in Christianity, where gender and sexuality issues had grown in importance. In the Moslem world, too, a mainstream tendency to disown radicalism had resulted in its own diluting end-results, where consumerism could grow unchecked to compete with western and oriental predecessors. Holy people of all faith persuasions were becoming scarcer. Islamic followings in the twenty first century, at first mainly linked to fossil fuel supplies, had been stopped in their tracks by the anti-religious power of the corporate bodies of Chinese communism as they exploited raw material contracts throughout the world. Older industrial nations no longer had the political will to impose the disciplines of a religion on individuals for whom increasing consumerism was now itself a state religion. Ben-Tovim mused that the destruction of the cult of Christianity as a fact of the past would be a devastating blow to the third world and its emerging nations.

The World States Council's 2131 Edict to begin a march towards global realignment of finance had indeed set off powerful reactions. These

253

southern alliances based their hope for the future on Christianity. A body blow such as that being prepared would swing votes back in favour of the northern world. Its financial hegemony would be restored, from Baltimore to Beijing. Ben-Tovim seemed satisfied. And yet......and yet; surely to a Jew the destruction of Christianity was just as important to a true believer as it was useful to the northern alliances. Why, in that case, should he and his country maintain this link with the Southern Brotherhood? Why should they continue to work with African and South American nations? This project in Turkey might work to Israel's advantage. If control of the world's financial institutions returned to Anglo-Saxon, Russian and Chinese centres of power, along with their sovereign wealth fund associates, surely Israel would find comfort in that arrangement? After all, the Jewish State had successfully manipulated the northern powers and their public opinion since the middle of the twentieth century. Whether it had been guilt over Nazi atrocities or something much deeper and more ancient, didn't really matter. The fact was that it had been easy to control western and northern opinion and keep it pliant to Israeli wishes. Yes, the Jewish State had done it before and it could do it again. Whether the message coming from Ms Smith could be believed or not, there were tangible advantages in Israel disentangling itself from its association with the Southern Brotherhood.

The diplomat smiled. Once again, his eyes focussed on the scene outside his window. The sun sparkled off the blue Mediterranean Sea. Hover-yachts smoothly crossed its surface, their down-thrusts sending the wavelets billowing outwards like shoals of flying fishes. Container tankers lay at anchor beyond the ring of artificial reefs that had been part of the security legacy laid down in the 2050s following the creation of the independent Palestinian nation. Ben-Tovim's thoughts and resolve hardened as the chain of connections moved on in his mind's eye. It was in Israel's nature to feel threatened and alone in the world. No-one would come to the defence of the Chosen Tribes if they did not defend themselves. Since the creation of their modern homeland nearly two hundred years ago now, their destiny had been in their own hands; two centuries of hard struggle to maintain, expand and nurture their settlements, and to grow to the point where they could geographically accommodate true believers from whatever part of the globe they wanted to come.

So, the starting-point would be the seeking of acceptance by the supreme internal power system of the policy that, whatever Israel decided to do, it would proceed in isolation from the Southern Brotherhood and without sharing the main secret of whatever purpose transpired to come from the Siverek connection. He would also need to enlist the support of Israel's senior scientists. Why had they not cracked this scientific problem first? Why had no Israeli scientists to his knowledge been involved in the work of the northern alliances? More importantly, if this was truly turning into a mission with a clear religious intention, where were the Jewish faith experts and what were they doing? He would need to check the universities and synagogue centres of power. The northern alliances would have needed to build up an impressive knowledge of biblical times in readiness for any kind of activity in the Christians' first century; how, where, when and from whom had they sought and obtained the detail they would have needed?

So, how should Israel become involved? Michael Ben-Tovim sighed. He conceded this was all predicated on the assumption that it was not all a stunt to deceive public opinion. The status quo was clearly not an option to be seriously considered. If it were not a stunt, but in deadly earnest, it might be unsatisfactory for the northern alliances to manipulate the situation to the point where they could decide what belief system was to replace Christianity. If Christianity could fall, the Americans and Europeans in particular might feel emboldened enough to try to belittle Judaism. Then Israel would be back on the full defensive again. Indeed, it could be worse. In the post-Christianity turmoil, other world faith systems might begin to crumble and all nations could turn on the small true believer lying exposed at the eastern end of the Mediterranean Sea.

The diplomat realised there was much to be done. Yet for a further twenty four hours he was helpless. There had been so many delays already, but he would have to wait for Shabbat to be over. Outside, a solitary seagull whirled around in an air current like an abandoned handkerchief to be carried away on wide wings towards the welcoming sparkling expanse where blue sea and blue sky merged to the vision.

***

While Tel-Aviv sparkled in its late winter sunshine, Norwich International Airport shivered under a gloomy leaden English sky in which indigo storm clouds threatened rain. While Michael Ben-Tovim's actions were being delayed by the Sabbath, John Devine's day was proceeding on time. He was happy. The slim luggage at his side contained ancient maps, lightweight cotton clothes and a swimming costume - he was off to Morocco! His retina scan completed, he moved through the security portal and on to the boarding gate. He checked the time on an overhead gantry - 14.15 hours. The flight to Paris to connect with an onward journey to North Africa would be on time.

As the Airbus 930 lifted its passengers into the bright blue heaven above the low cloud base the cartographer could barely contain his enthusiasm for what lay ahead. Maps of Tudor England indicating ancient woodland and the proposed sequence of their felling for the nation's warships would be of great interest to his international colleagues. The maps he carried had been found in a large country mansion in the County of Warwickshire and would be on show for the first time. On a casual enquiry from a fellow passenger he had gushed into speech. He had been accepted to present a paper to the International Conference on the History of Cartography, to be held from Monday 31 January to Saturday 12 February in the Moroccan city of Marrakech - the Red City, as he explained to his female listener. She also learned that these conferences were biennial affairs, and the 2135 event would be marking the one hundred and fiftieth anniversary of a successful conference held in the Canadian city of Ottawa in 1985. Certainly, the short journey to Paris was proving very exciting. As he pointed out, in addition to the professional days ahead, there was the wonderful prospect of exchanging the English winter for a mild fortnight in the foothills of the Atlas Mountains and on the edges of the Sahara Desert.

Many kilometres behind him, in apartment G7 of the Blakeney Apartments, the hologram receiver winked into life. The recorded message from Felixana Smith, intense and detailed, appeared in the apartment. Though it had been sent late the previous evening, as with standard holographic transmissions it would be processed and dispatched the following day. The message played to a room without its intended audience. The hologram receiver worked properly. It recorded the message and stored it until such time as John Devine chose to access it by remote receiver. The bug in the furniture worked properly. It recorded the message and stored it until such time as the Southern Brotherhood chose to access it by remote receiver.

Wednesday 2 February

The afternoon's presentation had been a success. John Devine had been elated; some international fame at last and in such a luxurious setting! Some celebratory slaps on the back, enthusiastic laughter, and then a burgundy-clad member of the hotel staff walked across the bar-room.

"Monsieur Devine, a message for you received today from your English forwarding service - marked as urgent - could you take it in our hologram room? Just come over this way, Monsieur."

Twenty five minutes later and his need had shifted from champagne to brandy, a large one. Despite the late hour, he knew he could not sleep; so many questions buzzed in his head. He was still in shock at having seen Felixana. How long had it been? He remembered the day in May, two and a half years before, when she had made a hurried departure for Oklahoma on the instructions of the Israelis. 'A short window of opportunity', she had said. Then - nothing. He'd assumed she must be dead, or at least captured and held by the Americans. He knew very little, had learned nothing else and almost forgotten everything. It had been so long.

He had thought about her, clearly. He had thought about her a lot, though perhaps he should be grateful that he had not been sucked into what might have been a murky global maelstrom. It had all gone dead. He had heard nothing from the BBC, for whom his brother still worked, and the State authorities had not contacted him. Even the Israelis had left him alone, and he had no idea how to contact Ben-Tovim. He had tried to maintain an interest for a while. The message from Felixana had mentioned Turkey. He recalled that some six months after her disappearance he had heard on the news that atomic energy inspectors had visited a secret base at a place called Siverek in Turkey. Now after all this time, she appears from this place called Siverek with an impossible story, a desperate plea, and a call for his involvement just when his cartography dreams had come true. Bloody lousy timing! And he was asked to contact Paul. His body shuddered, only partly caused by the cool February night air coming off the mountains onto his hotel balcony. What should he do? He was still agonising as the call to prayer sang out over the rooftops touched by morning light.

Thursday 3 February

The dusty outdoor tables of the Café Izmir were just being cleaned as he ordered a coffee. He checked his watch - 10:15 hours. He supposed he really ought to go to the conference venue again this morning to build on his triumph, but just yet he couldn't. He was tired, for one thing; best to stay away for a few hours. He decided that to attend might do more harm than good. He was still struggling with the plea to contact his brother. It suddenly occurred to him there was no way he himself could get back in touch with Felixana. Her request just hung in the air, with the implicit expectation of her trust and his compliance.

He took possession of his coffee - no pressure to pay for it, the waiter just went inside again. The morning warmth was slowly building. He guessed the temperature would reach about nineteen degrees today, perhaps a little more. He squinted up at the snow caps of the High Atlas - such a spectacular sight to the north of the city. It all seemed so normal today, while in his mind the turmoil was thrashing round. He thought back to the time when he had helped Felixana. He had been thrilled to do so, all that time ago. It had been a good puzzle to work on, and then to witness Felixana's anguish at hearing of Craig Landon's death......well, what was a man to do? There must have been a frisson of danger at the start, though no contacts had been maintained thereafter. He sipped his coffee. Morning activity all around him began to increase in tempo. The Café Izmir stood at the end of a narrow side alley leading into the huge expanse of the Djemaa el Fna square. He let his eyes wander over the picture. He saw market stalls, donkeys, spice sellers, one or two snake baskets to frighten the tourists; the noise and confusion was providing a colourful backdrop to café clientele. A man came to sit at the table on the left.

John Devine watched a young woman in a deep indigo-blue headscarf lead a girl of about five or six years across the square. He took another sip of the dark sweet coffee. Could he get in touch with Paul? Yes, of course, his brother still worked for the BBC. In fact, John knew he was somewhere elsewhere in Africa at the moment, covering the food riots in Tanzania. Should he get in touch with Paul? That was more difficult. He had scarcely believed the girl's story. The commercial activity around the café grew; another man came to sit at the other table on the right. John noticed that the first man, a middle-aged, well-dressed customer of Moroccan appearance, had received his huge cup of tea.

So, what to do about Paul? He would surely be too busy to respond, and it would mean sacrificing his career in the way that the girl had done. Felixana had specifically mentioned the need for security. Paul's BBC managers would not take kindly to another unexplained disappearance. It would be unfair to put him on the spot like that - throwing away a successful life in pursuit of a wisp of smoke. John's own career came back into focus. Suddenly, although he felt slightly guilty, he decided that he had spent so much time squeezing his brain round a past tentative relationship when he could still get to the conference centre and enjoy the rest of the morning's presentations in the real world. *Maps are my real reason for being here. I'm sorry, Felixana, but two and half years of silence have been too much for me. Too much water has flowed under the bridge.'* He looked around for the waiter; it was time to go.

The customer of Moroccan appearance was now sitting next to him. John smelt his after-shave lotion. His English was very cultured, his voice soft as his eyes still gazed out over the square, and not looking at the cartographer.

"Mr Devine, please come with us. We think it would be wise if you were to contact your brother."

John noticed the use of the words 'us' and 'we'. He also noticed the handgun in the lap of the other man on his right.

***

Pieter North's swimming style was more exuberant than technically brilliant, but the hormones that strenuous physical exercise released often lifted his spirits and helped him focus on priorities. The pool was part of the social facilities on-base in 2135. At all other stages of the long time-tunnel such luxuries had not been provided. The Dutchman had returned to the original station in response to a mysterious message that something of importance awaited him. He mulled over in his mind what manner of thing this might be, turning over and over who had wanted to contact him and for what purpose. At the end of the next length of the pool he pulled himself from the water. Now was the time for his appointment with the attorney who had been granted special permission to fly over to Turkey and enter the base. Pieter was slightly anxious but keen now to see the man.

"It's good of you to see me, Dr North. I've come a long way, but the instructions left to me made it quite clear that it is of great importance. I have not been told of the nature of this matter by my client's estate, however."

The tall thin man was a softly well-spoken American, very well-dressed in a dark blue suit and very precise in his manner. His handshake was cool, firm and dry. The two men sat alone in the airy room. The Dutchman relaxed a little; this lawyer seemed normal. After so long in the intense and surreal atmosphere across the centuries past, the scene was positively uplifting. Here was 'normality' again, what the American would have termed 'normalcy'. Here was a real person in a real room, bringing an air of reality. Pieter hoped his slightly-offbeat appearance and attitudes

259

would just be accepted as regular scientist fare by the in-comer. That seemed to be the case. After checking that the visitor had been welcomed into accommodation for two nights on-base, he invited the broaching of the subject in question.

"I represent the estate of the late Jon De Haag, who sadly died of a heart attack in Los Angeles in May of 2132. Though the main estate was settled within a year, there were side issues that required my company to investigate across the world, principally in the Netherlands and in the U.S. State of Oklahoma."

He paused. "A holographic message from the Professor and addressed to you has come to light."

Pieter North felt his stomach tighten slightly. A flicker of concern on his face must have been picked up by the American, who added quickly, "I am to apologise that this matter has taken over two and a half years to be brought to you. I trust it will not awaken old sadness after this passage of time."

His host felt light-headed; the juxtaposition of various periods of time involved in his life over the past thirty months of the American lawyer's life was so strange that he almost burst into laughter. Controlling himself with a jolt, he dumbly indicated that the lawyer should continue.

"I have brought the disk with me. Naturally, the seal has not been broken and it does require your fingerprints to activate. I must leave the disk for you alone. The terms of the estate are very clear. I am to take no return message in response, nor witness the viewing of the disk, nor to be involved at all beyond the safe handing over of the merchandise in question. However, we do know that it was recorded the day before his death."

North's fingers were shaking momentarily as the saucer-sized silver disk with its dark blue stripe changed hands. He dragged his eyes from the disk to the other man. "I am sorry in that case that I must continue with whatever secrecy this contains. I can only thank you and your company for the arduous work involved. Please relax as best you may while you remain on base."

The attorney smiled and left the room. North felt drained of emotion. After all this time, his true friend would return, albeit in an electronic form, to tap him on the shoulder and share something with him. The loneliness of the past few years gushed in. The Professor had guided him

260

well, yet there were mysteries afoot even now. He turned the disk over in his hands, almost willing it to reveal its secrets through the intensity of his stare rather than it needing a holographic player. He went in search of one and another empty room.

He set it up. In the silence, the soft background of the holographic picture gently hummed. A warm, wooden-panelled room came into focus in the centre of the small theatre. A library, perhaps, or a private living room; the scientist couldn't tell. It was furnished with little, but clearly gave an effect of restrained and high quality luxury. Then there was the image of Jon De Haag, feeling his way into an armchair. He smiled, sensing where the recording camera would be. Following human instinct, North smiled back. It was more effective a tool of communication if one took part in the deception created by the imagery. The Professor's voice was soft and melodic, the language Dutch.

"Pieter, I am recording this message on twenty six May." *That would be 2132'* thought his listener.

"I know your work will progress well, now that we have successfully moved a man safely in time. I am pleased with the success of last week's experiment. I am in Los Angeles; there have been people here I have needed to see."

He hesitated, as if in doubt as to how to continue. North waited. Then with a deep breath the image pressed on.

"Pieter, I apologise that I am not speaking to you in person. I am worried, and I dare not even come back to the project base. I have to see my contacts here again. I am worried for you and your team, for what you might find and now, even for my own safety. Since last January, when we moved that chimpanzee, I have been thinking and worrying. Remember that Saturday, Pieter? We spoke about Pandora's Box. I went back to my earlier notes on theoretical temporal movement; with all the uncertainty about starting a process we might not be able to stop, I felt uneasy about the possibility of releasing evils into the world."

The image seated in the room, itself in a room, screwed up its face. The watcher suddenly felt cold. The Professor's image continued.

"I don't know why I should have an instinct about the concept of evil; that's not very scientific, is it? It's just that I remember Paul Forbes mentioning the Box at the start of our project together last November. I wanted to check and re-check my earliest rudimentary calculations consistent with philosophical principles."

The image smiled ruefully. "Unusual for a pure believer, in science, I know, but I wondered if the approach might bear dividends." He paused. "It did. I started at the beginning, with E=MC squared, quantum theory and Potter's early work with the plasma cocoon. I played around with them in the contexts of different philosophical, pagan and religious criteria. Symmetry emerged that I didn't expect and it expanded along unusual lines. You may find, Pieter, that there is a natural limit for time travel, on the basis that we are testing it, at time intervals along multiples of three."

Doctor North sat transfixed, no longer feeling cold. His mentor continued.

"You remember the power differential we needed to introduce at three years' distance; you may find a temporal barrier at thirty, three hundred or three thousand years past, if you push that far. There may be a natural fault line aligned to the power of three."

North's stomach fluttered with confusion. Why had the Professor not mentioned these possibilities to colleagues during the early months of 2132? Yes, his untimely death had broken the chain of professional discussions, but an earlier intimation might have saved weeks of uncertainty that autumn as they struggled with the three hundred year conundrum. The image was talking again…

"And I simply could not leave my worries unvoiced. It seemed to me the symmetry that was forming in my work and discoveries was displaying coherence almost unknown in nature as we understand it. I have spoken with some people here in California over the weekend. It was possible that our political masters were pulling strings I did not know about. Yet to broach these matters with colleagues might have exposed you all to a situation I have increasingly come to fear. If we are touching a politically-motivated plan then we must be in some danger. There can be no other scientific explanation for the crystal-clear symmetry I now see in what we are doing. While I hesitate to believe the alternative mentioned to me over these past two days, I urge you, as a friend, please be careful Pieter in your future work. Whatever stage you have reached when you receive this message, you need to be vigilant."

The recording faded and disappeared. Pieter North gazed with his eyes out of focus onto the spot where his friend's image had just been talking.

Words without obvious meaning, yet pregnant with significance nonetheless, echoed in his brain. *'Coherence....crystal-clear....almost unknown in nature....the alternative mentioned to me'*. What on earth did all that mean? Who were the people De Haag had met and whom he had mentioned twice? What alternative? He could only hang on to the thought of a politically-motivated plan, and the clear warning he had been given to be vigilant. But vigilant for what purpose, and how would he know when he saw it? He thought of the security chief. Perhaps Simon Atkins knew more than was being made available, even to the top team of scientists. After all, the move to Turkey from Oklahoma had itself been shrouded in subterfuge and double-dealing. Nothing had been what it had seemed to be. The sequence of revelations in the time-travel objectives had been shifted to a political timetable and order of priorities. What was real and who could be trusted?

As he boarded the shuttle to the personnel TTUs four days later for the long return to the year 335, a significant part of his being was wishing he could remain in the relative certainty of the twenty-second century. He had swum in a pool, met someone from the outside world and listened to an old friend. Suddenly, he was feeling very tired.

Monday 7 February

He eventually found the courage to begin his journey back. Though the minimum rest period between transfers to another base was twenty four hours, he decided to give himself two days in each base to acclimatise. This would give him time to check calibrations, meet staff and think through how he might put into effect De Haag's warning advice. But it was more than that - he confessed to himself on arrival in 1835 that he had left a favourite chronometer at home base. Had that been an accident or was he secretly willing himself back home? He sat in the restaurant over an evening meal and gazed out onto the Turkish night, its inky shadows leaching out the last vague forms of rocks and skyline. *'Home was 2135'*. The thought as a concept was strangely comforting. He had no emotional place in what he saw as pre-history. The enormity of the challenge in his situation loomed up in his mind. He was going back to a woman who didn't want him, and a man who hated him, to finish a task that a trusted friend had warned him was laced with undefined danger.

What should he do when he got back to the year 335? There was only the science. He felt he understood why countless generations had termed it 'pure science'. No matter what the discipline, there was no right or wrong, good or bad, happy or sad. There was just the purity of truth. He decided the professional in him had a duty to his humanity to pursue the purity of his science to its logical conclusion, whatever that might turn out to be. History would then neither praise nor condemn him but merely record his achievement. His name would take its place in the annals of science - *'and quite right, too'* he told himself proudly. Yet he knew it was not a pure one hundred per cent pride; there remained a touch of regret over the BBC woman and a thin streak of nervous antagonism towards the South African.

His arrival in the 1535 base coincided with a gloriously-sunny day that thankfully lifted his spirits. The orange colour scheme in the base helped. His relatively rapid movement through the full tunnel was having some unfamiliar side-effects. He found he was noticing facilities, or rather the lack of them, that he had perhaps missed before. He already knew that the only swimming pool had been at the original base. That leisure centre had also housed the only anti-grav climbing wall, dream tent and indoor jogging track. Dream tents were new and very expensive. Few of them had been installed, mainly in luxury hotels. Pieter North reckoned the existence of one in Siverek had been an extra bribe to tempt tunnel workers to settle into their captive employment and carry on working. Tents consisted of a one-piece bodysuit with helmet and face visor, that gave to the wearer the total private fantasy experience of their choice. Coupled with sound, touch and smell elements the dream tent had proved to be very popular. Down-time workers were keen to be given the opportunity on vacation periods to return to the twenty-second century to take their turn in their fantasy world. It occurred to the Dutchman that for many of his colleagues their 'day job' of time-tunnelling merely provided a humdrum existence from which they were pleased to escape. The decrease in the number and complexity of leisure and social facilities also helped to explain how the opening-up of each new base occurred more quickly than the one before. By the year 335 things had become quite frugal, mused North.

The day after his arrival in the year 1235 he began to feel unwell. Whether the shaking and weakness were symptoms of something physical or something mental was uncertain to him. Certainly, he had been declared fit to travel by base medical personnel. Nevertheless, he completed the computer-led self-assessment, which he passed, and the personally-controlled body scan, which he also passed. He decided to delay his transfer to 935 by twenty four hours to see if his strength would improve, and in addition, sought out one of the centre's doctors. It had not occurred to him that fresh air might be beneficial; a walk outside was prescribed and by the next morning he was seated in a TTU and ready to face the green corridors of the next base. Unfortunately, the emerald-hued base was not one where strolls in the Turkish sunshine were allowed. All bases had been told of the murder of the four scientists in the nearby hills, but only the green base still denied outside activity. It made no difference to the number and nature of social and leisure outlets. These were decreasing with each base through which he passed.

The rainbow sequence of colours chosen had fitted the mood well; the human spirit became gloomier as the blue and then indigo backgrounds formed the backdrop to the scientific activity. On the twenty fourth of February Pieter North stepped gingerly from the transfer unit and was unnerved by what he saw. Unfamiliar TTUs now stood in a corner of the transfer hangar where previously there had been vacant space. On enquiry of a technician he was told "Those are new, sir. We now have our first construction staff in the year thirty five. They went over this morning."

***

"This is the closest the Brotherhood can get you to the base in Turkey, Mr Devine."

The reason was given as the jetliner from Cairo lowered through heavy black cloud into Damascus International Airport. The holographer shivered; it was the prospect of cool weather in the Middle East after the humid heat of lowland Tanzania. Paul Devine was nervous and excited as he thought back over the past weekend. Late on Thursday afternoon his whole team of four cameramen and sound recordists had been scooped efficiently off the streets of Mwanza. Two black limousines with diplomatic plates had lifted them from the Lake Victoria waterfront, left his colleagues at the local airstrip, and taken him alone on board a small aircraft lit with Kenyan livery. It was all over so quickly he didn't have time to worry too much. It was quite clear to his abductors that they had all been BBC personnel of European origin. It was equally clear to the plump Devine and his colleagues that government and not terrorist action was taking place. By Friday morning, he was sitting alone in a holographic studio in a government building in Nairobi, waiting for the image of his brother John to appear. The satellite connection to Rabat was established and his sibling told his ridiculous story.

Now barely three days later he was arriving in Syria with an assurance of personal safety, as far as it could be guaranteed, and facilities to follow a story. The government agents had been courteous, firm and open. He

265

was free to work from the BBC offices in Damascus. His abductors learned from his body language that he would thirst for exposing a story - *'it's just that I don't know which story'* he was telling himself as the hover cab hummed along the north bank of the Barada River towards the new commercial district. Much as he had respected Felixana's abilities as a reporter, there was no way he could believe the preposterous yarn conveyed to him. He had pressed John on the matter in no uncertain terms. 'What were her exact words? How did she seem? Did you get the impression someone was in the room with her? Had she sworn him to secrecy?' He put his own point across as well - *'you only received her message, you didn't speak with her'.*

Paul grappled with the options as the taxicab continued on its way. Clearly, the northern powers were concocting a massive project at Siverek, but everyone knew that was harmless solar research. If it really were otherwise, to break open the conundrum would indeed guarantee fame into eternity, but why should she entice him in such a ludicrous way? Obviously, Felixana was speaking in code somehow. The references to Christianity had been a cover that she expected he, Paul, would be able to interpret. He thought back over their years together. They had worked in Malta, Copenhagen and London - no clues there. She had seemed normal and gregarious; obviously frightened in the last few days when she was on the run and concerned for friends, especially Craig Landon.

Paul gazed out at the Syrian capital. The hover cab turned east into Faisal Street. He glanced over the river where the renovated walls of the old city ran along the banks. Damascus was an ancient dwelling-place, full of myths from the past, traditions kept alive today and engrained outlooks stretching into the future. He had never been here before, but it reminded him of Rome - dead yet vibrantly alive, a paradox existing in a mirage and floating on an ocean of individuals' private perceptions. What was real and what was not? He winced. *What was real and what was not?*

Back to Felixana.....perhaps her message was a cover for a religious assassination plot rather than a political one. The Southern Brotherhood was imbued with such people, moving in and out of religion and politics. Where to look first? They obviously felt threatened in a real way by the woman's viewpoint, but wouldn't open up to a mere holographer. Those who had transported him so secretly and luxuriously over several thousand kilometres in just a few days clearly took something seriously, and he would have to do the same. The history of these nations was known to him - they were the sons and inheritors of liberation theology, of 'Thy will be done on earth'. Felixana's message was leading him to think of which nation was the intended first target for a military strike. One further thought came to his mind with chilling finality as the hover-cab came to rest outside the BBC offices on Manamah Street. He had agreed to respond to Felixana's plea; his controllers had not placed him close to the borders of Syria and Turkey to film a travelogue. He would have to go into harm's way, confront the story and put his BBC employment to use.

Tuesday 8 February

It was difficult to know how to read the staff at the BBC offices. They seemed to be torn between a keenness to engage in an unspecified but clearly important assignment and reluctance to be seen to operate too close to the Syrian government. There were few of them, to be sure; just three part-time employees, and all Syrian nationals. In truth, their daily round had been short of relevance, and their ambivalence evaporated in the heat of excitement generated by the arrival of an outsider. Paul Devine suspected anyway that all three had been closely screened by the Syrian authorities and had been left alone as having been declared harmless. It wouldn't have mattered if they had been planted - he was in the hands of the Brotherhood at this point, anyway.

The contact with Felixana was now of first importance. He had gathered from John that she had conveyed a sense of urgency, though he didn't know of a reason for that urgency. Perhaps she felt in danger of exposure. He checked the timescale involved. Her message had been transmitted at 23:30 hours, local Turkish time, on Friday the twenty eighth of January. Nearly eleven days had now passed; without a contact she might reasonably assume he had not received her message or had decided not to act on it. He was to place a particular sentence in the newspaper personal columns of the English language daily in Turkey, the Hurriyet Daily News, to include a date and time of his choosing. She would meet him twenty four hours later, at specific latitude and longitude co-ordinates that she gave in her message. *'So, that was it,'* he thought. *'I choose the time and she chooses the place.' 'I am to come alone.'* It was melodramatic, to be sure, but hardly surprising. He checked the co-ordinates on a digital map; a steep-sided dry valley three and a half kilometres west of the dotted-line segment the map indicated as a military training area, but which he knew for certain was the Siverek Base.

He spent the remainder of the day preparing for what he knew would be a one-way journey. Getting into Siverek, either dead or alive, would be relatively easy in comparison with any attempt to get out again. Would the Brotherhood sacrifice him? *'Yes, most probably'*, he decided. Yet if he didn't get out the story, whatever it was, most certainly had to do so. Had the whole thing been a trap, anyway? No, that was unlikely - John had been totally convinced by Felixana and her sincerity. He knew he had to depend on the Southern Brotherhood at the moment, and admitted that without their detailed local knowledge and influence, even getting undetected within spitting distance of Siverek would be impossible.

Wednesday 9 February

His suspicions over the local BBC personnel were confirmed the next day. Ever helpful as they were, he was told a helicopter would be coming to carry him to the Turkish side of the border. He would be dropped some distance from his final point. He would then have to travel by horse. The newspaper entry was set for Thursday the tenth; the advertised time would be twenty three hours on Saturday the twelfth. If all went well he would be met by Felixana at twenty three hours on Sunday the thirteenth. 'Unlucky thirteen' crossed his mind. He had precious little time to leave contact details in a safe place before the government-organised aircraft conveyed him to Haleb for an onward helicopter lift to the border. He was told the European Union's southern border at this point was likely to be particularly-well protected. There was nothing he could do about that. The border from Antalya in the west to Nusaybin in the east would be constantly patrolled - a legacy of decades of dealing with economic migrants seeking access from Iraq via Syria.

***

The Israeli Internal Affairs Minister was incandescent. "We were told two years ago that this time-travel idea was a non-starter! Why has it taken so long for this message to come out? We are ill-prepared for handling it quickly."

His face reddened as he thumped the desk before him on the word 'why'. Several other members of the secret Israeli Cabinet committee nodded in vehement agreement. The hologram from the BBC spy had barely finished when the Minister exploded with anger. The two senior secret service agents present shuffled uncomfortably in their chairs. Their necks reddened. There was no natural light in the windowless lower rooms occupying the third basement level below the new Knesset complex in Yerushalayim. The Cabinet committee had been convened within ten days of the hologram to Ben-Tovim being received, validated and passed up the chain of command to the Prime Minister's office. One of the agents spoke timorously.

"The woman placed initially in the Base in America has only made contact within the last two weeks. We had no way of knowing she was even still alive. No military activity has been detected these past months. There has been no tangible and viable reason to recommend placing our military on alert."

Several other Ministers weighed in to press their case.

How seriously can we take this latest message?

Have our own scientists concurred with the likelihood of a successful time transit?

Why can we not take military action?

The arguments and anxieties throbbed across the round table. One hour after the hologram had been shown the Defence Secretary expressed his view.

"If we take this project at face value, the northern powers will by definition need to enter Israeli sovereign territory, albeit in a bygone age. I do not pretend to understand the implications of travel through time. I believe it to be impossible anyway, but I am a politician and not a scientist. However, if it is true we must remember this. This is our land, this was our land, and this has always been our land, even when it was occupied by Roman legions. The northerners have occupied our land before. Any hostile and unwelcome movement onto our land is an act of war and we must respond."

A ripple of applause, rare at Cabinet meetings, echoed round the room. The Prime Minister silenced it with the flat palm of his upraised hand.

"We should proceed with caution. You, yourself David, professed unbelief in the science. If we declare publicly that we believe ourselves to be under imminent threat of attack, with no discernible military evidence, the Europeans and even our Brotherhood allies will say we are doing no more than repeating what they say we have done several times over the past hundred years - dreaming up an excuse for precipitate and proactive aggression. To say the threat is real, but based over two thousand years ago, runs the certain risk that all the world's powers will laugh at us. The

American and Russian cartels will stoke that response against us. The Chinese would not even understand our viewpoint as theology is alien to them. Besides, the Palestinian and other Arab solidarity we have enjoyed this past thirty years are still only skin-deep. Imagine their reaction if we claim we are defending land on the legal ground that history has never changed. The whole basis of the present existence of the World States Council is that, regardless of the mistakes of history, we are where we are now in the twenty-second century and mankind must move on. All nations could say they once owned somewhere else!"

His cold logic bathed the room. "However, we can prepare for action by raising the tempo slightly. Perhaps some low-key military exercises across our northern borders?"

A nod from the Armed Forces Minister was followed by input from the man from the Religious Affairs Ministry. "This is a clear threat against Christianity, not against us. Why should we feel threatened?"

The Prime Minister acknowledged with a slight wave of his hand that a point had been made. "Yes, we would be wise to keep our options open at this point. We do not know for certain how far advanced this project has become, though from the BBC woman's statements the northern powers must be within striking distance of completion, perhaps no more than six months. At some point soon, there will possibly be a public relations campaign. We shall need our contacts within the northern world to monitor any growing activity on the media front; briefings, communication channels, satellite activity, that sort of thing. Certainly, there are no major world sporting events coming up in the next six months, so we should be able to detect any lifting of interest among media organisations. We must expect some attempt to grab world attention and steer world opinion. I agree that the defeat of Christianity would do our nation no harm. Our troops deployed on our northern borders, ostensibly on a regular series of military exercises, should contain the situation. We can also use it as a code for letting the northern powers be led to think that we are not averse to their intended target. Too much show of force, and we give the impression we feel threatened. Too little, and they might think we have no idea what they are planning.

"My personal view has already been touched upon by the Defence Secretary - I think this is only a scientific ploy, a bluff. We have no clear evidence that they really are travelling through past centuries. Our troops will also act as a gentle buffer against the Southern Brotherhood thinking it can achieve access to Siverek."

270

The Prime Minister leaned back in his chair as if emphasising the meeting was drawing to a summing-up point. He confirmed the impression with his next words. "We have therefore covered all the options. Either it is an expensive bluff, a public relations charade to weaken southern powers, or they really expect to seek to destroy the concept of Christianity. In that case, our Faith stands intact and stronger. Either way, we get to win by not upsetting the situation prematurely."

A lower-focussed discussion ensued. The Armed Forces Minister was already keying suggested troop deployment instructions into his hand-held satellite co-ordinator pad

Friday 11 February

"Thank you for seeing me. Mary is making good progress. We should be able to discharge her in a couple of weeks."

The psychiatrist smiled. Susan Poynton smiled back.

"That's good to hear. She can come here, of course. I have room. Saffron will be pleased to have her mother back."

The room in which they sat was warm and comfortable. The two armchairs in their soft indigo fabric were placed either side of a mock fireplace, a design feature he rarely saw these days. He mused that domestic design had taken great leaps over the past century, with technology and wall-width media screens now so standard that it was rare to see a room that reminded one of their great-grandparents' times. He sipped his tea again, placing the cup back on the little table his hostess had provided for him. He explained that such a visit was purely part of routine so close to a likely discharge. Susan nodded understandingly.

The man asked about the two women's childhood together. Susan began hesitantly, yet the story slowly emerged. Their mother had moved from Hunstanton to Northampton soon after Mary's birth. As a single parent in a society with so many single parents their life together in their new town caused no ripples. Mary's mother had begun living with a man in the new neighbourhood and their own daughter, Susan, was born in 2105. Relationships between step-father and Mary had soon deteriorated. Mary's mother had kept her maiden name of Trent. Mary had retained the name for her own life as an adult. As she grew into awareness the younger girl had tried to protect her half-sister whenever she could, though she

271

confessed this had been difficult. The chances to release her sister from the darkness of the cupboard had come so rarely. As she had grown towards maturity it had seemed to Susan that her father had been hostile to the thought of bringing up another man's child, especially so as times proved to be financially hard for them. Susan opined her mother had probably made matters worse by resolutely refusing to talk about Mary's father within the confines of the new family. Mary's experiences of being punished by her step-father for non-existent transgressions had ended when he died in 2115.

"What was your mother's first name and how did she die?" asked the psychiatrist.

"Linda. Linda Trent. She died in a hover-lane accident when I was sixteen," replied the woman. "That's another thing that made poor Matthew's death three years ago so hard for Mary to take. My sister has never been good at holding relationships."

"What can you tell me about Mary's real father?"

"Very little, I'm afraid. Except that I get the impression that Mum really loved him. She rarely spoke of him, of course. We learned from adult friends of Mum that she met him on a college trip at the age of nineteen. That would have been at the time of the Midwinter Festival in December 2099."

She rose from her chair, a thought having occurred to her, and left the room with a quick apology. She returned with a small silver box of holographic disks.

"There's no record of him, I'm afraid, but Mum did keep a picture of the friends she travelled away with at that time."

The small domestic holographic player was set up. The centre of the warm room was filled with the picture of a group of warmly-clad female friends laughing and smiling against a stiff sea breeze coming across the side rail of a ferry. Susan admitted she had no idea of the destination of that holiday trip over thirty five years before.

The psychiatrist said he sensed that Mary was sad that her mother had not been more supportive, and Susan agreed. He thanked her, indicating his pleasure that she would be willing to care for Mary on her discharge. He promised to return.

Sunday 13 February

By the time of seventeen hours, the evening sun leaving indigo shadows in the undulating landscape, Paul Devine was listening to the throb of helicopter blades fading quickly into the southern sky. A few moments later the eternal silence of the desert hills came down like a stifling blanket. He surveyed his surroundings and checked his satellite co-ordinates. He grimaced. As expected, they had dropped him with a horse some twenty kilometres from his rendezvous point. There would be enough power in the horse to take him to the final destination, but how would he obtain a recharge if no-one was there to meet him? He thought *'one of life's imponderables, no doubt.'* He gunned the horse to life; though the engine was professionally silenced, he was terrified by its modest sound relative to the absolute peace of the hills. Lifting to a cruising height of two metres he set off north-east towards Siverek following the river on his left.

The journey began swiftly and uneventfully. There was no-one around. Strange thoughts passed through his mind. He envisaged his possible welcome. A phalanx of European Union soldiers with weapons pointing motionless at his chest? A solitary sniper in desert clothing camouflaged in the scrub; someone he would never see? Or perhaps Felixana's tense and drawn face? His eyes dropped momentarily to the horse's navigation screen; there were four kilometres left to travel. It was now almost dark. Should he risk switching on a headlight? His speed had slowed to a bare crawl, gently passing over a rocky terrain with the occasional beep of the altitude sensor picking out a large bush below. Another flick to the navigation screen, which showed him three kilometres left to go. He succumbed to the headlight pressure, feeling too nervous to fly blind. There was absolute silence apart from the soft hum of the horse. He had entered a narrow valley, presumably the one he had identified from the map in Damascus. He longed to be able to stop and listen properly. He checked his watch, deciding there would be time to walk the final kilometre. He would hide the horse in a cleft, keeping sufficient power to reach the river behind and hope for a boat or small skiff if escape was called for.

Taking his small luggage, a hand weapon and his navigation pod, he set off on foot into the darkness. He smiled as he recalled the sentence of contact that Felixana had asked for in the newspaper entry. Tomorrow would be Valentine's Day - the contact message would not have attracted undue security attention embedded among many similar entreaties. In the silent desert darkness, He was feeling his lack of physical fitness. Though only forty years of age, his stout and florid constitution was telling against him. He was sweating freely with the exertion of the walk, the careful picking over of a path among boulders in the weak light of a torch, and the constant listening for a sound, from friend or foe, from the blackness ahead. His eyes were becoming accustomed to the night sky. He checked the time again - 22:40 hours, just twenty minutes to go and only a few hundred metres. What was the meeting place? Yes, a rocky valley, but would there be a large boulder, a stunted tree? *'Hardly a sign saying, wait here',* the thought caused an involuntary giggle. It was all so unreal. Just ten days ago he had been sweating for different reasons in the heat of the Tanzanian jungle, and now he was completely out of his depth on a strange and terrifying journey that might end with a bullet any moment now. Pushing a bead of perspiration from his eye, he tried to focus on the glowing satellite numerals. The pre-set instructions had switched their colour from red to green - he had arrived. He shivered as his eyes made out the form of a large boulder. No, surely not. Well, there had to be boulders everywhere in this hilly scrubland. He sat down, shaking like a leaf.

"I got your message, darling. I want you to do the same to me!"

A slightly joking, mischievous voice, but he could also detect the raw relief of seeing a friend after so long tearing through the impish tone. Felixana's words floated out of the darkness behind him. The short but heart-felt embrace barely quelled his shaking body. Then they were on a powerful tandem horse together, speeding into the night. As they moved away, she noticed his hand gun. Before he could protest, she had grabbed it and flung it into the night.

Friday 18 February

Felixana was getting excited. After months of waiting she felt a climax of some kind was approaching. Though she knew the final base had not been built, there was much to do in 2135 where the outside world surrounding their cocooned existence was a known entity. Other bases suffered a stifling absence of outside stimuli. No live pictures of the twenty-second century could be seen. Personnel had films and other entertainment but news of world events was filtered by the simple logistical operation of the TTU programme of activity. It took twelve hours in most cases for non-urgent information to travel the whole distance to or from the farthest reaches of the Indigo Base at year 335, the last one fully completed.

274

Felixana was busy. Getting Paul Devine into the base had been easy. She still held her senior personnel clearance, so assumed she was at least one step ahead of the security staff. Her media teams were centred on the original base, codenamed Caramel after the colour chosen for the up-time centre. Without some input from her BBC colleague she could not see a way of transmitting live images across the bases. Besides, until the scientists could reach Target Year there was no other natural centre from which potential publicity could effectively be broadcast. At present, the resources for her work had been limited, and the 2135 base held most equipment as well as personnel. There was much to do. She thought of the South African from time to time, nervous in case her deceit might somehow be discovered. Inexplicably, she nursed a slight sense of guilt. She thought of the Dutchman not at all.

Initiating Paul into the senior broadcast team and updating him on their work took several days. Her message to his brother had been a master-stroke, she felt, though almost an afterthought, and prompted by the technical demands of her task. The spin-off was tangible; she now had a friend on the base from the outside world. It gave her determination a distinct boost, a real anchor to counter the claustrophobic life awaiting her again down-time. She became conscious of having a foot in both worlds again, if only for a while. His few oblique references to the Southern Brotherhood she automatically took to be references to Ben-Tovim and his influence. There was no reason for her to know otherwise. Her erroneous assumption would have fatal and explosive consequences, but she could not have known that in the heady days of preparing for transmission of the project's cover story.

It was Friday, and she had been following world news for three days. The Israeli navy, army and air forces had begun military exercises north and east of Haifa on the previous Monday. All low-key stuff normally, and six hundred kilometres from Siverek, but political nerves had been jangled in the northern powers. A message was sent to the base that Operation Methuselah should move into a new phase. The publicity machine must now openly proclaim Siverek to be on the verge of success with the harnessing of the solar wind. Felixana should claim a world exclusive for the BBC; it would look more authentic, and the real Corporation in the outside world would hardly deny such a supposed coup.

If the middle days of February were proving a dizzy time for the female half of the BBC embryo, Paul Devine was finding them positively mind-blowing. Though an accomplished expert on holography and its associated equipment, he was now seeing sights he had never dreamed of before. Within the confines of the base dwelt vast hangars with throbbing machinery, twinkling lights and that indefinable presence of electricity which causes headaches. He was impressed; there was something going on here. It was not time-travel, of that he was sure. Yet the over-riding sensation on the base was of security, secrecy and subterfuge. He didn't understand the jargon he kept hearing, even in the social and catering areas. Perhaps that was why Felixana was so frustratingly enigmatic when she kept insisting that she herself had travelled into the past. Why would she be so deceitful towards him on this point? He told himself he mustn't blame her; just be patient and it will all become clear. In the meantime, he had to prepare the relatively-easy work of getting ready for the solar wind presentation.

Whatever the secret of the base, it soon revealed its dark side. After several days, he noticed that certain personnel seemed detached from part of reality. They were there, but they weren't there. He couldn't define it. Not that they wandered the corridors like zombies, with a glazed look in their eyes. No, it was more unsettling than that. Something about their demeanour set them apart from others. It manifested itself often as a highly-tuned impression of calmness, but with a sense of resignation about it, as if it carried a deep sadness. Not everyone seemed so confused. He raised it with Felixana in a quiet moment. She smiled knowingly, showing him her bio-plastic identity tag attached to her waistband. Turning it over, he noticed the clear red stripe across the badge.

"It's issued to all staff having to travel down-time. The disorientation sometimes grabs them and doesn't let go. We have a high turnover of people with mental problems; dissociative behaviour, severe mood swings, paranoia - you name it. We're all tested regularly for signs. In severe cases, people have been removed from the base, but they never go home, only to a series of medical facilities, I understand. We call it 'taking a sand dune siesta'. You might come across the term."

Paul's face was blank, as if he wasn't really registering her words. He did a moment later.

"Don't worry about it. It's never happened to members of my team, and you'll soon get used to it."

Alarm stabbed at his heart. He flipped over his own identity tag and stared stupidly at a clear red stripe.

Monday 21 February

The Israeli military exercises in the north had ruffled more than European and American feathers. Since a low-key start the previous week, they had grown in complexity and latent power. This was a major move, especially so in the context of relative peace within the Middle East and the onset of the period of Lent in the southern hemisphere. The broadcast from Siverek two days before, under the exclusive BBC tag, had extolled the virtues of solar wind engineering, heralding as it did a new era of potential cheap energy for all mankind. What to believe? How to read the straws in the wind? The world was in flux, with less than ten months to the transfer of financial resources triggered in Malta over three years previously.

In a world of holograms and virtual meetings, the Southern Brotherhood's high echelons retained their loyalty to human contact. Despite the distances involved, senior diplomats from Tanzania, Kenya, Sri Lanka and Chile had travelled to Cairo in advance of the World Faiths Congress meeting scheduled for the end of the month. Word had passed quietly up from agents in Morocco concerning the plea to the Englishman named Devine. The message, though quite unbelievable at first reading, was to be taken very seriously. The premise went to the heart of the Brotherhood's strength. The grouping had widened little from the ousting of the corruption led by some Brazilian elements under Romero Duarte. Within the wider World Faiths Congress, the Hindu, Moslem and Jewish blocs had never reached the highest levels of the Brotherhood's discreet inner councils, still controlled by Christian and Buddhist influences. These four diplomats would not be reporting to Congress leaders, only to Brotherhood ones.

From the high point on which stood the ancient Mehemet Ali mosque, the four were riding the new funicular down from the top. The view was breath taking, especially for the two non-Africans who had not been here before. Cairo was still the largest city on the continent, its statement of humanity insistent and clear. From the funicular cables across to the horizon, the streets, alleys and squares hummed with noise and movement. The pyramids at Giza were barely visible in the distance. The eternal mist of cement dust and traffic pollution hung in the air, turning the whole scene a miasmic toffee-yellow-brown. Centuries of development had spread the cities either side of the river Nile for many kilometres. Hover traffic was minimal, mainly restricted to Law vehicles, Corporation units and cars of a very few rich individuals who seemed to revel in bright garish colours. A random bagatelle of colour would flash out of the mist without warning and flash back in again. The afternoon

277

sun bounced off the funicular cabin. A large black crow of a Mercedes Corporation limousine was waiting at the terminal. The four were ushered silently inside, the crow flying away towards Congress headquarters. Their visit to the environs of the huge mosque on the hill had been undertaken to avoid listening bugs that it seemed to be impossible to eradicate, even in official buildings.

The quartet had been given four days to assess the likely impact on world power balances of a successful outcome to the European -led project at Siverek. Which nations would be likely to break ranks and go back into the Sino-American bloc? The report to go before a secret meeting of the Brotherhood's High Council on Thursday the twenty fourth of February was now complete, and it was serious. The four diplomats would be reporting to their political masters that most definitely there would be at least ten nations that would lead the way. Others would be tempted to follow them in a vote for a new World States Council Economic Summit. The list was world-wide - Mexico, Dutch Antilles, Barbados, Libya, Iran, Angola, Afghanistan, Singapore, Laos and the United Korean Republic. A pack of cards would tumble; bilateral agreements and understandings would topple a handful more for each of the ten target states. The Brotherhood could be under a real threat. Its High Council would need to assess how to respond to the developing situation. Options would be limited. This was not the concern of the diplomatic services. Politicians would need to grapple with such issues.

Nevertheless, personal thoughts had equal value, regardless of luxurious conference chairs, the pomp of speeches and interminable free lunches. Each of the four diplomats sat wrapped in private response to the possible outcomes as the cool cocoon of the limousine sped through the hot Cairo sky. The Sri Lankan had background training in the disciplines and outlook of a Buddhist priest. Regardless of a direct scientific assault on one of the world's major religions, his sense of calm and belief in reincarnation would carry him through any reappraisal of humanity.

The two African women were focussing on the world poor, dispossessed and hungry. Some progress had occurred over the previous one and half centuries. HIV/AIDS had become endemic across generations but its effects over one hundred and fifty years had been diluted. Sleeping sickness, yellow fever and polio had been eradicated, as had smallpox - again. Yet malaria had spread north and south to higher latitudes with climate change. Genetically-modified viruses had been developed militarily. Clean and plentiful drinking water was still a hopeless

278

dream and countless thousands of children paid the ultimate price every time the Earth spun on its axis. The women felt anger at the scientific diversion being pursued by the northern powers, when so much remained to be achieved.

The elderly Chilean woman was fearful. She retained a strong faith in Catholicism. She was not at all certain she could bear the pain involved in the loss of her Lord. A tear came to her eyes as she remembered her parents and her stable upbringing. A dull ache took possession of her stomach. It was not shifted by a surreptitiously-taken alcoholic-spirit pill. The Mercedes crow landed on green, manicured lawns at World Faiths Congress headquarters. Southern Brotherhood minders swiftly spirited the occupants away from possible prying eyes.

Thursday 24 February

The gates of Birchwood Community closed with an audible sigh of compressed air. They seemed to exhale with relief and finality. She sensed their mood; it fitted her own calm and mildly-positive feelings. She was leaving. The day was cool, but exceptionally bright. The growing strength of the winter sun welcomed her into the big wide world. She placed her bag of possessions on the ground and soaked in the scene, every nerve and sense alive to the day. Birchwood had been built on high ground on the eastern edge of the main Milton Keynes conurbation. Residential units stretched away to the left, but over to her right she could see trees and hedgerows, fields and sky. The air was clear and brittle. The sense of exposure was strong but certainly not frightening. She felt in control yet liberated. The taxi hovering three metres above her gently lowered to the ground. She recognised her sister sitting in the back seat. There was time for one last look with a feeling of gratitude towards Birchwood, and then the taxi lifted away into the air northwards towards her new home. She looked down on the neat dormitories, the green quadrangles and outdoor swimming pool, now empty for the winter and covered with a large brown tarpaulin. Then the community buildings were gone and Mary Trent's new life was beginning.

She spent the journey listening and responding to her half-sister's happy but mothering voice. How was she? Had she remembered her medication? Was she warm enough? Had she had enough to eat today? Was it OK if they went straight home? It was so good to see Susan; Mary was content to bathe in the overly-protective interest being shown. Just hearing the voice radiating concern was comfort enough. She had even settled sufficiently in her own recovery to find some gentle mild humour in letting the clucking mother-hen approach wash over her and bounce off without causing irritation. Mary switched off a little and let her eyes gorge on the wonderful expanse of countryside unfolding below while nodding every now and again in response to a well-meant question. There had been no snow for several weeks. Green was the predominant colour fifty metres below the taxi. And such a wealth of different greens despite the winter's day- the green of winter wheat, of fallow grass, of ivy-covered walls. There was even a huge green lorry parked at one set of buildings, its contents unloading by automated units to a wide barn in a farmyard below. The taxi crossed the ancient line of the former motorway, originally built in the days of the internal combustion engine, one hundred and seventy six years before, and now largely abandoned in this northerly section to environmental countryside regrowth. A flash of red caused her to notice two ramblers in their gaudy winter clothing; then the taxi banked gently towards Northampton.

"Far Cotton, wasn't it?" The taxi driver was given his directions and within the half hour Mary was resting in a warm armchair and basking in her half-sister's love. Suddenly, it was all too much for her. She burst into tears, gladly welcomed the tender cuddle, and took the advice offered of a short time alone to rest or doze. Alone for a while, Mary thought back over the past two years. She remembered the smells and the sounds more vividly than the sights. It seemed to her that the return to normality had been imperceptibly slow, yet some events and occasions had lifted her more than others during those days. The winter had frightened her the most. She supposed that had been the winter of thirty three thirty four, because now it was almost March thirty five. The journey from Birchwood today had been a sheer delight. She thought back over the previous summer, smiling inwardly. Now that really had been special!

Mary had learned much from that summer. She had sat entranced with her hand held by her doctor while she listened to his gentle voice recite a poem about why those specific colours had been chosen by Mother Nature and placed in that particular order. Mary tried to recall the poem as she sat in the silence of her sister's home. How did it go now?

'Red is for….' 'No, that's not it." She started again. *'Red is the…..'*

The door softly opened without a sound. The woman peeped in. Mary was fast asleep. Susan smiled and closed the door again.

Saturday 26 February

"You are not very fit, Mr Devine. You really shouldn't be travelling tomorrow. It would do you no good."

The Doctor's assessment over, she had announced the diagnosis and prognosis with the medical world's eternal presentation of opinion as fact. The holographer agreed wholeheartedly, but his relief was short-lived.

"However," she had added sadly," I suppose I must declare you as a green pass, even if a borderline one. I understand your value to the team makes your presence down-time essential."

And so it was that Paul Devine sat in a TTU in the personnel hangar on the morning of the last Saturday in February with not a little trepidation in his demeanour, the anxiety now crowding out his scepticism. What if it were true or not, what did it really matter if he was about to be splattered all over the inside of a glass cubicle? He took one last look around the toffee-coloured walls of the outer chamber and tried to remember his transit instructions. *'Close your eyes when you see the red light come on. Or was it off?'* The previous twelve days at Siverek had passed quickly. Familiarisation with the base, the checking of inventories on equipment, introductions to Felixana's team members - it had snuffed out his freedom to speculate. He had known why he was there, she had explained it to him, but he was at a loss to know how his skills could be brought to bear on the questions she had posed. Can we transmit live holography across two thousand years? If not, how can we provide a next best alternative? Can we give it global media coverage? He had listened incredulously as his BBC colleague had spoken calmly about the seven bases that the physicists had been forced to establish. Seven! And he had naively assumed that at most these science-fiction crackpots were merely wandering effortlessly around the universe like taking a walk in the park! Felixana had not for one moment taken his unbelief seriously. Perhaps she had been too busy to argue with him.

The base was certainly impressive. He had taken every opportunity over these twelve days to look around; his dreaded red-striped identity card had at least been useful for that purpose. He had dismissed the cargo TTUs as a silly expensive conjuring trick, though he was at a loss to fathom their purpose. Perhaps politicians were developing vaporising machines as a military weapon. Personnel TTUs had been strictly out of bounds to casual onlookers, even senior ones. He shuddered to think of them - surely they were not vaporising volunteers! Again, a military solution gave him comfort as he visualised armed soldiers popping into existence on a far-flung battlefield, or better still, an assassin silently appearing in the bedroom of an enemy General. That was probably it, at least he could..........

The instant of transfer hit him hard. A blinding light in his head forced his eyelids closed, bringing painful tears in its wake. Breath was squeezed from his body so fast he felt it must surely collapse backwards into the contoured padded chair and disappear for ever. He felt so bruised that he didn't dare take another breath in case his shattered body wouldn't stand the strain of expanding again. An eternity seemed to pass. His terrified imagination heard a voice. *'Breathe, please. You need to activate the air filter system'.* He realised at last that someone was talking to him. He gulped dry acidic air and opened both eyes, shutting them again almost immediately. The colour red! How could the walls of the outer chamber be red instead of toffee-brown? His stupidity at not remembering the instructions and not shutting his eyes had left them wet and bleeding! He felt sick and frightened - and angry. Why had he even agreed to sit in one of these boxes when the base commanders clearly had enough gullible volunteers for their military experiments? He opened his eyes again. No, he had been mistaken; with relief he knew his eyes were still intact. The outer chamber's walls really were red. Something significant had happened. It wasn't just the sheer size of the chamber - no-one could have shifted their colour from brown to red in an instant. He noticed innumerable small differences. There were new cargo boxes where none had stood before, a thick electricity cable snaked across one wall like an Amazonian boa-constrictor, and there were now more technicians present. No, this definitely was a different place from that of a few seconds ago. He had moved somewhere.

Then he saw her, looking relieved and concerned at the same time. Felixana smiled broadly as the transfer unit's door swung upwards.

"Well done, Paul. It's still the twenty sixth of February, but this is the year 1835. Welcome to Red Base." She laughed. He tasted bile.

27 February 1835

Security at Red Base was relatively loose. The outside world no longer presented a threat. There was no Southern Brotherhood, no air restriction zones, no wavelength interception and no fear of disenchanted personnel running away home. There was also not the paranoia of Green Base, nor the increasing tensions further down-time on the three-day old Violet Base, the final destination. The man knew none of this; he just kept walking. He was pleased that slipping away from the buildings had been so easy. The surrounding landscape of scrub and mountain lay silent in its isolation. The eagle swung round in a wide effortless arc trying to relocate the quarry it had lost sight of behind a rocky outcrop. Its eyes missed nothing. Ninety metres below a new, larger shadow appeared in the early evening sunshine. The eagle saw and dismissed it. It was clearly not cast by the target it was seeking. The eagle's wing shape changed in an instant, sending the bird diving towards the baby rabbit. The pressure of displacement in the hot air was not an experience wired into the brain of the land animal.

'Too bad,' thought the man, climbing to the top of a small ridge. 'It didn't stand much of a chance.' He stopped and sat down heavily. Perhaps the doctor had been right; perhaps he was not very fit. He shook perspiration from his forehead. Hell, it wasn't that bad. He must have walked over a kilometre from the base. The terrain was not ideal, and anyone would be slightly out of breath. Besides, it had only been yesterday morning when he had sat in that contraption against his better judgement. Now it seemed he had been transported elsewhere in the world to another mountainous area. Perhaps he was now in another base a few hundred kilometres away, or would that have not been worth the expense? Perhaps not an actual war-zone; of course, not a war-zone, these were still experimental activities and so still base-to-base and not yet base-to-General's bedroom. Nevertheless, he had decided, 'it would be wise to find out where I really am. No need to tell Felixana. She'll just laugh and carry on with that silly story. Not really sensible to keep on with that, especially with her senior staff. We all know something secret's happening, but it can't be so secret that it's being kept from even the top people working on it. I'm surprised she was taken in, or perhaps she doesn't even trust me yet. Well, I'm staying one step ahead.'

He lifted the global satellite locator from his pocket and placed it next to the palm phone, half the size of his hand, on the rock beside him. He looked around, squinting at the setting sun. 'Well, that's west. They can't fool with that, at least.' He didn't have a feel for latitude and certainly not for longitude. This scrub-filled upland could be in either hemisphere. He checked the devices lying beside him. They were both fully charged. Better to start with the satellite locator on general search for any satellite at its nearest position; that way he could check the nationality, orbit and decay details and know where he was sitting. He selected 'N' - the northern hemisphere seemed most likely as he had at least known he had started from Turkey. A string of small red lights glowed, pin pricks against a black ground. He frowned and selected 'S'. The appearance of red lights raised a sense of confusion. Surely he couldn't be exactly on the equator? His subsequent selection of 'sweep all co-ordinates' was almost a plea. It should have invoked an overload response as hundreds of co-ordinated satellite pulses would ask to be placed in a priority order. The red lights stubbornly refused to be extinguished. He checked the charge again. There was no mistake; according to his machine there were no satellites above him.

This was impossible. He grabbed at the palm phone in frustration, but hesitated. He couldn't put Felixana and probably others in danger with the risk of an interception. Still, an anonymous call to a BBC office would surely do no harm? They would be able to trace his location. He keyed a number. He nearly dropped the phone in alarm as it registered 'no signal'. There was absolutely nothing at all out there on the planet to connect with! The sun finally dropped beyond the horizon. A deep chill set in his bones. He hurried back in the direction of the base to surround himself with humanity again. Even the rocks in the indigo darkness felt alien to him. Suddenly he felt utterly alone and Felixana needed to be taken seriously.

***

European President Papandreou was gloomy. Twenty nine months had passed since he had indicated his support in the Hungarian Parliament buildings for uplift in spending on Project Methuselah. Now he was beginning to regret his decision. As the hard northern winter dragged on, social unrest was now becoming harder to contain. He reminded himself with little consolation that the original decision had focused on success being achieved within twelve months, with disruption and humiliation of the Southern Brotherhood at the time of the Midwinter Festival of 2133. A further year had gone by with no result. Now in ten months more, with the arrival of January 2136, one tenth of their wealth and assets would transfer by automatic process to nations in membership of the World Faiths Congress.

Often during February he would stand at the windows of his winter villa, his Winter Palace as the media mockingly called it, gazing out over the golden Algarve coastline, out towards Sagres and the Atlantic Ocean. He grimaced. Everybody knew that the Congress was a front for the shadowy bulk of the Southern Brotherhood, whose presence still gave succour to the vast populations in the southern hemisphere. If success

284

with Methuselah didn't come soon, it would be too late. He recalled some events from the past year; it did not make for happy memories.

Pay cuts in public sectors were already two years old. Owners of private hover-vehicles, no longer able to pay for safety checks, were driving them around in dangerous condition. The air accident statistics told their own grim story. In March 2134 a high-speed train crash occurred in northern France, caused by badly-maintained equipment. There were forty four deaths. In May, torrential rain in Sicily led mud-slides to flood into Palermo and Trapari. Media reports carried stories of hi-jacking, by Sicilian mobs, of aid sent by the Tunisian Red Crescent from Bizerte on the North African coast. The arrival of August saw more NVL marches in England and Cymru as local State unemployment statistics reached seven million. The level of violence was increasing, with numbers swollen by those still in employment but on their summer break.

The news from further afield outside the European Union had been even more appalling; with world economic dislocation having shocking results. By October 2134, the American States of Arizona, New Mexico and Texas had shut down their southern borders to prevent attempts by families to flee across to Mexico where adequate food supplies still existed. There was food in the United States, but no longer easy ways of transporting it. So it rotted. Hawaiian pineapples could not reach Vermont; Florida orange juice could not get to Oregon. A succession of bitter northern winters had left the northern nations neither able to grow green vegetables nor to pay southern nations for them. Kenyan green beans and Israeli sweet-corn no longer graced European tables at the Midwinter Festival. In December, the central Chinese provinces of Guizhou, Hunan and Sichuan were suffering from widespread outbreaks of a new strain of influenza. The Peoples' Republic was still refusing aid offered by the African Disease Research headquarters in Kinshasa, as it was rumoured that the Democratic Republic of Congo would include World Faiths Congress doctors in its mercy missions. Murders at barter-boot sales across northern continents were increasing as browsers fought over personal possessions.

The President watched the red sails of a yacht billow in the wind at a distance from shore, the foresail shivering as the yacht came about. Time was surely running out for the northern powers if they didn't make a breakthrough soon. Financial pressures were seriously impacting on social and political cohesion throughout the northern hemisphere. Of course, everyone knew that Siverek existed. Solar wind power would most certainly be cheap and plentiful. It would make a fortune for the developed world as they sold it on to the southern nations at the new high prices that it would surely command. People only had to wait a little longer.

As for the fact that Siverek was so secret, with no staff allowed out once enrolled and with external visitors kept to an absolute minimum, the official line centred on the existence of the Van Allen belts. The President had received a briefing on these two rings of intense radiation encircling the Earth at distances of around one thousand to five thousand kilometres and then fifteen to twenty five thousand kilometres. Media outlets had circulated their statements - *'The electrically-charged particles they contain are trapped by the Earth's magnetic field, and Siverek personnel are working with these volatile belts.'* Most sensible people on hearing this would want to stay away, in any case, thought Papandreou. He weighed up the options. Despite the publication in April 2133 of the Atomic Energy Authority report on solar wind research at Siverek Base, a succession of nations had taken every opportunity they could to complain about the matter. Perhaps allowing another visit might lance the boil, always assuming that they could keep prying eyes away from the crucial equipment. Responses to the first solar wind presentations, after all, had been generally positive.

Then at the end of February came the news that the scientists had reached the year thirty five. Now at last, given good and careful publicity, they could seek out the evidence that would turn the tide for them and change the world's balances of power and influence. They could finally belittle and demean the Southern Brotherhood and separate it from their poor deluded peoples. A new vote at the World States Council would restore nature's balance. The President put through urgent calls to Washington and Beijing, with the thought of good and careful publicity in his mind. They could now plan to go beyond the solar wind stories of the previous ten days.

VIOLET

3 March - Year thirty five of the Common Era

The six figures sat quietly round the edge of the room. They were surrounded by their four key advisers and together watched the presentation play itself out in the circular space between them. Project Methuselah was coming to an end-game. They held their silence, listening intently, their faces impassive, not giving any clue as to their likely individual or collective responses once the presentation had finished. With one or two exceptions of bare connection, those seated had not known each other, or even known of each other, prior to their disappearances over the winter of 2131 to 2132. All had disappeared willingly once apprised of the project offered before them. Even Philip Allen, former hand-weapons adviser to the US State Department, had participated positively in the fabricated 'abduction' in daylight along the Embarcadero on San Francisco's waterfront. The nuclear helicopter that had whisked him straight out to sea had never been seen again.

Outside the newly-constructed embryo of the final Siverek base, the isolated Cappadocian mountainsides baked quietly in the hot Spring sunshine. There was not a cloud in the mid-blue sky. Thickets of scrub, already tired in the heat, dotted the steep slopes of the high hills rolling down out of the Parthian mountains towards the Babylonian plain and out towards distant Nabataea. The silence was unbroken - only the vultures hung on noiseless wings in the heavy air, circling patiently in balletic performances as they waited for signs of death or misfortune in the rocks and ravines below. The appearances of emptiness were misleading - this was the first modern century in the extreme eastern edges of the western world and Nature's kingdom was unthreatened. The inhabitants, from insects and rabbits to antelope and ibex lived in fear of jackals, bears and lions. The winged squadrons of the sky would have rich pickings today, no doubt.

The shadows cast in the gullies and across the landscape were deep and violet, just like the sombre and almost mystical shades, redolent with magical spells and potions that painted the plasma walls of the new base's developing corridors. Bjorn Lundquist made a direct and potent connection between the magic evoked by the brooding shades and the magical power that the physicists and other scientists had woven to

287

achieve the objective that was playing out before him on the stage. He rubbed his hands through his long blond hair and screwed up his eyes in barely-disguised disbelief. He was experiencing a deep sense of foreboding. The sociological implications of this project were truly awesome, far worse and complex than he felt he could possibly imagine. Where to begin?

Strangely, it wasn't with the enormity of the age in which they sat, unique and fragile though that was surely to be. In the twenty second century of the Common Era the tapestry that was humanity was dangerously stretched. Despite the scientific advances of the previous three hundred and fifty years, or perhaps because of them, the thin fissures between peoples that had first been opened up in the days of European empire had gradually widened. The forces that were supposed to unite peoples had instead forced them apart. The industrial revolution, the division of labour, the urbanisation of Western Europe and North America, had created extremes of wealth and poverty that would never close upon each other. The phase of nation states that played out in two world wars, and the phase of world power blocs that followed them, had created a dangerously unstable cocktail of over-population and myopic policies in the context of the human condition.

The move into Earth, lunar and planetary orbits had not removed competition between the blocs of influence. During the course of the twenty first century the Anglo-Saxon heritage had corrupted and spent out its opportunities. The age of austerity had proved too high a mountain for peoples to climb; they just did not have the stomach for self-denial. Lands with convoluted and bulbous architecture had grown in wealth and power, lands which centuries before had been the stuff of nightmare in European children's nurseries. Strange and distant dynasties of silk and snow and dragons that had charmed and frightened the young to sleep now emerged into reality. Throughout the early decades of the new century they had worked their hypnoses innocently, but successfully nonetheless. Russia, India, Brazil, China, Indonesia, Malaysia and others had, by the year 2060, come to control the world.

Then they, too, fell to the moral corruption that had destroyed the earlier empire-builders. They had sought to learn from others' mistakes, but it had done no good. Whereas Europe and North America had sought militaristic world domination in the nineteenth and twentieth centuries, the oriental powers had tried economic domination in the first century of the new millennium. At first it had seemed to work; then a stronger power had come to ascendancy among them. Global warming caused by human misuse of greenhouse gases had become unstoppable. Out of the torment of flooded coastal towns and cities, submerged nations, refugee migration on a massive scale and food and water shortages, had grown a new potential master. The greed of over-production that had weakened the northern hemisphere in the years from 2000 to 2050 was countered by a return to European and North American imperial ascendancy springing from advanced financial instruments and a new sense of world domination based on scientific discovery. The new potential of the southern hemisphere was itself growing through its greater population, control of its own natural resources, and a return to religion and faith in divine salvation as a driving force in social cohesion. The Southern Brotherhood was turning from a social force to a political one. When the World States Council's resolutions of 2131 would finally take effect in 2136, that political force would metamorphose into a financial one. This completion of a new cycle was something the northern powers could not allow to happen.

The Swedish sociologist had never experienced or studied global social patterns of such immensity, power and unpredictability. Then again, he consoled himself; there had never been the release and confluence of such forces in history before. The world was bubbling like a cauldron of combustible liquid. He shuddered to think that whatever they discovered in the deserts and towns of Judea would be like throwing a firebrand into that cauldron. In three days' time they were to be briefed by the senior temporal scientist. Lundquist checked his notes again as the current meeting came to a sombre conclusion. It appeared that the theoretical physicist Professor Jon De Haag had died some years before. The briefing was to be led by the world's remaining senior practitioner in applied temporal displacement - a Doctor Pieter North.

27 January - Year 335

Simon Atkins had awakened to find his lover had gone. The smell of her body remained in the bed. He lay quietly for a few moments, breathing it in and out; thinking of her. She was good for him, he decided. She took away his nightmares. He showered and dressed, ordered breakfast to his room, checked his communication protocols until it arrived. There was nothing untoward, it was all boring stuff. He ran his hand through his hair and massaged his neck, aware he had to begin work. She was around somewhere, no doubt. His confidence was returning as he imagined her pining somewhere and thinking of him. It made him feel more virile and alive. Additional security personnel were arriving as the base reached its full complement of scientists and technicians. There were other, unfamiliar, faces appearing along the indigo-coloured corridors, people speaking strange languages and wearing strange costumes. That pathetic Dutch scientist was nowhere to be seen. *Just as well; only important people around at the moment,'* he decided. Early in February, he noticed on the arrivals and departures data sheets that Doctor North had returned to home base; 'for legal reasons', they had simply said.

The vetting procedures for a range of experts in numerous disciplines were now increasing in intensity - sociologists, nature conservation scientists, ancient language experts, military officers both in and out of uniform. All had to be cleared for pending travel to final destination - Violet Base. The hectic rounds of meetings and interviews chipped away quietly at his energy levels. Within a few days, he found he was not sleeping well again. The same horrifying dreams haunted him - spinning, falling, crashing to earth, suffering terrible injuries, trying to speak only to find blood pouring from his mouth. On the morning of the fourteenth he woke in a burning sweat, his chest was throbbing and his heart pounding. He tried to concentrate on his morning's duties. Monitoring the Base's general chit-chat he noticed it was Valentine's Day. Instinctively, he looked for a love-note from Felixana - nothing. He felt hurt and bitter, his mind turning to her continuing absence. What was she doing? Could he still trust her? He knew it would be impossible for her to leave the Siverek bases; no-one was allowed to leave unless on special medical grounds. Yet he still felt anxious. Were his feelings professional or personal? He couldn't disentangle them. She should be traceable. He checked the Base complement and its arrivals and departures, with no success. The temporal sealing process meant that he could only communicate directly with the adjacent Base; with current amounts of business in flow it would take at least twenty four hours for routine checking messages to pass to 2135 and back again with an answer.

Eventually, he found she was indeed back in 2135 preparing for an important global presentation as part of the deception plans on Project Methuselah. He took time on the twenty second of February to watch the BBC's solar wind exclusive, 'beamed direct from Turkey to your home', that had been broadcast three days earlier. Her colour moving image stabbed at his emotions. His suspicions evaporated. She was getting on with her work, and he must get on with his. He was soon at full focus, adrenaline driving him on. He slept exhausted, a dreamless slumber.

A warning tag he had placed on his arrivals and departures programme pinged and glowed forty eight hours later. He was aware immediately that the Dutchman had returned to Indigo Base; the same day that breakthrough to the year thirty five was announced. What a day! He read the accompanying detail on screen. Doctor North had been given immediate clearance by the Base Commander to travel on to the final base where his presence was deemed essential. *'Essential! And I'm still here vetting these never-ending incomers. Still, he's away from my woman.'*

Another ten full days passed before the security chief could find the opportunity to travel to Siverek final base. Stepping from the TTU, and angrily brushing aside arrival medical checks, he made his way to the conference hall. As he entered at the back he heard warm applause being given to Pieter North.

6 March - Year 35

Ten days after his arrival back in Indigo Base in the year 335, the Dutch physicist was facing the briefing of the travel team leaders as they prepared for their first foray towards the Judean deserts. He didn't know what to say to them. He had been tired during that previous week, but the prospect of finally reaching the target year had awakened a new strength of purpose. At last he would see the practical application of so many years' work. Thankfully, there had been no sign yet of that BBC woman, or of the security chief, Atkins. He had been pleased and relieved that he could concentrate on the stability of the transfer process without the worry of further down-time connections.

He moved in the awful gloom of a base coloured in shades of violet. One technician, with gallows humour had dubbed it 'deadly nightshade', a remark which hardly lifted the spirits of the small, but rapidly increasing, number of very senior personnel who were to be allowed to travel there. There was little time for sad reflection, however. The pressing scientific need now was to link the disciplines that would seek to move away from the base. Siverek would no longer be the sole home of the project's voyagers. Ways would need to be found to take co-ordinated action across hundreds of kilometres in a strange land with no practical experience between them of how to act or relate with the local populations. The senior team members had learned something of ancient Greek and Western Aramaic, plus a solid foundation in Latin. Colloquial speech would have to come the hard way.

It was with a considerable degree of disbelief and trepidation that Pieter North was told on the fourth of March that he would have to address the travel teams. His mentor was dead, and no-one else now knew more about the processes of time travel. But process was not practical effect; he was primarily a physicist. Yet there was no-one else who could tutor on logic and protocols for moving among humans from another time. Shaking with nerves he had vomited his breakfast, and only by ten hours that morning was he in a fit state to enter the conference room. He walked slowly to the lecture dais, and suddenly realised it was identical to the piece of furniture that had been sent crashing down on him by Simon Atkins less than three 'living' months before in the Blue Base of the year 634.

The memory somehow emboldened him. He told himself he was more than a match for the South African. He looked round at those in the room, their faces expectant with attention, even awe. With such an august gathering, how could he not rise to the occasion? He recognised he was more capable than he had let himself believe for so long. This was his moment. They were waiting and he would not talk himself down, or let destiny down at this crucial time. He managed a confident smile, deliberately hesitating for effect. Then he launched into his briefing.

"Good morning. My name is Pieter North. I am the principal temporal transfer and protocol officer for Project Methuselah. I am aware of your individual and collective skills, and many years of experience, in writing about, researching and speculating on the age and land in which we now find ourselves. I am grateful for your knowledge. I am here to provide a template against which you may more safely operate.

"First, some scientific technicalities, especially for those of you placed in the second or third teams for whom this may be your first lengthy period of operation. The only way in and out of this time period is via the temporal transference units, the TTUs. They are here in base. There will be no way we can replicate them and transport them. Remember that, please, when you are many kilometres away to the south. The air is safe to breathe. In fact, it is much safer than you will have been used to back home. Everyone has been given their inoculations, but there may be some mutant strains of familiar infections of which our medical teams are not aware. Don't go drinking the local water.

"Second, I must refer to communications and recording facilities. Short wave will be used, and without satellite connection it will be line of sight only. Small retractable booster aerials have been designed and produced to stake out a clear path for your main movement. Special teams will insert these into the landscape as you progress. They will be impossible for locals to remove even if they find them and know them to be newly-planted. Many will be disguised to meld with the area as trees or branches. Mountain-top masts will ease our work, but we cannot rule out the occasional signal shadow in some ravines. Logistics will support your travel with supplies. Recording teams will only join you from your second, longer journey, scheduled for the twenty second of this month.

"And finally, you need to know something about the interactive properties of having undergone travel to another age, and living among earlier peoples. We are not here as powerful magicians, getting our way by impressing the locals with loud noises and complicated machines. Our aim is to be as invisible as possible, consistent with our overall objectives. Rest assured, you will not 'change history' by inadvertent actions or cause chaos theory to break out, sending us all into a black hole."

Some nervous laughter bubbled up and cackled around the room with an eerie echo. The phrase 'tearing the fabric of time' came into North's mind again. He swatted it away like a small fly.

"The real danger is that you would trigger mob dynamics among a frightened population. That will not help our case. For those of you who have not majored in past civilisations, however, please note that these are not, repeat, not savages. The main inhabitants of Judea have a highly-developed sense of order and gentle respect. The Greek populations among which you will pass across the Decapolis are educated and well aware of Nature's strengths and characteristics. In order to merge successfully, you will have to have considerable respect for everyone.

"The Roman occupiers should be avoided like the plague. Rome can call upon nine Legions around the Eastern Mediterranean. That's about forty five thousand men at arms. Add in wives, children, servants and slaves, say around a quarter of a million people owing direct allegiance to their Emperor, Tiberius. Stories of strange beings with unfamiliar accents and mystical weaponry would spread rapidly and efficiently, and again, this will not help our case. We can also die. Though everyone will have hand guns, please believe me these will not protect you against spears, swords, knives and arrows, or even hand to hand combat with those whose lives are imbued from start to finish with the violent side of life. They grow up with these weapons and can use them as efficiently as if they were second nature."

Pieter North paused to take a drink of water.

"That is all at the moment. I understand your initial journey on the tenth of March will take you as far as Aleppo. As I indicated before, the second expedition is set for the twenty second, and will reach Galilee. Thank you for your time. I wish you well on your first journey in four days' time."

He bathed in the warm applause; then noticed Simon Atkins enter at the back of the hall.

10 March - Year 35

The tension had been there from the start. Was this a scientific, political or military expedition? Intense discussions had lasted for four days before leaving Siverek. The options that bubbled to the surface were plentiful. Now they were no longer dependent on the temporal physicists and the administrative infrastructure that ballooned in their wake, most of the other scientists and specialists felt emboldened to press their individual case for expeditionary inclusion. Lobbying for funding for specialisms had run for months, if not years. The extreme secrecy of Project Methuselah, however, had meant that outside Associations and Academies of Science had been given neither inkling nor opportunity to build and press a case. The central thrust was clear - to reach the point where Christianity could be proven to the world as having sprung from a minor and falsely-built premise. Any discipline not essential to this aim was irrelevant. Not that this reduced the field much. Sociology, linguistics, communication, media, diplomacy; they all jostled alongside medicine, disease control, supply logistics, biology, astronomy, botany and photography. Even veterinary science argued a case based round efficient and effective use of donkeys, asses, colts and camels, both as inconspicuous methods of transport and confirmation of evolutionary development. All had come to a head in those weeks of January and February as breakthrough beckoned. In the event, the initial foray for two hundred and sixty kilometres into Syria was determined to be a military operation. There were too many uncertainties and dangers, and too much at stake for the smooth running of later journeys, for it to be otherwise.

And so, on a brilliantly sunny morning, the six-day expeditionary force set out south-westwards towards the ancient city of Beroea, known to those travelling by the later name of Aleppo. Three days out and three days back, to test the electrical reliability in dusty conditions of the new sand-coloured horses and to experiment with the communication network proposed. The military were under no illusions as to the difficulty of what was to be undertaken. After initial daylight travel in isolated mountain terrain, already surveyed from previous Siverek bases, they would be expected to cover over eighty kilometres a night, skirt round settlements, maintain communication and avoid the Roman army.

Chuck Kowalski, however, had no intention of avoiding the Roman army. He was terrified, elated and calmly professional, all at the same time. He had been brought up in Wahoo, Nebraska, outside of Omaha, as part of an army family. His father and grandfather before him had served in the U.S. armed forces, his father in Tibet and his grandfather way back in Iran. Chuck himself had now been chosen along with eleven specially-trained comrades to travel as point outriders to the main column. The decision to initiate with uniformed personnel had been well taken. By two hundred hours during the night of the twelfth-thirteenth of March, the contingent of fifty American and European Special Forces, with their interpreters and logistical support, were encamped in Bedouin tents in a north-east facing cleft high on a steep rocky outcrop just outside their destination. Radio communication with Siverek was remarkably clear, as clear as the myriad of stars sparkling in the heavens. The blackness around was awe-inspiring.

A small group climbed on foot the rest of the way to the top of the arid plateau on which stood Halab Al-Shahba, one of the oldest inhabited cities in the world; the place where Abraham had milked his grey cows. Heavily-armed, shrouded in local robes, they reached as far as they dared towards the fiercely-flickering security beacons staked along the city walls. A few shadowy figures could be seen, walking slowly along the high fence atop the wall. Light bounced off the burnished sheen of a tinned bronze helmet. A murmuring of voices floated in the air, and then came a loud, cackling, ribald laugh. The sound was too far away to be identified as individual words. A distinct head full in the beacon's light, its face unshaven and sweating, appeared in view. It gazed for fully thirty seconds into the darkness. A small creature in the scrub was disturbed, its noisy exit deeper into the night drawing the attention of the Roman guards on the fence. The eight men below froze their bodies lifeless to the ground. It was enough. The defenders of Beroea returned to their dirty conversation. The interlopers into this strange world silently withdrew to their camp.

At sunrise on the thirteenth day of March, twenty of the squad's members with several of their translators stumbled dustily along the track to Beroea's wooden eastern gate. It was already open for traders. They

295

had come so far in such a short time; it was important to learn as much as they could. They mingled with the early-morning crowds. The trauma of jostling against men and animals who had lived and died two thousand years before their own time was overpowering. All would need some form of psychiatric counselling on their return to Siverek; some would never recover from it. As they passed through the market stalls their senses reeled in unbelief. One man described it later as being akin to standing too close to a television picture and falling in. The sounds, smells, colours and tastes came so fast that they couldn't be assimilated. Yes, tastes! *'You could taste the air, the sweat, the animal dung, even the joy and the indescribable excitement of living; even the grapes without having put one in your mouth,'* one of the soldiers recounted later. This was no deodorised, pre-packaged, timed, manipulated shadow that passed for life in the twenty-second century. This *was* life!

Feeling dizzy and intoxicated, the soldiers in their enveloping robes returned to their tents. As darkness fell, they began the long journey back to Siverek. For two nights, Chuck Kowalski lay on his bedroll and gazed up at the thousands of stars in the desert blackness. But he didn't see the stars. In his mind's eye he gazed upon the face that had looked out from the battlements for thirty seconds. A soldier, a real soldier; just like himself. It was time for battle.

Thursday 17 March 2135

There would be no reporters at the secret meeting. The delegates had entered the non-aligned diplomatic nation secretly; they would similarly leave. The Swiss diplomats responsible for the smooth running of the occasion were paid to be discreet, and paid handsomely. Gunther Friel had twenty years' experience of such events. The world's power blocs often came to his beautiful mountainous land to thrash out sensitive issues, or merely to posture. He looked out from the wide panoramic windows to the south of Interlaken, letting his eyes move up towards Lauterbrunnen and the peaks of the high Bernese Oberland. What would this day bring? There was an hour to go before the Southern Brotherhood High Council members and the Israeli national delegation met face to face.

The grey-haired German Swiss passed his hand over the sensor which played again the crucial moments from that final day of the World Faiths Congress meeting in Cairo. It was clear from the body language that both sides had been shadow-boxing. On the open agenda for Wednesday the second of March had been the Congress' likely response to recent successes in science around the world. Reference in the meeting's agenda papers had been pompous - 'how can medical and other advances be shared in contractual terms once the changeover on world finances has occurred in January 2136?' Would the Congress nations with their new wealth be under pressure to pay additional sums to the northern power blocs in exchange for using the new technologies? The solar wind breakthrough announced by the BBC at Siverek had come into the discussions as a case in point. Someone had questioned whether the unprecedented Israeli troop build-up around Haifa would be a hindrance towards the European Union being conducive to share the technology freely with the southern nations. The delegation from Tel-Aviv had responded quickly that the military movements were perfectly harmless; designed to calm the region and give the Europeans the space to complete their work. Other delegates had been equally quick to point out to the Israelis that their exercises had begun five days before the BBC broadcast from Siverek, not the other way round. This had caused some irritation. A huddle appeared round the Star of David flag on the conference table. The knife had been twisted with the comment that surely it was the responsibility of the northern powers to protect their own project if they deemed it needed it. The terse Israeli response mentioned a start to troop movements that had been planned for months, and upgraded and extended in response to the solar wind announcement. It did not escape the notice of the Swiss diplomat that senior Southern Brotherhood delegates had remained tight-lipped. Neither had it passed by the President of the World Faiths Congress; there was too much at stake in the financial sphere for such uncomfortable feelings to be left to fester among key parts of the Congress. Under intense pressure behind the scenes, the Southern Brotherhood and Israeli teams had agreed to meet under an independent Chair within two weeks to try to clear the air. The Interlaken meeting was just outside that deadline, principally because no suitable venue could easily be found earlier that had been acceptable to both sides.

Relations were cooling fast; it would be Gunther Friel's task to encourage a frank exchange of views. He pursed his lips in thought as he read again the briefing notes provided by the two sides. It seemed to his experienced eye that neither was prepared to take the Siverek announcement at face value. Their meeting now on neutral soil would perhaps throw more light on the matter. He and his colleagues would be sworn to secrecy in any case. A while later he welcomed his guests, surprised at the numbers involved. The Southern Brotherhood had sent fourteen senior politicians, including six from their High Council. The Israeli delegation counted in its number no fewer than four Cabinet members from the ruling government. Gunther Friel was not intimidated by the high political level of the occasion. In fact, it emboldened his resolve to press for an outcome. A short introduction was followed by an opening of the dialogue by the Vice-President of Gabon.

"Thank you for hosting us in your beautiful city, Counsellor. The President of the World Faiths Congress has asked that we attend, and are pleased to do so." He looked round, at the Israeli delegation as well as his own. "I will come to the point. All of us around this table are very concerned at European, American and Sino-Russian initiatives at the research establishment in Turkey at Siverek. My colleagues and I are not convinced that the declared aim of the work there is the real reason for their presence. We do not feel that the harnessing of solar energy is their true aim."

Friel looked over at the Israeli team. The Minister for Technology responded to the raised eyebrows. "We would have to agree, Counsellor. Our own initial research into solar energy in the Negev Desert, though not up to European standards, leads us to believe the northern powers would be at least ten years away from the position they say they are in now. It is not realistic."

Many nods around the table told their story. Friel spoke again. "Do any of you have any other evidence to suggest another reason for their research? It would be important if world-wide contracts for use of technology were to be sought in coming months."

Silence ensued. Friel took a deep breath. "Come, come, delegates. The President of your Congress has made it very clear to this arbitration that something runs deep here. So, I ask again. Do any of you have any evidence of other projects?"

Internal discussions prior to the meeting had left the Southern Brotherhood clear as to their aim. They knew from the Kenyan ambassador that Israel had been tardy in releasing information two years earlier about the Atomic Energy Authority report. They also knew that the BBC woman had contacted Ben-Tovim, as she had said as much to the cartographer Devine, adding that her call to Norfolk was off the record, an afterthought to enable her to prepare her work in Siverek more efficiently. Why had Israel not been open with the Brotherhood as soon as her message had been received? The Devine brothers were no problem to the Brotherhood - they would naturally assume everyone outside the

Siverek Base was on the same side. The Gabonese Vice-President smiled warmly and opened his hands towards the other side of the table. His voice oozed honeyed words.

"We are completely dependent on our Congress partners to find out what is happening. An assurance was given some time ago that Mossad would work on all our behalf to aid the poor people of the world. We only need some support here." Another pause hung over the room. The snows glistened in the far distance. The Israeli Minister for Cultural Affairs sought and obtained a nod from their senior Minister present. He coughed slightly and spoke softly, seeking to emulate the sweet reason that had flowed from the African's mouth.

"We can certainly reveal our latest findings, Counsellor. Only in the past few days we have learned that the Europeans are working on developing a gene that will disable those of non-Caucasian stock. It appears to be outside existing genetic warfare prohibition agreements. The impending transfer of financial resources this coming January is clearly too much for them to bear. We ask all people of goodwill to support us in our efforts to learn more. We shall, of course, inform the World Health Organisation as soon as we have a sample of the key gene."

The Gabonese Vice-President breathed a sigh of relief. "Thank you, Minister. At last we can move forward together." Counsellor Gunther Friel was equally happy. The March sun shone brightly on the eternal snows of the Eiger and their wheeling flocks of black choughs as the two parties of delegates flew out of Switzerland.

27 March - Year 35

The results of the expedition to Beroea had been crawled over exhaustively; six and a half days during which equipment, military communications and personnel had been tested in an alien environment. Nearly a week of exposure to a world that had only previously existed in scientific, cultural and historical text books had provided a mass of external data on which suppositions theories and hypotheses could be constructed and deconstructed over coming time. Yet so much had been set aside; the Siverek community had known that the next aim had been to prepare for the second, longer, journey. A journey of over six hundred kilometres needed to be made to the freshwater lake of the Sea of Galilee. More people would be involved this time - a total of around one hundred and fifty rather than seventy five, and this time to include facilities for some serious photographic work, and a team to test options for the embryonic publicity machine. Felixana Smith's senior group, though almost all assembled in Violet Base, had not been included.

The expedition had started so well...........

Bjorn Lundquist was perspiring. It seemed he was not yet acclimatised to the growing heat of the lower latitudes. His long blond hair was getting sticky and he had too much to do to find the time to wash it. Where was the shampoo, anyway? As the long hours of the afternoon of the twenty seventh of March dragged on, the civilisation sociologist heading up the Galilee scientific contingent was becoming nervous. They seemed to be getting nowhere. Camping in isolation had turned out to be the easy part. Coming from a century of over-population to one of humans barely scratching the surface of the planet, had brought a cultural shock that none of them had expected. It was all so different! Everything was so much slower, smaller and quieter than they could comfortably comprehend. Things were on a human scale. Only Roman horses could move more quickly than a man could run. Even they were rare at the moment in Galilee. The days were quiet and the nights quieter. Animals, birds and even insects became noticeable. The expedition members themselves would have difficulty in slowing down to the new pace of life now demanded of them.

The Swede's nervousness focused on this slowing pace. He considered that the one disadvantage of the first foray to Beroea had been the military-based obsession with security. That first experience had emphasised a recommendation on over-caution. The approach, when coupled with the slower pace of life now being encountered, had led to the expedition scientists becoming almost frozen into inaction. Nomads and strange accents abounded so much that no-one seemed interested in these particular newcomers. The whole world was a melting pot. Lundquist paused on the gentle incline back to his group of tents, and gazed back at the town of Tiberias.

Though only around ten years old, the new capital of Galilee gave the impression of having existed forever on the western shore of the sea. Tiberias had been named after the new Emperor. Old tombs had been uncovered during the digging of foundations, making the whole area unclean in Jewish law. Building work, however, had pressed on, meaning the whole town had to be peopled with non-Jews. The team's reliance at this point on the use of the Greek language was proving helpful. Neither Jew nor Roman, they were almost invisible. The town lay silent in the early spring heat. Scientists had spent that day and the day before almost disconsolately wandering the streets, trying to glean what they could from casual eavesdropping and talking with market traders. The Tetrarch of Galilee, Antipas the son of Herod the Great, was out of town for some reason. Coupled with a particularly low point in the totals of the Roman garrison, it had seemed the whole region was asleep.

Lundquist looked over the sea to the Golan hills in the distance. The land was so green, much greener than he had expected after the rocky slopes around Siverek. The Galilean countryside abounded with figs, olives, date palms and walnut trees. Yet the interlopers were not in the most fertile area of Palestine to undertake botanical research. Project Methuselah demanded greater things. They would have to find out what they could of this society's controlling currents. Most of all - was there, or had there been, a local teacher of religious ways with the name Jesus Bar-Joseph from the village of Nazareth way over to the west? Lundquist reached the tents.

A group of three horse mechanics emerged through a tent flap. They had the formal title of Transport Co-ordinator, but everyone knew them as horse mechanics, or more prosaically, horse doctors. *The hover jets have to be kept operational somehow,* thought Lundquist. They were needed to move around when away from the eyes of any locals and on night journeys away from the region back to home in Siverek. Big bluff Olaf Pedersen grinned through his thick unruly beard at the Professor's arrival. After two days of struggling with basic Greek, Lundquist heard again a much more familiar greeting from the red-headed Swede.

"Professor, may we have a word, please? We've had an idea."

Crouched in the large tent among several silent hover jets the three mechanics outlined their proposal. At its end, Lundquist burst into laughter.

"Yes! Yes! Sounds great! Just come home safely!"

28 March - Year 35: 'The Hillside Pond'

The spring snow melt continued apace. Across a wide expanse of the lower slopes of Mount Hermon the pure ice-cold water gushed in sparkling profusion down the open rock faces, through dark stands of pine trees and out into the meadows. The Hula Marshes at the northern end of the upper Jordan River filled up, spilling over into the Banias River and countless other rivulets, brooks, streams and tributaries. The regular course of the river beds couldn't hold all the snow melt. Further downstream, at the Sea of Galilee, between the small villages that nestled along the lake edge, numerous hillside ponds had formed among the vast forests of reeds. The sound of laughter rose up from one of these ponds. Many of the Siverek expedition members had gathered at the pond edge; Lundquist and the senior personnel among them. At a distance, the ever-watchful security staff kept a sober eye on proceedings. The huge pine tree-trunk bobbing in one corner of the pond was by now thoroughly wet - the next plucky contestants would not find it so easy to traverse.

Lundquist thought back over the reports he had received from the previous evening's escapade. 'Escapade' was the only word in English he could find to describe the occasion. The other expedition team leaders had shared Lundquist's concerns over lack of progress with their information-gathering. They simply did not have the time to remain in Galilee for weeks on end, and then return empty-handed to Siverek. Project resources would not permit that. Lundquist smiled at the memory as he watched events unfold before him. That zany Swede Pedersen had suggested to him that he was willing to go with a group of three like-minded colleagues into the first village north of Tiberias, to dive into the local inn, tavern, hostelry, *'or whatever they call it. If we take a large portion of the expedition's supply of local currency, I'm sure we'll be able to break the ice, make friends and learn what's going on. After all, men are men the world over and a public house is a public house.'* The plan had been approved. The four would pose as *'jovial traders from the far frozen north lands, passing through Palestine to offer their pelts to the men and their kindness to the women.'* Their unique mixture of Greek, Scandinavian, English and Latin would see them through, they were sure. That part of the gap in communication that could not be bridged by genuine bonhomie would be bridged by honest wine. The team commander had insisted that a back-up team of armed personnel would lurk in the shadows outside the chosen inn. The night had gone well, especially when some opportunistic thieves had later attempted to rob one of the local shepherds and Pedersen's party had come to his rescue.

Lundquist shook his head in stunned disbelief. He was now standing ankle-deep in cold pond-water, cheering on the Olaf men competing with a village team in log-rolling, a wager set up at the end of the previous evening's drinking session. Raucous laughter rang out across the water. Village supporters, men women and children, thronged the shoreline. Expedition members, garbed in their robes, broke into what sounded

302

suspiciously like a joyous football chant. The rhythm, cadences and volume were picked up readily by all onlookers, oblivious to the differences between them. *'Here was real happiness'* thought Lundquist; *'voices finding laughter and comedy in the continual falls from the pine log.'* His eyes moistened. In an ancient world of pain and short lives, the children especially found the morning's remarkable events uplifting. Their faces glowed and their thin voices squealed. On Olaf's final turn he nearly reached the end of the pond. As his heavy body hit the water the villagers whooped with delight. The Swede hugged his opponent with equal delight, the villager oblivious to the transfer of bitterly-cold water in the embrace. The local women on the shore were already preparing bread and fish for sharing as the bedraggled menfolk struggled from the icy pond. Olaf Pedersen caught the Professor's eye. Lundquist nodded and smiled. Bread was broken and wine was poured as the expedition's caterers brought strange but delicious foods to the feast. The women exchanged cosmetics and perfumes. The demands of daily life nibbled remorselessly at the humanity gathered at the pond side as the afternoon wore on. By seven in the evening, as candles and flaming torches began to appear, few were left to reflect on the day. Everyone went back to their allotted place in life; to humble shack, to field, to stone-walled shelter, to tents over the hill in which lay hover jets and radio communication equipment. Late that evening, Lundquist was approached by one of the expedition's senior linguists. She was clearly excited. The message she carried was conveyed in breathless tones as if she could barely bring herself to say such words of import.

"The women of the village say we should have been here three weeks ago to meet a special man. The preacher, Jesus from Nazareth was passing through their village with friends. He's gone south now, perhaps Samaria or Jericho; they didn't know precisely where."

When the village awoke early on the next morning there was no sign of the strange and wonderful people who had come from nowhere and gone back the same way. At the hillside pond, the pine log was motionless in the hot morning sun.

20 - 31 March - Year 35

Life in Violet Base was busy, shot through with a mixture of excited anticipation and extreme nervousness. Pieter North was no exception. Despite wielding an increasing control of one form of temporal continuity, he felt powerless in the context of upcoming experiences. His personal future was just as unknown to him as that of a prehistoric man. He came to recognise something that Jon De Haag had once said to him, but at the time didn't understand. A great enigma that he had not understood before - time is personal, it moves at a different pace for everyone, it cannot be shared, and without human intervention and consciousness it may even be an illusion. One secret of their success was revealing itself - that the movement through universal time granted by control over physics would merely allow common experiences to be replayed. Deep within each human, even for scientists who predominantly refused to recognise a spiritual dimension to life, a separate time clock was ticking away. He recalled early lectures about philosophers of the manifold. He also recalled that he had spoken of these things with Felixana Smith when he had escorted her round the central processor unit on Red Base. *Oh, Felixana! I still love you and want you so much to want me!*

The briefing of those travelling to Aleppo had gone well. He congratulated himself. His stock had risen. He did not envy those who had set out on the tenth of March. He was too much of a coward to blaze new trails in that direction. *Goodness, a man could get himself killed with too much bravado. Perhaps on another trip away to the south, if the chance should come....* He was still managing to avoid the security chief, Atkins, whom he had caught sight of at the end of his briefing. His own days were passing in the relative sanctity of the science laboratories and theory lecture rooms. One part of his role was new; to train a new generation of temporal physicists. A disturbing thought began to nibble at his mind in these final ten days of March. Young gifted physicists were arriving each day at Violet Base, arriving in the claustrophobic atmosphere of a secret military base, two thousand one hundred years from home. A base entirely devoted to a highly-speculative project that had been born of desperation, executed by trial and error, maintained by media deception, pushed by the greed of politicians, and now marching off into the Judean deserts towards an unknown and unknowable climax. It began to occur to him that this might be a one-way street. Was that what Jon De Haag had sought to warn him of in his final holographic message? Pieter thought back to that message, trying to divine new insights or a new angle to the mysteries it raised. One particular phrase jumped at him - *'I dare not even come back to the project base'*. He sighed in exasperation. He had been over all this before, with no sensible outcome. The phrase seemed warning enough. He began to wonder if it would be worth formulating an escape plan.....

It all went from his mind on the twentieth of March when Felixana Smith arrived. He was pleased when that plump but gifted holographer of hers came to seek his help with possible conflicts between the maintenance of the temporal cocoons and telecommunication clarity. Without power-boosting via an array of orbiting satellites, their systems were almost primeval again. Impressively, the Englishman had noticed very quickly that the Aleppo communications had been far from perfect. Unfortunately, the Galilee journey was on the point of beginning. There would be no time to make major changes before the twenty second of the month. Pieter's contacts with Felixana were cordial enough. She could sense from his shortness of breath that he longed for her, though he tried not to turn her rejection into coldness. *'Perhaps I'm maturing'*, he told himself. The sciences were beginning to grip him, anyway. He was still basking in the glory of the senior briefing he had given on the sixth of March. Any scientist or specialist he turned to seemed genuinely pleased to make contact. The month passed swiftly for him.

Felixana herself was feeling nervous and edgy. She was in completely uncharted waters. The solar wind publicity presentation she had fronted on the nineteenth of February had doubtless made her a household name in 2135. It would certainly burn her bridges with the BBC! She conjectured there might be a flicker of fame and support for a few weeks in her absence, but once the true nature of Project Methuselah was revealed to an astounded planet her subterfuge would quickly cause anger. She had deliberately lied in the name of the Corporation. She bitterly regretted now having agreed to use the BBC logos on that broadcast rather than generic European, American or Chinese ones. After all, these shadowy people were now her only 'employer'. She felt Paul Devine was still loyal to her; at least, she hoped he was. She had been honest with him throughout, and eventually he had come to accept the reality of their surroundings. She watched him. He was genuinely wrapped up in the enormity of his task. Holographic pulses and temporal cocoons seemed to throw up so many permutations for his delight. The still-far-from-perfect transmissions received from the Galilee expedition kept him busy. She assuaged her professional guilt by revelling in Simon Atkins' attention.

The South African security chief had passed a lonely fortnight on Violet Base until her arrival. The military ascendancy over the Aleppo expedition had not duplicated itself within the confines of the Base. His security personnel and procedures held sway. Felixana was making an increasing number of night-time visits to his quarters, their conversations in the darkness ranging from his safari experiences in Natal to her treks over the English Peak District. Only rarely during the month did his nightmare return. He was always alone in bed when it came and he could not bring himself to share it with her when they were next together. His awful secret still wrapped itself around his heart.

Life on Violet Base pulsed on as the heat of March gradually increased. People and materials came and went. Messages from Galilee were processed under Paul Devine's orchestral genius and syndicated around the Base. A rare and welcome humour lifted the Base as footage of the hillside pond competition entertained an avidly-watching audience in the main conference hall. The wide tapestry that had been the month of March had been fully woven and hung in history before their colleagues returned with their reports from Galilee conveyed from the women of the village.

CARAMEL

Sunday 3 April 2135 - Easter Day

Jesus Christ is risen today - alleluia! Our triumphant holy day - alleluia!

Mary Trent had never been to a church. In fact, by the end of the twenty-first century, only half a million of Europe's more than four hundred and fifty million citizens had done so. On Sunday morning, as the commercial shopping malls rapidly filled up with the arrival of the first Sunday in the new month, Mary and Susan had walked the half kilometre to their small community church building. Easter Day was still celebrated in the southern hemisphere as the principal Christian Festival, but for many decades now the northern world had treated it as a further shopping day.

The congregation of about twenty five predominantly mature men and women sang lustily in the small hall. The few who did not know the words of the hymn by heart watched intently as the lines appeared on the big screen at the front. The Pastor faced his flock, pleased that some volunteers had placed bright daffodils around the building. Spring had not come particularly late, but it had been only during the previous week that buds had opened in sufficient number to brighten the Festal occasion. A shaft of sunlight pierced downwards through a roof sky window, illuminating the singers, motes of dust swimming dizzily in its beam. The Pastor gave a mental cross to the dusting rota, counter-balancing the mental tick already given to the flower rota. At the close of the singing everyone sat before him. He cleared his throat and began his sermon.

Mary sat with her half-sister in the third row on the right side. Both were smartly dressed. Mary listened intently to the Pastor's words. His theme appeared to be 'renewal'. He spoke of 'beginning anew' and touched upon 'setting the daily clock to zero'. Mary thought back over the weeks since leaving Birchwood. The weather had not been especially clement, with squally showers through early March, but she had taken every opportunity to go for walks in the fresh air, and she had carefully noted each small harbinger of the season's changes as she went. The arrival of April had brought some welcome slight warmth. There was little real countryside around the western housing and commercial estates of Northampton, but at least Far Cotton did boast a community civic park, with a pond, trees and park benches. She always tried to finish her walks with a rest for reflection in the park, whatever the weather. Her psychiatrist had reminded her of the importance of Nature; 'green therapy', he had called it. Remembering his talks with her, she had not complained about the March showers, often keeping a special eye open for the possibility of a rainbow. None had appeared.

On Friday, the first day of April, she had been driven indoors by a distant rumble of thunder and a short sharp shower. As she wiped her hair on a towel, a colourful arc had lit up the dark western sky in a late afternoon burst of sunshine. Mary had counted the seven clearly-defined colours in rapt concentration. She found she could recall the rhyme.

Red is the one blood humanity bleeds

Orange the fruit for the food that it needs

Yellow for sunshine to warm and to tease

Green for the forests, the grass and the trees

Blue is the ocean, for river and stream

Indigo, darkness, to rest and to dream

And finally, Violet, the deepest of all

For when Man is ready to answer the call

On her way home, she began to weep with happiness for the world and for her life. Susan had come to meet her at the gate to give her the hug she often needed at these times.

"I'm sorry, Susan. I shouldn't be tearful. It's Comedy for Charity Day."

Her sister had smiled knowingly. "Never mind about that All Fools' Day business," she had replied. "I'll take you to Church on Sunday - it's Easter."

The Pastor's sermon of renewal came to an end. He noticed the few newcomers and was determined to extend a warm welcome and share a cup of tea before he had to move on to take his next service. Mary was pleased that he found the time to come and speak with her. She resolved she would sit on a chair next time that had been dusted.

4 April - Year 35

The Deputy Base Commander pointed to the calendar chart illuminated in a corner of the large screen.

"The supposed sighting was reported on the twenty eighth of the month, referring to three weeks previous to that date, so around the seventh of March. We can only assume these villagers can dependably measure three weeks.....?" The inflection in his voice turned it into a question. He glanced at one of the historians, who bit her tongue at such an uncomplimentary presumption and merely nodded agreement. The Deputy pressed on, oblivious to his clumsiness.

"So that means at ambling speed, and assuming plenty of stops for preaching, eating, socialising and sleeping, we're talking about a journey south at around ten kilometres every three days. Total distance travelled as of today, certainly no more than ninety kilometres and probably somewhat less. It's around a hundred kilometres to Jerusalem, so the target would probably not have reached there yet. That's assuming, of course, that Jerusalem is the intended destination. The villagers only mentioned Samaria or Jericho."

Many of the scholars in the room winced at the description of the Christian figurehead as 'the target', but held their counsel. Several considered it was perhaps best to keep the discussion objective, even cold, and they certainly conceded it needed to be couched in military terms. There was no time, and no more money, to spend it in a protracted period of trial and error. Pieter North had emphasised again the need for almost surgical precision. Project leaders had been relatively successful in keeping Project Methuselah focused. Nevertheless, every scientist, scholar and expert on the Base secretly harboured thoughts of moving on past the politicians' objective to undertake unique and possibly unrepeatable research in their own field. One of the Biblical team spoke.

"The likely route would be south through the Jordan valley. The road would be well used - I use the word 'road' lightly, of course - to avoid going through Samaria. At Jericho, they would be expected to turn west onto the road climbing up to Jerusalem."

Again, there was a nervous wince of unreality as he forced himself to speak in dispassionate, impersonal tones and terms about acts he had studied word for word from the Christians' holy book. No-one queried the avoidance of Samaria. Some knew the history. The huge curved executive screen glowed with a detailed map of the region, running from Gaulantis in the north to Idumea in the south. A series of indicators riffled and spun down the left edge to provide legend colours and symbols for viewers to activate by voice, for transposing information either to the main map or two smaller ones inset on the right side. These showed the first century detail of Jericho and Jerusalem. The Frenchman who headed the senior medical teams interposed. Doctor Pierre Lucas cut an impressive figure with his grey goatee beard and tall imposing stature.

"Why must we assume the destination is Jerusalem? Given that this sighting is of the man named Jesus, which I accept it is, we have no guarantee where he is on his ministry. A major movement south may be significant in terms of the activity no longer being centred around his home area of Nazareth, but it may be several years before that final journey to Jerusalem for Passover. Anyway, even if that is the case, we are too late to get there ourselves. Surely Passover is the same as Easter, and southern nations celebrated that occasion this past weekend in 2135."

Mumbles and murmurs around the gathering echoed much of the Doctor's scepticism. The senior historian responded, looking to the mathematicians and astronomers present to provide supportive nods.

"On a straight scientific count-back we are indeed in the year thirty five, measured from the departure base in 2135 in Siverek, from the wide range of atomic decay samples taken and the stellar picture, plus anecdotal historical evidence on the ground, as it were, gathered now in Aleppo and Tiberias. That does put the date at the end of the likely range for Jesus' ministry. The point about Passover is actually easier to prove, though mathematically more convoluted. Seasons and lunations, the cycles of the moon, are now taking place under the Julian calendar. In our journey from the twenty-second century we have left behind the Gregorian calendar, introduced on the fifteenth of October 1582. The Christian year is, or rather will be in due course, under a different cycle. The difference is increasing by three days every four centuries. Passover is a much older festival than Easter, obviously. We must take into account the Hebrew calendar. In order to link Passover with Easter, we must turn to the Julian cycle. In years three, eight, eleven, fourteen and nineteen of the Julian calendar, Passover would have taken place a month after the equivalent date for Gregorian Easter. We can project back, as it were, a theoretical Gregorian Easter. The range of dates for the Gregorian Easter is between the twenty second of March and the twenty fifth of April. So, if Easter had existed in the pre-Christian era, it would have been very late this year, on the twenty fourth of April. This means for the period immediately facing us, Passover will not occur until the seventeenth of May. There is plenty of time left, if you will excuse the pun, for both the target and us to reach Jerusalem."

Excited gasps shivered in the room. The project's potential began to open up before them in a way that it had not done before. In discussion earlier had been how and when to alert other bases to the report of a Galilean sighting. The expedition had returned forty eight hours before with its news. All scientific disciplines on base had now taken an opportunity to assess the significance of that report. The publicity officers under Felixana Smith edited the Aleppo and Galilee films for maximum effect, climaxing in the news gleaned from the women of the lakeside village. Some controversy hovered over whether to include footage of the log-rolling episode. Reports had been coming down over the past five weeks from 2135 that political pressure was being exerted to cut back on unnecessary expenditure now the time-travel elements had been completed. This was not well received by the wide range of scientific endeavour now immersed in such a unique research opportunity. They all knew with regret that an indication of a sighting of an itinerant preacher named Jesus would trump other considerations. The hilarity and seeming irrelevance of the water-sports might have appeared as an extravagant diversion without this golden nugget. In the event, the hillside pond episode was included.

A glossy and detailed holographic film was packaged as a test report for Paul Devine to dispatch via the cargo TTUs. Two days after the senior team meeting the package left Violet Base, travelling within the temporal sealing system. Twelve hours after that, the Commander at Caramel Base was on a security scrambler to the White House and the Berlaymont Building.

Tuesday 5 April 2135

Thousands of kilometres from Washington DC, on the African shores of the Indian Ocean, the High Council of the Southern Brotherhood was in

311

emergency secret session in a toffee-coloured low-rise building to the south of the central district of Mombasa. The ocean and its beach life buzzed away just a few hundred metres from the building. Bathers in reasonable numbers dotted the golden sands - a young couple naked with their daughter, two older women, possibly sisters, standing in the white shallows and sharing a conversation, topless women in sunhats striding confidently along just above the wave line, sun worshippers dressing and undressing, numerous heads visible as bobbing targets outside the breaker line, green pink and orange flashes of sail at several hundred metres' distance as local yachtsmen practised their craft. Several innocuous inflatable speedboats slapped the waves as they plied their way up and down this busy stretch of coastline. The security officers guarding the on-shore gathering were enjoying their sunny duty more than usual this day. Unlike the happiness on the beach the mood in the low-rise building was sombre and determined. After a period for prayers and reflection, the meeting began.

"We have all seen the latest news from our agents in Haifa. I want to give everyone the opportunity to comment."

The Ghanaian President, current Chair of the High Council, looked with some concern around the gathering. All fifteen High Councillors were present, an indication of the seriousness of the situation. The Gabonese Vice-President, having led the deputation to Switzerland nearly three weeks earlier, was the first to voice his feelings.

"The silence and inaction is ominous, in my view. The build-up of Israeli armour started seven weeks ago has stopped, but it hasn't gone away. Their soldiers remain significantly close to the northern base at Siverek, but not close enough to goad the northern powers into action. The European Union and its allies have referred to solar wind 'this' and solar wind 'that'. Nothing else has come out of the northern capitals, and even those solar wind announcements have been vague. Both Brussels and Tel-Aviv are waiting, but waiting for what?"

The Paraguayan High Councillor chose to answer the rhetorical plea, her response merely voicing what many were thinking. "They're waiting for some concrete news from the ancient world. The northern powers will announce something and then Israel will respond."

"We shall need to respond, too," chimed the St Kitts and Nevis High Councillor. "If their project is genuine, we could all face destruction as a force for good." The discussions ebbed and flowed, everyone taking an opportunity to speak when their turn came.

'There may be no ancient world. It may be an expensive bluff. Remember the fuss in the twentieth century when powerful voices claimed America had not landed men on the moon in 1969.'

'The BBC woman on the solar wind charade was the same person on the secret transmission to John Devine in England. She may indeed have been trying to mislead us.'

'We don't know for certain what message she passed to the Israelis. She may have been misleading them also.'

'I am angry that the delegation from Tel-Aviv tried again to confuse the Brotherhood by raising another red herring. The story about gene warfare seemed a mite desperate, especially with most international protocols on such weapons quite tightly drawn up as to detail.'

'I believe we cannot take any chances with the validity of a thrust against Christianity. We must assume it to be real, and respond accordingly.'

'We have a strong faith in God Almighty, my brothers and sisters. Surely our work will be recognised and our actions, whatever they may be, prove to be the right way forward.'

'How are we to respond, then? Surely it would be better to be proactive? We need to provoke the north into revealing its hand before it is ready.'

Agonising deliberations continued throughout the day, interspersed with prayer, refreshment, and more prayer. By the time the sun was setting a decision had been reached. The Southern Brotherhood would call the bluff of the northern powers and provoke a response from Israel. A delegation would make a highly-publicised visit to Brussels within the week. Delegates would carry the southern hemisphere's good wishes for a speedy completion to solar wind research and the offer of whatever practical help might be useful in support of all the nations of the world. The delegation would provocatively issue a press release while in Brussels expressing its great pleasure in expecting that Washington and Beijing would shortly be providing cut-price energy for hard-pressed northern consumers in advance of wider generosity. They would also announce an intention to travel to Turkey immediately after leaving Brussels. The Brotherhood would tell the World Faiths Congress only after the delegation had left for Europe, adding at that time for the benefit of Israel that a visit to the World Health Organisation headquarters in Geneva would be included in the tour to discuss possible contraventions of gene warfare protocols by un-named Governments.

It was also decided by the High Council that a rapid-reaction Special Forces unit should begin secret training in Ethiopia, just in case it might prove necessary to circumvent the Israeli cordon and disrupt the Siverek Base.

11 April - Year 35

"It's being caused by the new power levels in the lattice. We've checked the timings and there's no doubt of it."

Pieter North's principal electrical engineer held up his hands to emphasise his honesty. The group of senior physicists watched the graphs march across the presentation at the end of the room, synchronised with the time numerals glowing on the large screen. There was no doubt; the power level in the lattice was destroying outgoing communications.

"Why didn't we know this before?" North was fighting to conceal his irritation. The glow on his professional satisfaction was beginning to fade. The Communications Manager defended himself strongly.

"It's only just happened! The Aleppo expedition was primed to provide incoming data only, to maintain secrecy. It was entirely under the control of the military, anyway. We had no civilian input into their communications protocols. We had two-way communication for the second journey, but as we can see from the graphs, last week we were notified of plasma changes to the lattice and sealing walls."

North looked to Caramel Bondi. His stand-off with the Chief Plasmologist had never been resolved. He regretted not having sorted it out before, but realised it was too late now to have such feelings. The black woman was calm in responding.

"We had to strengthen the sealing walls. The frequency of transfers in and out of the Base had weakened them. We couldn't put personnel at risk, and we needed to build in the bounce compensation."

"I understand that," conceded the Dutchman. "What's done is done, but we'll need at some point to review inter-team working. One discipline can't work in isolation like this. It's more important to find a way to circumvent the problem. Perhaps we can contact the main expedition in the mornings and allow in-comers onto Base only in the afternoons."

North looked to the TTU controllers' link man. "Surely there are windows between each transfer?"

"No. The new level had been built permanently into the sealing walls of the lattice. It makes no difference if we use the TTUs or not. If we reduce the power, even by a little, the walls collapse. That would be disastrous."

"What do you mean?"

"At best, we are cut off permanently from all other bases. At worst, who knows? The whole edifice may collapse into a black hole, for all we know. This is way beyond our practical experience. It's like the first generation of skyscrapers over two hundred years before we left home base. They would have exploded if conventional demolition had been attempted."

Something in North silently died inside. Without Jon De Haag's guiding inspiration he knew he was left as Mankind's leading theoretical physicist on temporal transference, yet he didn't have a clue what to do. He realised this lonely exposure was the other, darker, side of the coin from basking in peer adulation. It made him feel weak and sick. All he could do was pretend he was not sick. That would be less easy when he would have to report to the Base Commander. He tried to keep his voice steady and calm.

"Then we have no alternative at the moment to managing with only one-way communication. Are the people off-base aware of it?"

"Oh, yes. They are now. We've received two requests for acknowledgement of information. We can't get through in reply. They should be in Aleppo by now. The expedition leaders tell us that in the absence of contact they will carry on moving south towards the Sea of Galilee."

One of the Communication Managers snorted with disgust. "That's very courageous of them, but most unwise. We shall have to see if we can set up portable transmitters at some distance from the base, to neutralise the effects of the lattice. Trial and error as to distance and level of signal will take some time. Meanwhile, the expedition is effectively cut off."

North's level of sickness increased. "Has it happened on other bases?"

Caramel Bondi cut in sharply. "It can't happen on other bases! Home base has access to a thousand satellites in orbit to boost signal levels. On all other bases there has never been the need to communicate out into the distant countryside like this. It's a one-off situation."

After the meeting, Pieter North cornered the plasmologist. "What on earth were you doing? This could be very serious if we can't solve it."

For some reason, Caramel Bondi was equally combative. She seemed genuinely frightened, and not by the Dutchman's attitude. Her eyes flashed her fear.

"Pieter, the situation is more serious than any of us thought. Our generation of electrical power is being affected by something in the environment, something we haven't come across on other bases. It's as if our use of positive and negative poles of current in this time zone is triggering-off an independent reaction somewhere."

Tuesday 12 April 2135

"Good morning, world! You're watching Timberwolf News Channel, live from Montreal, Canada, and I am Bradford Fletcher. Welcome to 'World in Focus'.

"International events have gathered pace this past week. A delegation from the bloc of southern emerging nations, the self-styled Southern Brotherhood, arrived in Europe Friday to offer support for the solar wind project that's been on everyone's lips. Yet while the Brotherhood has been talking peace, we also have the dark possibility of a new arms race. Today, 'World in Focus' will be discussing these events with key parties, and we ask, 'where do we go from here?'

"Timberwolf News is pleased to welcome to the studio the media representative of the North American Energy Association, Clarke Donnety -welcome Clarke - and from the World Health Organisation in Switzerland, we are joined by Suzanne de la Mare-bonsoir Suzanne-thank you both for agreeing to be with us at short notice.

"Can I start with you, Suzanne? Press releases from the Southern Brotherhood over the weekend have given quite a bit of detail on a report from their secret investigations into a possible contravention of gene warfare prohibition agreements. No nations have been named, but the communiques make it clear that the Brotherhood sees such initiatives as a worrying development at a time of peace. Can you confirm that you are taking these reports seriously?"

"Yes, of course. We must take all such reports seriously when they come from sovereign governments. Your viewers will know that there have been world agreements to outlaw GMWs- Genetic Malfunction Weapons-for some sixty years now."

"These agreements have been tenuous to say the least, surely, Suzanne. They have only related to domestic infrastructure - water supplies, that kind of thing; a sort of tampering via civilian-based terrorist action. The agreements never covered military delivery systems, such as guns or rockets, where aggression could have been expected in advance."

"That is true."

Bradford Fletcher leaned forward in his chair, focussing on the slight French woman on the colour screen in front of him. "Can I press you on this point, Suzanne? The media releases do emphasise the suggestion that the particular genetic weapon their agents have uncovered would most likely need to be tested by military exercises. Is the World Health Organisation monitoring any such exercises at the moment?"

Suzanne de la Mare's face was deadpan, though she was smiling inside. She knew a trap when she saw one and easily side-stepped it. "There is no reason to suspect any current exercise of being a cover for the testing of prohibited weapons. The reports are only a few days old. We are studying them carefully and thoroughly. We cannot assume a link to any government at the moment."

"Thank you, Suzanne. Can I now turn to you, Clarke, here in the studio? Update our viewers, if you would, in layman's terms, on the significance of solar wind power."

"In a nutshell, Bradford, it would be the holy grail of power harnessing. Up until now, the replacements for the fossil fuels of the twentieth century have been geophysical; wind, wave, tidal, direct solar heating, hydro-electric, that kind of thing. All based on the Earth's surface, and all adequate for the needs of the last century. Since Man moved off the Earth, however, to the Moon and beyond, the point of tidal power has been pretty useless. Global population levels have also reached the point where something more substantial and dependable has been needed for large-scale electricity generation. The stream of particles coming from the sun is limitless, so the whole planet would benefit."

"Would you say the offer of help from the Southern Brotherhood is significant?"

"Yes, most certainly it is. Those nations will have the financial resources from January next year, both to support the research and to buy the 'finished product', as it were. These are exciting times, and it's good to see the world coming together this way."

"What is your view, Clarke, of the suggested plans for cheap energy, hinted at by the Brotherhood as coming from America and China?"

"If it happens, then that's great. We have had no confirmation from Beijing or Washington yet, but we are certainly excited, as I said before. I guess we all are."

Bradford Fletcher spun in his chair as a red bar appeared across the bottom of his monitor screen.

"Can I ask both of you about some breaking news? We are getting reports this morning that the European Union has refused permission for the Southern Brotherhood's delegation to travel immediately on to the solar wind research base in Turkey. The Union's High Commissioner for Foreign Affairs has apologised to the delegates that approval cannot be granted at the moment. She had indicated, and I quote, 'the Union regrets that the current uncertain level of stability in the region would make it unwise at present to escort senior world leaders to such an important research facility.'

"What does this news indicate for you, Clarke Donnety?"

"Well, Bradford, it's a wise move. We're all keen to learn more about the solar wind project, but it shows that the Europeans do not want to jeopardise the safety of their future partners."

"Do you have a view, Suzanne de la Mare?"

"I agree with your other guest. But equally, I don't see a link between the two items we have been discussing. There is no evidence that the gene warfare suggestion points to the Middle East."

"Thank you, Suzanne de la Mare from the World Health Organisation and Clarke Donnety of the North American Energy Association. It's still looking good for the world. We would certainly appreciate an improvement in economic circumstances here in the north! Our next item concerns the proposed shuttle system for British Columbia. Join us after the break."

One angry wave of the hand switched off the transmission. The Chinese Premier was furious. The Peoples' Republic would not be misrepresented this way. The Europeans would be told to bring Project Methuselah to an early and successful conclusion, whatever the costs and sacrifices. He smiled to himself; there were few Chinese nationals in the range of Siverek bases. Their own nation's input had been overwhelmingly financial in nature. As for the Southern Brotherhood, well, their effrontery would be punished soon enough.

14 April - Year 35

The rain fell heavily on the Galilean countryside, flowing in rivulets then torrents from the hills into the villages and towns. The sounds of the downpour drummed on the tents pitched on the far outskirts of Tiberias, bringing a constant humming to the ears of the seven leaders gathered within. There was much to discuss. The remaining one hundred and fifty expedition members had reached the Galilean capital and there was still no word from Siverek. The commander had sent a message to the Base that they would continue going south. Whether it would be received or not, they couldn't tell; the drumming of the rain resembled the unknowing static of their useless receivers.

As a member of the expedition, Felixana Smith listened gloomily to the other leaders' reports. The problems over communication were putting additional pressure on her publicity and reporting team. She felt distinctly uncomfortable. She felt there was a conflict in her dual roles. How could she faithfully report the unfolding of events when she was working as a publicity agent to announce the project's success? It had all seemed so simple in theory; now it was pulling her in opposite directions. Several of her team had already voiced such concerns to her in private. She had merely nodded sadly. She also found that she was missing the company of Simon Atkins. Despite her attempts to remain detached, she found that she was falling for him. She knew what absence did to the heart. The present discussions round the huddled senior community only gave substance to her anxiety. They knew they couldn't hear from Siverek, so they didn't know if their reports going back were being received. She shook off her worries as best she could in order to put her energy into a

319

professional performance. She reminded herself this journey was unique in human history, and it fell to her to be its human voice and human face. Whatever the journey might bring, she had to hope that the high quality of her work would shine through. She resolved to lift her game to new heights of journalism. She nearly believed herself.

The subject in the tent changed; having talked out the options for communication they needed to decide if they should make contact with the villagers who had changed lives round a hillside pond. There were some personnel who had been on the previous visit, Olaf Pedersen among them. Yet he was not a party to this senior-level discussion. The third expedition was more highly-mechanised than the previous two had been. Half-tracks and two motorised cannon had joined the hover horses. There were also vehicles carrying a wider range of scientific equipment than before. The paraphernalia associated with the 'BBC' team was also extensive, though not particularly bulky. Felixana had seriously considered scrubbing out all visual references to the Corporation - who the hell would appreciate the advertising opportunity in an ancient Judean desert? She decided on balance that a comforting feeling of authenticity needed to be conveyed to her intended audiences, wherever they might be. She pulled her concentration back to the task in hand, learning that the leaders would conceal their presence from any villagers. Someone mentioned Pieter North's warning against the undue exposure of 'unfamiliar accents and mystical weaponry'. Felixana's stomach flipped; she had forgotten that lovelorn Dutchman and suddenly felt sorry for him. Yet the recollection also served to warm her inside towards the security chief so far away on the Base.

The expedition would skirt round the lakeside villages. It was agreed that the hundred or so personnel who were to press on southwards would strike out along the Jordan valley. Although they were still relatively-lightly disguised as Greek travellers - the larger mechanised transports would continue to move only at night - the leaders considered it wise to use rural and desert areas, avoiding the Decapolis towns of Gadara, Scythopolis and Pella. The long journey to Jericho lay ahead. It would take a further three days and nights to get there. Travelogue-style film reports had been recorded and transmitted; the publicity team could but hope that all the material was getting through. If not, those in Siverek would have to wait until the travellers returned with copies of the recordings. Paul Devine had remained behind in Siverek to boost any weak signals, edit the material and package it in digestible chunks for despatching up-time. Once he had solved any minor problems, Felixana knew he would start sending the physical packages away - *'if he had received them at all'*, she reminded herself. She mused on a possible return to Siverek, but quickly shook off the day-dream. It was far too painful a recollection to think of the Base and the people there.

In the late afternoon the rain stopped. The faintest hint of a rainbow brushed the sky, just sufficient to encourage some of the travellers to stand and watch. As the April sun set over the hills of Arbel to the west, the camera team began filming the orange and blue sky. One of the expedition's historians provided the commentary for the film. He related how, some seventy years before, King Herod had marched into Galilee to subdue the countryside. The local population had offered little resistance. However, some guerrillas had taken refuge in caves in the Arbel hills. The historian told how Herod had lowered his men in baskets over the ledges at the top in order to reach those hiding below. Using grappling hooks they were able to dislodge most of the Galileans. The remainder were burned out. The setting sun shifted its colour from orange to a fiery red, just as the story reached its climax. The chill of the April night clung to Felixana's bones as the expedition lifted camp and moved on.

17 April - Year 35

The expedition moved south for three days and nights, following the curves and bends of the River Jordan. The hover-horses travelled by day. The mechanised transports moved by night. After covering half the distance between Tiberias and Jericho the landscape forced a change of approach. There was far more undergrowth in the vicinity of the main watercourse than the scientists had expected. The botanists and biologists were reporting abundant wildlife - wild boars, antelope, bears, wolves, even lion scats were being detected. Snakes and lizards were encountered everywhere. The verdant undergrowth revealed willow and reeds that were too dense to navigate quickly. Extensive stands of fig and wild olive groves slowed progress. Date palms were beginning to appear in larger numbers. On the next level of higher slope the spreading branches of the Egyptian sycamore would catch the unwary horse rider with glancing blows if their automatic altimeter controls were not carefully pre-calibrated. South of Alexandrium, a diversion was instigated. The expedition rose to higher ground west of the Jordan. The rich soil was giving way to less fertile rendzina. The inorganic dusty marl of the Judean wilderness was becoming more prevalent. Though there was still ample fertile land at lower levels, the rocky hills and pale brown lifeless soil of the south began to be the predominant features.

The main road south towards Phasaelis was proving much easier to pass along, but using it meant exclusively night-time travel. The level of safety actually increased; marauding bands of brigands would stay well away from the huge black war machines that could outrun Roman horses and were larger than Roman siege towers. Non-interference with local traditions regrettably had to be partially sacrificed to ensure a steady speed southwards. As night fell on the seventeenth of April, the expedition encamped high on a lonely hillside to the south west of Jericho. The green vegetation below them rolled away into the darkness of the valley. At this height they could see the flaming torches along the watchtowers of the city away to the north east, pinpricks in the blackness. Jericho was the oldest and lowest town in the world, some two hundred and fifty metres below sea level, occupying a site on the only oasis in the lower Jordan valley.

The historians in the expedition knew this area well. A few kilometres to the north-west stood the high hill on which King Herod had built a fortress to defend the road to Jerusalem beyond. He had named the fortress Cyprus after his mother. Unseen below the expedition's encampment, the Wadi Qelt snaked its way north-east towards Jericho. Halfway to the city, invisible in the darkness, were the massive colonnaded extravagances of Herod's winter palaces. Many of those encamped on the hillside knew this was a dangerous place to be. The area should be full of troops. There were just over four weeks to Passover. Yet the expedition was by now well experienced. The setting of the dwelling, the drawing and guarding of the perimeter and the maintenance of a low profile were undertaken swiftly and quietly. The twenty-second century aliens melted unnoticed into their high base camp. Velvet darkness descended again on the mountainsides, accompanied by a heavy silence unbroken even by the unearthly wail of the wild dogs. The Earth spun on its axis, bringing in its due time the onset of a new day.

18 April - Year 35

Felixana Smith joined the other five discipline leaders in the expedition commander's tent as the hot sun struck the hill face above the camp. They all waited while the senior historian gathered the pieces of her presentation.

"Staying here outside Jericho is probably our best option at present. There are now just twenty nine days to the start of the Jewish Festival of

322

Passover. Our task is to locate Jesus and his accompanying band of regular followers. We can only assume we are ahead of them. The road to the west of here, running to the right of the Roman fortress of Cyprus, is the road they will take to Jerusalem. That's relatively easy to deduce; there are no other roads. Our main problem will be avoiding the Roman troops. Their headquarters for this Province lie to the north-west, on the coast at Caesarea. Normally, they would not be around here in large numbers, but in the approach to Passover, all that will change."

The Base Commander interjected. "You're right that our key focus must be on Methuselah. We have good military cover, but we don't have the fire-power to take out a whole army. Even if we had the will-power to try it, it would be unwise to wreck the delicate nature of our existence here. Tell us something about the Roman occupation. What is the likelihood that all these soldiers can disrupt our plans?"

"I'll deal with the first part to set the scene for us. It's important to understand the background. It colours how we may need to make progress from now on. The current troop deployment needs a military assessment."

The military commander nodded quietly, waiting his turn to speak. The senior historian continued with her own talk.

"It's a long and bloody history, but I'll keep it short. Rome's been dabbling in eastern affairs for over a hundred years now. Under Pompey they laid siege to Jerusalem in sixty three, before the Common Era, where the Jews under Aristobulus retreated to the temple fortress. Pompey had heard a great deal about this temple. Only the priests were allowed to enter. Anyway, Pompey's curiosity got the better of him and the Romans went in. They even entered the Holy of Holies which the Jews believed was the throne-room of their God. Although nothing was touched, the Jews never forgot, or forgave, the sacrilege they felt had occurred. It has soured relations between the Romans and the Jews ever since."

"How did we get to where we are now, and who exactly is King Herod?" One of the other scientists asked the question. The historian warmed to her story, excited by the juxtaposition of knowing history and yet living through it at the same time.

"Who exactly *was* King Herod, you mean. He died over thirty eight years ago. Anyway, the Jews continued to revolt against Rome. Herod's father, Antipater, was chief minister in Jerusalem soon after the siege. He realised his only hope of keeping real power was in playing up to the

Romans. Rome entered a period of civil war, with Pompey and Julius Caesar fighting each other. Antipater supported Caesar, as it happens that's the winning side, and in gratitude Caesar gave him the official title of Procurator of Judea.

"Antipater was moving up in the world. He promoted his two eldest sons. Phasael was made Governor of Jerusalem and Herod was put in charge of Galilee. Unfortunately, Herod got a little too rough with the Galileans, illegally executing his opponents. The Supreme Council of the Jews, the Sanhedrin, got upset and summoned Herod to Jerusalem to explain himself. Just imagine the indignity! The representatives of the occupied people ordering around a local puppet of the occupiers! Herod never forgot the humiliation. Sextus, the Governor of Syria, moved Herod to the border zones next to Judea to lower his profile a bit.

"In the spring of the year forty, before the Common Era, the Parthian empire to the east invaded Syria. Their local allies under Antigonus made a dash for Jerusalem. Fearing the worst, Herod escaped to Egypt. He appealed to Mark Antony, the Roman ruler of the east, for help against Antigonus. Mark Antony recognised in Herod the only person who could possibly keep the locals under control. The Roman Senate nominated him as King of Judea. Just as with Pompey before him, and like the set-to he had with the Sanhedrin, Herod didn't much care how he upset the Jews. He was only half-Jewish, after all. In the year thirty seven, before the Common Era, Herod married Miriam. He hoped that marrying into the local Hasmonaean family would make him more acceptable to the people of Jerusalem. Nevertheless, he still had to defeat Antigonus. In a bloody siege Herod eventually mounted the throne in Jerusalem in the summer that year.

"Remember the humiliation at the hands of the Sanhedrin? Well, Herod took revenge by executing forty five of its seventy members. These have been brutal times, to be sure. Nothing much has changed these past seventy years. Archelaus, Herod's son, proved to be even worse than his father. The Jews and Samaritans, normally not talking to each other, actually got together to send a delegation to Rome to complain! Archelaus was stripped of his title. Twenty nine years ago, Judea was placed under direct Roman rule.

"Herod's lavish building programmes had cost immense sums of money and taxes were high. The winter palaces just north-east of us were - are - famous for their opulence, even more luxurious than the palace on the plateau at Masada. Just as with the Herodean fortresses at Doq and

Cyprus, the winter palaces are only occupied as and when they are needed by the local Prefect and the senior Roman 'legionary legates'".

"Who is the local Prefect?" someone asked.

"When Tiberius became the current Roman Emperor he named Valerius Gratus as Prefect of Judea. Nine years ago, Tiberius replaced Gratus with Pontius Pilate."

A thought passed through Felixana Smith's mind, but she said nothing. The expedition's military commander had been patiently listening to the historical perspective. He saw his chance and broke into the presentation.

"You were asking, Michael, whether the current Roman presence can disrupt our plans. I think it best if I continue the briefing on that issue." The base commander nodded his agreement and the army man proceeded.

"I'll start with Pontius Pilate as he's now got everyone's attention." Humour bubbled around the room; the gathering was focused and fascinated with the wealth of detail. "Judea is considered as a third-rate province. No seniority there, then, as far as Rome is concerned. A Roman Senator would not have contemplated taking a posting here.

"Archelaus had about three thousand troops originally. They were taken over by the Prefect, trained towards Roman standards after a fashion, and organised into six Roman auxiliary units; say, around five hundred men in each unit, or cohort. I say 'after a fashion' because these were not legionaries, but conscripted in Samaria. There has been some strengthening in military discipline over the past twenty years, but numerical strength has dropped. The present totals, as far as we can tell, number around fifteen hundred, plus a cavalry unit. The three infantry cohorts are....." he consulted his notes, ".....Cohors I Sebastenorum, Cohors Secunda Italica Civium Romanorum, and Cohors Prima Augusta. This latter cohort is now predominantly Italian in membership. The three cohorts move around the Province in rotation, two being based in Jerusalem, in the Herodean palace and the Antonia fortress. The third is based in the Roman provincial capital, Caesarea, over ninety kilometres away. There is also around the province somewhere the cavalry unit, the Ala I Sebastenorum."

The military commander looked over at the historian. "As Susan has mentioned, the approach of Passover is likely to change the dynamic in the next few weeks. At present Doq, Cyprus and the winter palaces will be empty. The Prefect and his personal guard will be first to arrive. The one thousand men in the city will be augmented. The cavalry cohort will move closer to the built-up area but remain predominantly on open flat ground as a show of strength. We can expect they will be used to funnel crowds into the city through the open gates for Passover. As with all armies throughout history, plain clothes spies, informers and quislings will be everywhere, and not necessarily all in the non-Jewish neighbourhoods. If need be, in case of severe insurrection, the Romans would need to call on some of the five thousand legionnaires based further away in Syria. However, although the situation will be closely watched, it will certainly not be inflammable. There is likely to be an ordered sense of control.

"Susan and I have spoken at length about this point. Contrary to popular belief, Pontius Pilate is not an anti-Semite. Tiberius is much too wise an Emperor to send an anti-Jewish Prefect to Judea. The Syrian Governor, Lucius Aelius Larnia, spends much of his time in Rome. Without a Syrian Government to mint coins, Pontius Pilate mints them locally."

The military commander passed a coin round the assembled group. "You will see a staff of an Italian seer on one side and a bunch of grapes on the other. These are inoffensive symbols - there is no human head or animal depicted. The Prefect would not deliberately provoke the Jews. As long as we keep a low profile, we should have no trouble with the Romans. Only the Italian cohort, the Cohors Prima Augusta, is capable of giving us a military problem, and they may even be based in Caesarea at present. We shall need to find out. I propose to send a small unit into Jericho and villages to the north to see if we can find a trace of Jesus. Also, some of my more experienced troops will move on to mingle in the Jerusalem streets. There are still four weeks to Passover, so the crowds will not be too heavy. We should be able to track the Roman garrison and find out its pedigree."

The base commander declared himself to be well satisfied. The assembled group broke up.

Felixana agonised with the dilemma she faced. If she could get good footage, the politicians in Europe and America would be ecstatic. It would be her big chance. Publicity was what she had been cornered into providing in the first place. The decision on timing would not be hers, anyway, but her superiors couldn't release film they didn't have. She was a facilitator, doing what she was good at. Of course, she had to take extreme care, and remember the lives of her colleagues would also be on the line. The military units destined for Jerusalem would mingle unnoticed in the crowds; the 'Greek traders' setting out for Jericho would not attract undue attention. What would she do if her team were to be caught while filming?

Yet all members of the expedition were taking risks. Goodness, the whole of Project Methuselah was one big risk! She had taken a risk in hacking into Simon's security codes, in broadcasting her plea to John Devine, in waiting in the desert darkness to see if his brother would show. Hand weapons would get them safely away from aggressive interception - provided they would be willing to use them. Could she kill, or encourage others to kill? She really didn't know. But it wouldn't come to that. They would slip away without taking foolhardy risks if there was any danger of being seen. Could she risk the expedition? She appreciated afresh what Doctor North had said about moving through this alien world as an observer wherever possible and not becoming a participant. But the premise of Methuselah was that participation would be essential at some point in a messy and direct way; to prove to a sceptical but susceptible world that at the very most Jesus was just a man, a man who was brutally executed, who died - full stop, end of story, finito. Although she fully accepted the prevailing northern view that Christianity was based on a falsehood, she realised with sickness that she might indeed be required to film the crucifixion! The pre-requisite of such a trauma of broadcasting, by no means the worst that the Corporation had ever broadcast however, would be to convince the world that they were watching history and not a staged set. Risk was inevitable. She had to act. She laid her story before the base commander. He listened carefully, to her and to the concerns of the military side. She won.

In the heat of the early afternoon of the eighteenth of April, the publicity team set out to film the extravagant opulence of King Herod's winter palaces.

19 April - Year 35

Simon Atkins was a busy man. Not that there was much to do; with the departure of the main expedition on the ninth of April the bulk of the military presence had left the base. As before, civilian security held sway. It was merely that an illusion of activity was helpful in keeping his mind-set positive. Felixana had left with the two hundred or so personnel on the expedition. He had noticed her holographer colleague on base a couple of times since then. *'Who could miss that plump jovial man?'* he had thought. He knew the Englishman had not travelled with the expedition. Paul Devine's wizardry had upgraded quadrophonic audio to cubic video; the return of scientists to the Aleppo plateau and the Galilee lakeside had resulted in holographic images in colour arriving on base.

The security chief watched the films networked for colleagues. Felixana was in fine form, he thought, as he gazed on her guiding the test commentaries. She travelled with an experienced team, fully able to provide professional media reports. His thoughts remained on the woman; she would have reached Jericho by now. Small contingents would have stayed in Aleppo and Tiberias to undertake agreed research, releasing around one hundred men and women to move on down the Jordan valley. He found that his security duties took him conveniently past the photographic and holographic studios, checking the times of day when reports from the expedition appeared. Paul Devine was cordial. Whether he knew of Felixana's liaison or not the South African couldn't tell; certainly, the Englishman never mentioned it. He seemed to treat the security chief's enquiries as a mark of the vital importance of his work. Faithfully, Paul Devine would digitise, compact, edit and package the reports for onward despatch. Around mid-day on the nineteenth Simon Atkins nonchalantly asked if a message of congratulation would be sent to the expedition's publicity team on behalf of the security network. The holographer looked up from his work.

"That's not possible, I'm afraid. Since the expedition left, modern communication out-going from the base has been down. It's something to do with the new power level in the lattices of the TTUs. Engineers are working on higher ground off-base to try to set up a transmitter powerful enough to reach the expedition. Without satellite technology they can't boost a high enough signal here to overcome the lattice. We've still had no luck, though."

"How come we can still receive their messages and film?"

The plump holographer's eyes sparkled. He mistook the air of mild concern as a genuine interest in the technological conundrum he himself found fascinating. "Their signal level at source is not disrupted by other electrical interference. It starts off at full strength and gets lifted at stations on the way in. We can detect enough residual waves to be able to raise it on base. We now find we can get an emergency pulsed signal out, but no-one on the expedition can read Morse code. Morse code went out of use about a hundred years ago."

Neither man felt confused by the holographer's use of the past tense; both knew what was meant. Simon Atkins felt disappointment. He went about his business with his mild anxiety slightly deepened. "Dot, dot, dash," he mumbled to himself as he walked alone along the corridor. "What use is that when I want to talk to her?"

The message marker appeared on his console at precisely fifteen hours seventeen, base time. The orange, pea-sized icon in the shape of a theatrical eye-mask glowed silently like a harlequin's face at a masquerade ball. Simon Atkins had only seen this once before; when the European President had contacted his office in Windhoek in 2131 inviting him to attend in England 'in the forenoon of Sunday tenth November'. He remembered the hackneyed formality with a chill. At the time, the importance of being treated as a clandestine celebrity, courted by the top five or six people in the world, had appealed to his ego. So much had happened since then! Now, despite his panoply of security and fail-safe systems, he felt exposed and vulnerable. He had come to realise that the more layers of control he had piled on his surroundings, the more powerless he had become. Control! Why couldn't he control the communications networks? Why couldn't he control that damn Dutchman lusting after his woman? Why couldn't he control these shadowy politicians in 2135? Why couldn't he control this time travel magic himself and bring closure for his family in South Africa? Why couldn't he control the awful nightmares still stalking his darkness hours? With dread in his heart, he tapped the button marked 'open'.

The face of the President of the United States of America, Joseph L. Korda, appeared on the screen. Simon noticed his grey, bristly hair - what had once been known as a crew-cut. He also noticed the smiling eyes. He noticed them because even on a monitor screen he could tell there was no humour in the smile. He had seen soulless eyes many times with false friendship in them. They had been the stock-in-trade of politicians for hundreds of years. The face on the screen began with the usual procedure for the highest level 'harlequin' icon. "Please activate security."

Simon tapped in a nine-digit code. The screen went blank momentarily. He pressed his left hand to the plexi-glass and let it read his biology. The face of the President returned.

"Good day, Mr Atkins. We are aware of the successes so far achieved by Project Methuselah. Your own contribution has been invaluable.

Reports from the field, so to speak, are coming through. My fellow Presidents and other leaders are equally pleased in the knowledge that the expeditions are making progress. Our advisers tell us that we can now expect to have firm confirmation of the existence of this Jesus Christ fellow in the next two weeks, with complete success around two weeks after that.

"The expedition leaders have orders to press for a resolution. We need a solid message to reveal soon. My purpose in contacting you now on the highest level of security is to tell you that we are at a critical point. The Base here in Turkey may come under threat. You are to prepare for a withdrawal of yourself and the senior physicists. A list of key personnel at all bases subject to this withdrawal order will be sent to you shortly. I am aware that with normal rest periods it would take two weeks to get you out from the furthest base. That is too long. You will have to plan for a quicker return. Key scientific personnel at bases closer to us will clearly not take as long.

"I emphasise, Mr Atkins, you will need to prepare plans covering these senior scientists in the greatest of secrecy. Their travel sequences are not to be explained to them. Other personnel are not to be informed at all. Those involved must also be told not to speak of the withdrawal. You will need to lay in place a cover story. The whole operation is to be carried out in the highest secrecy. Your task will be to ensure that others operate as normal during the evacuation. Panic in the highly-technological environment of the bases must not occur. Once you have the plan in place, you are to notify the base commander in 2135. The list will be given the code-name 'viper'. If and when it is decided here to activate, you will be sent the code-word 'cobra'."

The President continued without waiting for comment. He smiled again, that insincere smile.

"We are also stepping up our investment in the project. We are preparing to send some additional equipment and two new teams of specialists. These will be arriving with you in the next two weeks. One of the teams of scientists will require their own accommodation in a separate part of your base. The equipment arriving will be capable of being assembled once on site. You should bring down some of your senior staff from neighbouring bases to ensure increased security for the new teams. You may add these staff to the names of those given on the 'viper' list. So that you can prepare for your new arrivals, I can give you some background detail."

Simon Atkins listened with increasing incredulity to the President's next words. As the picture became clearer his feelings turned to horror.

21 April - Year 35

Paul Devine made the final minor calibrations to his equipment and then looked at his audience. He was pleased with himself. The quality of the material was outstanding, its nature astounding. He felt he had added a certain something in preparing it for show. Taken together, he considered the three features would certainly impress the senior scientists and commanders present. He noticed the physicist, Doctor North, and the security chief Atkins in separate parts of the audience of around twenty or so before him. He started the presentation with a pass of his hand over the sensor. The lights dimmed and the holography began.

The heat of the Judean countryside seemed to grow in the centre of the large film theatre. The audience's gaze was directed upwards from the deepest part of the Wadi Qelt towards the twenty open ionic columns fronting the north wing of King Herod's winter palaces. The excited whisper rang in the room.

"We are about to climb onto the stone bridge connecting these two magnificent palaces. The one behind us is clearly the older of the two. We shall concentrate on the northern palace."

Felixana Smith's breathless whispered commentary held the watchers and listeners in a cocoon of expectation. The three-hundred-and-sixty degree cameras were picking up remarkable detail. Paul Devine smiled in the semi-darkness of the theatre; over eighty five per cent of the cubic waves had been received at the base. He had filled in the remaining fifteen per cent, and much of that only needed to go into deepening the background. The wealth of detail was astounding. Nothing stirred in the heat of the afternoon. The camera view lifted the audience in its wondrous eye to carry them through the open entrance into a courtyard surrounded on all four sides by rows of columns. The area covered was huge, extending away from the Wadi and along its bank by around thirty metres in both directions. Ahead and to the right of the courtyard were suites of guest rooms. To the left and south of the courtyard lay a grand triclinium decorated with breath-taking frescoes. The cameras moved south again into a new wing, accompanied by Felixana's almost musical and lilting commentary. The explorers found a pool with another large hall opening onto it, and a bath house paved with mosaics and walled with frescoes. Colourful designs on the floors were intricately woven with grapevines, creating a wonderful marriage of nature and geometric angles.

Parallel with the Wadi the camera carried the onlookers through the sequence of the bathing rooms. In turn, they moved through the frigidarium and the tepidaria, on into the hot room, the caldarium. The caramels, oranges and reds on the walls glowed in deep and bright pigments made of cinnabar. Turning back through the colonnaded courts the cameras returned to the great columned reception hall with its huge brown and cream Corinthian columns, then on to a wide open verandah replete with huge cacti in terracotta flower pots. There was no sign of occupation in the northern half of the palaces. The heat and silence were palpable.

"We can see all the way to the oasis from here."

Felixana walked into shot, shielding her eyes from the fierce sun and pointing north towards Jericho. The camera view followed her outstretched arm, its lens tele-extending into its eighty times enlargement and picking out movement in the distance.

"There is absolutely no-one here", she breathed, nevertheless hardly daring to speak above a whisper. "There are thin plumes of wood-smoke coming from the southern palace on the other side of the Wadi, so some-one's over there. Respected and trusted senior slaves, no doubt guarding the palaces until the Prefect and Roman soldiers return. There's no need to barricade the entrances. Nothing can be stolen from here; everything's just too big and heavy!"

The onlookers at Siverek gazed enraptured as the film ran through another fifteen minutes. At the end, the presenter beamed into the lens. "These palaces are truly magnificent, much more so than those we expect in Jerusalem itself, perhaps even more so than the great palace further south in Masada. They provide an excellent introduction for viewers into the wonderful ancient world we are now exposing to world view. As we move on to Jerusalem itself in coming days and weeks we shall doubtless see equally wonderful sights and meet wonderful people, straight from the ancient world. This is Felixana Smith, for the ......for the European-led expedition to ancient Judea in the year thirty-five."

Just a split-second's hesitation stopped her mentioning the BBC. It was barely noticeable in Siverek, where a spontaneous applause broke out. Paul Devine beamed again as the lights returned to full strength in the film theatre. The audience gradually dispersed. He began dismantling his equipment. Simon Atkins came over, his face grave.

"Any news as to whether we can contact them?"

The holographer knew who 'them' were. He shook his head. "The engineers are still out. It may be today, it may be tomorrow. We were lucky to receive such marvellous film."

His voice revealed his excitement. "I'll need to get it packaged up and sent on. As far as we know, there have been no global announcements yet. I guess they're waiting for a real sighting, not just village hearsay. Still, the footage is really brilliant. It'll be great….."

"I need a word with you; now, in private. It's urgent and vital." He glanced around. The room was nearly empty. The holographer sensed the mood and sobered immediately.

"Sure….yes….of course; I'll leave this equipment and come back later."

Simon smiled. "Thanks." He really meant it.

Ten minutes later, the two were sipping orange juice in the South African's quarters. The host looked grave and tired.

"Have you trained others in editing and packaging film?"

"Well, yes. But I prefer to do it myself, especially if the cubic wave ratios are low. It all depends on transmission shadows in the Jordan valley."

Simon really hoped the man would not get carried away on his technology 'high' again. He dived in.

"I need you to do something for me….for us….for all of us."

The security chief seemed genuinely frightened. It was a side of him Paul had never seen.

"Go on."

The blond-haired man reached across to his console. "I received a list this morning. No-one from the publicity teams is named on it, and that includes you. I need you to go back home."

22 April - Year 35

The expedition commander in Jericho addressed his senior team leaders, just as he had four days before. The six other people present sat nervously, wondering why they had been invited. They didn't have to wait long.

"We have good news and bad news. I won't waste time asking which you need first. Our forays into Jericho indicate that this Jesus man is indeed travelling down the Jordan valley. Yesterday, we gleaned from an innkeeper that itinerant market traders had been given reports from visitors coming from Alexandrium of 'the great teacher from Galilee' drawing crowds in the open fields above a village just two kilometres from the city; Alexandrium, that is, not Jericho. I know it's third hand, but the visitors were Greeks, not Judeans, so probably quite objective about their reports. Anyway, that puts our target around thirty kilometres or so north of us, and well on track to be coming down for Passover. Our next task may be to achieve a direct sighting of our own."

The commander pressed on without waiting for comment, explaining that they couldn't get communication established with Siverek. The audience shuffled nervously in their seats. The commander's voice sounded optimistic enough, but then, that was his job.

"As far as we can tell, the problem is not at our end. Our signal is as strong as we can get it for terrestrial purposes. We can't spare the time or resources to go back to check masts that have been erected. We can speak with the small contingent at Tiberias, but even they can't receive messages from Aleppo, and certainly not from Siverek. Something is blocking a signal, perhaps? We just don't know."

"Are our transmissions getting through?" Felixana felt she had to break in to the presentation.

"Sorry, Felixana, we don't even know that. We must hope Siverek is trying a stronger signal. The other piece of bad news, of sorts, is that the Roman garrison in Jerusalem does include the Cohors Prima Augusta. That's the crack Italian cohort, the fully-trained and disciplined Roman troops. They are based as we thought at the Antonia fortress. Our people couldn't get near the fortress, though naturally we'll try again when we move our main thrust towards the city."

The senior historian pressed for an answer on timescales.

"We've got just twenty five days now to the first day of Passover. We must decide if we all need to move on to be closer to Jerusalem, or if we should leave a group here. Does anyone have any suggestions? Please don't argue the case for your own discipline. They'll all be included to some degree. Like in Tiberias and Aleppo, some communication, logistics and research can continue relatively unexposed to main Methuselah business, with all that now entails for taking risks."

Discussion ebbed and flowed, ending in a decision to leave forty people in reach of Jericho. The other seventy three would move on to Jerusalem. Forty of these would be soldiers. Felixana tried to visualise how forty trained marines, even with unlimited fire-power, would manage against over a thousand Roman soldiers. She failed. How would any of them manage to survive if open conflict broke out? Her anxiety over being away from Simon Atkins, and even out of touch with him, began to take possession of her again. She tried to convey a sense that all was well with her in the commentaries she provided for the film packages they were putting together. She found it difficult and delicate. The dialogue would go through several vetting stages and she could hardly confess her love on film. Nevertheless, she knew that if her reports were really getting back to Siverek she could depend on Paul Devine to edit out anything too awkward. She knew she was fortunate in any case. The other people around her were not being permitted personal messages back to Siverek. Equally unsettling was the knowledge that the base commander and his two senior deputies were sending confidential reports back quite independently from her travelogue-style programmes. No-one would know if they were getting through, but it gave the impression that they had been pre-briefed on a course of action before leaving Siverek. Like ninety eight per cent of the expedition members, Felixana had no idea of how Methuselah would be carried to completion. It worried her.

Yet she was still required to be busy. It was agreed that a formal record would be attempted of the expedition's first encounter with the Nazarene group of travellers. It was felt they could easily film the Galilean from a distance with their telephoto equipment. She thought the encounter could be managed in the relative isolation of a Judean village, with her team dressed in appropriate robes. Until more was known of the likely progress south of their target the expedition would remain based on the Jericho mountainsides. Detailed judgements would need to be taken on which individuals would stay and which would move on to Jerusalem. Felixana noticed that the military personnel were practising hand-to-hand combat in their mountainous isolation. She was also not allowed to film it. Her nervousness did not lessen as the day wore on.

Thursday 28 April 2135

Deep within the bowels of the Berlaymont building in Brussels at a circular table, sat some of the most powerful politicians in history. The Presidents and Vice -Presidents of the United States of America, the European Union and the Russian Federation, sat alongside the Premier and Vice-Premier of the Glorious Peoples' Republic of Greater China. Such a gathering was almost unique in human history, but all knew this was a unique occasion. Their translators and senior officials sat in a wider circle beyond, in slightly less light. They had all been briefed in detail on a film report from Siverek dated two days previously. A European official was speaking as the assembled audience watched the film end.

"He's older than we thought, perhaps thirty eight or thirty nine, and darker in skin colour. Not clean-shaven but not bearded, either. He has long hair, very dark. He's shorter than expected, only a hundred and sixty five centimetres. His weight is estimated around sixty three kilos, so quite light. Knee-length tunic, dark cloth with a gamma pattern, tied at the middle. That's standard En Gedi expectation. In this heat, there's no cloak. There's a small leather bag worn across the body, and leather sandals, pretty well universal for the age. No sound recording was received because of the distance, but assumption will be standard Western Aramaic. No further data are possible from this angle, but the biggest surprise comes in the next bit of footage."

The listeners hung on the official's words. Then they gasped. The figure in the dusty road appeared to beckon his followers to the road-side field and walked off ahead of them - with his left leg dragging slightly in a distinct limp.

"Now that wasn't expected!" declared American President Korda. "Can we be sure it's him?"

"Oh, yes, Mr President. There's no doubt of it. These are pictures of Jesus of Nazareth, the Christians' Messiah."

Nods and grunts of satisfaction peppered the room. The Chinese Premier beamed and broke into applause, causing others to respond accordingly. The officials in the outer circle didn't know if it would be diplomatic to join with the politicians in expressing a view, so remained silent. Premier Lu Wan Tao oozed satisfaction.

"We can now move ahead quickly. Are the specialist teams on their way?" The question was addressed to the Russians, present Chair of the international organisation involved.

"Yes, indeed. They left Alexander Island on the sixteenth and arrived in Siverek on the nineteenth. We expect them at Violet Base on the third of May. The specialist transports are following the same timetable."

"Good, good. The Peoples' Republic suggests that we announce our findings to the world in two days' time, on the final day of April."

European President Papandreou's eyebrows rose in surprise. He reminded the gathering that no-one knew if the completion of Methuselah as planned could be carried out that quickly. The Chinese Premier snorted.

"We have the target and will soon have the technology in place. I remind fellow leaders that the Base may come under military threat. The Southern Brotherhood clearly does not believe the story about solar wind energy. We are all under pressure; forced to deny their unwarranted claims that we would lower energy costs. This has made us lose face in front of our people and the world. We must punish their arrogance."

"That doesn't mean, Mr Premier that we should act precipitately."

Faces furrowed until the American translator substituted with the word 'rashly'. Vice-President Lutz's caution was greeted with a few nods. He pressed on, looking to President Korda for support. "Might I put forward a useful compromise? We announce on Saturday as you suggest. We certainly have enough photographic material coming in to keep interest growing, and I agree with the Premier that until we grab that attention we cannot expect to maximise on Methuselah's inevitable success in due course. Yet our joint base in Turkey could be vulnerable. The Israeli military and naval exercises show no sign of slowing down. They are clearly operating at the behest of the Brotherhood, though they would deny it.

"I am willing personally to travel to Siverek in the next week to oversee Methuselah on our behalf. My presence there will, I believe, make the Brotherhood pause in its military intentions sufficiently long enough to enable us to carry out the final stages as planned. It would be beneficial if our announcements in two days' time merely refer to the great historical significance of our breakthrough and do not mention our final intention of causing humiliation."

A pregnant pause followed the Vice-President's words as politicians and officials digested the implications. Harold P. Lutz knew from their faces that he would soon be packing his bags for Turkey.

THE FINAL DAYS OF APRIL

10:30 HOURS

The TTU door swung up with an audible sigh of air. Paul Devine wasn't entirely comfortable with the physical anguish of transfer, but the thought of going home deadened the pain. His spirits were lifted by the Base decor - this was the year 1535 and the orange-hued walls and corridors almost beckoned him to stay awhile. Not that he was going anywhere in a hurry. Simon Atkins had suggested there was no need to draw undue attention to his journey by circumventing medical rest periods. His senior clearance was sufficient to deflect almost all interest. Base commanders would perhaps have been alerted to any show of haste, especially on a full-tunnel transit. As it was, he completed the post-transfer checks with increasing relief and excitement. He settled into his lunch-time meal anticipating a restful afternoon and a chance to plan the final crucial stages of his journey before facing the TTU jolt into Red Base on the second of May.

He thought back over the things the security chief had mentioned. None of it surprised him now, though parts turned his stomach. Corroboration of sorts had come four days before. While resting on Green Base, he had become aware of two new teams of scientists travelling in the opposite direction. One group had been shrouded in secrecy, though he knew of their purpose. He had managed to obtain a little information on the other, enough to confirm part of the picture that Atkins had confided. The team travelled in tandem with machine parts that he recognised. Engineers and pilots for fast, low-flying helicopters were on their way to Judea.

So, Felixana was just as much a victim as himself, and he had originally thought she was hiding things from him. If communication with the expedition could be secured, she could be warned. If not, Atkins had openly told him that he would set out for Jericho and bring her back. The holographer spooned another helping of apple pie into his mouth. Yes, he had read the signs well; the South African was besotted with her. No surprise, really. He had sometimes fancied her himself but found her too self-assured, too independent, for his own taste. She was a good boss, though, and deserved to be rescued. He would do what he could.

14:30 HOURS

The transmission was syndicated around the Base. Paul watched it with awe-struck technicians, scientists, caterers, medical staff; all the panoply of Orange Base personnel. The recording was on its way down-time to Methuselah's front-line, but everyone felt proud in his or her own private way. The chubby Englishman had wanted to share their pride, especially when the impressive results of his work came on display, but a cloud of darkness hung over him. The news conference had been recorded at ten hours, Central European Time. Senior northern politicians had gathered in Rome - a cynical ploy, he felt, though the significance would be lost on many. The honour had fallen to the European President to give the opening remarks. Paul watched the travelogue-style films of Aleppo, Tiberias and Lake Galilee like looking at old friends, hardly hearing Felixana's commentary. He did take professional pride in the global display of his editing arts, though noticed where they had truncated even further some of his favourite scenes to fit in with the politicians' own dark agenda. The hilarity and humour of the hillside pond had been cut to barely ten seconds, leaving his skills emasculated on a digital stripping-room floor somewhere. There was no mention of Methuselah, merely references to 'a major breakthrough for time-travel' - 'discovered as a side-effect of our work on solar wind energy' - 'further daily transmissions can be expected'. Paul's stomach churned as his thoughts projected his fears into what might happen next with the innocuous presentations.

17:00 HOURS

Far away to the south of Rome the Southern Brotherhood's High Council was beginning another meeting in Mombasa, their second in a month. They watched again closely the recording of the news conference from the Italian State Capital. The Chairman of the High Council, the Ghanaian President, watched with his face etched in a mixture of concern and puzzlement. At the recording's end he voiced his thoughts.

"There was no mention of the date for these transmissions. We are merely told 'ancient Judea around two thousand years ago'. That could mean around the year one hundred and thirty five, so clearly closer to our time than the strictly-Biblical era that would be significant for us." High Councillors contributed their own first impressions.

'There is a reference to daily transmissions. This is clearly the opening shot in a longer campaign. How much do they have to reveal? And again, it could be anywhere in the world, a film-set even.'

'I don't see the connection with solar wind research. It's a tenuous link that the rest of the world will doubtless also find scarcely believable. Unless that's merely an introduction to explain away what would otherwise come across as an expensive three-year deception. Their peoples would not take kindly to such an admission, especially given the financial pain they have suffered over this time.'

'Pain we have surely all suffered. The film they have shown is hardly better than a travel programme. They say it is Aleppo, Tiberias and Lake Galilee. Perhaps it is. Certainly, some of the lake-side vistas look realistic enough. Perhaps they have been filming there recently without Israeli permission.'

'The figure seen on the actual film looks like Felixana Smith and voice-print identification confirms her voice.'

'What can we do? There's no specific or even general threat against the Brotherhood. The motives for such a revelation have not been given. Perhaps the northern powers are seeking to convince the world by drip-feeding such articles; a kind of serial exposure. Perhaps they have their final chapters, perhaps they don't. What can we do to burst this particular bubble?'

'We could recall our ambassadors from Washington, Brussels, Moscow and Beijing, but on what grounds? Yet I agree we should not just sit back and wait for these following chapters. How are our Ethiopian preparations developing?'

The Chairman responded with a nod of satisfaction.

"We have around two hundred troops ready to be air-lifted to Turkey. They've been training on a detailed mock-up of the Siverek Base as described in the two-year old Atomic Energy Authority report. We can be confident that with the element of surprise they would secure the Base for Brotherhood purposes long before the European military could respond, or even the Israeli military for that matter. Once inside, we can hold the Base to ransom."

A delegate asked to what purpose. "We need to know their intentions in advance of them being revealed via news conferences. Our agent inside the Base, this Englishman Devine, the colleague of the BBC woman......what is he doing for us?"

"He's the holographic expert that the woman needed to facilitate filming. He was amenable to our suggestions to find opportunities to report back to us with information; however, it was clear from his briefing sessions that he was not convinced at all about the genuine nature of time-travel."

"Neither are some of us, Mr Chairman. But I fully accept the vital need to keep an open mind."

Nods and grunts of agreement bubbled up from a minority of the Council members. The Kenyan Deputy Prime Minister responded by articulating the High Council's majority stance.

"It is my view we can fully expect the northern powers to seek to humiliate us over our belief in Jesus Christ, our Lord. If they are not already in the first century of modern times, I think they soon will be." He lowered his voice, emphasising the importance of his next words. They were received in hushed silence.

"It is a question of belief, my friends. The dark arts of political deception are as ancient as the dust on which our Lord himself walked. Individuals are gullible. They can be persuaded to believe anything. The more often an untruth is spoken as a truth, the more it is believed. The greater the number of people willing to believe, the stronger will be the effect. It matters not whether this Siverek event of theirs is real or not. As far as the Europeans and others are concerned, it only matters that enough people can be persuaded that it is real, enough to swing nations against us, enough to stop the financial re-balancing of the world. If for only that reason, I feel we are in mortal danger. If the release of their films follows an expected pattern, we may only have a few days or weeks in which to neutralise their deception. We can only do that with a deception of our own. Just look at those images they have released to the world. Remember that Aleppo or Beroea as they have called it lies within our jurisdiction within Syria. That could be their great mistake."

He continued by outlining his plan.

THE FIRST DAY OF MAY

9:00 HOURS

A warm feeling of satisfaction bathed the room, tinged with just a sliver of excited impatience to help things along the allotted path. Those in uniform sat interspersed with those in civilian or religious clothing. All had been in the city throughout the Sabbath, so had been present to be called early to attend on this new Sunday work-day morning. The Prime Minister smiled broadly at a couple of colleagues, banging the table to call for the silence of prayer. Then the business began.

"I want to start with a military assessment, in particular a report on the troop deployment north of Haifa."

The Chief of Homeland Defence responded to the invitation by calling to the presentation screen a large coloured relief map of Israel. Icons danced before the eyes, abstract in their Jewish significance.

"We have built to full alert status over the past month. Co-operation in the field with the secular Lebanese army has been achieved to permit fly-through access for our Air Force. The friendship agreement has provided economic support to the new military administration in Beirut. The Lebanese are members of the World Faiths Congress, just as we are. Though they are still ostensibly loosely effective on the fringes of the Southern Brotherhood, we all know that money talks. We have bought the influence that we need. Syria remains beyond our reach, however. The government in Damascus is tied by the links it has with the African heartlands of the Brotherhood. Nevertheless, we now have use of airfields north of Tripoli. We can avoid European air-space around Cyprus and land troops south of Siverek if we need to do so. Assurances of non-belligerence are being prepared. We may need to convey this to Brussels to prevent them building their own troop levels."

The Prime Minister took up the dialogue.

"The reports yesterday from Rome make it clear that more revelations are to come. There is as yet no indication of the assault on Christianity we might have expected. Nevertheless, this is still their probable target. As to authenticity, well, I leave it to you."

342

He smiled smugly. Several other government members chuckled gently.

"They are clearly not filming in Galilee, or along the Jordan valley. I have obtained reports overnight that the areas in our eastern settlement lands are completely quiet and safe. It is remarkable how well they have recreated some mountain vistas. Our geographers have begun scouring the world to find out precisely where they have filmed some of the outdoor sequences." He looked to the senior religious leaders present.

"Do you have a feel for the faith side of this? What timetable can we expect they are working to?"

"It is hard to say, Prime Minister. It is clearly not related to Pesach or Easter, both of which have now safely passed. It strengthens the view that a deception is taking place. Which brings us to the heart of the matter, I feel. We must do nothing to upset this approach. It is clearly in our national interest to remain neutral and let the Europeans weaken the southern powers. The news conference in Rome mentioned daily reports. We can expect one today. It must follow that total denouement, or at least a clear indication of the line of attack, will come within weeks if not days. Perhaps we have two or three weeks? There would then be a period of intense political pressure on governments that are deemed soft on Brotherhood membership. Perhaps our Foreign Minister can enlighten us on which ones they might be?"

The bald-headed Minister took up the chance to shine. "Yes. We took discreet soundings during the World Faiths Congress meeting in early March. It would be likely that Mexico, Libya and Singapore, among others, would turn against the Brotherhood. That is significant, as all three are very wealthy nations already. What would be the point of securing a global shift in financial resources if much of the benefit heads even further south? No, the likelihood of a recalling of World States Council members to an autumn summit can be considered as very high."

The Prime Minister summed up quickly - it was the start of a new working week and there were other matters to discuss. The arrival of refreshments was welcome.

10:00 HOURS

"Good morning, world! You're watching Timberwolf News Channel, live from Montreal, Canada, and I am Bradford Fletcher. Welcome to 'World in Focus' for a very special Sunday edition."

The multi-view cameras panned round from the wolf logo, revealing a group of seven people seated in deep, caramel-coloured armchairs. The host's voice opened the topic for the thirty-minute television slot, popular around the English-speaking world. Podcasts beamed the programme to the orbiting stations above. The four women and three men, of varying ages and skin colour, smiled at the invisible viewers as each was introduced. The mix was impressive; Timberwolf executives had clearly worked overtime to assemble such contributors at only thirty hours' notice, allowing for all the time differentials. Bradford Fletcher was positively revelling in his conducting role with such a prestigious orchestra.

"You've all seen the films, including the new releases from Rome overnight. I think you'll all agree they provide pretty astounding suggestions. I want to ask each of you if you think these revelations can be taken at face value. And where is the linkage to solar wind energy; that's what we all want to know. Professor Leibnitz, from Massachusetts Institute of Technology, what is the significance for physics generally?"

"If it's genuine, then, yes, it's significant, very much so. However, there has been no world-wide, independent publication of peer research in this area at all over the past four years. I think it unlikely that the timescale is accurate; I am sure that laboratory research would have achieved a much smaller time shift, and certainly not involving the transfer of humans. The ethical implications alone would represent a major obstacle to what we are seeing. Still, we must remember it is well within the realms of possibility, and could very well be true. Ever since the Gran Sasso Revelation of 2011, confirmed by projects Borexino and Icarus over a hundred and twenty years ago, we've known that the speed of light is not the universe's top limit any more. We have certainly seen some theoretical and applied physicists move to the government's solar wind programmes, but as they've been highly restricted in terms of publicity, we do not get feedback from them."

"And what can you tell us of the historical perspective, Dr Lamb? Has the University of Montreal been able to assess the importance of the period they have ostensibly revealed?"

The man in his late sixties with a spare frame and steel-grey goatee beard lifted his bony hands in a gesture of uncertainty.

"The broadcasts infer a period around the year one hundred and thirty five in the Common Era. It was a time when Roman power was still strong. However, I have noticed some inconsistencies with the date inferred and the scenes on the ground, as it were."

Bradford Fletcher's ears pricked up. He dived straight in to ask what inconsistencies there might be. The Canadian historian was pleased to explain further.

"The pictures in and around Galilee do show a calm, peaceful and prosperous area, with Roman troops at a minimum. We have to remember that in the spring months of the year sixty seven around fifty thousand men under Vespasian and his son Titus put down the Jews militarily in no uncertain terms. For example, the town of Gabara in Upper Galilee was stormed, the adult male population was killed, and all the buildings reduced to ashes. Indeed, all the towns and villages in the area were burned and any people left alive were sold into slavery. It was very brutal, even by the standards of the time. The pictures released from Rome show happy, well-fed populations, no architectural damage and very few soldiers in full military uniform. If the films are genuine, as the Europeans claim, they have travelled back further in time than they are prepared to admit. If they have done so, they could have reached the time of Jesus of Nazareth."

A palpable buzz hummed round the studio. It was the first mention of the 'J' word on world television. Everyone wanted to contribute at once.

'That's preposterous! It's obviously a deception!' - The representative of the Board of Canadian Jews.

'Oh, hardly likely to be true, but what would the World Faiths Congress make of such a thing?' - The Senior Vice-President of Maple Leaf Financial Corporation.

'What a scoop for the BBC if it is in Biblical times.' - NBC's senior representative in Canada.

'Moving in Jesus' time would make it truly unique, and worth watching carefully.' - The Deputy Turkish State Consul to Canada.

'It may indeed be related to a time in history of importance to followers of faith. We should follow its implications as the revelations continue.' - The Cultural Attaché from the Chinese Embassy.

Bradford Fletcher could scarcely cope with his conductor's baton as the components of the orchestra before him pressed ahead with the own distinctive sounds. The thirty-minute performance came across the airwaves as a strident and discordant offering.

14:00 HOURS

Thirty three civilians accompanied by forty soldiers set out on foot for Jerusalem along the road past the Cyprus fortress. They presented as bedraggled a sight as they could muster; strung out in a line to mimic a loosely-organised village group making slowly yet purposefully towards the city for Passover. All were dressed in drab civilian clothing, almost rags, as would befit a group of poor village dwellers. The marine units concealed their weapons within their cloaks. The photographic equipment travelled in rush panniers on wild asses and colts gleaned from the hills and lonely hamlets. Fellow travellers were increasing in number. There were now only sixteen days remaining before the first day of the Jewish festival. Felixana Smith's senses soaked up all that came her way. After twenty three days of seeking to avoid human interaction, the change to an onslaught of human experiences was extreme. Strangers smiled and nodded; even the sight of matted hair and rotting teeth couldn't mask the joy of eye to eye contact. Each encounter lit a spark of spiritual purity across a divide of two thousand and one hundred years. And the sparks kept coming...... She began to respond willingly. Where her rudimentary but enthusiastic knowledge of Aramaic ended, she managed with grunts and facial movements.

The road steepened and the pace of progress slowed. A cloud of caramel-tinted dust and a clatter of hooves heralded the oncoming sight of a contubernium of eight Roman cavalry officers and men. The expedition members parted efficiently to let them by. It was a procedure they had practised many times, following Doctor North's maxim of minimum involvement. Deference and fear, laced with a slice of sullen intransigence, were deeply engrained in the local population. Compliance would ease their onward journey. The Romans rode past in imperious oblivion to the lesser mortals on foot below them. The huge and powerful dark brown thoroughbreds were an impressive sight. Their flanks glistened in the afternoon heat. The large red shields with the decorative golden whorls and bronze bosses were held professionally across each cavalryman's left side. Harnesses creaked and swayed as the party rode by; then came a dangerous moment. Most of the horses had passed the straggling travellers, their riders not even looking down to avoid trampling on inferior humans. The expedition's military escorts at the rear of the column averted their gaze - with one exception. Chuck Kowalski was determined to face up to the Roman presence. He had brooded for seven weeks on the soldier on guard duty who had gazed out from the Boroean battlements. That had been in almost complete darkness against the flickering light of torches. Now there was an opportunity in bright sunlight.

The career soldier from Nebraska looked up fearlessly into the brown helmeted face of the final Roman cavalryman. The spark that the BBC reporter had experienced flashed again for Chuck. The contrast was highly symbolic, though neither man really grasped the full significance of the moment. A long slashing sword and a javelin held in full view, would contrast with a lightweight programmable laser-guided hand gun strapped secretly within folds of fabric. Employment taken to avoid a lifetime of poverty with a promise of Roman citizenship at its end, would contrast with a career following in forebears' footsteps with a promise of a military pension. Yet there were similarities. Both men served in a foreign land, though how foreign neither of the two could begin to guess. The mounted man started at the other's effrontery in daring to stare. He wheeled his horse, its nostrils flaring as it felt the pain of the turn. Yet two pairs of eyes knew each other, gazing into knowledge of eternal conflict, the human condition that that only those who had served in subservience to controlled violence could feel. The eyes of both men could tell so much. A forest of arrows that could make a sky black; burning oil poured from a castle's roof; yellow-green mustard gas that turned lungs in trenches inside-out; the scream of jets that became indistinguishable from the scream of a child covered in napalm; a robot shaped like a human being that could explode with silver shards of glass into a crowded office foyer...... Yes, the two men certainly knew each other for what they were. The Roman smiled, wheeled his horse again at the shout of his commanding officer, and rode on after his colleagues. It was all over in an instant. But was it a smile or a flicker of fear? The group of interlopers continued on towards Jerusalem. Felixana Smith perspired in the afternoon heat as they approached the slopes of Mount Scopus. Chuck Kowalski shivered.........but he couldn't discern whether it was with the heat, or with tiredness or with excitement.

THE THIRD DAY OF MAY

8:00 HOURS

The day's life had already begun before the early morning heat haze had mixed with the dust thrown up by the surge of human life within the vast artificial platform of the Har Ha Bayit in Jerusalem. The Temple Mount dominated the city, occupying about one-sixth of the total area inside the walls. It towered over the northern end of the Tyropoeon valley and it looked down on the shabby streets and alleys of the lower city. The Temple in the middle of the platform had been King Herod's greatest building achievement. Only priests had been permitted to build the edifice so as not to defile the area. This had necessitated the retraining of around a thousand priests in the earthly skills of masonry and carpentry. Despite all the careful keeping of protocols, Herod had not been able to resist the placing of a statue above the main gate. A representation of a large golden eagle looked down its beak at the Jews bustling in the dusty squares below. The Temple itself had been completed in eighteen months, but the building and decoration of the outer courts continued for many years. Just nine years before, the Jews had been able to say to Jesus 'this Temple took forty six years to build......'. Yet in the north western corner of the platform rose a higher, more solid and imposing building. The Antonia fortress, built twenty five metres high on a natural rock, rose imperiously above the whole of Jerusalem, a tower at each corner. One of the towers was higher than the others, to oversee the whole Temple area.

The Roman guard on duty at one of this tower's window slots watched the black shape of the eagle wheel away in the sky above his station. Its wings were motionless as it circled the fortress. The guard's eyes moved away again to survey the seething mass of people below him in the Temple arenas of the platform. He had seen eagles before, many times. He had no way of knowing this wasn't a real eagle. Across to the north-east, beyond the Kedron Valley on the heights of Mount Scopus, the pre-set computer programs for the bio-drone automatically relayed colour pictures to the hand-held monitors of the expedition commander and the army unit controller. Felixana Smith peered over the controller's shoulder to watch the screen. Guards were changing within the Temple's environs. The commander nodded knowingly. The overnight Roman soldiers, forbidden to fall asleep on pain of death, would be particularly tired with

348

low vigilance if the interlopers were to move into the lower city via one of the furthest gates.

10:00 HOURS

The silence of Tuesday morning was shattered by the noise of forty hover-tanks of the Israeli Defence Army gunning into life. The sound echoed from the baking rocks around the narrow valley on the northern slopes of Qurnet es Sauda. From its three thousand metre peak the strike force commanders gazed northwards at the Syrian borderlands. The Force's insignia presented a miscellany of colours and designs - armour as red as fire, blue as sapphire, yellow as sulphur - regular Israeli forces, conscripted Lebanese units, mercenaries from the anti-Syrian hill dwellers among the Jebel Libnan ranges, well-armed Druze militia, volunteers from the Free Zion Defence League. In all, there would be over four thousand troops, fully mechanised and capable of reaching Siverek Base within thirty six hours. Surprise would be on their side; intelligence reports were telling them the European Union could only realistically put a few hundred paratroopers on the ground from Cypriot bases in Famagusta and Larnaca. Equally weak would be a Syrian counter-response from units based in Hama. Main Damascene forces were too far south to constitute a realistic threat. The strike force commanders felt confident. If they managed to keep below Syrian radar the main forces could traverse the Jebel el Ansariye marshes under cover of darkness and reach Turkish territory by sunrise. Siverek would be under siege before anyone was any the wiser. The intention would be 'to place the Base under protective shielding in the interests of world peace to prevent a terrorist attack on internationally-important research facilities'. Whether or not the world would believe the Israeli propaganda, the strike force commanders didn't care. They only had to march on Turkey. The order was given.

17:00 HOURS

As Israeli forces cascaded around the northern slopes of Mount Aruba towards the Syrian border at Telkalakh, three hundred and twenty kilometres to the south Professor Mark Henderson was sipping a late-afternoon cup of tea. The heat of the hour bore down on the excavation site, the harsh unremitting light washing out all relief and shadow into a caramel-coloured monochrome. The Professor's head ached slightly. His beverage was welcome and well-deserved; he had spent two hours in the late morning checking co-ordinates and distances across the archaeological site on which the joint Israeli-Canadian team was working. In all that heat he had managed to survey in digital detail only eight of the columns he had revealed in the reception hall. The Professor had hoped for more progress, especially as the four-metre deep column location had only been discovered that very morning, but there was always tomorrow!

He stretched his young powerful legs languorously in their denim fabric trousers. He certainly didn't look like a university professor. Twenty eight years of age and a professional life spent mainly in polar archaeology had left a thin wiry figure with blond-white skin and wide eyes. The large brim on his dun, linen-lined hat drooped in the heat almost as much as his demeanour in the chair. Why had he taken up this insane assignment? He breathed deeply, only succeeding in inhaling the sense of his own body odour. But of course it was a rhetorical question. He sighed again. He knew the answer fully enough - he was the world's leading practitioner in three-dimensional subterranean archaeology. Yes, he had told the university fund managers that ninety per cent of his work had been in permafrost, but they had somehow translated that to a potential for deep-lying artefacts anywhere, and 'underground was underground, wasn't it?' A boiling hot desert location could just as easily respond to his unique equipment and personally-developed skills. Besides, he was Canadian and available, and Ottawa had secured the contract with the Israeli government. Nevertheless, he longed to return to the clarity and beauty of the high Arctic, where there was no sunrise and no sunset for weeks on end in summer. Despite the disappearance of permanent ice-cover, there were still glaciers in places such as Svalbard to move the human spirit. The strident buzz on his lapel communicator broke into his reverie.

"Mark! Turn on your TV! New stuff's coming out of Rome on their ancient history road show, but this time you really ought to see it!"

His colleague in a nearby valley sounded nervous. The Canadian waved a hand in front of the visi-screen on his lap. The colour flooded his view. He recognised the presumed location immediately, his riveted attention dispelling the surrounding heat as he sat transfixed. He smiled to himself as he watched the vistas unfold. The European powers had certainly concocted a good story and background set this time he felt. Parallel with the wadi showing on the screen the camera carried the onlooker through the sequence of the bathing rooms. In turn they moved through the frigidarium, and the tepidaria, on into the hot room, the caldarium. The browns, oranges and reds on the walls glowed in deep and bright pigments made of cinnabar. Turning back through the colonnaded

350

courts the cameras returned to the great columned reception hall with its huge brown and cream Corinthian columns, then on to a wide, open verandah replete with huge cacti in terracotta flower pots. There was no sign of occupation in the northern half of the palaces. The heat and silence were palpable. A woman walked into shot.

"We can see all the way to the oasis from here."

The Professor suddenly stiffened. He shuddered despite the heat. "Replay - ninety seconds!"

His voice command quavered. He watched again as the camera passed slowly along the huge brown and cream columns. His single-worded instruction to freeze the frame seemed such an incongruous command in the heat of Jericho, given his professional history. Mark Henderson felt sick. He stared at the column left motionless on the screen. Calibrations clattered through his brain in smooth logical patterns.

Third column in sequence, two vertical cracks at three and a half metres' height, each half a metre long and two centimetres wide. No other blemishes or cracks in any neighbouring column.'

He turned to his equipment and ran again the measurements he had finished only that morning on columns he knew had lain buried in over four metres of hard ground for over two thousand years. His micro-resonance imaging had filmed the columns for the first time, of that he was sure. No-one, but no-one, had been disturbing this part of the palace's archaeological site. His was the very first virtual picture of something that had not seen the light of day since it had toppled all that time ago. He enlarged the column's picture, his lips moving in the words he had just read.

Third column in sequence, two vertical cracks at three and a half metres' height, each half a metre long and two centimetres wide. No other blemishes or cracks in any neighbouring column.'

His wild eyes returned to the frozen monitor. He knew he was really staring into the ancient past, now revived. It was not a film set at all! He felt afraid; for some indefinable reason, he shook with fear. It was just as terrifying when he realised he might make a fatal mistake and alert the wrong person as to what he now knew. His hands shook as he printed off a hard copy of his calibrations. He folded the sheet, putting it into his pocket. Deliberately, Mark Henderson erased the electronic record. There would be time enough to run his morning's work again on the next day.

351

He felt strangely calmer and safer as the power in the portable unit died away. Some things are better buried.

18:30 HOURS

Doctor Pieter North sat hunched up in his private quarters. He rocked back and forth in sick disbelief. His dizzying brain tried to make sense of the two scenarios in his mind. There was the news and orders he had just been given by the Base Commander, and there was the memory he held of Jon De Haag's holographic transmission from Los Angeles in February. Snippets of his friend's message spun in his mind like ghostly moths. Each time he reached to grasp one it dissolved into uncertainty.

'A coherence......crystal clear......almost unknown in nature'

'The alternative that has been raised with me'

'I have spoken with some people here in California over the weekend'

'A situation I have increasingly come to fear'

'You need to be vigilant'

There was no similar uncertainty over the instruction from the Base Commander. The Dutchman's memory was much more recent and clear on these statements and their significance.

"The two new teams have now arrived. Their work is to take precedence over all other considerations. We are about to bring Project Methuselah to a conclusion. Your own work has nearly finished. There will be little need to keep you and your senior colleagues here much longer. The information from Jerusalem is encouraging. In three weeks' time we can confidently expect to send a high-speed nuclear assault hover-copter south from here. It will be equipped with deep-freeze facilities. The newly-arrived cryogenic science team will freeze the fresh body of the person known as Jesus of Nazareth and transport it here for onward return to 2135. The whole sequences are to be filmed by the camera units in Jerusalem."

Pieter North could scarcely breathe as he listened to the matter-of-fact description by the Base Commander. How out of touch *was* this man? His recollection returned of Jon De Haag, but this time of their first reunion in the disused chapel at the English country house of Chequers on a bitterly-cold November day. His stomach now seemed as cold as the weather on that fateful Saturday. He remembered the Professor's calm and confident voice saying 'as long as no-one dies I believe it will work'. But someone *had* died; a science assistant who had been blown apart and left in a bloody heap in a back-transfer TTU. What would *that* have done to the logic of time's steady progression through history? And now there was the prospect of a snatch-and-grab raid on one of the most famous bodies in history! Nasty, thorny questions threw themselves at him like ravaging wolves.

What if the target identified as Jesus did not die in the first place?

Would they try to capture him alive, and then kill him to see if he would come alive again?

How would they know which body to snatch?

What effect would it have on the onlookers, on other scientists or on the local population?

What about the waiting world audience? What was supposed to happen when the 'cargo' was delivered to 2135?

Pieter North found he could not handle such questions. Surely putting a dead body on display to the world in a grotesque demonstration of mockery was too horrific to contemplate, even by the low standards of the twenty-second century? No! Enough was enough! He desperately did not want his place in history sullied or even denied by a shocking and shameful end to this story. He had to rescue his reputation, and that could only be done by going to Jerusalem himself. Yes, there were young and gifted physicists all around him - their day would come, but only if his own place in scientific history could be secured on solid foundations. He needed to find a way to get himself onto the high-speed hover-copter. He decided that regardless of danger or inconvenience he should pull rank and get himself aboard……..

Simon Atkins' mind was also in turmoil. The 'viper' list of personnel to be returned safely to 2135 had been received on the twenty-first of April, twelve days before the cryogenic and helicopter teams arrived. As expected, the list consisted entirely of names of some of the senior physicists, security staff and military commanders. Only the temporal physicists had been mentioned; other disciplines, junior military ranks and the media teams would all be thrown to the wolves……….abandoned in islands of history long passed, three hundred years apart, with no way of

353

returning to the twenty-second century. They would die out in their new surroundings in terrifying loneliness. He personalised the awful dilemma by imagining such a fate for Felixana, and in his fevered imaginings the South African could see what would happen to the castaways. Their prognosis was not good. He knew from the 'sand dune siesta' episodes on Base that all of them lived on the edge, emotionally-speaking. Surely the trauma of rejection and abandonment would easily be enough to trigger off mass suicides? Anyone managing to summon up enough courage to stay alive would be completely without basic life skills that had been lost over the centuries. Perhaps some of the military personnel would eke out a wilderness life for a few months, but these were precisely the men and women without language, social and community skills who could perhaps partially integrate for a while. In any event, no-one would pass their secret down even one generation. Safe pregnancy and childbirth were not offspring of the first century, or even of the nineteenth. He shuddered. He couldn't return home knowing that he had abandoned her to a terrible fate. He needed to find a way to get himself onto the high-speed hover-copter. He decided that regardless of danger or inconvenience he should pull rank and get himself aboard........

THE FIFTH DAY OF MAY

8:00 HOURS

After nearly a fortnight of travelling, with its painful transfers, the full tidal wave of twenty-second century life had burst upon Paul Devine's consciousness in sound, colour and complexity. He had stepped from the TTU at precisely 14:03 on Wednesday the fourth of May. Despite the physical similarity with other bases in terms of corridors and hatchways, the home Siverek base, Caramel Base, quickly overwhelmed his senses with its facilities and comforts. There was more here, so much more, than he could remember. He had only spent twelve days at Caramel on first arrival. Much of that time had been taken up with holographic work, though he had sought to explore wherever and whenever he could do so. Nevertheless, so much had happened around him since he had left on the twenty sixth of February to fall into that black hole of his recent experience. In just over nine weeks of life he had lived through a multitude of lifetimes, stared into eternity, been elated and terrified in equal measure, achieved the impossible - and, he had told himself shakily, still got back alive and in time for lunch. Well, at 14:03 a late lunch.

Over steak and fries in a base restaurant he had found he couldn't stop the shaking in his body. Had it all been a nightmare? Surely it would be so easy to walk away, right now? After all, he had slipped away before, into the desert. No! That was not true! He had slipped away so easily from Red Base in the year 1835, not from this busy, organised, noisy main centre. He had shaken his head to clear it, taking a slug of hot tea into his mouth to burn back some reality. How strange it was that he could think so glibly of centuries of history. Yes, his caution was right. It might not be so easy to slip off-base now. Felixana had got him in, but he would have to get out on his own. He longed merely to pick up a telephone and key in a BBC or Southern Brotherhood number, expecting the hover-taxi to arrive at the main gate in a cloud of desert dust. He had pressed on with his meal - it took two portions of apple pie and custard before his shaking stopped and he could focus his mind again. He had recalled the day in Damascus when he had checked co-ordinates on a digital map, deliberating on whether the Brotherhood would sacrifice him. He had smiled grimly - unlike his assessment on that distant occasion he was now convinced they would most certainly not reject him. He had a story to tell. Now, to business.........

He was pleased he had left contact details in a safe place prior to his helicopter lift over the Turkish border. One short phone call would be enough, if only he could leave the base. Then he remembered a holographic sleight-of-hand he had once performed as a party trick. As the sun rose from the eastern desert on Thursday morning, he was ready........

While Paul Devine took breakfast in Turkey, American Vice-President Harold P Lutz slept soundly in Washington D.C. as Wednesday slipped soundlessly into Thursday. The political decisions having been taken a week before, he had prepared himself for travel to Siverek. That journey would soon begin. A morning flight to the European base on Gibraltar would bring him within striking distance of Turkey. Then a military transport aircraft would complete the journey. If all went according to plan, the Vice-President's plane would be in Siverek Base by late on Friday afternoon. On his arrival in Gibraltar the authorities in Siverek would be instructed to prepare for his arrival with a total security lock-down.

In certain lighting conditions, it becomes impossible to distinguish between a holographic projection and a real entity. Paul Devine had mastered the technique. Throughout the progress of the morning he moved ahead with his plan. He remembered from his earliest explorations of the Base that levels of waste recycling at Caramel were lower than in subsequent centres. In recognition of the cardinal rule of leaving a minimal footprint at each new time-base, recycling had become almost total, with materials that could not be handled in this way being returned to home-base via the cargo TTUs. Paul knew that purity was not that much of a priority with home-base's own waste. It was a simple-enough administrative feature; regulators in different areas rarely talk to one another, even on similar disciplines. Temporal regulations for all down-time bases were drawn up and monitored by scientists answerable to Doctor North and his senior physicists. Regulations for Caramel Base, by contrast, followed standard military procedures, so in common with every military base throughout the world, there was always a certain level of waste disposal that was permitted, or at least tolerated, locally. At precisely nineteen hours each evening, several automated motorised skips would drive away non-toxic and non-perishable materials to be buried deep within the Turkish countryside in specially-excavated tunnels.

'The most effective way to hide something is in plain view'. Paul knew this truism and at 14:45 hours a holographic projection of him appeared on the flat roof of a waste skip. Visual monitors in Security Control picked up images of a plump person who appeared to be standing at a lectern and giving a presentation. A security guard was dispatched to investigate; on reporting a false alarm, with no-one in the waste area, the recorded image was scanned and the BBC media contact recognised. At 15:00 hours, a routine enquiry at one of the lecture theatres confirmed that Mr Devine was indeed giving a presentation to a few colleagues on his team. On being interrupted, he explained in embarrassed tones that malfunctions were occurring in electrical equipment and *'I'm sorry, but it seems I could pop up anywhere at any time and I'll try to get it sorted.'*

At precisely that moment, in a different country and a different time-zone, Air Force Two was lifting off from Andrews Air Force Base to carry Vice-President Lutz eastwards across the Atlantic Ocean on his five-hour flight to Gibraltar.

The officer on duty in Siverek's Security Control at 17:00 hours was certain he had seen a figure standing in underwear in the waste disposal area. Again, on enquiry there was no actual evidence.

The jet stream high over the Atlantic Ocean was speeding up. Air Force Two chose to take full advantage. The Vice-President was informed by the pilot that they would arrive earlier than expected in Gibraltar. Personal possessions and papers were gathered together.

When a security officer took a cursory look at monitor screens in Siverek Base at 19:00 hours he was treated to a view of a fat guy, dressed in green pyjamas atop a waste skip, studiously brushing his teeth. The officer's superior cancelled the monitor image with a smile, and merely pressed the release button for the evening waste departures.

The plane landed at 16:30 hours. An immediate instruction was flashed to Turkey to commence heightened security in readiness for the Vice-President's arrival the next day.

At 19:31 hours, local time, the whole of Siverek Caramel Base immediately responded to the message from Gibraltar and froze into lock-down. Several kilometres away, Paul Devine was stuffing a pair of green pyjamas into a rocky crevice and then reaching for his mobile phone.

THE SEVENTH DAY OF MAY

10:00 HOURS

Barely four days after Mark Henderson switched off his calibration machine to erase an electronic record, was he sitting in a large room in Ottawa preparing to open his findings to the world. He had not found the fortitude to continue calmly with his work on the Wednesday morning. He had told his colleagues about a serious illness of his brother in Swift Current, Saskatchewan, and how he felt he needed to return urgently. Who would check or query his word? Even the Israeli Antiquities Authority had not questioned his abrupt departure, merely rubber-stamping his exit visa. Nevertheless, he had been body-scanned on leaving the dig to ensure he was not carrying valuable artefacts from the country. Valuable artefacts! He had smiled inwardly as he thought of the print-outs included in his personal papers, print-outs that would mean nothing to a non-professional. Arriving at the Canadian Institute of Geodesy and Geomorphology this Saturday morning he had relished the cool freshness of the north wind blowing down from Mount Tremblant. Soon he could return to the Polar Regions where he belonged. He thought back over his visit the previous evening to the BBC offices in the Canadian capital. He knew this was explosive stuff. After several intense telephone conversations it was agreed a hastily-convened press conference should take place on Saturday morning.

Sitting alongside BBC executives, Professor Henderson felt hemmed in. He sensed the smooth and polished way in which they dealt with early introductions. Time enough to give his presentation first and only then deal with responses, he felt. Yet he had been beaten to the punch. The world's Press Corps had pushed before him the revelation from the previous day that Syrian authorities had declared the European project to be an elaborate hoax! Fully-believable film of Aleppo, with characters dressed in first-century clothing, had flooded the world's media with spectacular images. There was even a female presenter whose voice mimicked that of the English woman, herself fast becoming a world cult figure. After twenty minutes of startling urban scenes the façade was stripped away, leaving the bare bones of a film-set. It was only too clearly obvious to viewers. The Syrian President himself had appeared on camera to emphasise how easy it had been to counter the European Union and its cruel deception. There was even an allegation that the BBC itself had connived in such a charade. Yet the assembled press members sensed something more. They urged on the Corporation's explanation. Yes, an explanation was due! Who to believe?

The Professor's thoughts returned again to the previous evening. He now wriggled uncomfortably before the journalists' expectant stares. He felt his own contribution would only be a part of the picture; the executives seemed so assured. The politics had been way above the head of a mere Arctic scientist. He had not known of the conflicting tensions within the Corporation, and had only been able metaphorically to move his head back and forth like a spectator at a lawn tennis match as conversations that evening had swung from left to right and back again…..no, the Corporation had not been party to Felixana Smith's seemingly earth-shattering revelations…..yes, the Corporation had been silent in its acceptance of the travelogues ostensibly from the world of the Bible…..no, this did not mean that the Corporation was an arm of the European Union's foreign policy…..yes, the locations and dates were believable…..no, the BBC would not be drawn into taking sides in an increasingly-religious debate…..yes, the scientific evidence from the Jericho dig was overwhelming and could trump a stage-managed Syrian side-show. And yet….and yet…..

The Professor rose to speak. The audience hushed. Thirty minutes later, having fully and professionally convinced his listeners, he sat to loud applause. The Chief Executive of the North American arm of the Corporation quickly intervened.

"Ladies and gentlemen, please remain. We have more to tell you. I can introduce someone who has been to the heart of this astounding project in the Middle East. A close confidant and colleague of Ms Smith herself."

Mark Henderson stared with just as much excitement as everyone else in the room as a plump man walked to the speaking-point. Somewhat less than thirty minutes after that, pandemonium broke out as the world's press were this time permitted to complete their rush to the exits.

THE NINTH DAY OF MAY

6:30 HOURS

From separate panoramic windows Pieter North and Simon Atkins looked out at the activity within the base's wide outdoor area. The silence of the Cappadocian mountainsides disintegrated in brittle shards as the engine on the helicopter was started. Within the perimeters of Violet Base, support engineers maintained a cautionary distance, watching the pitch, roll and yaw procedures being tested at five metres, and then at ten metres altitudes. All seemed perfect. The first flight southwards could begin, just six days after the component parts and pilots had arrived. The building of a large generator on a hill-top some fifty kilometres to the south of the base had been completed. Direct communication with the off-base parties could at last be established. Simon Atkins was anxious and excited. Advance groups were in Jerusalem; Passover was less than eight days away! Yet there was still no plausible way he could alert Felixana to her danger. If test flights by helicopter went well, and the deep-freeze facilities completed on time, the principal thrust south would take place on or around the nineteenth of the month.

In a neighbouring room, Pieter North was letting similar calculations run through his mind. The Dutchman was frightened but resolute. Over the coming ten days he would need to devise a temporal argument to convince the base's military commanders that his presence on the final mission was essential. He was moderately confident of success in that regard. The 'cargo' to arrive from Jerusalem would need to be safely transported through the sequence of bases to 2135. He only needed to plant seeds of doubt in the commanders' minds, couched in complex technical terms and 'translated' with brutal simplicity; perhaps over whether a thawing process could be prevented at each transfer point, or whether more than one 'ancient' human needed to be transported. He shuddered. Dare he raise the possibility that the lattice might become unstable again? It might be worth the risk, even to his credibility, if that proved to be the only way to obtain a ticket south. He grimaced. It had always been a politician's shaky argument to suggest *'I got you into this mess, so I am obviously best placed to get you out of it.'* Better not to go there if it was avoidable……..

Simon Atkins also weighed up his chances with the military commanders. Guarding and escorting members of the advance groups was no option. He had rechecked the 'viper' list; only the commander now in Jerusalem had been named. *'So much for loyalty to those risking their lives for their country'*, he observed. He thought of the fate suffered by his grandparents. Their country had been just as precious to them as it had been to the terrorists charged with throwing them out. His gaze settled on the helicopter, now settling itself again on the ground. Its 'cargo' would need guarding, especially if it became known that only those definitely travelling back to Siverek with the frozen body would be saved. Perhaps there would be an advantage in showing through his presence the importance of giving senior and serious intent to completing the return journey. Anyway, whatever happened, he was determined that his woman would return with him.

Pieter North's desire to return to Siverek was equally strong. He had no wish to remain trapped in the past. What would be the point of protecting his scientific reputation if he couldn't return to 2135 to cement his immortality through a stream of personal interviews, physics symposiums, peer-led adulation conferences, text-book releases, sponsorship - the list in his mind elongated like a deformed worm - tickertape cavalcades, tropical villas, star-struck female students, and their mothers, offering favours for his attention or attendance on the after-dinner speaking circuit. He knew he wouldn't be the first scientist in history to be known as the 'thinking woman's crumpet'. The figure of celebrity danced in his mind. He knew from official restricted reports that the Vice-President of the United States of America had been on Caramel Base for three days. When he returned with the spoils of his journey he could shake hands and be welcomed by Harold P Lutz himself - a great start to his glittering scientific odyssey.

Simon Atkins watched the hover-copter's blades slow to a standstill. When exactly would the 'Viper' list be activated? The body of Jesus would need to be installed safely in 2135; not just in Siverek but probably in a key location. He recalled the opening global presentation made on the thirtieth of April. That had taken place in Rome. Would they, *dare* they even, transport the body to Rome? Why not? There would be no better place to destroy the cult of Christianity through the bright light of scientific reality. He felt light-headed; he realised he was getting ahead of himself. Once 'Viper' was triggered he would have to get Felixana on the holy list. In addition, an indefinable feeling of unease continued to gnaw away at his being. He turned and left his quarters.

11:00 HOURS

Mary Trent's arms leant to their duty in determined concentration. Monday was dusting day at Far Cotton Community Church and the latest recruit to the dusting rota was on her knees. The news from Ottawa had not escaped her attention, but then, there were few in the land who had not heard the details. Mary's eyes noticed the smudge of a dirty hand print on the otherwise-shiny end of a bench. Someone had missed that, and on the picture of an angel that it carried, too! She lovingly restored the shine. Her thoughts turned to the Canadian announcements, upset that her new-found sense of purpose and belonging seemed to have been thrown into a new turmoil. No! She would not let it happen! News media were famous for manipulating individuals' perceptions; had been for centuries. She gazed at the angel pictured on the bench-end as if searching for guidance. A short burst of sunlight through the side window caught the picture, the angle of refraction crazing the shaft into its constituent colours. Her intake of breath was audible in the silence of the building. Calm assurance returned to Mary's breast and she leant to her duty with renewed purpose.

THE SECOND WEEK IN MAY

News emanating from the Canadian Institute in Ottawa at around 11:15 hours on Saturday the seventh of May 2135 broke upon the

world like a tsunami. Details swept across continents. Governments, corporations, armed forces, religious bodies, men, women and children - they all listened, watched, cried, prayed and cursed in their own special way. At first, nothing happened; the news and its significance just could not be taken in. Policy-makers froze. With one exception, it took until Sunday, fully twenty four hours later, for the two messages to be distilled and understood. The facts were stark. The military base at Siverek in Turkey was sheltering a time-travel project that was actively searching for Jesus of Nazareth, and the northern powers were willing to sacrifice many hundreds of scientists in the closing stages of that project. The detail on these 'closing stages' was not known. The potential sacrifices were causing more turmoil and outrage than the concept of searching for a religious figure. The northern authorities were strenuous in their denials, though this merely added to the confusions and conspiracy theories swirling around the planet.

The one exception to frozen inactivity occurred at Caramel Base itself. A news blackout struck on the base before the Ottawa presentation even started. On his arrival on the Friday evening, the Vice-President had been informed of two key events; the unauthorised disappearance of the BBC holographer twenty four hours before and the arrival of a significant Israeli armed force on the Turkish border with Syria. The Israelis themselves were not far behind the Americans in terms of leaving the starting blocks. Barely two hours after the Thursday morning flight of Air force Two had begun, deep-cover Mossad operatives in the United States had informed Tel Aviv by coded message that Vice-President Lutz was crossing the Atlantic bound for Siverek. Though the news from Ottawa coincided with observance of the Sabbath, at first light on Sunday morning the troops along the Turkish border were already aware they were being ordered not to cross. The presence of a world leader nearby across the desert scrub demanded more than a modicum of caution.

Last to respond was the Southern Brotherhood.

THE SEVENTEENTH DAY OF MAY

6:00 HOURS

Gaza City sweltered in the summer heat, even as early in the morning as this moment. The muezzins' call to prayer rang out, its poignant eternal half-tones and glottal inflections hanging in the hot air for an instant, then spinning down into the ears of believers and non-believers alike. The Moslem world was beginning to feel the painful confusion and hurt being inflicted on Christian countries over the previous eighteen days. The predominantly-white skyline contrasted with the blue of the Mediterranean Sea. Born as a separate United Nations enclave under the Three States Agreement of 2046, the Gaza Republic, officially a secular, non-armed state, with its close economic ties to the completely-independent Palestine and the Arab League, had been totally rebuilt in the 2060s and 2070s. New mosques, hotels, apartments, schools, hospitals, parks and shopping malls had grown from the rubble of the former Gaza Strip. Enjoying the status of a World States Council open city it was possible for all nationalities to visit.

The three Southern Brotherhood army generals were sitting on a hotel suite balcony overlooking the ocean, pondering the fate of the small number of Ethiopian troops billeted on the outskirts of Bethlehem. Rosemary Sanchez, the forty-year old, English-trained Chilean, readjusted her sunglasses on her nose.

"They've been there a week now. We cannot be any more ready than we currently are."

A slow nod of the head, then a sip from a cold orange juice, and the Ghanaian officer was first to respond. "What news from Africa?"

"The High Council has given the three of us total authority to act militarily if and when we see fit."

The older Kenyan general spoke the words with a tinge of resignation. She felt the responsibility of high rank weighing heavily on her shoulders. The Ghanaian sipped her drink again.

"Oh."

363

The flat monosyllable summed up the dilemma they all faced so keenly. The South American woman looked up from holding her head in her hands.

"The film released yesterday from Rome gave them little choice, in my view. The Europeans are clearly committed to pursuing this action against us to maximum effect. Where on earth is it leading them? The assault by science on our Faith has now become uncontrollable. So many genies have been let out of the bottle!"

She sighed. Mary Poinsettia, the Kenyan woman, smiled on her gently.

"Ours is a military responsibility, thank the Lord; only that. We go into the Turkish base, we stop the films. We give the order if the Americans or the Israelis show clear signs of moving first."

Patze Mazuto, the Ghanaian officer spoke. "Then good intelligence is our pre-requisite. We need three hours' notice, and preferably six, to be in Siverek before anyone else."

Her white teeth gleamed in the growing early morning light. Rosemary Sanchez stood and stretched. The day could be a hot one - probably thirty eight degrees, the forecasters had said. She seemed particularly anxious.

"Will our Lord forgive us if we snuff out the threat but leave hundreds of innocent souls in previous centuries?"

Mary Poinsettia held out her arms. "We will not have killed them. Their lives will run their course..." she paused "....and God will be with them. There is no mountain so high, or dungeon so dark, or river so deep that it can separate them from His love. Only the person who deliberately and consistently turns away from God will run the risk of losing Him."

Patze Mazuto approached the dilemma logically. "Remember our training in military academy. We seemed to argue for hours over what constituted a Holy War. We studied examples from the Crusades to the Jihads, and on to the large-scale national suicides in Iran and Burma". She counted off the options on her manicured fingers.

"The numerical case when a small number of deaths might justify saving a larger number of lives. The nationhood case when God can be invoked to be on our side as shown by historical perspective. The redemptive case when every non-believer who dies in a conflict conducted for a religious cause is himself saved for salvation. The comparative case when sects and denominations can be laid against secular criteria. That one was particularly relevant in Ireland around a hundred and sixty five years ago."

She looked imploringly at her fellow generals.

"This is on a far greater scale and to a different set of principles. Plato and Aristotle saw no conflict of ideas. Newton and Galileo slept easily in their beds. Yet Darwin and Einstein were encouraged by outside forces to introduce edginess, a sharp side, a premature and unsubstantiated triumphalism. By the early decades of the last century science had parted company with morality. In its place was substituted ethics, action perfectly acceptable if it did not conflict with the law or with society's majority perceptions. Remembering the Lord's Prayer, and putting it bluntly - how can God's Will be done on earth if we don't get our hands on northern bank accounts?"

Rosemary Sanchez smiled. Mary Poinsettia stood up.

"We go. We put a stop to this madness."

14:30 HOURS

Chuck Kowalski had been picked for the security detail into Jerusalem. He was pleased. The whole final segment of the expedition had been based on Mount Scopus for seventeen days now, moving on foot downhill and into the city in the early mornings under precise daily target instructions. After each foray there had been an exhaustive debrief for all involved. Film obtained was screened by base commander and transmitted to Siverek. Chuck knew the pattern with its easy mnemonic - sweep, scoop, study, send - all in digestible packages. Today's work would be no different.

He clipped two more magazines of smart bullets to his waist-fixed bandolier. He particularly liked these bullets. Just over four centimetres long, each metal cylinder contained several computer bio-circuits. The bullet was fully-programmable in an amazing variety of ways. Fired in the general direction of a target, it would follow instructions. It would swerve and twist and change direction to hit the programmed target and only the programmed target. If it couldn't find this within a pre-set time limit, it would fly off into the air to self-destruct softly. 'Collateral damage' was a thing of the past. The programs could specify a man, a woman, a person over one metre fifty, a black girl, a Chinese person over fifty years old, a man in a green uniform, a woman wearing white clothing, a person carrying a weapon - the list was almost endless. How it could do all this, Chuck had absolutely no idea. He riffled through his belt programmer looking for an option resembling a metal-clad Roman centurion.

Jerusalem was filling fast as pilgrims arrived from all parts of Judea and beyond. The city would have a regular population of around seventy thousand, significant for its age. The arrival of pilgrims for festivals and other holy days would swell this number four or five fold. Those travelling from the coast at Jaffa had undertaken a three day trek. The Second Temple, in its gleaming white marble, shone in the afternoon sun as if it would at any moment burst into incandescent flame. The expedition members had listened intently to the briefings given on the Temple by the civilisation team. Quarries around Jerusalem had been plundered for giant ashlar stones and white limestone. Lebanese cedar forests had been cut down, to be floated south along the coast. The presenter had told how they could expect to see the edifice 'covered all over with plates of gold and at the first rising of the sun reflect back a fiery splendour.'

Standing on a relatively-quiet street corner, Chuck felt a wet bead of perspiration trickle down behind his left ear. He touched the small communicator device hidden above the lobe. The street behind was almost empty. He risked a glance at his wrist console. Even in the shade, the temperature showed as thirty eight degrees. He caught the eye of his unit commander. A hand and eye signal indicated imperceptibly that he should close up and stay vigilant. The commander and his four men ghosted through the growing stream of worshippers in the direction of the Temple. Their movements had been professionally practised; jostling and body contact with other people was being kept to a minimum. Though they had been taught not to make eye contact with the local population, this did not mean their eyes were not used. They darted everywhere, noting a constant flow of data on angles, distances, densities of the crowd, levels of compliance and assertiveness. High in the blue sky above several eagle drones circled lazily in the heat. The 'mother ship' voice of Base Commander calmly relayed key instructions in response to digital images being received from the drones at data headquarters on Mount Scopus. The instructions were targeted, either to specific unit commanders in the field or to all of them.

Chuck Kowalski and his immediate compatriots knew their day's mission well. They were to provide 'close and covert cover' to the main film unit under the BBC woman's control as it followed the Galilean's activities. After several days of such action the movements of the man named Jesus were well known. The soldier recalled the previous evening's briefing, words ringing again in his ears.

"Main target, code-named 'Gold', spends each night at the same dwelling in one of the poorer areas of the city. His disciples guard him well, indeed, very well; by our military standards we should be impressed. His key personnel know how to spot potential trouble-makers and informants - Temple officials, Roman stooges, and such-like. We are deploying a rolling sequence of close-cover operatives in support of the film units in order that a level of familiarity with our faces cannot be built up and responded to."

'So, that explains why I haven't had the chance before now to join the party' the man from Nebraska had concluded. The briefing officer had continued with a wry smile.

"Main target is code-named 'Gold' for a reason. We don't want any confusion in the heat of the moment engendered by such under-the-breath comments as 'Jesus' or 'Jesus Christ', or some similar natural every-day and common expletive. We are merely professionals doing a professional job. Remember that."

The toe of Chuck Kowalski's boot stubbed a raised flagstone, jerking him back to reality. The five-man unit was holding its shape well, but the stream of worshippers was turning into a stronger current as it approached the public entrances on the south side of Temple Mount. Chuck stifled a gasp. Through the monumental staircase of the Robinson Arch the Temple reared up ahead of him like a mountain covered in snow. The hub-hub and general noise of the crowd was rising. Roman soldiers stood silent and stern guard along the main thoroughfares, keeping clear of the religious areas. The Cohanim in their white linen robes were directing pilgrims towards the ritual cleansing and purifying areas.

Felixana Smith and her main cameraman had reached the outer boundary of the area known as the Court of Women. She was full of nervous tension, fizzing as if a carbonated drink was coursing through her veins. One of the linguists on the expedition came alongside, gripping her arm. The linguist herself, eyes wide with caution, lifted her gaze to the inscription displayed above the Court's entrance. Felixana's eyes followed, not understanding the Hebrew words depicted. The other woman leaned over and whispered the translation into her ear.

"Foreigner! Do not enter within the grille and partition surrounding the Temple. He who is caught will have only himself to blame for his death which will follow."

Felixana felt her legs turn to jelly. She felt cold, despite the heat of the day. Nevertheless, she whispered back, "Don't tell the others." The linguist was torn between envy and alarm for her female companion, but said nothing. She, too, felt sick with worry.

In the Royal Portico market place, with its upper viewing floor, stalls had been set up where pilgrims could buy a pigeon, or perhaps a lamb, for ritual sacrifice. The familiar scent of blood came to Chuck Kowalski's nostrils, his heart-rate lifting slightly with the soft gush of adrenaline into his arteries. Prices were being haggled over with a certain degree of aggression. The soldier sensed that something was not right. He had no way of assessing the religious importance of the occasion, or the layout of the scene. The Court of the Gentiles housed the main bazaar, but it was a busy day, with demand up and space at a premium. Tables were appearing far beyond, with riskier ones near, and even within, some of the ten entrances to the Inner Courts. Chuck felt himself being jostled onwards. He noticed the BBC woman in the crush ahead, indicating to one of her cameramen to take advantage of a higher viewing point on a vacant table at the end of the main court. The cameras were no bigger than a half cucumber and disguised as a small writing scroll, so could easily be pointed clandestinely in any direction.

"Target Gold present....target Gold present.....entering main court....and in a hurry! Close cover now, standard star pattern."

Chuck and his fellow unit members tensed as the message came over via their immediate commander's earpiece. Dressed in the same robes as most of the thronging crowd, the five moved expertly and silently to their allotted positions, each at two metres from Felixana and her second unit cameraman. The first camera would provide the mainstream footage from the vantage point of the trestle table. It would pan and zoom under independent control, while the second lens had to stay focussed on the provider of the commentary. A key feature of the later editing would be the switches between action and Felixana's face. The military protection therefore had to cover second unit and commentator, who would be devoting much of their concentration on each other.

Chuck Kowalski took up position at the right side star point, his eyes sweeping his quadrant from rear-point right to the unit commander at point itself. All seemed well. The intensity of the bartering and haggling over prices exhibited a fever made worse by the high temperature of the day. Chuck looked to his left; main target 'Gold' moved through the crowd with purpose, a look on his face of emotions that seemed to Chuck, only four metres away, to lie halfway between deep, sad exasperation and resolute anger. Chuck's experienced eye easily picked out the three - no - four 'minders' pacing slightly behind the target. It was the first time Chuck had seen the man named Jesus at such close quarters. It took all of his willpower to look away and focus on Felixana.

The crashing of tables began. Wood splintered, feathers flew and lambs bleated. The anguished and affronted wails of the market traders rose even higher. The newcomer was turning over the tables of the traders and money-changers, sending their contents spinning wildly across the mosaic-covered floor. Despite his obvious limp he exhibited great strength. As he moved through the court he strongly berated the men, and they were all men, calling out in a clear loud voice, pointing towards the holiest areas of the complex. Chuck had no way of knowing the words that 'Gold' was shouting, but it was obvious to him that the man was outraged at what he was seeing. Chuck noticed a small group of followers, perhaps five or six, wagging their hands in support and aiming the odd kick or two at a brass vase or startled lamb as they moved in the wake of their master. Felixana flagged a sign at her main camera as if to say 'are you getting all this?', and spoke excitedly as she looked at the second unit camera. The microphone clipped to the folds of her hooded cowl picked up her commentary. She knew well what she was witnessing and could scarcely control her excitement despite her professional training. Chuck's attention remained focussed on the BBC woman as the instigator of the mayhem continued to upturn tables nearer to, and then inside, the holy entrances to the other courts.

The turmoil had not gone unnoticed by either the Temple guardians or the Roman soldiers in the vicinity. The guardians readily stood aside to let the full weight of the nearby military make its presence felt. Yet there were too many people in the outer courts for the fifteen or so foot-soldiers to lock their shields into a straight phalanx to push the throng into order. The guardians shouted, gesticulating wildly that the soldiers should remain as a loose collection and pursue the limping transgressor. It was too late. Two knots of sympathisers had joined forces and spirited him away from the Temple area and down into a labyrinth of alleyways in the lower city. Somehow, the standard star pattern of five combat troops had stood relatively firm around Felixana. Together they swung forward towards the main cameraman, picking himself from the floor after jumping from the corner table as it was shaken by the departing crowd.

One of the nearest men in Roman armour, perhaps with special training in identifying controlled and disciplined elements in a crowd, stepped from the wall of the court. In a clear voice he ordered three of his number to intercept the expedition's men at rear-point left and rear-point right of the star. With their shields raised, the three soldiers in the service of the Emperor singled out their two targets. Chuck looked to his left. His nearest colleague was being harangued in Latin. Faced with a blank stare, the Roman then broke into stilted Aramaic, pushing the other back with short, aggressive movements. Further away, the man at rear-point left was being similarly harassed, this time by the two remaining Romans.

"The rear's in trouble, chief!"

Chuck spoke urgently into his microphone, at the same time gripping his hand-gun inside the folds of his tunic. His commander assessed the options rapidly - four hostile units in a chaotic crowd, against five expedition soldiers with obviously-superior weaponry. As long as they acted swiftly and strongly, the situation could be contained and the threat eliminated.

"Right side and left side, delete the close enemy!"

The crowd was pressing on all sides. Hand-fire at several metres would not be safe. It had to be blade-work. Chuck and his opposite number moved closer. Two of the Romans pushing with their shields seemed to consider this action would be enough to separate the two trouble-makers they had identified. The third had drawn his stabbing sword with its fifty-centimetre blade. The glint of sunlight on sharp metal caused an involuntary spasm in the knot of people around the incident. The locals clearly knew it would be wise to back off. Coming late to an understanding of what was happening Felixana Smith and her cameraman turned their focus onto the scene behind them. They both moved closer, drawn by the journalist's instinct to be nearer the action. Chuck closed the gap with the first Roman in three sharp strides, his senior officer's word 'delete' still ringing in his head. Now he was close enough for his knife; up through the tunic, twist and withdraw. The victim slumped against his opponent, his shield clattering to the ground. Chuck smelt garlic on the man's final breath. The noise of the shield on the flagstones distracted the attention of the other two Romans from their own quarry. The taller man, his stabbing blade still exposed, noticed an assertive figure standing against the shield of his nearby partner. A strangely-shaped lump of metal in the hand was pressed on the shield. A harmless pretence....some unknown Jewish incantation would follow....the Roman shield would laugh it off.....

A finger jerked, the lump of metal coughed, a small hole appeared in the shield, his friend's face glazed over in the unmistakeable eternal mask of death. The man nearly dropped his sword in terror. Why did he not feel safe? What was happening here? Surely no-one could be safe if a lump of metal could transmit death through a shield with an invisible finger? He sensed a pressure, a movement behind his back. His instinct for self-preservation overcame his training in his frozen brain; with a sound in his throat approaching a hoarse and violent wail he turned and thrust in self-defence at the perceived enemy behind him. Felixana Smith looked down at her stomach in disbelief. The pain of the sharp blade was excruciating. Her eyes widened. She saw the fear in the Roman's face. He pulled back with the sword, bringing glistening tendrils of muscle and blood into the open world. The cameraman dropped his equipment, grabbing at Felixana as she sagged. Chuck Kowalski switched off his silencer and pumped four bullets into the Roman soldier with four loud cracks of doom. The man in Roman armour who had initiated the fatal interception ghosted away into the screaming masses. The collective wail of a confused and frightened humanity rose through the oven of the sky where it was picked up by the circling drones, looking more like vultures than eagles.

GOLD

THE EIGHTEENTH DAY OF MAY

The bed where the lower stretches of the River Jordan had once flowed was dry - of that there was no doubt. The desert dust had blown across the southern valley for forty summers and forty winters. It wasn't for lack of trying on the part of the governments of the region. Despite scientific and technological advances of significant proportion the thinning snows of Mount Hermon could never melt into enough cool waters to overspill Kenneseret and move on to the Dead Sea. The sea itself was also almost non-existent. Yet the Jordan wasn't an isolated example of a former world river. Since the first banning of baptisms in the Jordan in the year 2010 there had been numerous occasions of sad moment. The Yamuna River in India, the Baghmati in Kathmandu and the Punjabi's Kali Bein had all disappeared into first a polluted state and finally a sad evaporation. The Israeli and Palestinian authorities in particular had felt pain at what was happening on the world stage. Day after day now the films released by the northern powers were creating new tensions and pressures. Not least among them was the sight of naturalists and environmental scientists moving quite solidly through lush river-side vegetation, disturbing myriad clouds of butterflies and dragonflies and filming such a wealth of plants and animals that at times the travelogues bordered on what older viewers had remembered as natural history programmes. The comparison with the Israeli-Palestinian hinterlands of the 2130s was stark to the point of embarrassment for both nations, uniting them at least on this clear shared ground of humanity. The keenness was felt particularly by those with a professional following linked to the former river. From university professor to game warden to humble peasant, the images from the ancient world, now shown to be genuine, caused many heads to hang in shame. Michael Ben-Tovim's was not one of them, but then he had much more on his mind. Nevertheless, he gazed with some sense of forlorn destiny as the dry river-bed in question sped past thirty metres below the rapid-response military hover-copter carrying him south towards Jerusalem.

He thought back over the tumultuous events of the previous ten days. He had been called by the Prime Minister's office early on the Sunday morning that had been the eighth day of May. The world was spinning

372

with the news released from Canada the day before. Suddenly, the northern powers were on the defensive again, but how to push home any advantage? The Mossad Director was pressed urgently to attend at the Government's internal security offices in Tel Aviv. The Europeans and their partners were preparing to self-destruct parts of a genuine project - and barely seventy two hours before had come the espionage information that American Vice-President Lutz was on his way to Turkey to oversee the process. It seemed to the Israeli high command that it was increasingly clear that the northern countries would risk military conflict to protect their now-less-than-secret weapon in the 'war' of ideas. Mossad had also discovered plans for American Marines to be landed at Kusadasi on the Turkish mainland, presumably under Chinese pressure for an aggressive stance in defence of northern policy. A defence force with significant potential could from Kusadasi be mobilised within a few hours to protect the Siverek base. It was obvious to Ben-Tovim that the Europeans intended to guard the grip they now clearly had on world attention. His first meeting with the Defence Minister had merely confirmed his fears. He had glanced at the outdoor temperature reading on his wrist console as he entered the Minister's office - twenty nine degrees. The Minister's topic was equally hot; what to do about the news from Canada.

Information two days later on the tenth of May increased his anxiety for some kind of homeland action. Reports were coming from the West Bank border with Palestine that soldiers with an unknown speciality were arriving from northern Africa. Whatever the answers to his questions might be as to their purpose, surely it would all focus on Siverek, and sooner rather than later. The military view in Tel Aviv was that their force in Lebanon and on Syrian soil was over-exposed. It should turn its focus southwards against the Brotherhood rather than continuing with psychological pressure on the north. The problem from Ben-Tovim's perspective was that the situation was not this clear-cut. He couldn't help feeling that there was something missing, some detail he had overlooked, or an angle hidden from his basic assumptions. Yet he couldn't pin it down....and still the images from the ancient world daily transfixed an international community of nation states and power blocs that had been fed on pre-packaged visual messages of deception and entertainment for over two hundred years. He sighed. The world would not change now. He thought back over the history of the subject in his mind. Flickering statements in monochrome of blond Aryan supremacy in the 1930s....ethnic conflicts in Africa, the Balkans and the Middle East....the rise and then fall of fundamental terrorism masquerading as religious fervour....state-sponsored air-brushing in the 2040s painting Chinese economic warfare and protectionism as necessary to placate the sleeping giant that was their rural poor. The power of the moving picture to embed an idea into the collective subconscious of the planet was indeed awesome.

Earth now accepted the vehicle bringing a message from the past, but the message was somehow out of focus to the Israeli's mature eye. He shrugged, knowing he had to put such fuzziness aside. The Defence Minister had made it clear at their second meeting on the twelfth of May that their prime concern now had to be the Palestinian problem. Ethiopian-trained combat soldiers were billeted in a specially-converted tourist hostel on the outskirts of Bethlehem. It was the opinion of the Israeli High Command that such action violated the terms of the Three States Agreement of 2046. The Defence Minister had grunted with irritation and controlled anger, his voice quavering with indignation.

"We are just eleven years from marking the centenary of the Peace Accord and now look at what they have done!"

Michael Ben-Tovim had winced invisibly as his superior spat out the word 'they'. He knew it meant the Palestinian government. He held his tongue, merely running his finger inside his shirt collar. His wrist console showed the outside temperature to be thirty three degrees. The niggling detail he had overlooked wasn't here in this air-conditioned room. It was increasingly his view that the Southern Brotherhood faced the same threat as his own nation, and was merely responding in what appeared to be a similar way. Yet he still couldn't lay his ghosts to rest. He knew the Minister was right in terms of global politics. The real tangible danger from the north was surely passing. The BBC's monumental exclusive story would play itself out. The Christian foundation underpinning the southern hemisphere would be ridiculed in a fresh wave of the science-led 'aggressive atheism' begun in the second decade of the last century. Israel could again resume its onward march. Their immediate concern was to turn the army southwards to face down the Brotherhood. If rumours coming from Mexico and Singapore were to be believed, an autumn summit of the World States Council's Economic Congress was only a few weeks away from being formally established. The next ten-year Plan would be reversed, the bulk of the world's financial resources would remain with China, Europe and North America, and Israel could prosper. Syria was already making noises about the build-up of too many foreign troops on its own soil along its border with Turkey. The excuse of protecting international research facilities devoted to solar wind energy could no longer be sustained. Ben-Tovim was informed that the majority of the armed units stretching out from Lebanon were unilaterally withdrawing in a gesture of goodwill towards the Syrian people. Mossad-trained operatives would instead clandestinely prepare to move south along the Jordan valley to block any early signs of an Ethiopian strike on the Siverek base.

***

And so it was that on day-break on Monday the sixteenth of May, as daily film releases on an ancient Jerusalem continued to astound and confuse the world in equal measure, the military forces representing the planet's differing power blocs were held in a delicately-balanced tripod of strength. The northern powers had installed American Marines at Kusadasi, the Israeli presence in occupied Syria was backing away slowly, and the Southern Brotherhood was making itself at home in Palestine.

***

On the same morning Michael Ben-Tovim had woken early in a sweat. In the summer heat of the dying night he turned fitfully and with perspiration in his bed. Anna, his wife, her own sleep disturbed by his unsettled movements, rolled over and wiped his forehead with a gentle cool hand. Their two children slept on in adjacent first-floor rooms.

"What is it, love?"

"I have to go to Jerusalem - soon."

"The whole world is going to Jerusalem!" she sighed. "We seem to be at the centre of things, but at the same time we are not. It is like the liquid soap in our bathroom; we reach to grasp it and it melts away into a strange shape. We are powerless to control the Jerusalem we see every day now on our home screens."

His gentle laughter hid the sad tension in his voice. "I need your insights around my desks, my dear Anna. Events are driving my superiors to distraction. It is an itch they cannot scratch."

"I worry for you, my love. I worry for what your masters may order to be done."

Why did he feel guilty and furtive at her remark? He knew it was meant with the deepest and sincerest of motives. "There is no danger to us, Anna," was all he could manage in response, but she was not to be deflected.

"It's only power-politics, Michael. You are used to that. Why are you so nervous?"

The diplomat knew his wife could read him like a book. Anna had been so perceptive during all of their time together. Perhaps this particular attraction of hers was coming to its most incisive, touching him to a point where he would be uncomfortable. Certainties of his upbringing were being tested, the knife-point of her life's experience about to prise open a shell he thought was solidly shut.

"I don't know, my love. The deceptions are becoming more reckless. It is as if the northern powers are prepared to destroy everyone. We could all fall."

"I don't believe that, my darling, and neither should you. Our homeland, our 'Promised Land' as you call it, is just that - land. When it boils down to it, in the phrase 'Jewish State', you see the word 'Jewish' and I see the word 'State'. It's nearly a hundred years now since the Three States Agreement gave us our peace. Remember our history books. The circle of eternal conflict could only be squared when we surrendered land in exchange for the title of Jewishness. The bargaining counter that proved to be the more powerful of the two was the physical, not the metaphysical. Europe and America can do nothing to harm us - unless we provoke them."

"I don't think our race is going to provoke them, Anna."

He could not reveal, even to his wife, that the more likely prospect was a delaying pressure on the Southern Brotherhood to allow the northern powers to complete their attack on Christianity. He had clung to his solid Faith throughout these murky years of bluff and counter-bluff. Yet he was nervous; she was right about that. He could not fathom the reason for it. Some vital piece in all this complex web of subterfuge was missing. Anna could read the conflict in her husband's face. She sighed softly.

"I've told you before, we are not a race. We are a nation."

His eyes widened. "Israel is the Jewish State, my dear."

"Judaism is a religion, Michael. It is only necessary that its adherents believe in its tenets, not that they have a particular strand of DNA in their bodily genetic make-up. We all have loyalty to our nation. Our history pulls us together in a way that few other nations can possibly know, but we are just that - a nation. It's the body of all humanity living within these borders who are watching what will happen."

He had remembered later that day, as Anna stepped from her shower, the transmissions from Rome that conveyed images of a jostling, excited humanity noisily crowding round a slightly-bearded figure riding on a donkey. Anna had confessed how she had stood naked and spellbound watching the wall-length screen. She had told him that surely it was sacrilegious for the Europeans to continue with this series of revelations. Yes, it was revealing aspects of the Christian New Testament and not her husband's Holy Scripture, but to her the project had a distinct air of brutality about it that lifted pity into her soul. The liquid soap had slid noiselessly through her fingers, gathering in an equally-pitiful pool on the shower floor. He recalled that he had kissed her tenderly and gone to meet his official car.....

A shout in his earphones woke him from his reverie. Once again, it was the eighteenth of May and the dry river bed of the Jordan was speeding past thirty metres below the hover-copter's spinning blades. The pilot's voice crackled in his ear to remind him that he had twenty minutes to prepare for arrival. He heard the final sentence. "Local temperature in Jerusalem is thirty nine degrees. Storm clouds are gathering."

***

Within precisely the same geographical air-space, an almost-identical hover-copter was also speeding south. Though this one flew over a verdant river-valley, its occupants were tormented by anxieties quite similar to those of the Israeli diplomat. Simon Atkins and Pieter North were travelling towards their own destinies along an identical path, separated from Michael Ben-Tovim only by the gossamer curtain they all would call 'time'.

The light from the setting sun bathed Jerusalem in an awful colour, mid-way between blood-red and mustard-yellow. The orb itself was only visible as a bright spot within the thick cloud-base that had built up remarkably quickly in the dying hour of the day. The base commander, standing alone on the rocky outcrop, shielded his eyes with his hands as he surveyed the city below. The heat was not dissipating; in fact, the build-up of the cumulo-nimbus storm clouds was acting as a blanket, sucking moisture from lungs and energy from legs. What a day it had been! His gaze swept northwards in the expectation of catching a first glimpse of the in-coming hover-copter. Nothing appeared. The achievement of a two-way communication link with Siverek base had only been temporary, but it had been enough to confirm that Methuselah was still to be enacted. Yet that would be more difficult than ever now; now that filming had stopped. The mask of anonymity for their task had been ripped away by that awful incident yesterday in the Temple. Romans would be everywhere now. Bloody reprisals would erupt regardless of the diplomacy for Passover. The base commander thought of Felixana over in the field hospital. A different kind of mask was now delivering bio-engineered, oxygenised, replacement muscle-lining to support the vocal chords that had linked this world so well with the one they had left behind. He passed his hand over his sweat-sodden head. He had not slept since the teams had returned from Jerusalem the evening before. He was dizzy with fatigue. The surgical team had worked all day. They were generating enough blood to stabilise the poor girl, but that damned Roman blade into her stomach had carried several ancient infections which the expedition's computers had been unable to identify. If they couldn't bio-engineer a counter-action, he feared they could lose this particular battle.

A sound carried on the burning air as the fading light flickered in the sky. A faint rumble reached his ears. It stopped. He strained to listen harder. The thunder repeated, slightly louder this time. His eyes swept the heavens. There was no sign of lightning, yet it could not be far away. A different throbbing emerged. Far to the north he saw the pulsing light that accompanied it. The shape grew against the backdrop of the storm clouds. The heat and tiredness had worn him down; there was no sensible reason for the ghostly image of a second hover-copter reflected in the cloud alongside the one he had expected. He dismissed the trick of the light. It was gone in an instant, seeming to peel away from the edges of his eye. The single machine from Siverek threw up a pale curtain of red dust in the evening darkness. Then it was down. He ran towards the opening door.

THE NINETEENTH DAY OF MAY

07:32 HOURS

Up...down, up...down, up...down. The gentle rhythm held a quietening comfort of its own, a soft reaffirmation every few seconds of a life continuing. *'Only a heart-beat from eternity each time'*, he thought. Simon Atkins' eyes followed the rise and fall of the pure-white linen surgical gown covering Felixana's breasts. The computer lights on the medic-console twinkled silently. He matched his own breathing sequence to hers, a conscious attempt to twin with her life, to will a slow recovery. He recalled their love-making. The patina of perspiration on her beautiful neck was no longer there. The pallor that faced back at him spoke of skin and flesh, hair and sinews, not of lust and desire, perfume and enticement. No matter. He only knew he loved her. The boom of nearing thunder could just be heard, or sensed, through the theatre's plasma walls. Though only a few centimetres in thickness, the constant electrical charge pulsing through the bio-plasma acted as a good sound-proofing.

"What are her chances?" he had asked earlier.

"Here, less than thirty per cent. Back at Siverek, I suppose fifty or so. Problem is we haven't got her stable enough yet to travel safely."

The leading surgeon had been honest. At least that helped. Simon's conscience pricked when he recalled the number of times in his life when he had been deliberately dishonest himself. There was little more they could do now other than wait for her to regain consciousness. They had welded the gash in her stomach and replaced her upper intestinal tract. New blood had been manufactured and pumped through her body. The artificial kidney was operating satisfactorily. Seven of the nine infections introduced on the Roman's blade had been identified and countered.

"And..?"

The red-haired surgeon had shaken his head, anticipating the question.

"No luck on the other two, I'm afraid. Obviously, we can't get samples to home base hospitals. I'll leave you alone with her for a while. If she comes round, press this button."

Silence returned to the room. Now as he looked at the white-clad torso on the bed before him, a burst of horror came into his mind. He experienced a flash-back to the bleeding stomach of Paul Forbes, the way the blood of his victim had soaked his clothing, the dead weight of the body as he had dragged it to his room, that awful interminable journey up the hot dusty slope outside the Pichot Base. Guilt and self-loathing welled up inside him like burning bile rising from his gut. Previously-meaningless sayings from his mother in his childhood spoke in his mind.....'*All the world's a circle*' and even more enigmatic '*as ye sow so shall ye reap*'. His throat emitted an involuntary whimper of awful fear and shame.

The cadence of breathing below him changed with a quiet dry cough. Felixana woke. In the silence of the room, with just the two of them, the atmosphere changed. No longer was the space a cold operating theatre. The walls of consciousness closed in to envelope a man and a woman looking at each other. Simon's gaze was serious, of a 'look what happens when I take my attention off you' kind. Felixana merely smiled weakly. She had seen him again, and felt 'I can die quietly, knowing I am safe.' She saw the glistening in his eyes, which she read entirely as love. Her left arm lifted. The computer lights blinked and danced with the new vigorous movement. He held her fingers gently.

"Sorry."

She mouthed the word, forcing her eyes to stay open as if willing the response from the mouth hovering above the bed.

"We'll get you fixed. I've come with a helicopter."

"I don't think so, my love. I've come to the end." She squeezed his hand strongly. "I'm afraid, Simon. I miss England. I don't want to die in a foreign country."

"It's not going to happen! We'll solve this problem together."

He could sense her level of distress rising. The computer lights danced to a more chaotic tune. Part of the tune must have carried resonance to a distant circuitry; a figure in a white overall appeared as if from nowhere to check the patient. A small pad of gauze was laid on the beautiful neck. The computer lights resumed their former guard-duty as the prostrate figure fell asleep again.

"You'll have to leave a while, Mr Atkins. Too much movement will speed the infection round her body. She'll sleep. You can come back later."

The South African's jaw set firmly as he left the room. How could he tell her there was only one hover-copter?

13:15 HOURS

Pieter North scarcely believed the numerals that swam before his eyes in the semi-darkness of the pre-storm light. Forty degrees centigrade was a temperature he had rarely experienced. The breeze in his face on the exposed slope was certainly hot. The clouds were darkening the sky, yet the expedition's meteorologist had told him the main storm would not break for a further twenty four hours. Fitful spots of rain began; then stopped. The hillsides were silent, bereft of wildlife. The sick colour of mustard-yellow clung to their contours. No birds hung against the dark curtain of the clouds. He looked down towards the city. Flickering brands of fire had already been lit in several quarters. No sound floated up to the mount. The few expedition members who had been allowed to travel down during the morning had returned with a sorry tale. The turmoil and fear following the mayhem the interlopers had caused two days before had not dissipated. In fact, it was getting worse. No-one had been permitted to visit the city immediately after the near-fatal stabbing.

His thoughts turned to Felixana. He was upset at the terrible turn of events. Why did these things always happen to him? Diane, his French personal assistant on the lunar base, had died in May 2130, just a few months after they had taken tentative steps towards having regular sex. Now there would be no happy ending with the English woman, even if she recovered. The South African had won her heart, not himself. She had chosen not to put herself under his protective wing and now look what had happened to her. No-one had ever loved him, he told himself. Yet he mustn't be bitter. All was not lost. If he could achieve the scientific stardom he felt sure was now almost within his grasp, she could yet turn her head his way in right and proper adoration. He must stay focused. He had learned from the senior staff briefing at noon that filming would resume that afternoon, though now under even more strict military control. The city was far too dangerous and unpredictable for any other course of action. Project Methuselah had to be concluded successfully. Contact with main target 'Gold' had to be re-established as soon as possible. The scientist felt that there was no way of knowing the precise sequence or timing of events that had only been recorded by hazy recollection later in the century by those he had been taught had less than objective viewpoints and motives.

Pieter had taken some issue with the opinion of the military personnel that scientific input could now be reduced to a minimal level. He had reminded those in the noon briefing that here was an opportunity to maximise advantage for the northern powers in the post-theology world they would inherit. Once the Southern Brotherhood had fallen apart, and the financial future of Europe and her allies had been secured, northern science would be in a supreme position. A gem in its crown would be the monopoly control over time travel. They could, for example, journey back a mere eighty or so more years and glean the lost secrets stored in the

Royal Library of Alexandria, so terribly destroyed by Julius Caesar in an accidental fire. Resurgence in scientific endeavour now would in no way jeopardise the success of Project Methuselah. The world was tied to its view-screens, waiting for leadership. Science would deliver Methuselah and then science would be the salvation of the world. So much money and effort had been invested in the current project - surely it should be built on and not left to rot away?

His argument held sway, so successfully that he now found himself sucked into the afternoon foray into Jerusalem. Despite the deteriorating weather, and the equally parlous level of social unrest to be expected in the city, the expedition needed to resume filming. The images recorded two days previously had not been forwarded to Siverek. Uncertainty surrounded their value as a publicity tool. Certainly, the chaotic and disjointed flashes of film depicting the Roman aggression on the expedition could not be released. That left two pressing issues - keeping up global interest with further film and tracing main target 'Gold' sufficiently closely to ensure an interception under Methuselah conditions. The Dutchman shuddered with anticipation. He knew now that the senior cryogenic scientist, like a high-technology vulture, was preparing to welcome a very important corpse into the expedition's midst.

THE TWENTIETH DAY OF MAY

05:49 HOURS

Daylight arrived, though it was barely discernible as such. The hot sticky night surrendered to a new dawn that was almost indistinguishable in terms of light and humidity. Occasional bursts of sheet lightning lit the steep slopes of Mount Scopus. Further down the boulder-strewn rock faces into the Kedron valley the electrical discharges hardly touched the stygian darkness lurking there. The wetness of the night was giving way to a heavy drizzle of warm rain as the inevitable storm approached. The few expedition members on duty were coming to the end of their vigil, though the many they had guarded had scarcely slept; it had been too hot a night. Throughout the encampment people were stirring. It would prove to be a long day. Most of those stretching and dressing sensed this to be so. Twenty second century mankind would need to confront its demons again, disguised in their many ancient forms.

The Base Commander, accustomed to order and good data-flows, had no communication with Siverek because of the growing electrical storm activity. The senior military officer, accustomed to discipline and a known enemy, faced the prospect of taking his soldiers back to a city where unrest, distrust and terror were running rampant among different social groupings, tearing at each other's throats. Pieter North, accustomed to the ancient laws of scientific method, was unnerved by a set of circumstances in which there would be no control experiment running alongside the hypothesis being tested, no likelihood of a back-up option, and in which the number of unknown factors far exceeded the number of known ones. Simon Atkins, accustomed to the total command of a life as 'puppet master', stood helpless as all the pieces of his jigsaw were melting away like morning frost on the high South African tablelands.........And in the silence of the base hospital unit Felixana Smith, accustomed to being surrounded by family, colleagues, friends, lovers and her ever-attentive public, lay on her back and gazed up alone into the face of death.

The foray into Jerusalem on the afternoon before had brought back a miscellany of livid violence and dark intrigue. The Roman garrison was scouring the streets for the ring-leaders, the persuasive and the powerful. Summary executions were beginning, despite the closeness of the height of Passover........and the whole of humanity thronging within the walls was haunted by the spectre of a devil within their midst, an interloper from beyond their experience, a presence they could neither touch nor comprehend, but which nonetheless demanded to be placated in some way. One or two individuals on Mount Scopus, perhaps with a background of philosophy or ancient history, sensed their rocky home could more closely be likened to Olympus than Scopus. The gods would look down on their playthings, but was there satisfaction, amusement or shame in what they were doing? But these individuals were not senior enough to swing deals for history. As the morning light gradually increased, the professionalism and training in everyone on the mountainside came to ascendancy. The teams would again set out for Jerusalem. It was thought that main target 'Gold' had been traced on the previous early evening to a private house on the outskirts of the city near an oil-press known in Aramaic as Gath-smane, though no-one could be sure of this event. A Roman military presence had appeared and the teams had lost track of him.

The heat of the day continued to build; by ten hours thirty it had reached forty one degrees. The cumulo-nimbus clouds, building from the south-west far out over the ocean at Joppa and Ascalon, were now delivering sheets of steady rain. Rivulets and swollen streams poured down the hill-sides in chocolate-brown torrents. The base commander ordered a delay in the hope that a break in the downpours could appear. At eleven hours ten the rain eased. The military and scientific teams moved down the mountain. Simon Atkins watched them go. He turned and went back to be with Felixana. She was awake, her eyes glazed with the effects of pain-killing drugs. Despite the numbness showing in her eyes, her face was wracked with torment and doubt. Desperately she raised a hand.

"Simon, have we been doing the right thing? I couldn't bear to die not knowing if we've been playing with fire."

"Hush. It's fine, my love. We know the films have been getting through. You're famous. The world will be stable again. Teams are going back to Jerusalem. We're nearly there. When the 'copter goes back to base, you'll be on it safely with me. I promise."

She recalled the words of a woman when she had first arrived on Pichot Base. *'You should save yourself for someone who loves you.'*

She passed out again. He listened in the silence. The rain was starting once more. He went outside, letting the stinging sensation in his eyes wash away as he looked out over the Kedron valley, mostly hidden in the hot stormy mist.

14:13 HOURS

Michael Ben-Tovim stood on the flat roof of the government building. Despite the heat he felt he needed to be in the open air. The persistent rain of the previous twenty four hours had finally stopped, but no-one knew for how long. The yellow orb of the sun had returned, hazy and shimmering with its own fear. Michael looked eastwards, out across the Kedron valley, his eyes trying to give shape to the movement way out over the far slopes of Mount Scopus. It was nothing, just a shaft of light glinting on a robotic crane working on the new housing settlements over there. It was Friday, so Jerusalem and its Jewish environs were mostly busy with commerce. Only the Moslem areas baked silently under the watery sun.

He heard again his wife's words echo in his head. She had not known she was being prophetic, yet perhaps she had sensed the kind of event that now seemed to be rolling out before them. Anna had said *'the whole world is going to Jerusalem'*. He knew she had meant 'in its mind's eye, via television, in spirit not in flesh'. He suddenly felt the urge to look in every direction, both near and far. The high-rise buildings, the old and new settlements, the hover-highways; everything seemed normal. But of course he couldn't actually see the problem the Minister had raised that morning. A large-scale civil emergency had been declared. Tens, perhaps hundreds of thousands of foreigners were starting to converge on Israel. The Minister had revealed film taken by the State's own operatives to complement and reinforce that of the world's media outlets. From every direction they were coming, to press against the borders of the Jewish nation in ever-increasing numbers. *'The whole world is going to Jerusalem'* his dear wife had said, and it was coming to pass.

Michael Ben-Tovim winced. It had been his secret pact with the slender English woman that had led step-by-step to her face being seen on every screen across the planet. He had been left in no doubt why he had been ordered to the ancient city. The emergency committee of the Israeli Cabinet had been convened in Jerusalem so rarely in recent years that he could scarcely remember the last time. The Prime Minister's cold rage burned brightly in the room to which the diplomat had been summoned. Michael could see it clearly in the politician's face despite the low lighting accentuated by the lowering clouds beyond the windows.

"There's been nothing since Tuesday! No more film released from Rome in three days! Now we have this perversity of a growing civilian invasion! The two are clearly connected, but what are we going to do about it?"

The diplomat took it to be a rhetorical question. It was spat out with such exasperation that it seemed to be the best approach, with no answer required immediately. Perhaps when the initial storm had passed.......Ben-Tovim's judgement was accurate; the Prime Minister continued without waiting for any answer from anyone. He fixed Ben-Tovim with his stare, his voice lowered by a notch as the rest of the committee sat silently.

"This seems increasingly less like an attack on the Southern Brotherhood and more like an attack on us. The northern powers are toying with us, taunting us with their storyline. Have they deliberately stopped filming to emphasise uncertainty as to the outcome of this absurdity?"

Again, there was the need to decide if to respond. Ben-Tovim's face remained passive. The Prime Minister was in full flow and would get to the point soon, he was sure. The Prime Minister's mouth opened again.

"The civilian influx seems to be the anticipated defence mechanism by southern Christians, but if so, why hasn't Europe pressed its advantage with further revelations towards the coming humiliation?"

He evidently loved speaking his rhetorical thoughts out loud, thought Ben-Tovim, and his anxiety dropped a little. He sensed the others in the room were no more in the light than he was. The egocentric rambling continued.

"As it stands, we're now about as popular in Rome as we were in the days of Fulvia!"

Michael Ben-Tovim knew his history. In the year nineteen of the Common Era there had been a scandal which had led to the expulsion of the Jews from Rome. Eastern religions had become very popular with the women of the city. Amongst those attracted to the Jewish Faith had been a noble-woman named Fulvia. She had been persuaded by four rabbis to send a large donation to the Temple in Jerusalem. This donation never got farther than the four rabbis. It had been reported to Tiberius, who was also dealing with complaints against Egyptian priests. The Emperor had acted swiftly to restore Roman purity of religion.

Nods and murmurings around the committee were followed by a question that most definitely was nor rhetorical in nature.

"You've met this BBC woman. Is she a threat to us?"

Michael Ben-Tovim was taken by surprise. He had expected a focus on the Europeans' project itself, or on his duplicitous dealings with the outer edges of the Southern Brotherhood. His delay in replying was barely noticeable and could easily be put down to a diplomat's natural caution in framing answers to be as accurate as possible.

"No, Prime Minister, I don't believe so. She is a standard northern atheist. She has a personal axe to grind, it is true. Her close BBC colleague was disposed of by the European government in their attempts to conceal the time project. She can be expected to follow the BBC's traditional left-of-centre line - hostility against Christianity, courtesy towards Islam and supportive neutrality for ourselves. But clearly, the current hiatus in filming is not helpful for our nation."

The Prime Minister harrumphed. "No, indeed not; we have waited three and a half years since this whole affair began. Three and a half years wasted!" The Prime Minister's final comment was a humiliation for Michael. Thankfully, he was dismissed from the room without further mauling. As he watched the black storm clouds gathering again over the sun he reflected on the two painful hooks on which the Prime Minister had so wanted to impale him.

What would be the outcome of the European project?

What would be the Southern Brotherhood's response?

The twin horns pressed on him in the heat. He honestly had no answer to either question. He checked his watch - fifteen hours. He decided it was best to phone Anna to tell her he would not be leaving for home until the Sabbath. As he walked back down the steps from the roof a great flash of lightning tore across the darkened sky. The clap of thunder that was its partner shook him visibly. He was still shaking as he reached the bottom of the staircase.

20:45 HOURS

The base commander's tone was sombre, as befitted the fast-fading light outside. Pieter North listened in an equally-downbeat mood. He looked round. Simon Atkins was not in the room. Outside, huge violet shadows cast in strange shapes crept up the bare slopes of Mount Scopus, like a vampire's fingers crawling up a virgin's neck. The breathing of the small audience surrounding the Dutchman was slowly being strangled as the listeners absorbed the news. The afternoon rain had first reduced to a solid drizzle, then had stopped completely as the clouds scudded away to the east. The setting sun was blood-red. No-one had yet recovered from the awful clap of thunder that had struck at one minute past fifteen hours. The base commander tried to clear his throat with a dry cough.

"The last of our survey teams returned at just after fourteen thirty hours. I accept they had no alternative. The rain was constant, beginning to affect some of the electrical equipment. However, that was not the main problem. Following our major incident three days ago the city has been turned over by the Roman garrison. Fearing a Jewish insurrection of some size the military have been rounding up known trouble-makers and community leaders in equal measure. Summary executions have been taking place. You would not like much of the film we have been able to record. Certainly, it is not fit to return to Siverek for global use. Only the less unpalatable bits have been edited here to give a general idea of what we've been up against."

He indicated for the footage to be run. Pieter North's black mood deepened as he recoiled from the sights. Many of the surrounding hillsides, including the one the expedition had identified as Gulgalta, had been turned into effective killing-fields. Wooden posts, hastily-purloined tree-trunks and large branches had been erected in a haphazard fashion across the landscape. Several senior scientists stumbled from the viewing theatre to throw up in the darkening gloom outside. Pieter wished he could join them, yet felt rooted to the floor as if he too had been nailed like those desperate unfortunates displayed before him. He recalled briefing held in the sterile harmless atmosphere of Siverek, surrounded by the comforts of a scientifically-advanced and self-confident civilisation. Crucifixion was described by the Roman orator Cicero as the most cruel and frightful sentence. Clearly, the garrison leaders and the Governor's senior staff considered the unexplainable sorcery invoked by a magic that could charm its way through a Roman shield needed to be neutralised by as much blood as possible. Yes, crucifixion could be inflicted for murder, banditry and piracy, but it was most commonly used for rebellion. Rebellion stirred up with witchcraft was evidently particularly heinous. Pieter knew that the Romans used the punishment on a vast scale, but until his own eyes had seen the hillsides across the valley, he had no way of comprehending what the adjective constituted.

Scores of writhing, pitiful bodies had been nailed to the wooden scaffoldings and crosses that had been set up. Sometimes the weight and movements of the victim caused the erection to crash to the ground. Sometimes a nail would shatter with a misplaced blow, prompting the executioner to slit the throat of the sufferer with an impatient shrug. Sometimes an artery would spurt into a centurion's eyes, provoking a swift sword thrust in revenge. The heaving, roiling horrors rose and fell across the hillsides in discordant disharmony with a satanic soundtrack. The farmyard cacophony of screams, moans, squeals and shrieks was barely human in its form. A blind listener, indeed blessed without sight in this gathering, would deem the noise to be hell incarnate. No technological recording medium invented by mankind had ever frozen such butchery in the history of the world. Pieter North was appalled by the bestial sights the unthinking camera lenses had scooped like dog droppings into their maw.

The base commander's hand swept again. Barely ninety seconds had been more than enough to convey the problem they faced. His voice quavered outside of his control as he continued with his presentation.

"The sheer quantity of executions here will cause us some severe difficulty. We know from covert intelligence that main target 'Gold' was one of the key figures sought for rounding-up last night. If he was taken, if he was fast-tracked for treatment, and if he was summarily sentenced for execution, then he is likely to be in this extensive carnage somewhere, but we can't say for certain. Our filming didn't locate him. All we have to act on is the further shaky assumption that his body was somehow recovered from the hillsides and entombed somewhere safe nearby. If that proves not to be true, then indeed our cause is lost. We all know from the local gossip over past weeks that this person was definitely named by common parlance as Jesus Bar-Joseph, that he was expected here in the city at Passover and that the populace expected him to be a leader of some kind in a rising against the occupation. Our cryogenic team has been in the upper reaches of the far hillsides this evening checking for freshly-prepared rock-tombs. They have reported finding seven possible locations."

A few groans rose from the gathered senior personnel.

"Yes, I know that's disappointing in itself, but by applying further factors we can narrow that down. We start from the nature of 'Gold's' relationship with his followers. Given his extensive network of connections with a range of local leaders and influential men it must be likely that at least some wealthy individuals would be close to him. Three of the tombs are far too close to the communal grave for paupers situated in the Kedron Valley. One rock-tomb is not yet completed. There's no sign of pre-activity. The other three have been more interesting. There are reports of a Roman guard patrol on the nearby hillside. They may be taking a particular interest in those three tombs. I'll hand over to Bjorn to set out the burial protocol information we're working on."

"Thanks, Michael. So…….a quick resume of burial patterns. The body is washed and anointed with perfumes. The dead were originally buried in their most expensive clothes, but clearly we are not expecting to look for that feature in this case. Current procedure, however, is for the body to be wrapped in shrouds containing spices, the face to be covered with a cloth and the hands and feet bandaged. Our teams would have to break into a tomb and cut open quite a wrapping."

Graphics appeared on the main screen in response to the presenter's voiced instructions.

"A simple tomb normally consists of a rectangular room set out either with ledges, known as arcosolia, or with shafts, called kokim, cut into the walls. The body might be placed in a coffin, but that is unlikely given the speed and secrecy involved here. So, it will simply be laid out on the bare rock."

At a nod, the base commander resumed the presentation.

"The cryogenic equipment has been prepared for transportation. In view of the uncertainties we're faced with, I suggest the wisest course of action will be to gain access to all three chambers under cover of darkness and only then decide which body to place in cryogenic suspension."

The senior historian present looked puzzled. "Why not freeze all three?"

The base commander shook his head in response to her question. "We don't have the materials or equipment for more than two bodies. We have planned to have one shell as a contingency in case of equipment failure."

The historian spoke up again, her voice insistent and confident. "In that case, I have to accompany the second journey to the tombs. We shall need to cut open all three wrappings and try to decide which body, if any of them, is likely to be target 'Gold'."

THE TWENTY FIRST DAY OF MAY

01:45 HOURS

Pieter North couldn't sleep. It was all getting out of hand. He recalled reports received throughout March and April that political pressure was being exerted to cut back on unnecessary spending once the time-travel elements had proved successful. He had listened to the complaints of the scientists. Was all this scientific achievement to be sacrificed for world political advantage? He turned in his bed. Surely science had been the handmaid of politics too often in the past? The achievements of nuclear fission had been hijacked by politicians. He recalled the advantages being brought by high-intensity battery farming, by genetically-modified crops, by animal cloning, by stem-cell industrialisation, by longevity and euthanasia trials. He especially remembered from his childhood the stories told by his parents about the Great Flood of 2085. Scientists had warned for years that dams along the Waddenzee had needed replacing. Indeed, the new 'smart technology' that would have saved the coasts had been available in embryonic form. It would have been easy to have employed it. Politicians, however, mindful of public disquiet about the potential for letting self-programmed bio-concrete loose to decide which communities were 'worthy' of being saved and which were not, had overruled the pilot projects again and again. There were some citizens who had tried to argue that the abandoned network of former church buildings on low-lying land should have been spared as part of the State's heritage. Saboteurs working against some automatic dam-building programs were not even taken to court. The result of all that squeamishness was that thousands had died anyway, lost to the cold unforgiving waters of the North Sea.

The Dutchman sighed. A fully post-theology world was at last within mankind's grasp. The potential for a wide range of sciences to maximise the opportunities that now presented themselves was surely not to be missed. He thought of the immediate band of senior colleagues huddled together here on the outskirts of Jerusalem. He had watched as the blood had drained from their faces at having to witness the crucifixion scenes. Indeed, several had stumbled from the viewing theatre to give their stomach contents to the Judean soil. That was not befitting of such beautiful minds! What would happen if this downgrading of scientific endeavour were to continue beyond a new World States Council resolution? The momentum would be lost if he, Doctor Pieter North, did not declare publicly to the world that only immense scientific advances had made it all possible. The hover-copter would return to Siverek with a body once daylight returned. Goodness, they didn't even know for certain if it was the right body! In a way, he felt, that didn't matter - the smooth publicity machine of the northern world would wring maximum advantage from the situation. The Brotherhood would crumble. He just had to be back in 2135 as soon as possible with a new team around him. It would be the core of, how could he put it, *'a new scientific foundation for the post-theology age'*. Yes, that sounded good.

He lay on his back in the darkness, trying to recall the disciplines of the senior scientists on Mount Scopus. Medicine.....botany and nature conservation.....bio-engineering.....physical engineering.....post-quantum physics.....nutrition and food technology. Was there another? The young French woman with the short dark hair and the pert breasts came to his mind. Yes, history and civilisation. That made seven in total. Not a bad foundation. Now…how and when could he speak with them? *'As early as possible in the morning',* he decided. Having reached a good decision, he settled into a shallow sleep.

06:30 HOURS

"How is Felixana?"

The base commander's face was drawn as he questioned the overnight doctor emerging from the medical facility. He didn't need to hear the answer; he could see it in the man's face.

"She's near the end, I'm afraid. The infections have proved too elusive for us. I've given her a sedative. The security man spent much of the night with her. I think he's in his quarters now, though I doubt he's sleeping much."

"Thanks." Commander Michael Donaghue turned towards the residential tents and then stopped. Sensing a greater priority, he strode instead towards the nondescript building housing the cryogenic unit. There was little to show for the immense potential significance of what lay inside. It felt surprisingly cool in contrast to the early morning heat beyond its walls. Air-con units hummed obediently in their roof-mounted housings. The scientist on duty looked up from his small control console as Commander Donaghue entered. He gave a twitch of his hand which may have signified a wave, before returning his attention to the meters in front of him.

'Cold fish, indeed,' thought the newcomer. *'They're in the right profession.'* He surveyed the scene. The silver casing of the shell in use was completely solid. Just as well - part of him wanted to look inside and part of him didn't. He couldn't tell if the casing would be warm or cold to the touch; no-one could get near. Four armed guards stood silently in the room, one at each corner of the shallow platform on which the shell rested. The stand-by shell stood a little distance away, with no wires, no guards and no twitching cold fish. He didn't know what to say. He just stood and looked for a few moments. The only sound came from the air-con units. Had he expected something, perhaps a surreal buzzing, or a rhythmic blipping, or a fizzing of ice? He remembered the overnight briefing.

392

The real drama hadn't been here, but in the tombs below on the hillsides. The historian had indeed travelled down, as she had threatened she would. There had been no sign of the reported Roman guards. The expedition's soldiers had broken into the three located burial sites, finding a newly-prepared body in each of them. A fourth, overlooked, burial nearby was also entered. Infra-red night vision had supported the grave-robbing. The commander had previously cautioned respect for the dead, though had no way of knowing if the wash-up briefing's 'by the book' approach had marked the real events or not. The night-time visitation had not offered easy-to-read clues as to likelihood of success. All four bodies were those of males aged from around twenty five to forty five. All had suffered crucifixion and displayed collateral injuries. The Romans were nothing if not predictable. The historian knew her work. Two of the four finds had spear or sword wounds to the torso, though whether either could have delivered the fatal blow was pure conjecture given the absence of a proper autopsy. Some hesitation and disagreement among those on the raiding party as to how to close down the options had been interrupted by a warning of flaming torches and voices in the far distance coming up from the stygian darkness of the Kedron valley. The historian had quickly chosen the body with what appeared to be some signs of a deformity to the left leg. Freezing chemicals had been injected. Some fifteen agonising minutes later, as the torches meandered onto a separate path on another part of the hillside, the preserved body had been hooked up to a portable cryogenic harness and being carried carefully back up towards the summit of Mount Scopus.

The base commander stared at the active cryogenic shell as if to grant himself x-ray vision to see beyond the silver enigma and rest eyes on the contents. He had re-read the scientific summary on rising from his bed. The physical work had been successful; one body, riddled with trauma, but thanks to knowledgeable local preservatives, skilfully-administered high-technology bio-engineered fluids and a swift return to the mountaintop laboratory, a body in astoundingly-good health, considering it was most definitely dead. Computerised diagnostics and prognostics had confirmed that minimal deterioration had taken place. The base commander set his jaw firmly. A global audience would be waiting. He sighed deeply, setting out for his own quarters. Behind him, the air-con units continued with their humming.

07:15 HOURS

Base Commander Donaghue was taken aback by the dishevelled appearance of the security chief Atkins when the latter came to visit his quarters. The South African had not shaved in over two days. A clear growth of untidy stubble spoke volumes to Donaghue, who had only ever experienced the other as a smarty-presented perfectionist, whose obsession with control had always extended to his physical appearance. He had hitherto found the security chief to be brittle. Yet Donaghue recognised that Project Methuselah had progressed this far in no small measure because of the efficiency of security operations. No, it was more than that. Hand in hand with security had travelled safety; the safety of people, materials, equipment, finance, scientific research. Indeed, every aspect of this great project had fallen at some time under the orchestration of this blond enigma. Atkins had seemed unwilling, or perhaps unable, to disentangle security of purpose from security of person. In a highly-controlled environment, control can sometimes be comforting as well as restricting. Donaghue felt that they both stood at the pinnacle of an immense mountain of achievement. They had come so very far and probably both knew that it could still spiral into a black disaster, should security in its most benign sense not be maintained. Michael Donaghue noticed the red-rimmed, tired eyes that met his own. He sensed desperation in the eyes, and smiled gently.

"Simon. These are not good times."

"Not good times at all - Michael."

There was a slight hesitation before the name, no more. Atkins felt a twinge of embarrassment at the informality. He fully sensed the reference to the personal and not the professional. The commander spoke again.

"I understand it is not hopeful - with…."

"No."

"I'm sorry. No-one could have foreseen such a disaster, even with a project as dangerous as this one."

"Michael, I've come to request use of the stand-by cryogenic shell. We need to keep Felixana safe for infection studies at home. A re-animation may be possible."

The commander sighed. "Simon, you know as well as I do that the global centre on Alexander Island is the only place we could hope for that. There have been decades of research, private sector investment, any number of trials, and even the Antarctic's record with re-animation has been patchy at best, and horrific at worst. The brain just doesn't pass muster most of the time. It may be just an old wives' tale, an urban myth."

Yes, it had been desperation in the security man's eyes. They glittered now. Was it a trick of the light? Donaghue couldn't tell. Yet he knew of the 'viper' list, of the pressure that Atkins must be under. His hand passed over his communication sensor. He punched in three numbers.

"Doctor Gonzales. Is 'Gold' stable?"

"Yes, Commander, we're ready to leave whenever we get the word."

"I want you to activate the stand-by unit. When we leave, we leave with the BBC woman's body."

He ended the call and looked up.

Atkins simply said "Thank you". He left to resume his painful vigil.

08:17 HOURS

Felixana died. She closed her eyes and just died. Simon sat by the body feeling numbness creep over him. It was almost an anti-climax, really, after hours of anguish mixed with so many other emotions. The two technicians in the cryogenic team pushed past him to begin the freezing process. He felt the flexible tubing brush his arm, a sense of polar cold as brutal as death itself. It forced his thoughts back to reality, pulling them away from the temptation of dwelling on what she had meant to him in life. He swam instead in the bitterly-cold lake of the moment, telling himself there was work to be done. Part of him was upset that he didn't have the time to grieve; yet part also was whispering words of hope, reminding him that these tubes were keeping alive chances for the future. He stood back, letting the twin wizards in white work their magic. He swallowed hard, closing his eyes as the technicians forced open the dead mouth. Then curtains were drawn. He saw no more.

09:00 HOURS

Pieter North introduced himself to the man busily checking laser communication ports on the underside of the hover-copter. He made sure the man knew his senior role in the mission, not having been able to speak to crew members on the outward journey down from Siverek. It wasn't really necessary. The navigator was pleased to have someone to talk with; as far as he was concerned, the sooner they returned to Siverek, the better.

"What's your human pay-load on this?"

The navigator stopped work, wiping sweat from his face to convey the information that seventeen could be carried. "Plus the two shells, of course," he added. His voice lowered, though there was clearly only the two of them around.

"Word is - we'll have two horizontal passengers on the way back. The BBC woman's died and we're taking her back, too. That's why I'm re-setting the laser ports; heavier pay-load means different channel angles."

The Dutchman wasn't interested in channel angles, whatever they were. He felt a wave of sadness wash over him, a lonely sadness. *'So, my dear Felixana is dead. She won't come to me now, that's for sure. I'll never know what it's like to have her love me. Well, there we are - silver again and not gold.'* The coldness in his genes reasserted itself. He would have to live alone with his eternal glory as a leading scientist, perhaps never again sleeping with the intimacy of a warm female body. Biographies written about his famous life might need to touch gently upon such subjects. He hoped they would be kind to him. He wondered briefly if Archimedes, Galileo, Newton, Einstein, Potter, even De Haag himself had struggled to reconcile scientific fame with personal loneliness. He really couldn't remember whether he had learned such things in studying these giants in college. No matter; he had to get back to business. He took up the navigator's parlance with practised smoothness.

"So, max is seventeen, eh?"

"Yes, sir, base commander gets to choose. I guess you'll be OK, being so senior and all. Most people here will have to walk or ride back."

He smiled without malice. North smiled back. "I guess so. Thanks for your help."

His mind was rapidly calculating numbers as he walked away.

09:45 HOURS

The gentle rain that had rolled around the Judean hills overnight was coming to an end. The heat returned, but not before a rainbow had thrown its arm out across the city. Its colours arched away to the south and north, losing their focus in the fuzziness of the dusty brown slopes. After so much rain there would be green shoots again in the desert. Simon Atkins stood on a rock, watching the hover-copter's blades slowly turn as the pilot tested the engine. Surely soon, very soon, he would gun the engine in earnest.

At a few hundred metres' distance, Pieter North ducked into Michael Donaghue's tent. The base commander looked up from a holographic contour map of the region. He waved a palm over the projection, causing it to collapse into oblivion. Pieter introduced his grand plan obliquely.

"Well, Michael. Methuselah is nearly over. This is a good stage completed."

The other man tilted his head sadly. "Yes. You will have heard about Felixana's death?"

"Terrible thing, but good that we are taking her body back. One never knows these days what wonders science can perform."

The base commander was surprised that his decision on the body had spread so far so quickly. He remembered that two and a half hours had passed, so let it go without comment.

"We've got to get her there first, Pieter. Can you be ready to leave in ninety minutes?"

This is going well,' thought the Dutchman. '*Off by eleven fifteen, or thereabouts, but I need to speak around further.*'

"No problem; in fact, that's what I came to see you about. I'm hoping there's no fixed passenger list. I have a few important suggestions which should help us."

The base commander's face gave nothing away as he blandly gazed at the balding scientist. North bit his tongue, waiting for a response.

397

Donaghue knew that his colleague's name was on the 'viper' list - the distraught security man had told him so. Now, as base commander, he was still trying to come to terms with the awful responsibility of having to deceive almost everyone now trapped on this ancient Judean hillside. He knew the hover-copter carrying 'Gold' would also be the rescue vehicle for no more than a few fortunate souls. Seventeen living humans and two dead ones would not be a generous salvation, to be sure. Everyone else would set out on foot or land vehicle for Siverek, yet once there they would surely find a deserted shell. He couldn't visualise the horror this would bring them. He indicated that Pieter North should elaborate further. The Dutchman was eager to oblige.

"We have to think and plan for what comes beyond Methuselah, Michael. The advantages for science after the destruction of the Southern Brotherhood need to be built on and not frittered away."

Michael Donaghue held his patience. The scientist came to the point relatively quickly.

"There are key scientific leaders in the expedition who now have valuable experience of time travel. They ought to return rapidly to home base. If I can keep a core unit together, we stand a good chance of recruiting others in more disciplines essential to world improvement. I've already spoken with three colleagues about my ideas. I think there are four more that could benefit from an early return; just seven in total. I understand the hover-copter carries seventeen."

Michael Donaghue stood, walked to the tent flap, and stared out. For the second time in a few hours he faced an unorthodox situation. He tried to do the calculation on numbers, tried to give a logical numerical bias to a decision he knew he had to make in any case. Who to choose for life and who to choose to leave behind? His conscience lay heavy. Perhaps he could, after all, wash his hands of the guilty burden by letting it fall on the enthusiastic shoulders of the man with him in the tent. There would be two pilots, four cryogenic doctors, the security man Atkins, North, himself of course, plus one of his senior deputies, the other to remain behind to take charge of the expedition. That made ten. So, there it was - he had a justification now for the final seven places. He turned.

"Make sure you're ready by eleven hours - and for pity's sake don't speak out of turn with anyone. If someone is not sold entirely on your 'scientific foundation' argument, just let the offer drop away lightly. We need those on the slow route back to Siverek to stay content."

North was already half way out of the tent. He didn't understand the other's final comment, but didn't care. His foundation would take a step closer. Michael Donaghue watched him go. He realised with a twinge of panic that he couldn't absolve himself entirely from responsibility. Which of his two senior deputies would he condemn to death?

11:21 HOURS

The hover-copter lifted from the ground at precisely eleven hours and twenty one minutes. It was a few moments later than planned, but no more than that. The occupants strained against their harnesses, their faces watching the ochre dust swirling around outside the window ports. A sudden surge of power and the craft was in the clear air. It banked to the north, gathering speed.

"Hell!"

The pilot's shout coincided with a yanking of the control stick. The instinctive jerk nearly threw the craft into a stalling climb that was only just corrected in time. The hover-copter's passengers barely had time to react before it was all over. The co-pilot stared blankly at his colleague.

"What the.....!"

"Another 'copter! Well, I thought so, but there's nothing out there - nothing on sweep, nothing on visual."

The pilot was shaking, though the craft held steady. His trained breathing was nearly back to normal. "As we passed over Scopus....just a shadow....rising on the edge of vision....but it seemed to be our familiar shape!"

He shook his head to dismiss the picture, wipe it from the memory. The co-pilot rapidly scanned the slopes below. Nothing there now; just housing settlements, automatic cranes, ground traffic highways, the large silver disks of the new desalination generators pock-marking the horizon. The cabin door opened and Michael Ben-Tovim staggered in.

"Are we under attack?"

The co-pilot shook his head. "No, sir, it was just a trick of the light. Sorry about the jolt. We should sight the first waves of international

399

migrations soon. Reports of over two hundred thousand spread out west of Amman into the Jordan valley."

The Mossad chief returned to his seat. He ducked to peer eastwards through a nearby port. Large groups of people, each perhaps several hundred in number, were milling around makeshift camps in the desert. They shielded their eyes upwards as the engine of the hover-copter roared past. Michael Ben-Tovim sensed no animosity, merely excited interest. But they were too far below to have caused a danger in any case. He sighed deeply. The seat recorded his settling weight, locking his restraining belt automatically with an audible hiss. He closed his eyes, recalling the previous hours. They had culminated at dawn as the military powers had responded rapidly to the Prime Minister's call for martial law. The leader's broadcast echoed in his mind.

'A situation has developed on our borders which brings me to take steps to defend the integrity of the State of Israel. Large and unsustainable numbers of mobile migrants are bringing intolerable pressure to many sites. Water, food and accommodation cannot cope. There is the possibility of a danger to public health. I have instructed our military forces to hold back the civilian intrusions as peacefully as possible. We know that the declared intention of many is to reach Jerusalem, though for what purposes it is not at all clear. Some may be subversive to our long-term interests. We call on all northern states to clarify their intentions in Turkey, and on all southern states to desist from military actions not conducive to peace in our region.'

'That should take care of everyone', thought Ben-Tovim with sad cynicism as he had drained his morning coffee cup. He had dressed and packed hurriedly. The martial law ruling meant that a different, more foreboding, hover-copter than the one he had arrived in was waiting on the departure pad. The logged flight-plan had included Tel-Aviv, though Michael sensed it might be diverted to anywhere on the way there. Would he see Anna today? He couldn't tell. He felt as stateless and helpless as the faces staring up at him from the ground. He longed to be back in his lovely apartment in Neve Tzedek where he could look out over Charles Clore Park and the sea-front.

The previous day's torrential rains had done little to dampen the nomadic urge of the flood of humanity. He had played no part in the political and military developments overnight, having to be content with the media's own offerings delivered via his Jerusalem hotel room. He knew he had been deliberately excluded by the Prime Minister and the government. Despite his assurance that the BBC woman would not be likely to cause trouble for Israel, his decisions over past months had not carried the stamp of sure-footedness expected of his office. He found these only too easy to catalogue.

He had not reported to his political masters that he had placed an informer into the American base. He had declined a chance to tell the Brotherhood of the agent in the AEA inspection team. He had not taken seriously the report subsequently made by the Nigerian agent. He had not pressed strongly enough for the homeland science community to keep pace with the northern experts on time displacement techniques. The Israeli Cabinet had not been given sufficient warning of the European Union's true abilities and intentions. He had continued to advise Ministers as recently as the mid-March meeting in Switzerland that the Southern Brotherhood could be deceived with impunity, and would never act independently from Israel. They were sins of omission rather than commission, to be sure, but sins nonetheless in the eyes of the shadowy intelligence community. Yes, the Prime Minister had been right - three and a half years had slipped through their fingers. He would be punished. He thought of Anna and a warm secluded beach. He felt tired.

After less than an hour's flight he heard the note of the hover-copter's engine change. He glanced out of the window port, recognising the smooth low outlines of Mount Tabor. The hover-copter began to descend, permitting the serried ranks of orange groves within the valley of Jezreel to be identified. Michael's blood chilled. They were landing in a military settlement on the plain of Megiddo.

20:35 HOURS

The primary science laboratory on Violet Base was strangely silent. The sole person present welcomed the solitude. She needed to be alone, to be able to think. Her long, well-manicured fingers tapped rhythmically on a stainless-steel table top. It was her thirty-third birthday, though she told herself ruefully that her scientific skills had woven a spider's web of journeys back and forth over time that would make her personal biology irrelevant. One feeling burned in her breast. Caramel Bondi wondered if Doctor North would support her in a crisis.

She knew she was partly to blame for the stand-off in their emotions. She recalled sparks of conflict; in November 2131 on Pichot Base - *'there will be equality for poorer nations one day'*, and later in December 2132 at the inquest on Siverek Base - *'we consider lattice instability to be virtually impossible'*. She had made it clear over many months that she was not entirely convinced of the need to destroy the Southern Brotherhood. The method chosen was not the key issue for her - unlike Paul Forbes she was in no way religious - but she did feel for her sisters in Africa and South America. The end was unworthy and the means to that end would make no difference to that. Her dissatisfaction had bubbled gently, until a discovery had come her way.

One of the outcomes of the December 2132 inquest into the TTU fatality had been the insistence that timetables should be prepared and followed that did not dangerously overload daily activity in either direction within the time tunnel. As Chief Plasmologist she needed to monitor planned TTU traffic for several days in advance. She held final responsibility for the integrity of the lattice. The totality and frequency of both cargo and personnel journeys were within her gift. On occasion, she chose to exercise this gift. Messages could only transfer up and down the tunnel by physical movement within the TTUs. While initially she could have no need of access to the content of messages, it had become increasingly clear to her throughout April and May that certain features were coming into focus, features that intrigued and then concerned her.

She had colleagues within translation and encoding departments who were willing to feed her disembodied snippets of information. These were innocuous by themselves, just single words lost in a meaningless jungle. She already knew Methuselah, though not its final intentions. The stringing together of other words opened up a clearer picture - Gold, Lutz, Rome - she gleaned them with interest. Then the messages from home base stopped completely on the sixth of May. For two weeks now, there had been silence from the future. Indeed, even more alarmingly, film from the expedition had stopped five days ago. The blank communication screens spoke eloquently of mystery. Nerves were beginning to fray, even among the Siverek faithful, and most certainly with the plasmologist herself. It was during the empty period that she had become aware of a new word in the lexicon of political deceptions. Earnest enquiries among her secret network of friends had traced the origins of 'viper' back to the twenty-first of April. No-one at her level and below could find out what it meant. It had been reluctant to give up its secrets. Then she uncovered its significance, but she couldn't find out at first if her name was on the list or not.

Late this very afternoon the hover-copter had returned with its astonishing story. She visualised the great domed amphitheatre housing the cargo TTUs just along the corridors from where she sat. The finger-tapping abruptly stopped, frozen by the enormity of the decision she needed to make. If she was expendable then she would bring down the project around her own sacrifice by preventing the return of their cargo to the year 2135. She owed this at least to her countless sisters in the southern world. Yet she still felt some loyalty to her colleagues. What should she do? She left the science laboratory to its silence, returning to her quarters with a heavy lump of worry in her stomach. A simple change to one of the computer programs would be enough.

***

The scene was different in the cargo TTU amphitheatre itself. The units, thirty in number in two rows of fifteen, were not in use. The plasma walls were switched on, but nothing was transferring in or out of the base. Technicians moved with studied purpose between the units. Armed guards stood at the doorways. White-coated men and women watched screens. Support trolleys rolled noiselessly in obedient patience alongside the senior technicians, kept in tow by radio pulse units at their masters' waists. Set between the two rows, at the end of the amphitheatre, rested the two cryogenic shells transported from Mount Scopus. A hush had descended that no-one could explain or sought to interrupt. It was partly perhaps the high technical content of the work being undertaken. When the time would eventually come for the plasma walls to be activated, and the largest TTU prepared in readiness for transfer, the power feeding into the body shells would need to hold steady. No-one at this stage could be certain as to the outcome. All would be subservient to the lattice. The silver skins of the shells contrasted with the matt black covers of the transference units. Individuals seemed to tense a little as they passed by a shell. Whether this was a reverence for the dead, or an invisible, involuntary genuflection in awe of the power of science to maintain bodily integrity, no-one could tell. It was there nonetheless.

Neither Pieter North nor Simon Atkins was present. There was much to be done elsewhere. The Dutchman was hard at work in his quarters reviewing outcomes from time transference experiences. The mass of detail was staggering. It threw up strange conundrums. Why did light objects move position slightly within the TTUs compared with heavier ones that stayed still? Why did younger travellers exhibit a sense of skittish nervousness, even an adrenaline rush, while one elderly woman was actually found to have fallen asleep at the end of a transfer? And over it all, the enormous mountain of inexplicability that was the three hundred year barrier. Despite all their ingenuity and experimentation the barrier had remained in place. The more he shuffled through his data, the more Pieter shivered with delight. He was now the master of a new science,

403

thrusting with imperious power through virgin landscapes towards glorious consummations of achievement. Many phenomena would even need to be given names! This was exciting stuff!

He had been remarkably successful with the seven scientists to whom he had spoken on Mount Scopus. All had strapped with enthusiasm into the hover-copter, watching with grateful eyes as it had lifted into the ochre dust swirling around outside their window ports. He sensed many were even now scrolling down through data banks of their own, garnering key facts and findings that could accompany them in their onward journeys back home. Pieter called to the screen the current status in the cargo TTU· amphitheatre. Power was down, the individual cocoons switched off. No matter; he surmised there was much to do. The next day would surely see the body shells transported.

Felixana came to his mind. In the optimism engendered by his new mission in life he imagined he could see her in full health again, somehow changed by her experience into loving him. Goodness, he even felt his penis stir! He switched off his console, stripping eagerly to take a hot shower.

***

Simon Atkins walked in the darkening evening a stone's throw from the rocky eastern perimeter of the Siverek base. He looked back at the now-familiar outlines of the storage sheds, silhouetted against the dying light. He had set out on a journey to Jerusalem to bring back the woman he had come to love. Now it was the end of the third day since that journey was made. All he had been able to achieve was to bring her back as a dead body. He sat on a dusty, uncomfortable boulder, watching the faint glow of day finally give up the ghost. Grief and anguish came over him. The sorrow in his heart was so great that it almost crushed him, and he felt utterly alone. Gone was the sense of control that had orchestrated his life up to this point. Yet he resolved he owed it to her memory to get her body back home to give the Antarctic base a chance to save her. General knowledge told him that the chances were slim, but he was certain his achievements on Methuselah were now so close that, once secured, his political stock would soar like an eagle. He could surely claim beyond the three hundred million euro in his contract. The extra would be to salvage dear Felixana's life, to press for a no-expense-spared attempt at her re-animation, once the remaining infections had been identified and neutralised. Then he realised the work she had done in appearing as the human face of the story sent back to please the politicians. Although only early feedback had been received on the three weeks of global transmissions successfully forwarded to 2135, it was clear that Felixana was a celebrity. How fitting it would be for them to save the star! More than anyone else, she could corroborate the evidence and convince the ordinary viewer. Such power! The line of thought gave him renewed hope. It burned within him as he sat in the darkness.

In control of his senses again, he began to plan. The total number of names on the 'viper' list was thirty seven. In addition to those scheduled to travel alongside the cryogenic shells, it would give an average of only four people from each of the intervening bases. The uncertain factor in all this, he felt sure, would be the extent to which Paul Devine had been able or willing to reveal the human sacrificial elements of the project. When he had confided in the holographer he had expected that he would lose Felixana as part of the overall deception. Now there might be a realistic chance of saving her and of taking her back with him, he hoped that the successes of Methuselah were not going to be compromised by unstable circumstances within the world to which he desired to return. He expected that once the cryogenic shells had been received in 2135, the code-word 'cobra' would be activated. Though there were many imponderables, at that point surely he would be safe.

Far to the south, a faint rumbling of thunder could be heard. He stood up quickly with confidence and resolve. He needed to take command of his world of security again. As the human scale of measurement recorded the arrival of the twenty second day of May, many sparks of will began to converge on their final explosion.

THE TWENTY SECOND DAY OF MAY

02:30 HOURS

"How many cylinders were left there?"

The senior deputy with responsibility for the Mount Scopus expedition felt his breath catch in his throat with exasperation as the report came in. He stared somewhat stupidly at the junior officer, whose reply did little to help his demeanour.

"Two, sir, and both filled with liquid nitrogen, primed for use. It only came to light when we - when the equipment audit for departure was done. They can't be found anywhere. The remains left by the cryogenic team were checked. There's no doubt of it, sir. Twenty litres of concentrate are missing."

The senior man felt sick. "Could they have got onto the hover-copter?"

A shake of the head was accompanied by confirmation that this was most unlikely. "The gold-coloured markings in the top glass receptacle would have triggered an alarm. They might even have blown with the vibration of take-off."

This was getting worse. There was no alternative but to go and look. He fully remembered the exhortation given by Doctor North. *'We are not here as powerful magicians, getting our way by impressing the locals with loud noises and complicated machines.'*

He shuddered. There would certainly be loud noises if a cylinder exploded in the confines of a rock tomb. "Send a team immediately to get them back, and don't wait until morning!"

***

Early in the morning, while it was still yet dark, the small group of women climbed gingerly over sharp pointed rocks towards their goal. Climbing was not easy - as well as the absence of light, they dared not drop the expensive and rare oils and embalming solutions they carried. The woman in front held a flaming brand to show the way and to frighten off animals. All were fearful of encountering Roman guards. In the pre-dawn darkness they were not at all sure they could find the correct entrance. What would happen when they got there.....and what would happen when they returned, their men finding out where they had been without their permission?

A groan of recognition, yet surely this couldn't be it? It must be farther up the slope than this. The covering boulder has been removed. The torch-bearer stooped to thrust the flame inside. Three pairs of eyes were close enough to the opening to glimpse what seemed like two human forms inside, both draped in light-coloured burial wrapping, yet glowing funereally in the gloom. Fighting off her fear with a loud voice, the leading woman cried "There are two here, both dead!"

The white-suited chemical engineers, certainly mortified with the intrusion, stepped back and faced the newcomers. Their basic knowledge of Aramaic wouldn't help them, yet one recognised the word for 'dead'. Trying to recall how to formulate a negative, he called back very clumsily what he thought was the challenge, 'We're not dead, and we're alive!'

The women sobbed with terror, falling back down the slopes into the darkness. The expedition members grabbed the two nitrogen cylinders to clamber up the slopes in the opposite direction. The encounter had meant nothing to them - these locals were only women and they appeared to be unarmed. The repetition of the challenge in the retreating group sounded recognisable. Its originator was proud of his little knowledge, though he had no way of knowing they were screaming the word for 'he' and not 'we'.

11:30 HOURS

Ferry records over thirty years old had not been easy to track down. The psychiatrist had so few clues to work on. The holographic image he had borrowed from Mary's half-sister had merely shown a white ferry rail. He had checked the Irish Sea and Scandinavian routes before he struck lucky. Now he was on his way to meet one of the only three women still living in England who had accompanied Linda Trent on that fateful college trip. His hire-car lowered through busy hover-lanes as it approached the outskirts of Portsmouth. Half an hour later he was sitting in a café on the dockside. Opposite him with a glass of coffee in front of her sat Amanda Paul. She smiled when he produced the three-dimensional hard copy of one of the main frames from the ferry image. It was a warm smile, yet haunted with a touch of sadness, as if lamenting the loss of so much youth, so many memories. She sipped her coffee, replacing the glass carefully in its saucer with barely a sound. Her eyes met his, her voice soft and wistful.

"Yes, that's me there, and that's Sonia and Doreen, and there on the end, Linda, lovely Linda. I'm sorry to hear of the troubled times of her daughter."

"Tell me about the trip. What do you remember?"

Amanda Paul fingered the ferry image delicately, turning it softly in the light to accentuate the three-dimensional effects. Her eyes glazed as her memory drew her back.

"We were all students at Art College in Reading. It was our first trip to the mainland. We wanted to celebrate the Midwinter Festival at the Van Gogh Museum. I remember the hostel we stayed in. 'Hostel Good Sleep' seemed such a charming name. It wasn't far from the Singel, so in a good part of Amsterdam. We met up with a group of science students from Rotterdam, and it was clear from the outset that Linda was strongly attracted to one of the boys. The two of them spent a lot of time together, I mean, a lot of time," she emphasised meaningfully. "Well, it was no surprise to us when Linda finally announced at the February half-term break that she was pregnant. We all knew who the father would be, and we were pleased for her. Linda clearly loved him, but despite several attempts to contact him, there was no luck. It never stopped her loving him, and when she gave birth to a girl, it seemed that she would be the best souvenir Linda could have of true love. Is her daughter really trying to get in touch?"

"We don't know if it would be a good idea or not just yet. I'm just piecing together the parts of the picture to see if anything will help us strengthen Mary for the rest of her recovery. By the way, you don't happen to remember the name of the father, do you?"

Amanda nodded. "As it happens, I do. I remember it because it was an English-sounding name, even though he was obviously Dutch. Perhaps it wasn't spelt the English way, but his name was Peter, Peter North."

***

The earth turned. Daylight spread its warmth over the northern hemisphere. Hour by hour new capital cities blinked into wakefulness. In rapid succession, responding to the continuing press of humanity on the move, Palestine, Egypt, Jordan, Syria and Iraq all closed their borders. States of emergency were declared in Iran, Libya, Tunisia and Lebanon. In Israel, where martial law was now twenty four hours old, the country's substantial numbers of reservists were called up. Further afield, at ten hours local time, an announcement from the South Sudanese capital of Juba was issued 'in the name of God's Southern Brotherhood' to urge 'all those conscious of their creation in God's image' to 'keep calm, keep faith and keep praying'. At eleven hours, Eastern Standard Time, American President Korda also called for calm. He declared that 'northern powers do not wish to take military action. We fully expect further clarification from the film units in ancient Judea to lessen tension between our nations.' No timescales were given.

At precisely that moment, late afternoon in the Middle East, the rains began to fall.

***

In contrast to the global political and military turmoil seething throughout humanity in the twenty second century, the atmosphere in Siverek's Violet Base exuded focussed but expectant calm. Events were making progress. Work had been undertaken all day on ensuring the power supplies to the largest unit in the cargo TTU amphitheatre would be stable. The base commander visited the amphitheatre every hour like a mother hen checking on her chicks. He wasn't alone in this…..

Simon Atkins nervously hung around the chamber like a disconsolate lover, needing to be near Felixana's body. Pieter North ensured his seniority did not go unnoticed, talking with technicians and security guards alike as he sought to impress on anyone who would listen that he was a man for the future. The two had seemed to have reached a kind of uneasy fragile understanding that they did not need to fight each other. Their agendas were diverging, even though they fished in the same pond. Caramel Bondi waited for her chance, and while she waited, she watched. She watched the men, she watched the dials, but most of all she watched the weather. Throughout the long afternoon the electrical storms in the south came closer. A power spike aroused alarm in the chamber. The plasmologist gave precise instructions in compensation. The moment passed. The base commander paced and paced, his brow furrowed. Question marks buzzed around his head like ghostly bees, each carrying a fatal sting. Would the lattice hold? Should they send the BBC woman's body first to test the system? Who should travel immediately behind the cargo? Why were messages from home so guarded and infrequent? Yes, he knew he could not send film, it was too horrifying, but he had otherwise given assurances on progress. Then shortly before seventeen hours he reached a decision. The fateful message set out.

***

"God damn it! Are the crowds coming our way or not?"

American Vice-President Harold P Lutz was not a happy man. The aide could usually tell as much by the way the politician chewed his gum. The violence of mastication increased with its frequency whenever 'VP's' happiness levels fell. Now they were positively plummeting.

409

"There's no sign of that, Mr Vice-President. Migrations towards us have been minimal. Most attention is on Jerusalem. The Israeli decision yesterday to call martial law seems to have bought us valuable time. Wisely holding the Marines at Kusadasi certainly keeps our powder dry."

Harold P Lutz was mollified - just. He harrumphed. There was no point in getting tetchy. He was the only person on base who knew the truth of the 'cobra' instruction. Only trusted aides were monitoring world traffic. Though many at home base would be clearly not affected by the implications of 'viper' for the down-time bases, there was always the possibility that the news could spread there with tumultuous effect. So, Siverek remained sealed off. It was time to act. Perhaps the time had come to send an encouraging, prompting message. He barely had time to express his decision to the waiting aide. His desk console self-activated with a soft 'ping'. He immediately knew the significance of the sombre-hued background it displayed - a communication at last that had its origins on Violet Base. He snapped his fingers, calling the aide to share the incoming message. It was text, not visual, but accompanied by the correct user password and graphics codes. The white words dazzled with their brilliance and their import.

'Methuselah complete; intact body to be sent ASAP, arriving Caramel Base by 0200 hours Monday. Strong probability body is 'Gold'. All transit bases alerted to journey. Close support medical team following in sequential TTU. Request you notify safe arrival.'

Both men sighed with satisfaction. A second 'ping', a second text...........

'BBC woman is also dead. Her body is following after 'Gold'. Request you notify cryogenic authorities and guard both pieces of cargo accordingly.'

The Vice-President's constitution jolted. So many unanswerable questions remained, but the time for action was now clear. The aide spoke first, asking if it was time to alert Kusadasi.

A shake of the Vice-Presidential head responded. "No, just notify the President on the security line. We have much to do here before two in the morning." He glanced up at the bright red numerals glowing at the top of the wall opposite. 18:33, - in less than eight hours now he would be custodial guardian of a package of frightening proportions.

"Send in Head of Security - and not a word to anyone else! Stay close until I call you again."

410

Harold P Lutz put his elbows on the desk, his head in his hands, and felt his heart lump in his throat.

***

The electrical storms in the south had begun to cause lights to flicker in some parts of Violet Base. Although only taking effect in storage and waste areas, Simon Atkins was becoming unnerved by the occasional flashes of lightning. In the evening gloom accompanying the darkening skies the flashes stung him out of his inertia. There were security points to be covered and a small grip to be packed. He looked at his desk console - no sign of the orange, pea-sized icon in the shape of a theatrical eye-mask that would presage arrival of 'cobra'. Still, he had to be ready. A need to insist on a final security check would get him into the chamber to be close to Felixana again. The guards would have left to make way for the dangerous and delicate work of moving the body shells into the two largest TTUs. Now even the technicians themselves would have moved to a safe distance. The chamber would be empty of life. At 21:55 hours he entered onto the balcony overlooking the deserted cargo amphitheatre.

***

Pieter North had learned of the Base Commander's message nearly an hour after it had been sent. He read it, and then read it again. 'Close support medical team', it had said. No mention of an early transfer of other senior scientists. *'Strength in numbers'* he told himself. He made sure his new foundation colleagues were told of the impending transfers of the body shells, now set for 22:30 hours. A twinge of alarm nudged him - where was Caramel Bondi? She would be personally responsible for the efficiency of the TTUs on such an important journey. The gathering storms might well affect the individual plasma cocoons, even perhaps the main lattice itself. And *was* she still dependable?

He tried to picture the power topography in his mind. The nearest seal on the tunnel was located in Indigo Base, not here. They were the weak points, the seals. If they popped.....he preferred to find her rather than merely worrying and hoping for the best. Still unable to track her down, he entered onto the balcony overlooking the deserted cargo amphitheatre at 21:57 hours.

***

Caramel Bondi sensed her heart beating. She checked her watch - 21:59 hours. The time had come to initiate the individual plasma cocoons.

411

Walking quickly along a glass-sided corridor she glanced outside. The storm clouds were darkening. The strong winds were whipping up clouds of sand, throwing them against the base. The flickering of lights in the storage bays had spread to inter-level elevators. She could only access the corridors to the TTU centres on foot. Time was pressing; she was still some way from the chambers. A young female came running in the opposite direction, clearly agitated.

"We can't get in to the plasma controls! The whole amphitheatre is locked off! Power transmission is unstable."

The plasmologist thought the woman was going to burst into tears. Her stomach churned.

"Is there anyone inside?"

"We don't know. Screens are out. It's light-proof and sound-proof. There's no way we can break in. Even if we could, we don't know if the lattice or cocoons are compromised. If they are…..!"

Caramel sensed the woman was going to become hysterical.

"Stop it! It's going to be OK. We can go in on manual over-ride from the personnel TTUs. Come!"

Together they turned down a sloping corridor towards the lower part of the section. The storm seemed to be directly overhead. A blinding flash of lightning was accompanied by the terrifying noise of a huge thunderclap. The base shook. All its lights went out. Caramel and her assistant stopped as if they had hit a solid wall. They could see nothing, just the smudgy after-image of the corridor in their eyes. After what seemed several minutes, but must have been only several seconds, the back-up circuit of the emergency generators restored the lights.

Others had joined them in the flight to the huge rooms housing the personnel TTUs. Wailing alarms indicating miscellaneous and unknown malfunctions swirled round the base. Automatic doors opened or closed as if in response to a maniacal poltergeist. As the small but growing group reached the first outer set of doors, the emergency procedures had run their course. Stability returned, if not yet sanity. Human nerves jangled far beyond the time limits for computer programs that were robustly designed. Eyes swivelled wildly, seeking consolation and support. Caramel keyed the master code and pressed her left hand to the central plate. She breathed into the entry port. The BBI light glowed red.

'Calm down, woman; take a deep breath and do it again.' Still red; a sense of unreality wrapped around her like a fog of dark grey cotton wool, smothering and tilting her universe. One of the technicians behind her asked if anyone had seen Doctor North. Eyes turned to the security screens connected to cameras on the inside of the complex. They showed nothing. Caramel ran back towards the base commander's quarters, not quite understanding why she was feeling flushed with guilt.

***

The door had closed behind him. Silence in the huge chamber descended like a comforting blanket. Simon Atkins welcomed the feeling - he was alone with Felixana, sharing their special intimacy again before the scientific mumbo-jumbo took her away from him on her long journey back home. He remembered the times he had spent with her, and the memories that were theirs. In the silence he had moved slowly to the right along the balcony, heading for one of the two stairways leading down onto the chamber floor. His footsteps made no sound. In the sealed chamber the lightning storm outside could not intrude into his surroundings or his thoughts. As he walked, he gazed down into the circular chamber. Over to his left, at the far side of the circle, the two largest TTUs stood with their doors lifted like huge bird wings. Behind them, leading up to the balcony, ran the second stairway, and in front of them stood the two cryogenic shells. He knew the one on the right held Felixana. He had stared down onto it, trying to imagine her form lying at peace inside. The silence seemed to fortify the human sense of imagination. He paused at the top of the stairway. No, he wouldn't go down, not for a few moments. Up here, he could stand guard above her, quietly watching, thinking and yes, even still carrying out his security function. Security was all, now. If he held his nerve and stayed calm, he could yet see her awake again. He held the balcony rail and took a deep breath. As the air had gently left his lungs a loud click signalled the opening of the balcony door way over to his left. The sounds of the base rushed in, followed by the sounds of the storm. Then the shape of Pieter North appeared in the doorway. The spell of silence broken, the South African looked up sharply, his knuckles white on the dark golden brass of the balcony rail. He finished exhaling and stood still.

North left the door open, looking quickly round the chamber, his eyes searching for his uncertain plasmologist. *'She's not here, it seems - but Atkins is! Over there on the other side of the chamber!'* He turned as if to leave, but instead he closed the chamber door. *'Do I pretend I haven't seen him? Can't do that - it would be too obvious.'*

413

North gripped the balcony rail, staring down at the array of TTUs as if still searching. He stood rooted to the spot. The security man was evidently here to be with Felixana's body. *'Perhaps he thinks I am, too. Yet I was looking for Caramel. Can't wander round and explain that! Still, it's best to keep the situation low-key. There's too much at stake here to provoke him. My foundation is so close. It would be pointless, anyway; she's dead.'*

He felt a sudden burst of sadness wash over him, whether for himself, for Felixana or for Atkins, he couldn't tell. Perhaps the profound silence in the amphitheatre was amplifying his feelings, plunging everything into a deeper intensity. A parallel sense touched him of the chapel at Chequers, so long ago in his experience now. He looked down at the balcony rail, sensing for a moment how he had traced with his fingers the ornate curled wooden end of a pew. He looked up, into the roof of the amphitheatre. There was no stone angel there to return his stare. He held his position.

Atkins sensed the man on the opposite side of the balcony posed no immediate threat. *'Why would he, anyway? At the moment, we have both lost. Perhaps our conflict will continue into the future again. If events play out as planned, we're all destined to travel home, as an eternal triangle spinning into eternity.'* A shiver passed through him. Perhaps the silence in the amphitheatre was giving him a depth of philosophy he never knew he had. He could see the newcomer was making no move towards either stairway. They would soon be joined, anyway, by the personnel whose duty it would be to put the bodies into the TTUs ready for their journey. Should he now go, or stay a few moments longer? His body tensed, undecided whether to step towards the second stairway or back towards the exit.

The lights went out.

There had been no flickering or dimming. It was total and absolute, as if both men had suffered instantaneous blindness. The after-image of the huge amphitheatre ghosted across their retinas for a few precious seconds. Then even that was gone, leaving a poor memory of what the chamber might look like. Despite frequent visits over many months, the amphitheatre would not respond to easy recall. The memory does not provide a photograph. It plays tricks. It tempts, deceives and points only where you wish it to point. Though it can be trained it does not generally possess the acuity of those who lived before the nineteenth century invention of photography. In common with most of their sighted fellows within humanity, both Atkins and North had brains that had become lazy. The instant of being alive and fully receptive to outside stimuli could no

414

longer be appreciated once photography had begun its innocent data base. Yet this didn't need to register in those first seconds. Both knew the procedures; the second circuit of the emergency generators would cut in very soon. The word 'lattice' threw itself across the Dutchman's consciousness. He brutally ignored it; if they were still alive then the universe hadn't imploded. They were merely inconvenienced for a moment. It was a good opportunity to be professional with the other man when the lights returned, he decided.

They waited. Nothing happened. Darkness remained.

Coupled with the absolute silence it began to assume almost physical proportions. It began to affect the rhythm of breath. Too shallow, and flashes would appear in the brain. Too deep and slow, and the darkness would be taken into the lungs, to smother and suffocate entrails in its nothingness. Pieter North lifted one hand from the balcony rail and raised it to his nose. He could smell the metal. He dared not remove the other hand. He felt powerless. Indeed, he knew he was almost completely so. He tried to think. *What options do I have? Wait for the return of light….inch round the balcony rail to a stairwell (to what destination?)….call out to Atkins to make human contact….turn from the anchor of the rail and reach out for the chamber door to see if it will open….wait for outside intervention…..that's about it, really.'* He had a sudden thought that lifted his spirits. What would Jon De Haag have done? He waited for inspiration, trying to imagine his mentor's face.

Across the darkness on the other side of the amphitheatre, Simon Atkins was in a worse state. He knew he was further from the exit door. His ethos had drilled control into his life, yet here there was no control at all. He had no torch, and gathered that Doctor North was in the same predicament. Where was the array of security cameras sited? *'Think, man, think - you installed the damn things!'* It was no use; he found he couldn't judge distance, elevation or direction. His brain took him through the same options as his fellow captive. Calling out was the sensible thing to do. At least they could face the darkness together. How to introduce the approach? He knew he had to move to the left, yet began to imagine hurdles and impediments in the way. Perhaps there were cables or boxes, or even the end of the balcony and a fall into oblivion. He remembered the salient features of his nightmare and felt sick.

"Simon……Pieter."

'Ah! He's broken the silence before I did.'

"Yes, indeed, Pieter, what are we going to do about it? Have you any ideas?" called Simon Atkins.

The South African's voice sounded louder in his ears than the original whispered contact. There was a momentary delay as he waited for the scientist's response.

The Dutchman remembered how he had played the whispering gallery game with Felixana, so was not taken aback by the low volume of the first words. In fact, he thought he had imagined the contact entirely. But why had the South African spoken his own name first and only then the word 'Pieter'? No matter; he had actually opened his mouth to reply when the louder, different sentences echoed across the chamber in the darkness. His blood chilled. He felt cold, confused, even a touch of, what was it, not fear, perhaps just a trick of the darkness teasing with his emotions, surely? The security chief couldn't be responding to his own words. Yet the Dutchman was gripped by two certainties - he had heard, or imagined, the two names himself, and the man on the other side of the chamber had heard, or imagined, them as well.

The use of first names at least was by now well-established. Pieter would find a weird, comforting anchor in continuing with their use. He felt compelled to put the other man on an equal footing of awareness. His irrational fear was beginning to grow and it might yet expand out of control if he didn't share it. He kept his voice at what he hoped was an even tenor; not as soft as to replicate that awful first contact, nor as loud as to betray the fear bubbling up inside his body.

"Simon. I agree we can't wait for ever for the lights to come on. The transfer teams will be trying to find a way in. Did you see anyone else in the chamber when you came in?"

He was pleased he got the balance in volume and cadence right, but then Pieter's balance was knocked when he heard the puzzlement in the other's responses.

"There was no-one here, unless they were hiding for some reason. You did speak our names, didn't you?"

"No."

"That's right, Simon....Pieter. I called you both."

The whisper again; they both heard it. The security man shivered. He wished he could see Pieter North. How close was the voice? He couldn't tell. Who was in the chamber without permission? He tried to imagine, and failed. His brain had frozen. The Dutchman was first to recover.

"If you're part of Caramel Bondi's team you'd better identify yourself and find the lights. They'll be here any moment now."

"Pieter, Caramel's outside. They all are. It's just us here; you and Simon, me and Felixana."

It was the way the whisper had spoken in couplets that blew apart any sense of reason in the two men. Simon Atkins clearly showed his nerves at this point. They manifested as exasperation.

"This is a serious situation. Identify yourself! If you're responsible for the lights going out, I'll have you arrested!"

Silence…..

Pieter North's mind, struggling to be logical, was determined to reinforce the security-based answer. The interloper was clearly part of Caramel's plot. There must certainly be a plot. Hadn't he expected it all along? No wonder he hadn't been able to find her. The accomplice had been hiding behind some machinery waiting his chance. Had sabotage occurred already? Nevertheless, he wasn't going to be fooled by a pathetic red herring. It irritated him that the whisperer could assume such gullibility….and he a scientist as well! He put two and two together in his mind and deliberately deduced four hundred to display the preposterous alternative significance of the words he had heard. His voice carried more than a touch of sarcasm into the darkness.

"Don't try that one! Nothing mighty about you! This dangerous deception must end. If you don't show yourself there'll be no mercy given on your arrest. Who are you?"

The darkness was stripping both men of a layer of their facades. The whisper spoke again, in soft honeyed tones, yet dripping like acid on onion skins in the ears of the two listeners.

"Pieter and Simon, please calm down. I think you know me as 'Gold', so that is the name I shall go by."

"Rubbish!"

The Dutchman spat the word into the void. No response came from the other side of the chamber. Simon Atkins was trying to locate the position of their whispering tormenter. His skills were more finely tuned than those of Pieter North. He decided the voice had come from somewhere near the second stairway, behind the large TTUs. 'That's a long way round', he thought. Still holding the rail tightly with both hands, he silently took a step to the right.

"If you move again, Simon, I will move. Please remain calm, both of you. There is nothing to be afraid of."

Simon thought he could feel a warm wetness on his left leg, but perhaps that was just imagination, too. Silence again.

Pieter's brain was working furiously. Somehow the interloper could see them, or at least could hear Atkins moving. He was close. Did he have a hand-held radar-based retina screen? The scientist spoke out.

"The transfer team's outside. I'll let them in." There was now less violence in the Dutchman's voice. He turned, fervently hoping he hadn't strayed too far from the exit door. 'Yes, here it is!'

He yanked on the controls. The door refused to budge. Frustrated, he leaned back against the door, squeezing his eyes shut, despite the fact that being open or shut made no difference. 'Think, man; think!' There were two of them; perhaps if they worked together....The darkness might yet prove to be an ally. Surely a security chief would be carrying a weapon?

"We are armed. It's only a matter of time before you surrender to us." Was there a whispered sigh? What would it sound like, anyway?

"I agree it is a matter of time, Pieter. But we have time, at least a little of it. Time together."

Simon Atkins also digested the enigmatic response. There had been no welcoming inrush of light from an opening chamber door in Pieter North's direction. He knew they had both had a display of resistance neutralised with as little effort as a butterfly's wing-beat. His training led him down the negotiating route. Perhaps they had time to recover and strengthen their positions; a Stockholm syndrome in reverse.

"What do you want with this time?"

"To talk."

The security chief tried to set aside the disturbing disorientation of the darkness. He could now go to work on something familiar.

"So, you have chosen the name 'Gold'. You could easily have picked up the word anywhere. Perhaps from the team coming back from Jerusalem yesterday? It's a big responsibility we have, you and me. I can see to it that you travel back early on. I will need to be convinced that you mean no harm to the project, so leave the body shells alone."

"Ah, Simon, trust me."

"Not good enough! You put the lights out and then refuse to reveal yourself. What are we supposed to think? Trust can only follow actions, not words."

"Well said, Simon. But where has been the trust in your relationships?"

The security officer winced in the darkness, as if he had been prodded hard in the stomach. This was queasy. He needed to change tack; the whisperer was trading question for question. This man perhaps wouldn't open up, or lower his guard, unless a more probing attack made progress. He took a deep breath.

"As Head of Security I'm in a strong position. I'm willing to trust you with highly-secret information. There are only a limited number of allocations set aside for early return to home base. If you give me some idea of your particular skills and training, I am sure we can do something for you."

Across the darkness Pieter North had not been idle. Mention of the body shells must surely have been deliberate. He decided to act. The whisper resumed its steady path.

"I can do much more for you, Simon. It's your particular skills and training that matter, and how you've used them over your lifetime. Everyone takes a personal journey. You tell people to take personal responsibility for their own security and then you don't trust them to do so. How many times have you broken in to others' lives and then not followed through?"

Despite himself, Simon Atkins' memory threw up numerous examples of interference. His lack of trust in John McWilliams' work for Doctor North; the hastily-organised visit to Los Angeles to chase Professor De Haag; the anger he had felt when the Controller of Federal Security Services had admitted the assassination of the BBC man, Landon; his almost-violent impatience when told of the death in the TTU; his rude brushing aside of medical checks on first arriving here at final base.

"Every time you fail to trust another human being without due and prior cause you demean them, and then you demean yourself."

"I trusted Paul Devine with the knowledge of 'Viper'!"

His hand flew to his mouth. 'Why did he say that? This man knew nothing of such things. 'Goodness. I don't even think Pieter North knows! What is it with this damn whisper?'

He began to shake with fear. The earth seemed to become jelly underneath him. Yet strangely it was directed at himself and not at his invisible host.

"Your attempts at self-aggrandisement and personal projection have left you incomplete. The more you have struggled for self-identity, the farther away it has moved. You were forced by love to confront and acknowledge Felixana's identity in preference to your own. Trust followed."

Pieter North listened breathlessly to the continuing psycho-babble. It was proving to be a good distraction. Surely he was getting close now? His sly movements to his left around the chamber balcony were going undetected. The saboteur was focusing his attention wholly on the other man. It didn't matter what he was saying. 'Some rubbish about security and trust, though it would be helpful to know what 'viper' is.' Silence again. The whisper had stopped. Pieter paused with his left foot tensed to move. He lowered it noiselessly to the floor. His left hand reached out. The balcony rail bent downwards at the start of the second stairway!

'Surely I should be able to hear him breathing now. I must be so close!'

"As I was saying, Pieter, the farther away it has moved."

He was not here! The scheming, devious traitor had moved again! Had he walked past him in the darkness? Pieter North gripped the handrail and shook with impotent fury. There was no other way to let out his anger. The darkness was still absolute, its totality making him light-headed as imagined forms and shapes, words and concepts, rattled around in his fevered brain, ghosting before him in the ether of his mind. Far away now, on the other side of the chamber, the whisper resumed its gentle, insistent course.

"You think yourself a scientist, Pieter, yet you do not analyse carefully enough what you perceive. You say to yourself quite readily 'I am composed of electrical and chemical components', but you do not say 'I use electrical and chemical components to move'. Why not? You know from experimentation that humans are the only creatures with the ability to imagine, to project, to surmise, to move thoughts through time. Why is this? You have never even asked yourself that simple question. I am who I am. The mere thought of wondering what it would be like not to be alone was sufficient to create what you have called very inadequately the Big Bang. But it is too late for regret. It is time to come together again."

The words fixed both listeners to the spot. 'This is a very deranged saboteur', thought Pieter North, who alone held enough violent energy to do battle in the darkness.

"Identify yourself!"

The whisperer ignored the challenge.

"I need critical mass to return to oneness. Every splinter of DNA carries eternity. When the surrounding bulk perishes, what you call individual death, that piece of the eternity returns to me. It either decides to re-integrate into the whole, or it rejects itself as having consciously decided it no longer belongs. Each piece of eternity carries my volition, but I cannot save what does not consciously want to be saved."

Pieter North's hostility was becoming brittle.

"We don't save mad traitors! Where is the evidence for all this?"

"Pieter, there is a mass of evidence everywhere, every time the earth turns. I meet even your scientific community's critical and suspicious criteria. I am detectable, measurable and retainable. I grow and gather strength. I shine in eyes, in the sparkle of a stream, in the warmth of community, in self-sacrifice for a human stranger. Your criticism at times has become bitter, mocking cynicism, over-defensive even, as if you fear the unknown because you cannot explain it."

Pieter North found he could not easily find the precise words to fling back in reply. This was a moving target, not yet revealing sufficient detail on which to focus. Even the face of Jon De Haag in his mind's eye was impassive, as if thinking profound thoughts itself. More shockingly, the face of his own father seemed to appear in the darkness before him, smiling with confident kindness. The juxtaposition of the image and the next words of whisper became even more unnerving for him.

"Ask yourself now - why have you never discovered life on other planets in other solar systems? Your SETI programmes have not delivered results. Why have you found the universe to be mathematically finite but not know what lies beyond it? Why did you cling so stubbornly for so long to the belief that the speed of light could never be exceeded? Why have you never discovered that elusive sub-atomic particle that you always tell yourself will be the final one? Why are you prepared to believe in little green men, but not a loving father? I have patiently waited over seventeen billion of your years for parts of my identity to coalesce. What you have named biological evolution has merely been that process in operation. Early physical life took hold on this planet because enough fragments of will came together. It could have begun anywhere, at least where the conditions were right. Yet it didn't. There have been no guarantees. Near extinctions have been random and beyond my control. There was never any need for crowing of Darwinian supremacy as a vindication of science. Charles Darwin was astute and perceptive, reverent towards spirituality, but he couldn't explain why there are no half-completed species in existence. When slivers of eternity reach a particular critical level they make the jump into a new branch of evolution. Biology has been the first step in an onward journey. Volition has needed a method of movement. What you call evolution has been the start of a homeward journey."

Simon Atkins had guessed that his colleague was no nearer the whisperer than he was himself. It was no use. He slumped to the floor of the balcony, his back leaning against the solid comfort of the chamber wall. He could hear the conversation taking place, but felt frozen and unable to contribute to it. He knew his tormentor had moved on to focus on the scientist. He himself was grappling with thoughts of ego, identity, trust and Felixana. He was finding few nuggets of comfort swirling about in the muddy waters of shame in the prospecting pan of his memory. Pieter North would have to fight his own demons in his own way. He heard the Dutchman's confident voice echo out from the direction of the second stairway over to his right as he took up 'Gold's' challenges concerning the Victorian Englishman's theories.

"The origin of species has been proved scientifically. Nothing can stand in its way!"

The scientist's proud assertion rang out. Simon Atkins sighed as the whisper showed no sign of altering its volume or cadence.

"There is nothing unnatural or strange about evolution, Pieter. The steady move from physical to mental to spiritual has been the upward journey I have sought. I have watched and waited over these aeons as splinters of eternity have struggled to make contact with their purpose. I set a sign and waited for a species to develop that would display enough of my image to reassure me that progress was being made.

It started well. Over two hundred and forty thousand years ago, an early primate on a hunting trek paused to look up at my rainbow. His eyes became moist with tears. He was tired, frightened, injured, hungry, cold and alone. He had caught no animal that day. Yet he stopped on his way to shelter. He consciously directed the strands of existence that had evolved into his eyes to gaze upwards at the beauty of the arc of brilliant colour. Yes, Pieter, beauty. Its component parts do not require life as you perceive it to be. Yet a rainbow is not merely an optical effect.

"You see, Pieter, a rainbow can only be seen when enough of my being has coalesced into a form to detect it."

A long pause filled the darkness. Both men found they could visualise the sharp colours of a rainbow in their minds' eye. They experienced a longing to see one in reality. They waited for the whisper to continue.

"Once that longing gaze had taken place, I knew that a life form had evolved at last that was capable of bringing me home."

Pieter North's brain kicked in. He thought of Jon De Haag again, throwing a taunting challenge into the darkness.

"What about blind people, then? Are they to be denied your bounty?"

"Oh, Pieter, sight is more than light. All humans communicate and all humans can detect me if they wish to do so. It took more of your years, but counter-currents meant I had to intervene more directly in the affairs of Man."

"What counter-currents?" Pieter North's strident tone had lowered a notch. Simon Atkins could detect it.

"Violence as an aspiration began to manifest itself. Empires and armies sought self-gratification. The spread of the Roman Empire reached a point where humility needed to be re-established in the affairs of nature. I broke into the evolutionary journey. But you have also used science as a tool to reinforce and perpetuate your perceived self-worth. You have turned the humility of that upward gaze, symbolically made towards what you once described as 'the heavens', into a questing for knowledge for self-gratification. Many of you have even begun to exercise a skill in genetic control that has had the effect of bringing an end to your own evolution. Selective breeding was rejected with revulsion in your twentieth century, yet you continued with selection. Every time you consciously denied a life to come into existence, or orchestrated a death to occur that should have been prevented, or forced to occur before its allotted time, you altered natural selection. Evolution does not belong to one species. You have even taken the evolutionary truth of a 'right to live' and forced your World Councils to create a totally-opposite 'right to die'. You cannot reverse the universe, and you should not even try. The

closer to ultimate power and knowledge you thought that science was taking you, the farther away you actually drifted. I knew we would never come into oneness if the splinters began to believe in their own individual self-importance. Can you honestly say, Pieter that you have always taken responsibility for your own actions, and always taken into account how you have behaved in your youth?

"So, you see how, by your own actions, the worship of self and the worship of science have brought us to this point. Something you have described, Simon, as finding your own way, on your own terms and to your own desires."

Simon Atkins curled back in numb surrender against the wall. His fellow captive fought on, though the tone of strident confidence was ebbing.

"No more of this stupidity! Identify yourself! What do you want?"

"You can predict the weather by looking at the sky, but you cannot interpret the signs concerning these times."

"The security forces will break in. You'll be arrested or killed. Don't you see that?"

Simon Atkins sighed. His numbed brain silently began to work. 'Unfortunately, they won't do that. They're probably in darkness themselves. Even if they're not, they can't tell whether our temporal seals are damaged. They wouldn't take the risk. The personnel TTUs may be locked off. We could be the nearest people to the only way back home.'

The realisation in the final thought served to lift his spirits. He thought of his mother and what she had been through as a child. There was no need for him to crumble now. He pulled himself to his feet. There seemed to be only one way forward towards a proper resolution. He would have to stand tall and open before the entity he sensed. Could he trust his voice not to waver? He coughed to clear his throat.

"We seem to be in your power, Mr Gold. The absence of light appears not to concern you. You may have brought it about. In that case, may I suggest you restore it? We need to talk further."

"Do you trust me, Simon?"

"Please don't play games, Mr Gold. It's not a question of trust. This is a business transaction."

"You still see that you have never been willing to trust anyone - except perhaps for Felixana. Would you have trusted her, Simon?"

The security chief wriggled helplessly on the fishing line of his own making. What else to do but go along? *'Be honest, boy; nothing else to do.'* He thought to himself.

"Yes, I did trust Felixana."

"She is dead, Simon."

The finality of the statement sliced into his heart. Something deep in his being welled up with a soulful, anguished groan.

"I have nothing to offer you, Gold." He had dropped the 'Mister' without realising it.

"Give me back some light, I beg you!"

Imagination began to weave its web again. Simon blinked, feeling moisture begin to move in his eyes. He imagined he could see Pieter North over to his left, a burly figure out of focus in the almost complete darkness. He looked around further. Yes! The shells of the cryogenic units were outlined in the chamber below, just distinguishable from the looming hulk of the cargo TTUs. Pieter was finding his eyes too were coming back into use. The saboteur was being tricked into responding, though where the light was coming from, neither man could be sure. The Dutchman was impressed by the negotiating approach. He had no way of knowing the inner turmoil ripping the security man apart. He only thought of how he could get closer, perhaps even jump the traitor.

"I can give her back to you, Simon."

The whisper again....Pieter held his breath. Why did he feel a strange pang of jealousy? How close was the whisperer now? The darkness lifted a notch further. Atkins' voice rang out.

"I can't trust what I can't see!"

The total darkness returned like the blade of a guillotine. Neither was left in any doubt of that. The whisperer pressed insistently, asking for a second time.

"Do you trust me, Simon?"

"All right…all right! I trust you! Please give us back the light!"

He had included Pieter North in the plea without a conscious effort. The darkness began to lift again. Huge shapes became clearer in the chamber below. Pieter thought he could make out a human form standing near one of the cryogenic shells, partly hidden by the machinery from Simon on the far balcony. He couldn't summon the energy to fight. His mind was in turmoil over the possible significance of something the interloper had said to him. Something about taking responsibility for things he had done in his youth. Yet perhaps that was psycho-babble, too.

"Walk to your left, Simon. Back the way you came, back to the door."

The voice carried up from the chamber floor. The security officer began to move; his legs were shaking, even though he could remember this was the way he had come. His right hand guided him along the balcony rail. He called back as he moved through the deep gloom.

"Give me Felixana, then!"

The reply stopped him in his tracks as if he had walked into a solid wall.

"It's not that easy, Simon. Look inside yourself. Don't you have a terrible secret that you need to confess first?"

'No! Not that! How could he know?' He just had to trust that somehow this man did know; did know of the awful act he had carried out when he had killed Paul Forbes. He could carry the guilt no longer. Tears burst from his eyes, rolling down his face in the dark. Pieter North couldn't see them, thank goodness! His legs finally gave way. He knew what he had to do as he slumped to the floor. His voice somehow regained a dignity between the sobs.

"I killed Paul Forbes, Pieter! I murdered your friend! He was a Christian….a good man….he wouldn't take part….what we were doing….I buried his body on a hillside….outside the base in America….early on. You wondered what had happened to him….now you know. I'm so sorry! I'm so very sorry!"

The sobs overcame the stuttered confession. The Dutchman was confused. He wanted to stay focused on the interloper below, yet found his memory ripped back to the riddle of the engineer's unexplained disappearance from the Pichot base. Anger welled up inside him. He might have expected such a thing from the security chief, his rival for the girl. But why did he also crumble before the insidious mind-games spun by this talented tormentor in the darkness, this traitor using the name 'Gold'? It might or might not be imagination, but he remembered a young girl in Amsterdam. Without realising it, he heard himself saying

"I believe you can give us back the light."

It seemed to work. A lessening of the total darkness began again. The sound of the sobs had stopped. Pieter North held his breath. A t the foot of the stairway a slender figure was standing between the cryogenic shells below. One of the shells appeared to be open, but he couldn't be sure. Though its face was obscured in the gloom the figure looked up, whispering for a third time,

"Do you trust that I can give you a second chance?

It was not clear this time to which listener the question was addressed. Each man felt it strike personally. Both replied.

The sudden return of light was brutal and violent. After so much time irises, retinas and optic nerves just couldn't cope. Both men were temporarily blinded, falling to the floor with the excruciating pain that was felt even through closed eyelids. Pieter North passed out first, but not before his youth and the canals of his homeland came to his mind. Simon Atkins felt cool fingers close around his hand. He distinctly heard his name lovingly spoken in an English accent, just once, before he too fainted. He felt at peace as he lost consciousness.

MONDAY 23RD MAY 2135

THE FINAL DAY

03:30 HOURS

Vice-President Harold P Lutz could wait no longer. The cargo had not arrived. The one message from Red Base had indicated that nothing had arrived there, either. Beyond Red Base - well, who would know? He had to act now. Despite numerous denials about sacrificing past bases, the developing world's communities had not believed the northern protestations. The carefully-constructed picture of humiliation aimed at the Southern Brotherhood could still succeed quickly - but only if Siverek had a body to subject to independent scientific examination. Without it, a succession of travelogues from ancient Judea might take ages to de-mystify and belittle the beliefs of nations set to inherit the world's financial resources in less than eight months.

While turmoil, speculation, fear and aggression bubbled on the outside, the life on Siverek's Caramel Base was tightly controlled. The base was on shut-down, a situation nearly everyone accepted, given the expectation that a very important cargo from due from down-time bases. All were proud to be part of such a venture. They had worked for many years to make it so. The scientific community on base still displayed a strong professional camaraderie. Harold P Lutz was pleased they were so gullible.

Only ten senior executives surrounding the American Vice-President knew of 'viper'. Even fewer knew of 'cobra'. These select five had gathered in the silence of a small ante-chamber next to the cargo TTU amphitheatre. Through glass windows they could observe the few technicians still working in the main chamber. The plasma walls were active, but nothing was coming up from Red Base.

"There is talk of Mexico and Singapore being about to call for a reconvening of the Economic Forum. We are nearly there."

Susannah Wong was Head of Finance. She pushed her flowing dark hair behind her ears. Her electric blue eastern clothing shimmered under the ante-chamber's lights. It contrasted with the no-nonsense khaki dungarees worn by Monica Langley, senior scientist over all the temporal transference teams. Ms Langley could not have been more different in other ways, either. Her close-cropped masculine hairstyle had always caused the Chinese accountant a certain level of distaste. The scientist voiced her response.

"Without the body of 'Gold' we have nothing to bargain with. There is no sign of a build-up of power coming from down-time. We have irreplaceable scientists down there."

A picture of Doctor Pieter North came to her mind.

"We need 'cobra' to be activated to get them back, and as soon as possible."

The Vice-President looked for an opinion from his Head of Security. Pierre Chalon had worked closely over the years with Simon Atkins. He knew the pressure the South African would be under as he prepared and waited for 'cobra' to be announced.

"I suggest we move now, Mr Vice-President, while we can still get messages down the line."

Monica Langley winced visibly. She was fully expecting her scientific missives to be getting through. There was no need for this security man to raise doubts on that front, just because she had refused to go to bed with the Frenchman....

The military commander was the last to speak. The others could tell that the politician would weigh his opinion carefully. Force of arms was still carrying a big stick in the twenty second century.

"We are not well-equipped here to defend against an armed national force. My boys will do their best, but we couldn't safeguard Methuselah for long. We need the Marines from Kusadasi."

Harold P Lutz didn't take long in reaching his decision. The chewing gum moved round and round as he looked into four anxious faces.

"OK. We call in the Marines." He looked at Major Douglas.

"Get 'em here fast, Roger. I'm going to activate 'cobra'."

04:15 HOURS

Michael Ben-Tovim hadn't slept. There was too much noise for one thing. He also held a terrible thought in his heart. He thought back over the immediate past. The military build-up at Megiddo was immense. The hover-copter had landed at twenty minutes past noon nearly two days previously. During the first few hours after landing he could be forgiven for feeling that he didn't exist. There was no explanation for the diversion from any officer who stood still long enough to be asked the question. He had dressed in his military uniform to face the Prime Minister. Now in civilian clothing he was virtually invisible as troops, vehicles and armaments rushed around him. The hover-copter pilot had merely pointed to an olive-coloured tent when asked for guidance after landing. The sound of the rotor-blades had drowned out the diplomat's questions,

429

though it had been clear what had been asked. Michael picked his way through the army traffic towards the tent. The stern-looking guard at its flap, much taller than Ben-Tovim, had stuck out a pudgy hand into his chest. Fumbling inside his jacket, the diplomat handed over a bio-card. Little green lights flashed when the guard slipped it past his belt computer. He thumbed an entry and stood aside. There was still no word from his mouth.

A group of officers, perhaps six or seven, had been bunched over a three-dimensional battle plan. The holographic quantity of units had looked from the tent entrance like horrendous over-kill to the practised eye of the newcomer. One officer had straightened his back, instantly recognised Ben-Tovim, and held out a hand in welcome. Another officer killed the hologram with a finger sweep.

"Michael! They said you were coming! Have some coffee."

No further clarification; nothing as to who 'they' were, nothing about the hover-copter's diversion or of the numbers on the ground. The dark-haired diplomat had forced a strained smile.

"Hello, Joseph. Yes, coffee please; that would be good."

He waved a hand back out beyond the closing flap.

"Megiddo, Joseph."

"Yes, Michael. Megiddo. Scary, isn't it? This is the first time we've broken the 2005 UNESCO world heritage agreement. Let me introduce you round."

The other officers gave their names and a random selection of smiles. Michael could recall none of them now, forty hours later. He had obviously not been listening. The seniority and security clearance of the international diplomat were evident; the hologram had been recalled in all its gory splendour. The senior officer summarised the position for his guest.

"We're waiting, basically. There are four hundred American Marines in Kusadasi on the Turkish coast. The Southern Brotherhood have around a hundred insertion units holed up in Bethlehem - mostly Ethiopian, but some are Southern Sudanese from Juba. They are very highly trained; geared up to take Siverek Base faster than a laxative!"

430

Dirty chuckles bubbled round the hologram map.

"We're told to expect action within forty eight hours. Either the Marines or the laxatives go first! Our orders are to bring down the Ethiopians on over-fly with Syrian weapons so it looks like an accident."

Michael Ben-Tovim's concentration had lapsed at that point, early on in the briefing. He had found he was dreaming of his wife and children, wishing the hover-copter had taken him home rather than to this ghastly-historic battle plain. He knew the significance of Megiddo well enough. Every Israeli did. Late that evening, he had lain on the bunk-bed provided for him in a single tent, somewhere near the edge of the vast array of armament. He was trying to clear his brain of the mist that had clung so persistently over the past months. He laid out the bare bones of argument across his mind's eye.

One, the northern powers were going to dismantle the cohesion of the Southern Brotherhood by belittling, then destroying, their faith in Christianity. Two, it was in Israel's long-term interest that their plan should succeed. This had a two-fold advantage; that Israeli investments in the northern hemisphere should be protected and that Judaism should emerge stronger in the remainder of the Faith world once belief in Christianity was over. He considered this important in the middle of a geographical Moslem region. So far, so good....

He grimaced. It had proved important to play both sides during the past three years, regardless of what the Prime Minister had said. Yet the Prime Minister had said something else of significance and he couldn't recall what it had been. If the northern plan had been a hoax, a deception, then Israel could have continued with its slow infiltration of the higher levels of the Southern Brotherhood. Over the past few weeks the dynamic had changed. The northern scientists were actually about to deliver. Israel was still allowing the northern powers to proceed. Yet something was missing. What had he overlooked? What if....? What if....? He had fallen asleep with the mist still clinging to his mind.

He had woken late on Sunday morning with a recollection of the PM's words, and their significance that had eluded him. 'Three and a half years wasted'. That's what the man had almost shouted at him. 'Three and a half years wasted.' Three and a half years was forty two months. Why did that length of time mean something? He had rolled to a sitting position, plugging his personal belt computer into the tent's world organic web connection. Strangely enough, about forty two minutes later he had his answer.

He had dressed hurriedly and had run to the commander's tent, gripping in his hand the special download package he had pieced together. His unshaven and frantic appearance had evidently unnerved his military friend. The few other officers around had looked up quizzically from their consoles. It was around eleven in the morning, and with no immediate prospect of action the alert status on base was low.

"Michael! What's the matter? You look terrified."

"Joseph, can we have a quiet word, please; just the two of us?"

The commander indicated to a colleague to take over. He took Ben-Tovim by the arm.

"Over here; there's a small briefing room." They sat alone. The diplomat spoke softly, in an intensely-focused voice.

"Go over again for me the sequence of action you're preparing for, Joseph." The serious tone was communicated to the commander, who responded likewise.

"Intelligence speaks of a rising level of preparedness among the Americans in Kusadasi to bolster defences at Siverek. The Union's time project must be close to climax. Another film release later today from Rome, perhaps, as it's Sunday? There's been nothing since last Tuesday, so perhaps they've been preparing a spectacle. Politicians will tell us nothing, of course. We could speculate, but it's not our job. Our orders are to wait for clear evidence that troops are leaving Kusadasi or Bethlehem. We are to monitor the Americans, but to destroy the Southern Brotherhood's attempts to thwart the release of the spectacle."

Michael looked anxiously round the room, even though he knew it was empty.

"Joseph, what if the Siverek project can only prove Jesus to be real? Not just a human body, I mean, but something else."

The commander looked blankly at his friend, as if he had spoken in a foreign language.

"What, you mean a figurehead to rally round, for instance?"

Ben-Tovim searched for a word. "No; something supernatural, I mean."

"Michael, you know that's impossible!"

"Yes, yes! I know that!" Ben-Tovim waved his small hands nervously as if swatting an invisible mosquito.

"But, please, just assume for a moment that it's a theoretical option."

"Why should we, Michael?"

Joseph had lowered his voice in reply, an uncertain edge appearing. This was not only muddying the military waters. The significance of questioning army orders was dangerous enough in itself, but this was bordering on questioning a much deeper law running in Jewish veins and arteries. But Ben-Tovim continued.

"Let me show you something." He held up the small disk. "This is something only very few people have seen and mainly in America."

The change of geographical emphasis caused the other man to pause. He nodded, even taking the disk to slip it into the small silver unit on the table-top himself. He was determined to confront this circular devil and exorcise any power it might hold. Ben-Tovim keyed the necessary commands to play the sequence. The Seal of the President of the United States appeared, floating above a short message addressed to 'Officer Commanding, Pichot Base. 479 OK'.

The message consisted of two words. 'Methuselah approved.'

Ben-Tovim's eyes flashed. "Note the date."

The commander replied out loud. "Saturday, November, twenty three, 2131. So?"

Ben-Tovim's voice quavered slightly. "Tomorrow will be the twenty third of May. That's three and a half years later. Notice, exactly three and a half years. Forty two months. Not one day out!"

"So, what's the significance?"

Fingers flashed over the keys again. Words and their context appeared on the screen.

The beast was allowed to make proud claims which were insulting to God, and permitted to have authority for forty two months.'

433

"Sounds biblical; what is it?"

"Book of Revelation; Chapter thirteen Verse five."

The commander snorted softly. "That's no good. That's the Christians' New Testament."

"Ah! But just look at this." New keys, a new presentation, and this time Michael Ben-Tovim spoke the words out loud, slowly and with feeling.

'Then I saw two men standing by a river, one on each bank. One of them asked the angel who was standing further upstream, "How long will it be until these amazing events come to an end?" The angel raised both hands towards the sky and made a solemn promise in the name of the Eternal God. I heard him say "It will be three and a half years".'

The commander hesitated. Ben-Tovim could see in his face that his brain was working. The diplomat concluded by saying "Our Book of Daniel, Chapter twelve Verses five to seven."

"That's just coincidence, surely? You could pick any number of quotations and get them to fit. You know you can read anything you like into our Holy Book."

"But it's worth reminding our masters. You yourself said how scary Megiddo is! If we don't stop the Americans and the northern project somehow, they could uncork a bottle we cannot handle!" Michael was getting wound up; he was mixing his metaphors.

"I'm sorry, Michael. This is way beyond my pay grade. I'm a military man following orders. You were yourself, once. Surely the politicians, the Rabbis and the professors would have gone over these matters time and time again. There's no danger here; just the chance to keep things stable so the Palestinians and their southern allies can't get their hands on our money! And anyway - what do you mean by 'supernatural'? That the 'beast' is the northern coalition? That this Methuselah thing might actually resurrect in some way? Honestly, Michael, I can't see it!"

Ben-Tovim pressed the keys again. "Then look at this! See if *this* will convince you!"

The scene displayed the scene at the Ottawa conference on the seventh of May. The world's press was listening in rapt attention to the man who had escaped from the Siverek base. Michael Ben-Tovim skipped a few lines and then re-set the speed of the presentation. Normal speech flowed from the earnest, florid face of Paul Devine, explaining why it had taken him nearly a fortnight to travel up from the farthest base. The Englishman laboured the point that each transfer had been physically painful for him. The diplomat paused the recording to ensure the military man was listening. He lifted a finger. "Now comes the interesting bit….." Paul Devine's voice continued.

The scientists had to build seven bases to overcome a temporal barrier at three hundred years. Each transfer punches a fresh hole in time. I don't understand the science, but basically there's a plasma wall in place whenever transfers occur. Movement then takes place behind a sealed wall.'

Michael Ben-Tovim spun round.

"You see, seven bases so seven seals! I know it's the New Testament again, but look at Revelation, chapter six. Seven seals! The Europeans are tampering with our ancient homeland through seven seals!"

The commander cupped his chin in his hand. "I don't know, Michael. It could still be conjecture." Uncertainty had crept into his voice. Michael pressed his point.

"My dear wife, Anna, has flirted with Christianity. She says it's important to hold to a Tree of Faith by learning from its branches and leaves as well as its roots. 'Looking at evolution', she calls it. I'm different. Only our roots matter to me, but we could be destroying our Tree of Faith if this project runs its course."

Joseph was breathing heavily, torn by the strong dilemma facing him. His military side was still in ascendancy.

"We must follow orders. You know that and I know that! Even if this Jesus existed he was just a dead body all those years ago. There can be no threat to Judaism."

Michael Ben-Tovim exhaled loudly. "At least pass these issues on."

***

As he turned fitfully in his bunk in the small hours of Monday morning, Michael recalled his final words to the commander as he had left the tent.

435

"If we don't destroy the Turkish base, we must pray that proves to be the right call. I can do no more to give warning."

***

His sense of powerless frailty was shared by many in the dying night, even though some were wrapped in cloaks of action, energy and determination. Whistles in the dark....

Four hundred soldiers from America's elite Marine Corps left the military airstrip in the green hills around Kusadasi. They were newly-equipped for computer-assisted low-level parachute entry, a technique never before employed in potential conflict situations. They had no way of knowing what would meet them at Siverek.

General Mary Poinsettia watched bullet craft carrying a hundred and twenty insertion troops lift off from the outskirts of Bethlehem, heading north. She had no way of knowing if and when they would encounter opposition.

Harold P Lutz was informed that the 'cobra' instruction had gone out, but as far as the scientists could tell there was no way of knowing if it was being acted on, or even if it had been received.

Michael Ben-Tovim lay in the gloom of the early dawn, his imagination gripped by the words he had now almost learned by heart. Throughout Sunday evening he had read and re-read awful pronouncements in chapter six of the Christians' Book of Revelation. His sombre mood reflected off the pre-dawn banks of grey cloud appearing over Mount Tabor. He thought back over his own knowledge of the Bible from school. Names and figures marched before him like gaunt army generals, each with a mission to carry out. Nehemiah, Job, Jeremiah, Ezekiel....the list went on. He had learned them all. One stood out; there was Daniel in his mind, with his tales of war, lions, victory and defeat. Michael's father had taught him that Daniel was a great prophet for boys and men. Then there was that angelic prediction in chapter twelve. He had been attracted as a youngster to chapter twelve because it mentioned his own name. Michael sometimes felt it was talking to him. Classmates had laughed. He supposed his attachment to the verses explained why the mention of three and a half years had struck a chord once the Prime Minister had first dealt the blow. Yet all his youth-time lessons had never carried the deep terror he was now finding in the Book of Revelation. Nothing in synagogue was as doom-laden as this!

He re-ran the BBC's broadcasts from Galilee. They carried a constant reminder to him of what he had done in placing the English woman in harm's way. Yet he had done what he had to do. Perhaps they would meet again, and he would have a chance to explain. He thought of the year of origin for those broadcasts, and read the Christians' New Testament against them. He felt an icy core to his stomach as Revelation spoke to him of violence, destruction, disease and judgment. There could be no mistaking its message, as he saw it. The seals would be broken in sequence, each bringing a three hundred year tide to completion. The seven stages swirled around in his mind, each one bringing a theme that merged with another, yet each more disastrous than the one before. What horrors would appear from the past if an unknown force broke through into his world? Fabled horses in stark colours….he could read no comfort in the narrative.

Dawn broke….He heard the roar of missiles setting out in sequence, their noise eclipsing the whoops of excitement lifting from the nearby battery personnel. He had no way of knowing their target. He rose bleary-eyed, looking through the flap of the tent. Army vehicles were revving into life, their mounts eager to flood north in pursuit of the missiles. Michael watched them, stunned by their enthusiasm. He noticed their corps insignia catching the shafts of early morning sun. Words echoed in his brain….'Near the great river Euphrates, horses and their riders, breastplates red as fire, blue as sapphire, and yellow as sulphur.'

***

Mary Trent knelt at prayer in the quiet church building in Far Cotton. No-one else was present. The turmoil of traffic pouring out of centres of population towards the perceived safety of rural isolation could not be heard here. Here she would be safe. Susan waited with Saffron in the hover-car outside, content to give her sister a few moments to seek inner strength and guidance. Then they, too, would have to flee. Susan was ever vigilant against the new threat of looting. A large group of young men and women had already rampaged across western Northampton that very morning. The terrifying news from the Middle East of a violent explosion had set in train tens of thousands of such events throughout England alone. Other European states were suffering similar traumas. The church building creaked softly in the wind. It seemed to the kneeling figure that it would even breathe if it could. She prayed for the safety of Susan and Saffron. She prayed that the three of them might stay together without harm through the coming world storm. She prayed for the safety of the world and its peoples. Tears came to her eyes, blurring her vision.

Mary heard a soft noise at the back of the church. Susan must be coming to urge her to come away. She became conscious of a figure. There was nothing threatening about him. He seemed to be walking gently with a slight limp, but she couldn't be certain. He breathed quietly. She couldn't see clearly, but thought he was the caretaker, asking him "I mean no harm. Please let me stay a little longer."

The figure said to her, "Mary. Don't be afraid. I've come to bring you good news."